**THE G**

Delia lay in her narrow bed in the dormitory and wondered if she would be happy at St Agatha's. Suddenly she felt a touch on her arm and discerned a figure standing by her bed in the dark.

'I say,' a girl's voice whispered, 'it's me, Thelma Fanshawe. I hope you're not feeling too lonely on your first night here. Let me slide in with you for a few minutes.'

Thelma put her arms around Delia and held her body close. Both girls wore identical nightgowns, the cotton thin enough for Delia to feel Thelma's belly against her own, and also Thelma's bosom, the small hard buds of her nipples clearly perceptible through the material.

'There's no need to be lonely here,' Thelma whispered, 'we love getting into bed with each other for a cuddle after lights out . . .'

*Also by this author*

The Royal Scandal

The Pleasures of Women
The Secrets of Women
The Delights of Women
The Mysteries of Women

Love Italian Style
Ecstasy Italian Style
Rapture Italian Style
Erotica Italian Style

# The Girls' Boarding School

Anonymous

Copyright © 1993 Richard Arlen

First published in 1993
by HEADLINE BOOK PUBLISHING

A HEADLINE DELTA paperback

10 9 8 7

All rights reserved. No part of this publication may be reproduced, stored in a retrieval system, or transmitted, in any form or by any means without the prior written permission of the publisher, nor be otherwise circulated in any form of binding or cover other than that in which it is published and without a similar condition being imposed on the subsequent purchaser.

All characters in this publication are fictitious and any resemblance to real persons, living or dead, is purely coincidental.

ISBN 0 7472 4039 6

Printed and bound in Great Britain by
Caledonian International Book Manufacturing Ltd, Glasgow

**HEADLINE BOOK PUBLISHING**
A Division of Hodder Headline PLC
338 Euston Road
London NW1 3BH

# The Girls' Boarding School

# THE GIRLS' BOARDING SCHOOL

Being a true narrative of the depravity and perversities to which a virtuous young English gentlewoman, named Miss Delia Sempill-Shand, was subjected, and the means by which her moral character was tainted, when, at the tender age of seventeen years, she was enrolled as pupil at a well-known boarding school for young ladies. This history of unredeemed licentiousness, and the dire results that sprang therefrom, is here presented in fearful and nigh-on unbelievable detail, as a warning to the public.

# CHAPTER 1
# A Young Lady is Used Indecently

The pages that follow contain a true narrative of what befell a young English gentlewoman, named Miss Delia Sempill-Shand. The author will not shrink from presenting the reader with the fullest explanation of the depraved acts that were done to her when, at the tender age of seventeen years, she was entered as a pupil at a well-known boarding school for young ladies.

In the public interest every particular shall be exposed here of the practices now carrying on without any moral hindrance or intervention of the law in certain educational establishments, to which the very best families in the land entrust their young daughters. Loving parents will be shocked to learn how, on the very first night of her arrival at her school, the innocent and hitherto untouched person of Miss Sempill-Shand was seized upon and used for a debauched purpose by a fellow-student.

Also laid open to public view shall be the artful plans made by particular members of the female teaching staff, who were in a position of responsibility towards their pupils. The shameful reason for these nefarious schemings will be shown to be merely the gratification of vicious desires, perpetrating an infamous abuse on the modesty of Miss Sempill-Shand, and the other young ladies caught in a like predicament. To state the case plainly, not one girl at this highly respected establishment escaped the ignominy of being subjected to the disgraceful discipline held in esteem by the head mistress and her teaching staff – namely, smacking on the bare posterior, followed by manipulation of the female parts.

This tale of perversity and unredeemed licentiousness begins on a spring day in the closing years of the nineteenth century, a day when, after the Easter holidays, Miss Delia Sempill-Shand arrived at her new school – namely, St Agatha's Boarding School for Young Gentlewomen. At Paddington Station in London she had been put on an express train bound for the West Country, and at Midsomer Rackham she had, all by herself, changed trains and even platforms, for the local line to Tuppington, which was the nearest stop for the school.

A groom with a smart pony trap was waiting for her outside Tuppington railway station, and in this she journeyed the final few miles to her new abode. Her first impressions were chaotic, for there were so many unfamiliar faces and voices, so much she must try to remember. She was introduced to Miss Jardyne, who would be her form mistress, and put by her into the care of the form prefect, Miss Thelma Fanshawe, a red-haired young lady of Delia's own age.

After supper Thelma showed her the Form V dormitory where she would be sleeping. It was a large and pleasant room furnished with twelve beds, six on either side, well spaced and divided off for privacy from each other by curtains that hung down from ceiling to floor. Delia unpacked her boxes, which the groom had brought up earlier, and put away her clothes.

The day had been long and tiring, and Delia was pleased when the hour of retiring came at last – half past eight. It was hard to suppress her yawns, but politeness required it, and she removed her clothes and donned her long nightgown, hidden for modesty's sake from the other girls in the dormitory by the curtains between beds. The chattering ceased at once when Miss Harriet Jardyne's voice made itself heard, bidding them a goodnight, whereupon the lights were extinguished and near-darkness fell on the dormitory.

Delia lay in her narrow bed with her hands under her head and thought about all she had seen that day, of the persons she had become acquainted with, of the impression they had made on her. She wondered if she would be happy at St Agatha's – whether she would be accepted by the other girls, whether she would find a special friend or two, and whether she would be clever enough to cope with the classroom work well enough to win good marks from the severely beautiful Miss Jardyne.

In the unfamiliar bed sleep refused to come, and whilst Delia was revolving these questions in her mind, she felt a touch on her arm and opened her eyes to discern a figure standing by her bed in the dark.

'I say,' a girl's voice whispered, 'it's me, Thelma Fanshawe. Are you all right, Delia? I hope you're not feeling too lonely on your first night here. You're not blubbing, are you? Move over and let me slide in with you for a few minutes.'

Delia thought it very kind indeed of the form prefect to take so much trouble over a new girl, and she slid sideways a little to make room for her in the bed. Thelma got in, covered herself with the bedclothes, put her arms about Delia and pressed her body close. Both of the girls wore identical long nightgowns, a school uniform requirement, the cotton material thin enough for Delia to feel Thelma's belly against her own, and also Thelma's bosom pressed close to her own bosom. She blushed to think that the small buds of Thelma's bosoms were perceptible through her nightgown, and therefore her own must be equally perceptible to Thelma.

'There's no need to be lonely here,' Thelma whispered, soft tresses tickling Delia's cheek lightly, 'we love getting into bed with each other for a cuddle after lights out. It's easily the best and nicest part of the day, and we sleep sounder as a result, believe me!'

She kissed and hugged Delia very lovingly, pressing mouth to mouth and tickling the corners of Delia's lips with the tip of her tongue. Delia became somewhat confused and agitated when it dawned on her that Thelma had brought her hands up between them to stroke her maidenly bosom through her thin nightgown. Delia found this so very unfamiliar that she was all in a flutter to realise what liberties were being taken with her person.

Though darkness reigned in the dormitory, Delia felt her face covered with fiery blushes as Thelma's hot kisses on her mouth, and the searching of her hands inside her nightgown, caused her limbs to tremble with emotions incomprehensible to her youthful inexperience.

'But how you shake, dearest Delia,' said Thelma. 'What can it be you are afraid of? Surely you like having your titties felt by a friend? Give me your hand – there, put it up my nightgown between my legs and give my pussy a feel.'

Whether she would or not, Delia's wrist was seized and her hand pushed up underneath her bedfellow's nightgown, until her palm lay over a warm and secret split, where a light sprinkling of curls could be felt. To touch the privates of another was so astounding a thought to Delia that she became quite breathless, and was robbed of the power of speech for some time.

## The Girls' Boarding School

In the meantime, Thelma had opened the front of Delia's nightgown and was playing freely, without permission of any sort asked or given, with Delia's delicate and hitherto untouched bosoms. It is needless to say that Delia would never even dream of giving consent for this act of indecency – not even if her closest and dearest friend had asked it!

Thelma was no friend – she was an acquaintance of a mere half day, and to judge by her forward behaviour, not even likely to be accepted as a friend! Nevertheless, Thelma blithely stroked the sensitive pink buds of Delia's bare bosom, her fingertips skilled in arousing lascivious emotions in young ladies.

Poor Delia had never heard or read the word *lascivious* or any other like it, and had no inkling of the emotions for which it is in general used. Yet as all the world testifies, innocence has no protection against a skilled and determined seducer, as countless unfortunate young women without husbands but with big bellies prove.

If only some older and wiser female relation had explained to ruined young women with swollen bellies the commonsense reasons for keeping their legs close together in the presence of males, they would not have succumbed to temptation when a lewd finger pressed itself into their slit and tickled their fancy – to be followed shortly afterwards by a thicker and longer part of the masculine anatomy, a part most dangerous to young maidens!

Not that Thelma had the needed apparatus to give another girl a big belly, of course, but her caresses set Delia's blood on fire. *Oh, oh!* Delia gasped, not knowing what was happening to her, and her body shook in her bedmate's clasping arm. Struggle with all her might though she did to regain her breath, knowing that she must tell Thelma to desist from her improper action, a failure of will held her helpless in the ravisher's grip.

When at last she regained, by great effort, the power to make her voice heard, it achieved nothing.

'I beg you to remove your hand from my bosom,' she gasped.

'Bosom!' Thelma said with a giggle, 'it's your titties that I'm feeling – you've got pretty ones, Delia. Shall I give them a suck – do you like that?'

'My *titties*?' Delia repeated faintly, and only to speak the hitherto unknown word brought to her cheek a faint blush unseen in the dark.

Thelma was as good as her word – she slid down the bed a way so that she could press her face in between Delia's uncovered *titties*, as Delia now found herself thinking of those charming mounds upon her chest, instead of the proper word she had used previously. *Titties* – it had the ring of a lower-class word, in Delia's opinion, and it was an extraordinary description of the female anatomy to find a young gentlewoman like Thelma Fanshawe employing in her conversation!

Not content to shock Delia by the coarseness of her choice of words, Thelma embarrassed her further by placing her open mouth over the right-hand titty of the pair, and sucking at its dear little bud. Meanwhile, her fingers were playing skilfully over the matching bud of Delia's left-hand titty, and this doubling of immoderate and reprehensible sensations set up in the startled girl feelings she had never known in her life before.

'What is it, what is it?' Delia gasped in her bewilderment, 'what is happening to me, Thelma?'

Her slender limbs stiffened in convulsive shudders, and there raged through her entire body an overwhelming paroxysm. Lost in astonishment, it seemed to Delia that

## The Girls' Boarding School

an unseen giant hand had gripped her belly and squeezed it tight, then reached up inside her and turned her belly inside-out! These strong and strange feelings were frightening in intensity, yet also delightful.

'Oh my!' she sighed, her limbs relaxing in the soft lethargy of content.

It was only then that Thelma understood she had caused Delia to experience the deep thrill of the sensual spasm for the very first time. Had Thelma Fanshawe been a young person of decency and sense, she would have been ashamed at this moment, for she had introduced an innocent young woman to guilty pleasure – and this was a wicked course, which in due time, would produce dire and wholly deplorable results. Alas, it was not so, for Thelma herself had been seduced from the path of maidenly virtue and a strict regard for chastity some years before by another girl.

In consequence, she now felt a perverse pride in what she had achieved, coupled with surprise that so pretty a girl as Delia could reach the age of seventeen and remain completely unaware of the possibilities for pleasure of her own body. In some corrupt way Thelma felt she had taken Delia's virginity, though in fact she had touched so far only her *titties*, as she called them.

In an access of improper delight, she covered the new girl's burning face with hot kisses, and waited eagerly for her little tremors to subside and her body to lie still again.

'Oh, Thelma – what have you done to me?' Delia whispered, 'I thought I would die.'

'I made you fetch off,' her companion replied proudly, 'and I believe it was your first time! Was it? Tell me, Delia.'

'I have never before undergone an experience like

that,' said Delia, still unsure of what had been done to her.

'Isn't it absolute bliss?' Thelma whispered. 'I started when I was ten or eleven to do it to myself – and never let a night pass without doing it a time or two before going to sleep. But since coming here to school, I've no need to play with myself – I get my special friends to fetch me off at bedtime.'

'Every night?' Delia gasped, still bemused by the faint but highly pleasant throbbing that lingered in her belly.

'In the daytime too,' Thelma replied boastfully, 'never less than six or eight times a day usually – sometimes more.'

'But surely that is impossible!' Delia said in amazement. 'I cannot believe that the human frame is strong enough to undergo sensations of that intensity so often.'

'Ninny! Of course it is,' said Thelma with a giggle.

'But I feel a lassitude spreading through my limbs already,' Delia answered, 'I am certain twenty-four hours must elapse at the least before any organism could sustain that shock a second time and not collapse utterly. Perhaps even forty-eight hours would be required to regain one's vital forces after so huge a drain on them. In fact, thinking plainly of it, I believe once a week must be the absolute limit of human endurance.'

'What rot!' said Thelma with another giggle. 'You have much to learn – that was only the beginning of it, Delia. Open your legs and I will teach you the proper way to do it. And as this is your first night at St Agatha's, it is your honeymoon night. I'll fetch you off half a dozen times before I let you sleep.'

Before Delia could reply, Thelma had pulled her nightgown up to her belly-button and was pushing her thighs wide apart, into a disgracefully immodest posture. In yet

## The Girls' Boarding School

another moment her hot hand took possession of Delia's tender private parts, virginal and untampered with until this moment. Thelma pushed a finger between the soft lips, ignoring Delia's cry of panic at finding herself invaded in this way.

'Your pussy is so beautifully warm and wet,' Thelma murmured, 'the only other girl in the dorm who can fetch off from having her titties felt is Myrtle Fookes. Her bed's the one nearest to the door on the other side. When I tell her you can do it just like she does, she'll crawl in beside you one night and you can suck each other's titties, to see who fetches off the fastest.'

Delia's mind was in a whirl at the lewd suggestions that were being made to her. Suck another girl's bosoms, indeed! How very unseemly a thing to contemplate. And yet another improper word had been used to offend her modesty – *pussy*!

Very obviously it had been employed by Thelma to indicate the portion of the female body for which there existed no word that decent young persons knew. Nor was one necessary, it being out of the question ever to refer to the parts *down below*, situated where the legs were joined to the body.

'Lie on your back,' said Thelma, 'I'll show you how it's done and you'll love it!'

'How what's done?' asked Delia, timidly.

Thelma made no reply, but pushed against her hip until Delia turned on her back as requested. In spite of her very natural feeling of revulsion at the indecency of being touched between the thighs by Thelma, she was intensely curious. Her new friend had caused her to feel sensations she had never in her seventeen years experienced before.

Thelma most obviously understood many things about

the female person and its private parts that Delia did not, and surely it was never wrong to want to acquire new knowledge. Necessarily there was an element of immodesty in permitting Thelma to touch the secret parts of her person, but it was undeniable that the blissful tremors now fluttering inside Delia's maidenly little belly seemed reason enough to overlook for now the inconvenient considerations of seemliness and decency.

'Oh, Thelma, I feel so . . . so . . . I cannot say how I feel – it is so strange!' Delia sighed, spreading her legs wide apart to allow Thelma's fingers to dabble freely within her pussy, 'I do believe that something astonishing is going to happen to me in another minute. I know it – though I know not what it is . . .'

'You're going to fetch off again, that's what you feel,' said Thelma cheerfully, 'and this time it's going to be a corker! I mean to make you fetch off so hard you'll think I've pushed my hand up your pussy to the wrist – but don't squeal, or everyone in the dorm will know what we're doing.'

'But you said that they all do these strange things to each other,' Delia sighed, 'so how can it matter?'

'They're paired off and playing with each other now,' Thelma assured her, 'but if they hear you screeching as you fetch off, they'll come rushing over to join in – and I want you to myself tonight. Tomorrow you can pick your own bedmate.'

Delia thrust a knuckle into her mouth and clenched her teeth on it to suppress the cries of joy that bubbled up inside her, at the instant the sensual spasm gripped her belly. Her slender back arched high off the bed, until she balanced on her head and heels, her rigid body shaking in ecstatic delight.

'Yes!' Thelma hissed fiercely, her eager fingers ravishing

## The Girls' Boarding School

Delia's wet little pussy, 'That's a lovely fetch off – a real beauty. Don't let it stop!'

Yet end it must when nature had run its appointed course, and with a long exhalation of breath Delia sank down again, limbs trembling in the sweet aftermath of her bliss. She lay limp and half-swooning, murmuring incoherently to herself, amazed by the intensity of the pleasure she had felt. Thelma chuckled while she moved her hand from Delia's pussy to her quivering belly, and massaged it slowly and very lightly, with a rotatory motion of her palm.

'What did you think of that?' she whispered. 'That time was a real fetch off – your pussy's wet through! I felt it sucking on my finger like a little mouth.'

'You must leave me now,' said Delia faintly, 'I am spent from what has been done . . . I must sleep.'

'We'll have no selfishness of that sort here, Miss,' Thelma retorted firmly. 'I've shown you how it's done, and now I want to be brought off. So rouse yourself and get on with it at once – my poor pussy is yearning to be tickled!'

'No, I cannot,' Delia sighed. 'Please return to your own bed and let me sleep.'

Thelma expressed her displeasure by pinching the tender flesh of Delia's belly and thighs cruelly, endeavouring also to rouse her from the lassitude that had overtaken her since her second coming-off. Delia winced and uttered soft little groans at the sharp nipping she was forced to suffer, but gave no indication of being brought back to full wakefulness. That being so, wily Thelma desisted from applying torture and approached the matter from a different direction.

She licked at Delia's bare titties, starting first round the circles of rosy pink that graced the milk-white flesh, though of this nothing could be seen in the dark. After that she moved on to lick over the tiny buds themselves, and despite the state of exhaustion in which Delia lay, these libidinous attentions caused her rosebuds to tingle and grow firm.

When Thelma felt them reach this condition of arousal, she at once opened her mouth wide and drew into it as much of Delia's left-hand titty as she could, filling her wet mouth with tender flesh. Then after some time she dealt out the same treatment to the other titty, then back to the first, and so back and forth, until Delia was in a daze of resignation, moral revulsion and blissful sensation.

Without a word of explanation, Thelma sat up in bed to pull her nightgown over her head. That done, and her body as naked as the day she was born, she straddled Delia's belly with her legs, holding her down on the bed while she rubbed her wet and hairy pussy up the smooth flesh.

'Thelma – what are you doing?' gasped Delia, dimly aware of some new depravity being practised on her innocent body. Yet if all is acknowledged, few would contend that Delia's young body had continued in a state of innocence after she had experienced the female orgasm, even though it had been without her consent and most surely without her understanding.

Once felt, the body can never forget that most intense of all sensations humanity can experience. The memory lingers forever along the nerves and in the secret recesses of the brain and in the depths of the personality. Though Delia loathed the thought of what had been done to her, she was utterly without the power to dismiss the memory of how delicious it had felt.

As she rubbed her bare and wet pussy along Delia's soft belly Thelma slid herself forward. Delia neither understood nor cared what Thelma did, so long as it was

## The Girls' Boarding School

soon over, and she was left along to sleep and recover her self-esteem and composure after the ordeal she had undergone.

By now Thelma was right over Delia's titties, trembling and sighing while she positioned herself above the pink bud of her victim's right-hand titty. Through the dim half darkness of the dormitory, Delia stared bewildered at Thelma, not guessing what she was at. By peering hard, she discerned the lips of Thelma's pussy swallow the firm little bud of her titty.

'Ah, that feels nice!' exclaimed Thelma, and moved herself a little backwards and forwards in a rocking motion.

The rosy-pink bud of Delia's titty was being pressed against the rosy-pink little nub inside Thelma's pussy, sending throbs of pleasure through the youthful exponent of this perversion of nature. Delia's entire soul rose in revolt against so abnormal and vile an abuse of her sweet and untouched body – but not for long was she able to remain unaffected. The slippery and gentle rub against her tender titty-bud sent tremors of bliss coursing through her, from her misused titty down through her throbbing belly to her own pussy. That word again! It had lodged within Delia's mind and she now found herself making use of it, even in her secret thoughts.

It was quite impossible then for Delia, no matter how much her untainted instincts rebelled against this physical abuse of her person, to ignore or silence the clamour of her young body for immediate sensual gratification. Every fibre of her being craved the intense delight of the spasm – it was as if she were a drugged slave to an opium habit. Indeed, it would have been a far better thing for her moral welfare if the drug she craved had been opium, and not the drug of sensual excitement, which is insatiable, once it has taken hold.

She reached around the girl seated above her, and plunged her fingers eagerly into her own pussy – a shameful action she had never performed before. Even when she washed it daily, she had always been careful to use a face-flannel, to prevent her bare fingertips from coming into contact with her private parts.

Yet now, all moral purity cast to the winds, she was touching herself eagerly – and she found that her pussy was slippery-wet and highly sensitive, the merest rub of her finger sending soft little throbs of pleasure through her. Meanwhile, as Delia was making these indelicate discoveries about her own person, above her Thelma rode rapidly to and fro. Her crisis was approaching, and she pressed close together the two buds joined in this strange act of bodily debauchery.

She gasped out that she was coming off, and beneath her Delia felt the sweet convulsions passing through Thelma's body. Then her own responses robbed her of all awareness and swamped her mind with incomprehensible emotions. She fetched off herself in perfect unison with the lascivious violater of her young body, her fingers fluttering in her own wet pussy, to raise her to an even more ecstatic climax.

When both girls were done, Delia collapsed again and lay very still and quiet, too involved with her own whirling thoughts to pay any attention to Thelma's hand resting between her legs.

'It's no use going to sleep,' said Thelma, her sharp fingernails digging into the flesh of the inside of Delia's thigh. 'I haven't finished with you yet.'

'I beseech you to be kind,' murmured Delia. 'Let me sleep.'

She moved her legs to press them together and prevent further access to her pussy, but Thelma was too quick for her, and had a hand over it in time to stop her thighs meeting.

'No more!' Delia insisted. 'If you do not release me at once I shall scream for help – think of the scandal!'

'Don't be silly,' Thelma replied, 'if you do that, what will happen is that two or three of the girls will come to play with you, instead of just me. They'll fetch you off until you faint clean away. Make up your mind, Delia – give me what I want now, or give it to half the girls in the dorm. Which is it to be?'

'Then do with me as you wish,' said Delia wearily, 'for I no longer care what happens.'

'You'll change your tune in a minute,' Thelma promised.

Her fingers probed within Delia's pussy, teasing and feeling, tickling and stroking, and after some time the results became apparent in the agitation of Delia's breathing. With a movement quick as a tabby-cat pouncing on a mouse, Thelma rolled herself on to Delia's body.

'I can't any more,' cried Delia, feeling Thelma's weight lying on her, bare belly on bare belly, bare titties pressing on bare titties.

'Open your legs very wide,' said Thelma, 'as far as they go – I want your pussy to be pulled open.'

She arranged herself with a hand thrust down between their two naked bodies so that her pussy lay over Delia's, the tender lips of both open, so that wet bud touched against wet bud.

'Oh!' Delia exclaimed in surprise, her weariness forgotten when Thelma began to move lasciviously on her. Very quickly her passions became inflamed, and she agitated and heaved herself beneath Thelma to make the sensations yet more intense.

Reader, pause and consider the implications of what has been divulged in the last few lines. This well-bred young

English gentlewoman had lost the ability to distinguish between moral good and moral evil – and all in the space of a half-hour! The truly innocent and virginal Delia Sempill-Shand had passed into a veritable frenzy of lust, and was moaning and sighing openly as she twitched and shuddered and waited eagerly for the female spasm to seize her.

For Thelma, an old hand at this desperately depraved game of bedtime indulgence, what was happening was less satisfactory to her than to Delia. With violent movements she raised herself up and reversed herself on her victim, head to foot, so her mouth was now in command of Delia's pussy, while her belly lay on Delia's soft titties and her legs lay outside Delia's head.

It is needless to say, the attentive reader of this shocking and scandalous account will have understood immediately that as a result of taking up so very impure a posture on top of Delia, Thelma had also poised her own wet pussy above Delia's face. To many it will seem impossible that a young lady of good family, not above the age of seventeen years, should have the least knowledge whatsoever of the mechanics of the unmentionable bodily action she was contemplating, but, fearful to say, the young ladies of St Agatha's were all too well acquainted with practices that in a low Parisian house of ill-fame would have been forbidden!

'What on earth are you doing?' gasped Delia, taken aback by the sudden cessation of sensation when she had been so close to her moments of bliss. Thelma said nothing, but lowered her head and ran her tongue up and down the lips of Delia's pussy.

'Oh yes!' Delia cried, shaken from head to toe by the sheer violence of the sensations aroused in her. She jerked her belly upwards madly to meet Thelma's tongue, and that young lady took full advantage of the moment she had schemed for – she lowered herself, to bring her own pussy down to Delia's mouth.

In the sweet confusion of her sensations Delia did not guess at first what this warm soft and hairy thing touching her lips could be – nor did she care. In wild excitement she thrust out her tongue to lick it, as she was being licked herself, to her immense satisfaction. Then though not fully aware of what she was doing, she thrust her tongue between the soft lips pressed close to her mouth, darting into the depths of warm moistness, licking and sucking.

From Thelma's lips came a long soft groan of ecstasy as the female spasm gripped her belly at last, and she came off fast and furious. She wriggled her person voluptuously and hotly on Delia's searching tongue, and rammed her own tongue deep within her companion. In an instant she felt Delia's loins and bottom jerking fiercely beneath her, and she guessed the new girl had achieved the delicious crisis once more.

As the blissful sensations ebbed gently away from her, Thelma rested her cheek on Delia's thigh and bethought herself with an inordinate and utterly debased satisfaction of what she had in so short a time achieved – for scarce an hour had passed since she stood at the bedside and asked to be allowed to get in with Delia! In Thelma's estimation, the new girl had been properly broken in, and now knew what was expected of her, in giving and taking pleasure. Henceforth Delia was to be available to any in the dormitory who wanted to abuse her body, on the nights when Thelma chose to take her pleasure elsewhere.

# CHAPTER 2

## A Doubtful Kind of Friend

On the day after Delia's shameful ordeal at the hands of Thelma Fanshawe the rising bell sounded at seven o'clock and the first lesson in the classroom began at eight. In the hour between it was necessary to rise, to wash and to dress, to take breakfast, and attend to whatever other matters required attention before the day's work could commence.

There was so much to occupy Delia's thoughts that the events of the night had no place in her mind. The classroom occupied by Form V was light and pleasant, and well equipped with blackboard, easel and a large terrestrial globe. For the dozen girls there were plain wooden desks, arranged in three neat rows, and facing them was the tall desk of Miss Harriet Jardyne, form mistress.

Red-haired Thelma sat in the front row, at the desk nearest to the door, as befitted her important position of prefect. She it was who indicated to Delia that she should take the middle desk of the back row, and she it was who reported *All present and correct, Miss Harriet* when exactly on the appointed hour of eight o'clock the form mistress entered the room, and the girls stood up to greet her and bid her *Good Morning, Miss Harriet*.

Luncheon was taken at midday, after which the girls had

an hour of freedom before lessons recommenced at two o'clock. When Delia had eaten her fill, she went out into the school grounds for a walk in the clear spring air, to clear her mind and raise her spirits. Behind the main building lay an extensive flower garden, in which she walked with pleasure, eyeing the daffodils and early blooms.

'Wait for me!' called a voice behind her, and Delia paused.

A slender dark-haired girl came skipping towards her across the grass between flowerbeds, a girl she had noted that day in the classroom. Delia knew her name to be Maria, for that was how Miss Harriet had addressed her in class. Maria was the one who always knew the answer to whatever question the form mistress asked, and almost every time it was Maria's hand that went up first to reply.

'You're Delia Sempill-Shand,' said the other girl, when they stood facing each other. 'Are you related to the Staffordshire Sempill-Shands, by any chance?'

'I believe I am, though distantly,' said Delia.

'I'm Maria Wendover,' said the other, her smile charming. 'I shall show you round the gardens – we've plenty of time.'

They strolled on together, engrossed in the exchange of small talk, until they were some distance from the school buildings, a clump of ornamental trees intervening between, to screen them from it. They came further on to a green wooden bench set under a tall chestnut tree, affording a long view across fields to a distant rising slope.

'How pretty the vista!' cried Delia, enraptured by what she saw of the countryside. 'I shall come here often when the sun shines, for it is so peaceful and quiet.'

'It is a very pleasant spot for a quiet chat,' Maria

agreed, taking Delia by the hand to draw her gently to the bench.

They seated themselves upon it, Delia very eager to ask her new friend many things about the school, and the curriculum of studies. Maria was very willing to answer all her questions and behaved in so very amiable a manner that Delia took an instant liking to her. For this reason it may be noted her astonishment was so much the greater when Maria, during their conversation, as casually as could be, slipped a hand under Delia's dress.

All the horror of the night before came back to Delia at this moment, when dark-haired Maria Wendover felt up her thighs, and she turned pale and felt quite dizzy.

St Agatha's boarding establishment prescribed what its pupils must wear; dresses, shoes, stockings, and also their underwear. Whoever had been responsible for the choice of the latter must, in Delia's opinion, have harboured old-fashioned views on what garments should enclose a young lady's modesty. Young persons of taste and position wore wide-legged underwear of fine muslin threaded with coloured ribbon, and with flounces – a garment known by the terribly modern name of *knickers*.

At St Agatha's girls were required to wear old-fashioned drawers of white cotton, held about the waist by a drawstring and open from front to back between the legs, thus enabling the wearer to perform her natural functions without pulling them down, as she would if she wore closed knickers.

Delia found this characteristic of open drawers of little or no advantage, compared with the distinct unease she experienced from knowing her private parts were – a thought that never dare be spoken aloud – virtually unprotected beneath her skirts! In truth, these parts, for which she had learned the name of *pussy* from Thelma, were *accessible* to a prying hand by reason of her open drawers. Accessible, in fact, to Maria's hand, as it slid up her thigh in a most suggestive manner.

'No, no, you must not!' Delia exclaimed in confusion, bright red of face at the memory of the ravishing she had endured the previous night at the hands of Thelma Fanshawe.

'Why ever not?' enquired Maria, a knowing smile on her young and pretty face as her hand passed in through the front opening of Delia's drawers, to rest at last on her soft curls. 'We are all the best of friends in Form V. Surely Thelma told you that?'

'What do you mean?'

'She must have told you we all play with each other, when she got into your bed last night,' said Maria.

'Why do you suppose she was in my bed?' Delia asked in some dismay, for she had hitherto thought and hoped that the brutal violation of her person was a secret shared only by herself and wicked Thelma.

'It was your first night in the dorm,' said Maria with a sly smile, her fingers moving daintily on the lips of Delia's warm pussy. 'Naturally Thelma got into your bed to put you right on how we like things to be between us in Form V.'

'She may have hinted at something of the sort,' Delia said, a blush on her pretty cheeks, 'but whether to believe her or not, I am unable to decide. To say the very least, the circumstances were suspect, and my opinion of Thelma Fanshawe will not bear repeating. I shall be obliged if you will remove you hand this minute from my person.'

'Suspect? How can that be?' Maria enquired pertly, keeping her hand between Delia's thighs.

'She forced herself upon me after we had gone to bed and the lights were extinguished,' Delia admitted in mortification, her blush deepening to a fiery red. 'She proceeded to take the most astounding liberties with me – even now my head whirls to think of it! What her motives may have been for what she did to me, I cannot even begin to guess.'

'Poor Delia,' said Maria with a little laugh. 'But to speak candidly now, was she cruel to you? I do not believe she was, not while my sense of touch informs me you have a most delicate little pussy, worthy of the most tender cherishing.'

'O mercy me – what a thing to say!' Delia exclaimed, unable to believe such words could emanate from the lips of a charming young lady like Maria.

'That's what I mean,' said Maria with a smile, 'your pussy is worthy of every possible act of mercy one can imagine. I shall touch it very gently, like this, so you are not distressed.'

'It is exceedingly rude of you to touch me there,' said Delia with caution, for she did not wish to offend the lively girl to whom she was inclined to offer friendship. Yet Delia was unsure of what was implied by this fingering of her person.

'Ah, we are going to be the best of friends,' Maria assured her. 'I think you're very pretty, Delia, and I already begin to dote on you. We must have no secrets from each other.'

'Will you truly be my friend?' Delia asked, 'I should like that very much.'

'You may rely on me in everything,' said Maria with a tender smile. 'I have been here at St Agatha's for almost two years now and I can advise you and help you to find your way, if only you will give me your trust.'

'I trust you,' said Delia, trying to press her thighs closer together to evict the intruding hand that lay between them.

Maria took note of the movement, and hastened to calm her new friend and give her reassurance.

'You are somewhat agitated still, Delia, by the thrills that you enjoyed on your first night here,' said she, 'and moreover by your sudden introduction to our ways by Thelma. Although she is a nice person at heart, and a delight to be handled by in bed, there are times when she takes her position as Form V prefect a little too seriously – and then she can become a bully.'

'She forced me into unmentionable acts,' Delia confided, her eyes bright with unshed tears at the memory of her humiliation. 'I blush for shame even now to think of them.'

'Then let me comfort you while you regain your self-composure and drive the memory from your thoughts,' Maria suggested, very loving in her manner. 'Lean back and open your thighs, Delia. I know exactly what is needed to calm you.'

Though the request was an immodest one, Delia did as she was asked, but with some lingering reluctance. She allowed Maria to raise her skirt and petticoats into her lap, and then part the opening of her drawers to uncover her person.

'As I thought,' said Maria, 'a superb little pussy – all pink and blonde! It shall have a kiss from me.'

So saying, she pushed Delia's legs wide apart and leaned over to kiss the soft lips between her legs. A moment later she went further – she parted them with her fingers and thrust in her tongue, to touch Delia's secret bud – the little rose-pink bud that had been so viciously abused by Thelma's prying hand.

It has to be said, as a part explanation of why so pure and right-minded a young gentlewoman as Delia Sempill-Shand allowed herself to be seduced from the paths of true virtue, that Maria was very unlike Thelma Fanshawe in her approach. Whereas Thelma had been most forceful in the way she had abused Delia's maiden body, Maria was all loving kindness. Her wet tongue-tip licked over Delia's hidden button softly and tenderly, arousing sweet and gentle sensations of bliss.

Nevertheless, Delia ought to have fled from the temptation at once, for she knew it in her heart to be dreadfully improper – but alas she closed her eyes and gave herself up to the caress. She felt Maria's hands stroke her bare thighs, the touch of her tongue within her open pussy, she heard her own sighs of bliss. Because she did not resist this perversity at the very outset, she condemned herself to sinful impurity.

The pulsating sensations mounted within her body, she opened her eyes to gaze downward, and saw Maria's pretty dark head was bobbing up and down between her spread thighs. The movement was not furious, nor in the least menacing. It was, in truth, very reassuring in its warm friendliness, so much so that Delia was rashly immodest enough to part her legs wider yet.

She noticed how her own thighs were trembling uncontrollably, not from cold, for a wholly delicious heat was coursing through her body, especially in her *pussy*. Without being aware of what she did, Delia arched her lower parts upwards, to meet the soft thrusts of Maria's darting tongue.

Soon the first thrills of the sensual paroxysm flashed along Delia's taut nerves, and it seemed to her astounded mind that her secret bud had swollen up to twice or thrice its usual size in anticipation of what was to come.

'Oh, Maria!' she cried, going into spasms of sheer delight as she fetched off.

When she was calmer, Maria took her in her arms and

held her close while she kissed her, and whispered endearments to her in the golden after-throes of her pleasure.

'There, dearest Delia,' she said at last, when she felt that the girl pressed to her own young bosom was tranquil, 'you will be much better able now to talk to me and unburden yourself of what distresses you so very unnecessarily.'

'How kind you are, how understanding,' Delia whispered back, determined to close her mind to the indecent nature of what had just been done to her. 'I feel I can lay my heart fully open to you, Maria.'

'Assuredly you can – and you may start by telling me how many times Thelma had you last night. Was it three or four – or more even? Did you return the favour each time, one for one?'

'I cannot tell,' said Delia in a hushed voice, ashamed to be asked about the improprieties that the form prefect had forced on her. 'She did things to me for hours and hours – such things I never imagined could be done by one human being to another! She compelled me to do things to her that I blush to recall.'

'Don't be a goose,' said Maria, giggling at her. 'All she did was to make you fetch off a few times. There's no harm in that, and it can't have been the first time you'd done it.'

'Nothing of the sort had ever happened to me before, alone or with another,' Delia declared firmly. 'I was shocked beyond all belief to be handled so freely by another. And so far as this *fetching off*, as you call it, is concerned, I swear it almost undid me, the sensation was so violent.'

'My!' said Maria. 'You were virgin when Thelma fingered you, is that what you are saying? But you should have told her that and she would have broken you in gently.'

'How could I know what she intended when she got into my bed and laid her hands on me?' said Delia, trembling to feel Maria pass her hand lightly over her pussy again.

'Thelma is a good sort and I'm sure she made it very pleasant for you,' Maria replied, ignoring the repulsion in Delia's tone of voice. 'When I first came to St Agatha's I was had by a girl who was older than me, and form prefect then. She took a fancy to me, though she was in a higher form. Properly speaking, she ought to have stayed in her own dorm with friends of her own age – but before I had been here a week she came by night into Form IV dormitory, where my bed was.'

'Were you very frightened, Maria? I know I would have been quite petrified!' Delia gasped.

'Not frightened exactly, now, for I knew all there was to be known about what girls do to each other, but a little nervous. Petula Dobson-Skimpole was the prefect's name, and she had huge plump titties and a backside like a dray-horse. She told me that she'd watched me at meal times, and had fallen in love with me because I was so pretty.'

'In love with you! Lord!' Delia exclaimed.

'It was very flattering to be admired by an older girl,' said Maria, her hand stroking Delia's warm little belly. 'She held me in her arms and kissed me a thousand times and told me that she was going to take me in hand, and show me what true lovers did together. She opened the front of her nightgown and made me suck her titties while she felt my pussy. She was so clever at it that she could do anything she wanted to me.'

'Oh Maria – surely some qualm of conscience pricked you, some doubt entered your mind? True lovers do not commit indecencies on the person of the one they love,' said Delia, remembering at last the dictates of morality. 'The novels of Miss Austen teach us how affianced couples behave – with respect and courtesy for each other. Even to kiss on the lips is frowned upon.'

'Petula kissed me on the lips and put her tongue inside my mouth,' said Maria, a glint of amusement in her sly brown eyes at this new evidence of innocence on the part of Delia, 'and in her loving embrace she fetched me off eleven times that night before she went back to her own dorm. She desisted from making love to me only when I swooned away from pure bliss at last.'

'Did she have no care for your health?' asked Delia. 'Your delicate constitution might have been debilitated and ruined for the remainder of your life by excessive stimulation!'

'When I awoke in the morning I was so wrung out that I could hardly stand on my feet,' said Maria with a chuckle. 'I almost collapsed during breakfast. They thought I was ill and sent me to the sickroom. I had two lovely days in bed there before it was decided I had recovered. If only they knew!'

'Knew what?'

'That Petula managed to slip in to visit me on both evenings, when everyone else was busy with prep. She hugged me and kissed me and said I was a martyr for love and she adored me the more because of it. She put her hand in the bed and up under my nightgown, and fetched me off so beautifully that I worshipped her with all my heart.'

'Is she still here at school?'

'Of course not – she left at eighteen, like everyone else. But that first year she used to slip into the Form IV dormitory whenever she could get away from the girls in her own dorm who wanted to have her at night. Once I even went into her dorm, although it is strictly against the rules, but I did so long for Petula and her lovely cuddling that night! We took off our nightgowns and I lay on her bare belly, sucking on her titties – enormous and soft they were. But then another girl from her dorm slipped in bed with us, and found me there.'

'Heavens! Did she report you?'

'No, she was too keen on Petula to cause any trouble. She let me stay while they were fetching each other off, and then I had my turn with Petula, and then with the other girl – Hermione Spalding was her name. She was wonderful, the way she used her tongue!'

It was in Delia's mind that being handled and *fetched-off*, as the young gentlewomen of St Agatha's named the sensual spasm, was a kind of initiation ceremony, adopted by the young ladies before admission to friendship could be allowed. That being so, she had completed all required of her, and was now secure from further molestation.

She had read in a book by a devout Anglican missionary that African tribes required their youths to undergo some ordeal or other as a rite of admission to full membership of the tribe – horrid ordeals that involved making patterns of scars on their bodies, and thrusting thin sharp bones through their noses.

Her own ordeal at the hands of Thelma Fanshawe had been awful beyond anything she could have imagined previously, but it had left no scars on her body, for which she was thankful. She said as much to Maria, who burst into laughter and began to draw up her own skirts. When they were up as high as her thighs so that her white cotton drawers were revealed, a dreamy look appeared on her pretty face. She gazed at Delia from half-closed eyes.

'Oh Delia, I cannot believe you are quite as innocent as you make yourself out to be,' she said. 'Perhaps you had never done it with another girl before last night, but you must have used your fingers often enough to pleasure yourself. Everyone does.'

Maria's skirt was round her waist and her fingers had entered the opening of her thin drawers, exposing to Delia the sight of a patch of dark curls.

'Really, Maria!' Delia protested. 'The suggestion is highly improper. I have never in my life tampered with my person!'

'Never even once?' asked Maria, smiling in disbelief.

'Never! And you ought not to expose yourself in this way to me – you know that it is reprehensible in the extreme. Why then are you doing it? Do you entertain the hope that you will draw me into I know not what acts of immodesty?'

Nevertheless, although Delia's sense of decency was outraged, she was unable to tear her gaze away from the sight of Maria's slender girlish thighs and the little thicket of dark brown and silky curls where they met. Yet for all her interest, she could not prevent herself from blushing scarlet to view Maria glide her own hand along the smooth pink lips that peeped shyly out from the curls.

'Ah!' sighed Maria with a dreamy smile, pressing her fingertip into her own pussy. 'You may protest your innocence until you are quite black in the face, but you will not be able to persuade me that you never played with your pussy before you came to St Agatha's. It feels too nice for anyone to resist.'

Delia stared dumbfounded and open-mouthed, to see her friend continue in her shameless behaviour. Maria's legs were spread apart to allow her fingers readier access into her pink-lipped split, where they slid up and down in a rapid motion. A gasp indicative of pleasure escaped Maria as she rubbed, her breath came quicker, and then a look

## The Girls' Boarding School

of indescribable rapture appeared on her pretty face as the sensual spasm took her.

When the delicious throes had passed and Maria was calm once more, she laughed to see the disapproving expression on Delia's face, and moved close to her on the wooden bench.

'Silly girl,' she said, 'to be so put out to see me fetch off – anyone would think you'd never seen it done before.'

'Of course I haven't!' Delia exclaimed, her face crimson.

'I do it half a dozen times a day,' Maria informed her, 'and sometimes more, if I am in a frolicsome mood. We all do, and no one thinks it in the least unmaidenly or improper, as you seem to suggest.'

As she spoke, she put her hand up Delia's skirts again, and rested it on the bare skin of her thigh, the mere touch sending inexplicable thrills through Delia's body.

'I cannot believe you are telling me the truth,' said Delia, sorely puzzled by all that was happening. 'Properly brought-up young ladies do *not* interfere with their private parts! And as for your absurd suggestion that the girls here do so, and many times daily, it is utterly and unspeakably indecent.'

'Well then,' said Maria as she stroked Delia's thigh gently, 'what befell you on your first night in the dorm? I'm sure you can't have forgotten the hand of welcome on your pussy.'

'How can I ever wipe that memory from my mind!' Delia cried.

'You will never be allowed to,' Maria assured her, 'for there will be someone in your bed to play with you every night.'

'There was a shameful assault on my person,' said Delia, her voice low and her face pink, 'but I am convinced it was only an aberration by one particular girl who has abandoned all decency and good manners. It was, I now believe, a disgraceful type of initiation ceremony, and I am of the opinion that it ought to be put a stop to. I mean to report it to Miss Harriet.'

'Yes, do!' said Maria with a giggle. 'You will get quite a surprise – you'll find Miss Harriet's hand between your legs for a feel, before you've finished complaining about Thelma.'

'What a horrid thing to say!' Delia exclaimed, 'I wonder you dare impute such low motives to Miss Harriet. She is the very model of what a teacher ought to be.'

'You'll find out soon enough,' replied Maria with a pout. 'As soon as she thinks you've been properly broken in by the girls in the dorm, she'll send for you in her study.'

In some unexplained manner, during this exchange between the young ladies, Maria's hand had again insinuated itself right up Delia's thigh and into her loose undergarment. Delia gasped to feel fingertips slide along the lightly-furred lips of her – oh impossible and scandalous word, but so handy! – her *pussy*. It aroused in her sensations for which no adequate description was known to her.

Unfortunate young woman, trapped in a predicament of her own making. She knew these sensations were forbidden to her, as to all decent females, but she could not but admit that they were remarkably pleasant.

'You must stop this at once, Maria!' she cried, summoning up all her strength of character. 'You may do immodest things to yourself if you choose – that is not a concern of mine. But you shall not tempt me into these base habits!'

She would have snatched Maria's intruding hand away from her person, but just then a knowing finger was pressed slowly into her split, setting up so delicate a thrill that poor Delia was rendered quite helpless. She could do

## The Girls' Boarding School

no more than remain where she was, her better nature overwhelmed, and shudder in nameless emotion brought on by the lubricious finger that sought out her secret bud and tickled it lightly.

'There now,' said Maria impertinently, 'you didn't make all this fuss before and I'm at a loss to know why you make it now. You'll change your mind when you've been fetched off a time or two, and you won't think it indecent when you get the taste for it – you'll be fingering yourself three or four times a day.'

'Never!' gasped Delia, her legs straining apart of their own volition, in spite of her wish to bring them decently together. 'I shall never allow myself to sink to the despicable depths of interfering with my own person.'

'You'll sing a different tune soon enough,' Maria said slyly, her busy fingers fluttering away expertly inside her friend's slippery pussy.

Delia uttered a faint shriek and shivered as if seized upon by a high fever. Her bright blue eyes almost started from her head, her belly heaved in and out, and Maria chuckled to watch her fetching off again.

When Delia had recovered from the tumultuous emotions of the sensual spasm, she stared reproachfully at Maria, who smiled at her knowingly.

'It felt nice, didn't it?' Maria whispered fondly, bringing her head close to Delia's.

So saying, she clasped her hand about Delia's wrist and laid it over her exposed pussy, urging her to return the compliment. Delia was reminded of the shameful moment in the dormitory when Thelma had forced her to put her hand on her bare split.

In some way, Delia knew, she had been changed at that very moment – her maidenly innocence had been sullied by the feel of another person's private parts under her hand.

However repelled she had been at the time, the fearful truth was that the feel of another's pussy had undone her, and set her feet on a slippy slope towards a fate of which she had not the least heed.

'Come on,' Maria whispered, 'we've got to go back to lessons in a minute or two – fetch me off first, Delia.'

Delia was dumbfounded at the suggestion, and knew herself to be incapable of complying with it. Maria held her wrist tightly and moved her hand up and down, so that Delia's fingers trailed along the warm lips of her pussy.

'Feel me!' Maria ordered her.

In Delia's startled soul was a turmoil of remembrance she was unable to shut out – the remembrance of how Thelma had made her feel her, and then later inveigled her into kissing it by lying reversed on her, each of them with her head between the other's thighs! Thelma had forced her own tongue into Delia's pussy so expertly that she had caused all sense of propriety to become suspended – Delia had put her own mouth to the soft pussy lips pressed to it and thrust in her tongue!

Shameful, shameful! The fearful scene had burned itself into Delia's memory as if with a branding-iron on tender flesh, and never would be eradicated. She felt that her very soul had been scarred by the dreadful experience. Yet, though she refused for even a moment to admit it, the sensations that had been aroused in her bosom by the touch of tongue on pussy had conveyed her to the utmost pinnacle of bliss . . .

She must never allow herself to think in that way! What was done to her was against her will, she assured herself, and what she had done to Thelma was done in ignorance and under duress. It had been infamous!

After so monstrous an experience as that, it seemed to Delia that it hardly mattered if she tickled Maria's secret

## The Girls' Boarding School

bud with her finger, especially if it brought this unwelcome affair to a quick conclusion. Alas, morality was sacrificed to expediency – she flicked her fingertip over the slippery bud till Maria gave six or seven gasps and shook all over.

Soon the two young ladies quitted the bench under the tree to stroll sedately back to school, both appropriately demure of appearance, despite the indelicate pleasures they had indulged in beneath the shade of the chestnut.

'I say – you won't breathe a word about this, will you?' said Delia to her companion, alarmed by a sudden thought that Maria might inadvertently betray the secret of their actions together and bring ridicule – and reproach – upon her.

'About what?' Maria enquired.

'That I was weak enough to allow you to involve me in certain acts of vice back there on the bench. If we are to be friends I must solemnly ask you to respect my privacy,' said Delia.

'Oh, look – there's Edna Calthorpe-Brunton!' Maria cried and pointed to another seventeen-year-old charmer in the light grey school uniform frock of St Agatha's.

Edna was somewhat ahead of them, strolling on her own towards the school building.

Maria called out, and Edna glanced back, before halting while they caught up with her. Delia had noticed her earlier that day in class, for Edna was creamy-pale of complexion and her hair was of the lightest ever yellow shade. It grew straight and was pulled to the back of her neck in a bun.

She smiled at Maria and then at Delia, when they reached the spot where she stood on the path.

'You've seen Delia Sempill-Shand, the new girl,' said Maria, by way of introduction.

'I saw you both,' yellow-haired Edna replied, with a

smile at Delia. 'You sat for the longest time on the love seat with your hands up each other's clothes.'

Delia blushed crimson, from her forehead down to her neck – and under her clothes too, down to her titties, though happily no one could observe that. Maria giggled and linked her arms in the other two girls' arms, and they moved on in a threesome to the school buildings.

'Were you jealous to see us having a feel, Edna?' she asked.

'I thought about coming to join you on the love seat,' said Miss Edna, sounding as sweet and innocent as an angel, 'then I remembered that two's company and three's a nuisance.'

'Not always,' said Maria with a lewd grin no seventeen-year-old girl should be capable of. 'Sometimes six hands are better than four.'

'If you say so,' Edna replied, 'but one hand can do the trick as well as four. So I sat down in the sun, with my back to another tree, and played with myself till I fetched off.'

# CHAPTER 3
## An Injustice is Perpetrated

Kind reader, imagine with what apprehension in her heart Delia retired to the Form V dormitory on her second night at her new boarding school. Was it possible, she asked herself, that she was expected to receive another girl into her bed *every* night, as Maria had said? Surely that was a gross overestimate of the base appetites of the seventeen-year-old young ladies of St Agatha's – these misguided young persons who permitted the base promptings of nature to set at naught the canons of decency?

Every night? No, it was manifestly impossible, and absurd to believe that tender young girls of seventeen could sustain the sensual spasm nightly, without a total collapse of their constitution, however degraded they had become.

Somewhat cheered by this conclusion, Delia closed her eyes in gentle repose and was on the verge of sleep when the bedclothes covering her were lifted for a moment, and someone got into bed beside her.

'Go away!' Delia whispered.

To protect her maidenly modesty she crossed her arms over her bosom, and clamped her legs tightly together in her nightgown.

'It's me, Edna,' a voice whispered back, close to her

ear. 'I only want to talk to you, Delia – don't send me away.'

At first Delia was suspicious of what this newcomer intended, for all her meekness. Then there came into her mind a memory of what Edna had said earlier that day, when they were introduced by Maria Wendover. She had confessed without the least trace of shame to having sat on the grass with her back to a tree while she tampered with her own private parts!

Delia now took this shocking admission to imply that Edna had fully exhausted her base lust, and for that reason alone could be trusted not to make any attempt on the person of another.

This remarkable conclusion, it need hardly be said, was based on Delia's proper ignorance of the female capacity for sensual thrills. She herself had experienced the spasm twice that noon, at the hand of Maria Wendover – though much against her will – and therefore she believed herself fully sated. In her belief it followed that Edna was in a like state, and could be trusted when she claimed she had come only to talk.

'Do you like my hair?' Edna asked, cuddling close. 'I don't – I hate it because it grows straight, and not in lovely little curls like yours.'

'I think the colour very pretty,' said Delia, calling to mind in the dark the pale yellow of Edna's tresses, 'and the texture is very fine.'

To make her point, she brought up a hand and smoothed it over Edna's hair. Edna had unbound it for the night, and it hung in long straight hanks down to her shoulders. To Delia's touch it felt like spun silk, and she stroked it several times without a bad thought in her head. How very shocked she was, how amazed, when she felt Edna's warm hand slide up inside her nightgown and clasp her between the legs – for in her mood of confidence she had let her legs move apart.

'Stop that at once!' said Delia, 'or out you go!'

'Don't be mean,' Edna pleaded, 'you let Maria feel you on the love seat – so why can't I? I'm better at it than she is.'

'Enough!' said Delia, rolling over to put her back to Edna. 'Can you not understand that Maria cajoled me into letting her use me for her degraded pleasure to the point of exhaustion and despair? I will not and I cannot repeat that shameful action, so you may as well leave now.'

'Fiddlesticks!' said Edna, pressing her body against Delia's back. 'That was hours ago!'

She had her arm over Delia's side and was trying to insinuate her hand between Delia's legs. To balk her, Delia drew up her knees as high as her chest, but by doing so she lost the advantage of her former posture. Edna pulled the back of Delia's long nightgown above her bottom, so baring those tender cheeks to her own roving hands, before feeling between her thighs from behind.

'The hair on my pussy is palest gold,' Edna murmured close to Delia's ear. 'Can you picture that? No other girl in the dorm has pussy-hair half as pretty. I'll show it to you in daylight – we will walk up to the love seat tomorrow.'

'Certainly not!' said Delia. 'I have no interest whatsoever in examining your person. Nor do I mean to let you abuse mine, so be off with you!'

'Maria said you were a shy one,' said Edna, and her fingertip tickled gently at the soft lips between Delia's legs. 'She said you'd never been fetched off by another girl before and Thelma was your first – is that true?'

'Please, I beg you, go back to your own bed and let me sleep in peace,' said Delia. 'I do not wish to discuss these indecent matters with you or anyone else.'

'Why not?' asked Edna, and she pressed her fingertip slowly into Delia's pussy to seek out her hidden bud. 'There's no need to be shy with me.'

Delia's mind was in a turmoil – her natural modesty demanded that she put an end to this perverse titillation of her private parts and send Edna Calthorpe-Brunton packing. All the same, so blissful was the thrill that ran through her from the touch of the invading finger that she was tempted to lie still, her back to Edna in disapproval, and accept whatever would happen.

This weakness was unworthy of her, she told herself fiercely, it was demeaning to let the matter go by default – self-esteem demanded that she take action. Moreover, there was the fearful consideration that if she let Edna do this to her, and bring on the sensual spasm, she would be expected to return the favour. To finger another's privities was out of the question! She had forced herself to do it to Maria on the love seat, but only to get away from her, not because it gave her any sort of pleasure to handle the other girl. Heaven forbid!

With hindsight, it was blameworthy in the extreme to tamper with Maria's person, and she was ashamed of herself for doing it. Never, in any circumstances whatsoever, would she agree to interfere with Edna Calthorpe-Brunton.

Even while these feverish thoughts were passing in dreamlike fashion through Delia's mind, Edna's attentions to her proved the truth of the vile contention that she was *better at it than Maria*. Waves of delight coursed through Delia's belly from down between her thighs right up to the pink tips of her *titties*. It was impossible to resist further, and she uttered a little mewl of a cry in her delicious spasms.

'Got you!' exclaimed Edna, her fingers fluttering in Delia's wet split to prolong the ignominious bliss.

After this dreadful ordeal of shame, could worse happen? It could – and it did, in a very short space of time. Delia lay on her side, gasping to recover her breath, and then as her sense of propriety returned, she turned quickly over to face Edna and push her away. It was at this moment that the bedclothes were dragged to the foot of the bed, and there, bending over the two girls, stood Thelma Fanshawe, the Form V prefect.

'Hah!' she exclaimed in high dudgeon. 'I'm too late, am I? You couldn't wait for me, Delia – you invited someone else into bed with you. Look at you – your nightgown round your waist and your belly uncovered!'

Delia lay paralysed with fear, to be discovered in this way. Before she had time to draw down her nightgown to her ankles and cover herself, Thelma's hand darted out to feel between her thighs.

'Wet with fetching off,' she said. 'You're no use to me now tonight. As for you, Edna, go and get into my bed and wait for me – I'll have you begging for mercy before I finish with you. You'll lick me till your jaw aches and your tongue is worn out – then I'll have you on your back and ravish you till you swoon unconscious. Off you go.'

Edna slid quickly out of the bed and sped up the dormitory to the prefect's bed. Delia lay uncovered, hardly daring to move or to breathe. Thelma reached down to grasp her right titty and squeeze it painfully hard.

'You may be new here but there's no excuse for breaking the rules – it's up to you to find out what they are,' she informed Delia in an unpleasant tone of voice. 'You belong to me for the first week you're here, do you understand that? Your pussy's mine – and nobody else is allowed to touch it without my spoken permission. You'll have to pay for not obeying the rules.'

'There can be no such indecent rule!' Delia exclaimed.

Her protest angered Thelma, who was not used to being spoken to in that way by girls she considered her junior. She showed her displeasure by hitching up her nightgown and getting on to the bed, where she knelt heavily on Delia's uncovered belly and used both hands to maul her soft little titties most cruelly.

'Shut up!' she said, 'Not another word out of you. Take a warning before you are in worse trouble. If you get into my bad books your life will be a misery. So be warned – tomorrow take your punishment and keep your mouth shut – not a word about me, do you understand?'

The pressure of Thelma's knees had almost driven the breath from Delia's body and she was incapable of responding. Not that Thelma stayed for an answer – she slid off Delia and was gone, to where fair-haired Edna lay in her bed awaiting her coming.

Troubled and confused though she was by the strange events of the past half-hour, Delia at last fell asleep. She rose to the ringing of the morning bell, and proceeded with her companions about the daily routine of the school. At the back of her mind was an uneasy memory of what Thelma had said to her, but as the day passed and nothing came of it, she began to think it was no more than bravado and idle threat by the form prefect.

Her illusion was shattered at the end of the final class of the afternoon, when Miss Harriet stood up to dismiss the girls. Judge of Delia's astonishment when the form mistress announced in a severe tone of voice that Miss Sempill-Shand would attend in her study in five minutes' time, for punishment.

## The Girls' Boarding School

'Oh Delia,' said Maria, when they had left the classroom and were walking slowly together along the passage, 'what have you done that Miss Harriet means to punish you?'

'I don't know,' Delia confessed, 'it must be a mistake.'

'Don't keep her waiting,' Maria advised, 'she gets shirty if you're late, and that will make it worse. I'll show you where her study is. I'll be in the common room so you can tell me all about it afterwards.'

Miss Harriet Jardyne's study proved to be a pleasant room, as much a sitting room as a study, with a desk by the window, and a sofa and several armchairs arranged cosily before the fireplace. Miss Harriet sat in one of these chairs, with her hands folded in the lap of her severe black dress. Her gaze was stern and unbending when Delia stood before her with downcast eyes.

'I regret to say I have received a disturbing report,' Miss Harriet began. 'It concerns your misconduct, Delia, and this is all the more disturbing as you have been here at St Agatha's no more than two days. Unless your wrongdoing is checked now, no one can tell to what extent it may taint the other young ladies of Form V.'

'But what am I accused of?' Delia asked pleadingly. 'I have done nothing wrong, I assure you.'

'Then you deny you had another girl in your bed last night?' Miss Harriet demanded, her sleek black eyebrows rising upwards in disbelief.

'But . . . but . . .' Delia stammered, at a loss how to reply.

'You do not deny it. Then be so good as to inform me for what purpose the other girl was in bed with you. I see you blush and look down in shame! That is a complete confession, there is no need for you to say a word. The purpose was immoral.'

'It was not my doing, Miss Harriet,' Delia said miserably. 'I begged her to return to her own bed and leave me alone.'

'So you try to shift the blame on to another's shoulders. Do you suppose I am so gullible as to believe your feeble excuse? You are to be punished, Miss, punished and shamed – and I want no more of your weak and despicable untruths.'

It was very obvious to Delia that Thelma had reported her to the form mistress in revenge for her own disappointed desire to share her bed. To attempt to unmask Thelma before Miss Harriet would surely make matters worse and give rise to an accusation of lying. There was nothing for it but to accept the punishment that was imminent.

At the time of her enrolment into St Agatha's, Delia had been informed that the school's humane and progressive regime banned absolutely such old-fashioned and severe forms of discipline as birching the posterior, caning, flogging, or any other violent infliction of pain. Young gentlemen at public schools might be beaten senseless every day of the week, but bodily punishment was quite improper for young ladies of birth and breeding.

Only now, with mingled feelings of astonishment and dismay, to say nothing of embarrassment, did Delia learn the methods by which discipline was maintained among the pupils of St Agatha's boarding school. They were subjected to a brisk smack upon the bare bottom, as is done to small children!

The reasoning upon which this humane but strange system was based, Miss Harriet explained, was that mere physical pain was easily discounted and forgotten when it had passed. The effect of a severe caning was gone as

## The Girls' Boarding School

soon as the red weals on tender flesh faded – a day or two at most.

On the other hand, the moral, intellectual and social shaming experienced by a young lady who had her bottom smacked lingered on in her memory, as a warning to mend her ways.

In view of the fact that Delia was a newcomer to St Agatha's Miss Harriet displayed a fine degree of compassion that partly reconciled Delia to her fate. Instead of commanding her to bend over and touch her toes for the smacking, she took Delia by the wrist and drew her down to lie across her knees. Whilst she did this, she said that discipline must always be enforced, but it should be tempered by mercy.

Having arranged Delia across her lap to her satisfaction, her clothes up over her back to reveal her bottom in white cotton drawers, Miss Harriet did not hasten to inflict the punishment she had promised. She said it was needful to ensure there were no physical infirmities or deformities to render a smack risky to health. Delia was therefore not outraged when she felt Miss Harriet's hand inside her drawers and smoothing slowly over the bare cheeks of her bottom.

In the opinion of Miss Harriet, it was a promising bum, with big round cheeks. Reader – it is necessary to disclose at this point that the form mistress was depraved in her nature just as surely as Thelma Fanshawe or Maria Wendover, and took a vicious pleasure in handling the secret parts of young ladies' bodies. In pretending to examine Delia for infirmity, she continued her handling of the girl's posterior for so long that the touch of her hand roused in Delia's bosom emotions of humiliation.

These emotions did not prevail unchallenged, for in

some way Delia found to be inexplicable, they intermingled with another emotion – an emotion to which she was unable to put a name, but which made her breathe a little more quickly, as if in pleasure or the anticipation of pleasure to come.

'Punishment at St Agatha's is dealt on the bare flesh,' said Miss Harriet in stern warning. Delia blushed to feel hands pass beneath her to find the bow that tied the narrow string of her drawers. The knot was pulled open, and cool fingertips traced an arabesque on the bare flesh of Delia's belly. A moment more and her drawers were stripped right down her legs to her knees, to hang there pathetically, exposing the rear parts of Delia's body from waist to stocking-tops.

This uncovering of her private person raised in Delia's bosom yet another emotion to compound those already there – a natural curiosity to know what it was Miss Harriet intended. She meant to smack her, that was obvious, but the elaborate preparations and preliminaries seemed to hint at something more than that – though what it might be was beyond poor Delia in her innocence to imagine.

Delia's face-down position confined her field of view to the carpet, and she was therefore mercifully unaware that the sight of her bare young posterior was producing an effect upon Miss Harriet that might well be described as *stirring*. A pink flush had risen to her beautiful face and her eyes gleamed brightly. She drew in a long and slow breath, very deeply, that made her full bosom rise, then she raised her arm and brought down her open hand smartly on Delia's bottom. The blow could hardly be said to be fierce in impact, but it was sufficient to bring the dull redness of physical chastisement to one white cheek.

Delia clenched her teeth together to stop herself from any unworthy outcry, and wriggled her tingling bum under the hand. In Miss Harriet's flashing dark eyes could be seen, if there had been a third person present to note it, the fire of lust, a burning lust kindled by her cruel treatment of the young lady across her lap. She raised her arm again and dealt a smack to the other bare cheek, forcing a sob from Delia.

The violence was over, and Miss Harriet's hand, disgraceful to report, slipped between Delia's thighs to touch her pussy. A relentless finger pressed between the plump and pouting lips to discover the rosebud within. A sigh escaped Miss Harriet's perfect mouth as she plied her lascivious finger to bring on a sweet moisture beneath its manipulation.

'No, oh no!' Delia murmured as throbs of perverted pleasure passed through her belly with ever-increasing intensity. It was only now she recalled the words Maria Wendover had spoken under the chestnut-tree – that before the week was out Miss Harriet's hand would be up her clothes to feel her!

At the time she had denounced Maria's prediction scornfully as monstrous and unthinkable, the shameful figment of a warped imagination. Yet it had been truthful in every particular. Even now Miss Harriet's fingers were interfering with Delia's *pussy*, giving rise to overpowering emotions.

Ah, what respectable and righteous-minded person would ever have believed that the severely beautiful Miss Harriet Jardyne, with her glossy black hair tied back, her long straight nose, her slender hands with long thin fingers – who would believe this paragon of classic loveliness and high intelligence would defile herself by taking a corrupt pleasure in stimulating to a sensual frenzy a pretty seventeen-year-old girl?

The awful truth could not be denied. In less a minute she

had raised Delia by her libinous attentions almost to the top peak of sensation, drawing sighs and sobs of embarrassment from the girl. Not even another full minute elapsed before Miss Harriet had her victim squirming across her lap and gasping wildly in the convulsions of the sensual paroxysm.

When Delia lay all a-tremble across Miss Harriet's lap in the after-throes of the female spasm, the form mistress removed her hand from between the girl's twitching thighs and rebuked her for what she was hypocritically pleased to call her *misconduct* with another pupil the previous night.

'I know very well what it is that young ladies do together if they are not pulled up sharply,' said Miss Harriet. 'They touch each other between the thighs in a misguided attempt to provoke spasms of pleasure. If they continue in this habit, for soon it becomes an unbreakable habit, and thereafter an addiction, their health will be severely impaired.'

She paused and shook Delia slightly, to compel her to say she understood what was said.

'Mark me well,' Miss Harriet continued. 'No doubt you have a female relative, for almost every family of means and substance has such a one – most usually a maiden aunt – who at the age of thirty-five years or thereabouts has become a martyr to the vapours. These miserable creatures spend their days stretched out feebly on divans or settees, sipping at herb infusions or other remedies. They lack strength and will power to leave the house and walk out in the fresh air. Their eyes are dull, their complexion is sallow, and their appetite is enfeebled.'

She paused again in her exposition, and Delia at once said, 'Yes, Miss Harriet.'

'These unfortunate creatures are none other than the victims of unrestrained self-gratification, the indulgence

## The Girls' Boarding School

in solitary vice,' said the form mistress in a doom-laden voice. 'They have ruined their constitution, which never will recover. They remain semi-invalids for all of their lives. Take warning from their desperate plight, Delia.'

'Yes, Miss Harriet,' said Delia dutifully.

She was at a loss to reconcile her teacher's dire warning of the natural outcome of sensual indulgence, with the undeniable fact that she had just perpetrated the fearful act upon her own pupil. Perhaps the effect of enduring the performance of it upon one's person by another female was less harmful than if the act were carried through alone. Yet, thought Delia in a puzzlement she could not resolve, young ladies of Form V performed the act upon their own bodies, as readily as they submitted to having it done to them by others, as for example Edna Calthorpe-Brunton, who had no scruple about admitting her solitary pleasures – and she was hale and hearty as anyone in Form V.

'For your own sake, so that I may best advise and guide you away from the pitfalls of sensuality, you must reveal the whole truth to me,' said Miss Harriet, placing her hand on the right cheek of the girl's burning bottom. 'When did you first begin to abuse your person?'

'Never!' Delia gasped, in horror that she should be accused of so dreadful and very immodest an act. 'No hand ever touched any private part of my person before I arrived at St Agatha's and was rudely violated on my first night in the dormitory.'

'Come now,' said Miss Harriet, 'let us be frank – perhaps you had no opportunity for playing with other girls before you came here to school, but you cannot expect me to believe you did not discover at an early age the method by which the female parts can be manipulated in solitary vice. How old were you when you first did it to yourself?'

Delia's repeated denials that she had ever done such a

thing did not convince the form mistress, but had rather the opposite effect – she became short-tempered at what she believed to be her pupil's resolute lying. After giving Delia due warning that telling an untruth was a serious offence and would be severely punished, she gave her one final chance to confess.

For Delia there could be no choice – her nature compelled her to adhere to the strict truth, even if it would attract results unfavourable and painful. Whereupon Miss Harriet pushed Delia's head down with her left hand, whilst with the right she resumed the discipline by delivering a forceful smack across the right cheek of Delia's bare posterior.

In the agony that overwhelmed her, Delia had no time or wish to observe the effect of the smack on the form mistress who so vigorously delivered it. Nonetheless, if there had been in the room a witness of an independent turn of mind, that astounded person would have surely commented that Miss Harriet's emotions were stirred deeply by the sight of Delia's bare flesh, and the manner of her wriggling and gasping at the smack laid on it.

Indeed, the darkly-beautiful Miss Harriet's heart beat faster in her swelling bosom, her blood had mounted up to her face and coloured her cheeks a bright pink hue, her breathing was quick and shallow. While her arm rose and fell again to bestow on the left cheek of her victim's bum a smack equal to that administered to the right cheek, she spoke to her, albeit with difficulty because of her rising emotions.

'You will remember in future to conduct yourself with proper decorum,' she cried. 'Do you hear me, Delia? You will refrain at all times from touching other girls' bosoms or between their legs. You will not manipulate your own private parts – are you heeding me well?'

## The Girls' Boarding School

'Yes, Miss Harriet!' cried Delia, between her sobs.

She lay limp across the knees of the form mistress, her bum displaying dull red hand-prints. Unseen and all unnoticed, Miss Harriet smoothed the thin stuff of her own dress down over her rounded belly, while her knees moved a little apart underneath Delia. She gazed down at the bare bum she had abused so cruelly and leaned back in her chair, sighing silently.

An onlooker of a lewd turn of imagination, had it been at all possible for any such person to be in the room, might even have interpreted the position that Miss Harriet had adopted as an offering of her own superb loins and unseen *pussy*, as almost an invitation – but to what? Or to whom? To a probing hand? To a lascivious touch?

Her lovely eyes were closed, having glutted themselves to the full on Delia's sweet young flesh. A certain feebleness was now making itself apparent in Miss Harriet, a delicious lethargy in the way she allowed herself to sit slackly in the armchair. Her dainty white hand remained lying across the soft cheeks it had reddened.

'We will leave it at that for the present,' said Miss Harriet languidly, 'but before you have been a month at St Agatha's you will answer my questions about your earliest experiences of the sensual spasm. You may go now, Delia.'

Greatly relieved that the ordeal was at at end, Delia rose to her feet, wincing at the smarting of her bottom as she drew up her drawers over the hot and stinging flesh. She smoothed down her skirts with a shaking hand, and turned to go.

'Wait!' Miss Harriet commanded. 'There is something you have omitted.'

'I ask your pardon for any lack of duty, Miss Harriet,' said Delia quickly, not relishing another smack, 'but I do not truly understand what it may be.'

'How could you?' said the form mistress. 'This is the first time I have had occasion to punish you. I doubt it will be the last. Listen then, and learn what is required of you.'

'Yes, Miss Harriet,' said Delia dutifully, gazing with due respect at the woman's face and attributing the pretty flush of her cheeks to the exertion of smacking her.

'It is the custom at St Agatha's for young ladies undergoing punishment to kiss the hand that metes it out, as a token that they understand that the shame inflicted upon them is for their own good.'

She extended her long-fingered hand, and at once Delia bowed herself almost double to press her lips in a respectful kiss on the smooth back of it.

'Good,' said Miss Harriet, 'now you may go.'

As Delia straightened up, her eyes were fixed in admiration on her form mistress. How very lovely Miss Harriet was, thought the enraptured girl, how perfect her complexion and figure, how rich and glossy black her tresses. How creamy-white and smooth must be her skin under her severe clothes. Oh, but that was a forbidden thought – the bodily attributes of another lady could never be a fit subject for a young gentlewoman to think on!

Delia left the room, her mind in a whirl as she struggled to rid herself of improper thoughts. In her confusion she pulled the study door to behind her, but not tight enough to make the lock click. She was halfway down the stairs on her way back to the common room to render an account of her ordeal to Maria and whoever else might be present, when it occurred to her that she had not closed Miss Harriet's door completely. Fearing that it might be held against her for a fault, she at once turned about to go back and rectify her omission.

It was as she feared – the door stood just a fraction ajar.

## The Girls' Boarding School

She reached for the brass knob to put matters right, and heard from within the room a sound that halted her. It was a long and deep sigh, a sigh from the bottom of someone's heart, a sigh of a captivating type, not of sorrow but of some pleasant emotion.

Although she was perfectly well aware that to eavesdrop on others was extremely rude, Delia was so entranced by the sigh from within Miss Harriet's room that she chose not to heed the principles of her upbringing and education. She stood close to the door and put her eye to the crack that was open.

What she saw brought a flush to her face and a gasp to her lips that was hurriedly suppressed before it could be heard in the room by the occupant.

Miss Harriet had risen from the chair on which she had sat to take Delia across her lap, and she stood before the mirror over the mantelpiece. Even whilst Delia watched in open-mouthed astonishment, the form mistress undid the buttons all down the front of her high-necked white blouse, and tugged it out of her skirt waist. What could be the reason for this divestment was utterly beyond Delia's comprehension – there were no reasons of any kind she could even imagine for a female to disrobe herself elsewhere but in her bedroom, before retiring for the night.

In another second she was astounded beyond human belief when she observed Miss Harriet take the blouse right off!

Miss Harriet stood admiring herself in the mirror, and there was in truth much to admire – her bare shoulders above her thin chemise, her long and slender neck, her uncovered lissome arms. Then in a gesture that Delia found almost impossible to believe she was truly witnessing, Miss Harriet raised her hands to her full bosom and ran her palms over the fleshy globes contained within her chemise.

Delia's face glowed a deep red to see Miss Harriet slip off the narrow shoulder straps and let the chemise slip down to her waist, baring the most magnificent pair of *titties* the girl had ever seen. They were full and rounded, the flesh a cream-white, the pretty pink buds prominent and well-developed.

*Titties*, Delia murmured under her breath in youthful devotion and respect, *lovely lovely big titties*!

For some little time Miss Harriet let her hands wander gently over her abundance, emitting further deep sighs expressing her delight in what she saw. Then she let fall her skirt, down to her ankles, and with it her petticoats. She wore no stays, the spying girl observed, that narrow waist and belly requiring the aid of no whalebone or binding to sustain a superb slenderness of appearance.

For some minutes Miss Harriet leaned with her elbows on the mantelpiece, staring closely into the reflection of her own beautiful black eyes, clad only in her fine linen underwear and transparent stockings, her chemise having gone the way of her other garments. Her graceful rounded bottom jutted out behind, splendid in its fullness and charm. Greatly to Delia's delight Miss Harriet was wearing not the old-fashioned drawers that the girls were compelled to wear, but wide-legged, frilly knickers threaded with pink ribbons.

By now a familiar sensation was making itself felt between Delia's own thighs as she spied upon Miss Harriet. How fearful, she thought in confusion, how inconvenient and improper that so very unwanted an emotion should manifest itself now! What can this degraded desire for the sensual spasm have to do with her admiration for Miss Harriet?

## The Girls' Boarding School

To calm the unwanted thrill, Delia pressed her skirts between her legs, until her palm lay over her well-covered *pussy*. That seemed to ease it, and she returned to her eavesdropping with keen appreciation. If only Miss Harriet would divest herself of her remaining garments and stand completely nude, like statues of ancient Greek goddesses Delia had seen in the British Museum – for surely full nudity would reveal only what Delia believed already, that Miss Harriet was more than worthy to pose as a sculptor's model for Aphrodite!

Miss Harriet quit the looking-glass and returned, wearing no more than her frilly knickers and stockings, to her chair. She seated herself in a most ungenteel way with her legs stretched forward and well parted, her head resting on the chair back, a position that could be described as slumping – a reprehensible way of sitting, one that she would have punished any young lady in Form V for adopting in her presence.

The chair in which she sat did not face full-on the door where Delia stood in breathless wonder, nor did it face to the side, but it was set at an angle. Delia thus was granted a view of all that took place, whilst running no great risk of being discovered, even if Miss Harriet had looked towards the slightly open door.

Her total interest was elsewhere, as Delia quickly saw. Miss Harriet pulled down her *knickers*, uncovering her belly, leaving them halfway down her thighs. In so doing she exposed a bush of glossy black hair, split by a pair of long pink lips, the sight bringing a silent sob to Delia's throat. Never till this moment had it occurred to the girl that a *pussy* could be an object of natural beauty.

Without a pause, Miss Harriet parted the smooth lips with one hand and plunged two fingers of her other hand inside. At this Delia could scarcely stifle the gasp that rose to her lips when she finally realised what her form mistress was doing.

'This cannot be!' thought Delia, her heart beating faster at the rare sight. 'It is impossible that she should abuse her own person in pursuit of the sensual spasm so soon after she issued the sternest of warnings to me against it!'

Whether it was impossible or not, the solemn truth was that Miss Harriet's bare belly was twitching to darts of sensation provoked by the movement of her middle finger in her pussy. Her long and slender legs in their transparent stockings shook, and spread still wider apart. Now Delia had a perfect view of open lips, full yet elegant, and the moist rose-pink inside of Miss Harriet's enchanting person.

Long and loud sighs racked the form mistress as the inevitable approached, and she submitted to it with a tremulous and gentle motion through her belly and thighs. Delia knew that the female spasm was upon her and stared wide-eyed.

'Oh yes – I feel it taking me!' Miss Harriet gasped aloud to herself, and then her body squirmed and twisted in the chair as the overwhelming emotions within her found their release.

Her thighs opened so wide that into Delia's feverishly racing mind came the incredible thought that she could at that moment plunge her whole forearm up into Miss Harriet's throbbing wet pussy! Although the very thought was indecent beyond words, it so fascinated the girl that she imagined herself doing it again and again.

# CHAPTER 4
# Friendship Betrayed

After the humiliation of being punished by Miss Harriet after being reported for allowing Edna Calthorpe-Brunton to get into her bed, Delia's mind was set firmly against being trapped in this manner again. Edna attempted several times to speak to her in order to apologise, and to claim it was not her fault that Thelma had reported them to the form mistress.

Whatever it was Edna wished to say to her, Delia was resolute in turning away, although in her heart she pitied the girl and would in other circumstances have been most sympathetic towards her evident sorrow. It was impossible not to notice that Edna's face was pale and that there were dark rings beneath her pretty eyes – evidence enough that red-haired Thelma had carried out her threat to ravage her all night long. A prayer of gratitude escaped Delia's lips that she had been spared this debased and repugnant ordeal herself.

'Please, Delia, let me speak to you,' Edna pleaded tearfully on her third attempt to break the ice between them. 'I have so much I must tell you – I too have been punished by Miss Harriet after Thelma reported us.'

'Leave me,' said Delia, 'you have nothing to say to me except about shameful matters concerning the sensual spasm. Though you and I might otherwise be dear friends, I will not tolerate more molestation of my person.'

With that she walked away from Edna. Neither did she have any desire to converse with Maria on the subject of her punishment, but Maria was kind and sympathetic and refused to be put off in so cursory a style. Moreover, she proved helpful in a way Delia could not imagine – for she gently spread a cooling lotion upon the reddened cheeks of Delia's posterior.

For this purpose they went up to the dormitory together, and Delia lay face-down over Maria's bed, her skirts up around her waist, while Maria applied the soothing unguent.

'Did Miss Harriet feel your pussy after she'd smacked you?' Maria enquired as casually as if the matter of violation was in no way extraordinary. The very thought of what Miss Harriet had done to her made Delia's face blush redder than the cheeks of her bottom.

'I refuse to answer so demeaning a question,' she replied.

'Ah, then she did feel you!' said Maria cheerfully. 'Did you like it? The first time she smacked me and then fetched me off I couldn't believe my luck, it was so very nice. Sometimes on purpose I make silly mistakes in my class to get myself called to her study for punishment – it's so utterly gorgeous to feel her fingers playing with your pussy.'

Whilst she was setting forth the shameful pleasures of being manipulated to the sensual climax by Miss Harriet, Maria let her own hand wander from the creamy-white cheeks of Delia's bum to the softness between her thighs. In short, she attempted to insinuate her fingers into Delia's maiden split, and for the purpose of provoking base lust.

'No, Maria!' cried Delia, pushing herself up off the bed at once and pulling down her skirts. 'You shall not touch me. I'm sure you believe there is nothing wrong in what you wish to do, but I cannot accept your view. We shall be friends, but only if you understand that I do not share your depraved weakness for constant physical sensation.'

'I was only trying to cheer you up with a quick feel,' Maria answered, quite put out.

'Do not be angry,' said Delia, kissing her friend lightly on the forehead. 'Let us return to the common room and play a game of Ludo together.'

That night, determined that there should be no reason for her to be reported to the form mistress and punished again, Delia made herself stay awake after lights out, ready to repel anyone who came to her bedside. Events soon proved that her judgement of the position was accurate, for noiselessly in the darkness a girl in a nightgown appeared and sat on the side of her bed.

She reached out to stroke Delia's face, and she whispered, 'Delia – it's me, Amy Gore-Boothby.'

'Go away,' replied Delia, and hugged the bedclothes tightly up under her chin to thwart any attempt to get in with her.

'It's all right,' Amy whispered, 'you don't have to be afraid of Thelma catching us – she's in Edna's bed and the two of them are going at it hammer-and-tongs! Half the dorm's listening to the moans and sighs – you can hear it from here if you listen.'

'I have no wish to listen to the sounds of immorality,' said Delia. 'Go back to your bed, Amy, for you are not coming into mine, not if you sit there all night.'

It took some considerable time before Amy was convinced that Delia meant what she said. She pleaded, she cajoled, she tried to get a hand under the bedclothes to tickle Delia's titties – but all in vain. Eventually Amy rose to her feet and, uttering a snort of disgust, she went away.

Delia kept watch for another half-hour, lest Amy return to bother her, then fell asleep and was undisturbed for the whole night.

The following day passed without disturbing incident. Miss Harriet's demeanour in class was normal, just as if the curious events in her study had not taken place. Delia was bewildered to recall that the calm-faced form mistress who asked her the date of the Battle of Naseby had only the day before interfered with her so very thoroughly as to compel her to experience the sensual spasm against her will.

As to what followed, when Miss Harriet thought she was alone and had bared her own body to manipulate her private parts to a full climactic convulsion, Delia blushed even to recall it. How dreadfully degraded an action it was! Yet Delia could not help but think how lovely Miss Harriet's body was to view unclothed. Her smooth lily-white belly, the glossy black curls between her thighs, the rose-pink lips of her pussy! All was divine – but Delia blushed in shame to remember these things.

At bedtime Delia retired with a quiet mind. She had secured for herself a night of undisturbed rest by speaking very firmly last night to Amy Gore-Boothby, and she intended to repeat her rebuff if any foolish girl came to pester her tonight in hope of slaking her depraved desires. Comforted by this thought, she began her preparations for the night.

It occurred to her as she removed her dress that there was a most unaccustomed silence in the dormitory. In the general way of things the girls chattered to each other up to the moment of lights out, when Miss Harriet came in briefly to see that all were in their beds, and to turn out the gaslight. A great hush pervaded the dormitory this night, for which Delia could in no way account.

After her dress, off came her underskirts and petticoats,

## The Girls' Boarding School

her shoes and stockings and her thin chemise. She pulled her nightgown over her head to conceal her body modestly before she took off her drawers. She heard Miss Harriet's voice in the dorm and jumped quickly into bed, and covered herself before she could be seen by the form mistress.

Miss Harriet walked the length of the room, counting heads on pillows, before saying goodnight in a clear carrying voice, and after her pupils had responded in chorus, *Goodnight, Miss Harriet*, off went the lights.

For the space of about ten minutes there was silence through the dormitory, as if all twelve girls had on an instant fallen deep asleep. Then Delia heard a pattering of bare feet on the floor, and a moment later her bed was surrounded by shadowy figures. A safety match was struck, and two candles lighted, to reveal to the astonished girl that all her classmates stood at her bedside in their white nightgowns.

It is unnecessary to record that Thelma Fanshawe was right to the fore – the ring-leader and guiding hand.

'Sit up and listen, Delia,' said she, her red hair shining in the candlelight. 'You are on trial and must make answer to the serious charges against you.'

Delia sat up in bed astonished, and clasped the bedclothes to her bosom.

'What charges?' she demanded. 'What silly game is this you are playing, Thelma?'

'It is no game,' said the other, 'we are in deadly earnest. A very serious accusation has been made against you by Amy. Last night she asked my permission to have you. But for some reason none of us understand, you refused to let her into your bed and sent her away. Do you deny it?'

'Deny it? Certainly not!' Delia exclaimed. 'As for reasons, I told Amy plainly that I would have no part in her vicious and immoral habits.'

A groan arose from all eleven girls who stood about Delia's bed, and a hiss of disapproval. Thelma raised her hand like an orator delivering an address to an expectant audience.

'You were warned,' she said. 'I explained everything on your first night at St Aggie's. You've broken the rules and have to pay for it. Strip her, girls!'

At once the young gentlewomen of Form V pressed forward like a mob about Delia's bed. Hands seized her wrists and neck, the bedclothes were snatched away, her ankles were gripped tightly – and she blushed and twisted left and right to escape when she felt her nightdress pulled up over her head, revealing all her naked body by the flickering candlelight.

For all her struggle, she could achieve nothing, so many held her. She was forced down on her back and heaved over ungently, then stretched out at full length on her bed face-downward. She moaned in horror and despair, but was helpless to resist or to break free. Then use was made of two pairs of cotton stockings, to lash her ankles and wrists to the bedposts.

'Thelma – what do you mean to do?' she cried out in dismay.

Her answer was a lewd chuckle and the injunction to *wait and see*. She was not kept long in suspense, for as she had feared, the plan was to shame her. Her legs were held wide apart by the lashings that affixed her ankles to the bedposts, and therefore her thighs were also open and her virginal parts exposed.

She heard the girls about her giggling, and passing comments on her person. A shriek escaped her ruby lips at the touch of unknown fingers in the crease between her bum cheeks, tickling her knot-hole. *O shameful, shameful!* she cried out, at which there was more giggling. All too soon,

## The Girls' Boarding School

as she had feared would happen, the ultimate advantage was taken of her helplessness – she felt impudent hands groping between her thighs, where silky curls covered the slit of her bare pussy.

Thelma asserted her right as form prefect to assume charge of the proceedings again. She ordered the other girls to stop what they were doing, but in words ominous to Delia's ear – for the girls were informed *there would be time for that later*. For the present, said Thelma, Delia would be punished severely to teach her she was at the disposal of her form-mates at bedtime.

By twisting her head to the side, Delia saw that Thelma had chosen Rhoda Fitzwalter to aid her. The two ranged themselves on either side of the bed, facing each other across poor bound Delia's upturned and bare posterior. Then at a word from Thelma they both began to smack her with an open hand in regular time. The chastisement meted out by the young ladies in the dormitory was not by any means the same as the single smack on each cheek delivered by Miss Harriet. That was to humiliate, this was to hurt! Thelma and Rhoda followed each other in delivering hard and stinging smacks on Delia's defenceless backside, almost as if they were a pair of bell-ringers at their work.

The other girls watching about the bedside fell into fits of giggling and whispering to hear those resounding smacks ringing out, and to observe poor Delia wince and sob under their cruel punishment. Her bottom felt as if it was on fire, and indeed it had taken on a rosy hue where the smacks were falling. Yet more painful still was the sight of her friend Maria standing by the bedside with an arm round the waist of Myrtle Fookes – and the two of them giggling to see Delia's discomfiture.

Thelma was gloating over the chastisement she was

inflicting and did not call a halt at the twelfth blow, although had Delia but known it, *a dozen of the best* was the recognised limit of dormitory punishment. Rhoda, however, did cease from the vile and degrading punishment when her share of the smacks had been accomplished.

'Carry on!' Thelma cried. 'She shall not get off lightly. If you are fatigued, stand aside. Daphne, take her place!'

Big-bosomed Daphne Grenville, fresh and untired, quickly took up her position by the bedside, and the relentless smacking was continued. By the thirtieth smack Delia was writhing on the bed continuously and crying out between sobs for mercy.

'Very well, cry-baby,' exclaimed Thelma, 'we'll call it quits for now. But take heed, if you again refuse to play with a girl when she asks you, the punishment will be repeated. And mark my words, next time it will be fifty of the best for you!'

Delia turned her tear-streaked face to the side to stare most piteously at her tormenter. Through the pain that wracked her tender body from the smacking, she could not but help noticing that Thelma was in a heightened state, her face flushed bright pink and her eyes a-sparkle. Her prominent titties heaved under her nightgown, and it was obvious to all who saw her then that the punishment she had dealt out had excited her emotions.

Without a word spoken by either, Daphne ran lightly round the foot of the bed and placed herself on her knees before Thelma's feet. A moment later she had raised Thelma's nightgown to her hips – whereupon all the watching girls drew in their breath in appreciation of the form prefect's ginger-haired bush exhibited so freely between her strong bare thighs.

Delia stared spell-bound at it, as on an earlier occasion she had gazed in wonder at Miss Harriet's black-haired

## The Girls' Boarding School

treasure. In the dormitory on that frightful night when first at St Agatha's Delia had been interfered with by Thelma, it had been too dark to observe the full glory of Thelma's flaming bush. Though she had kissed and tongued Thelma to a fetch off, this was Delia's first plain sighting of her parts.

A gasp was wrung from Delia, whether of shock, dismay, horror or admiration, not even she herself could have said, but within her bosom there was lighted a flame of the strongest and least worthy of emotions, merely to consider which would be enough to appal and disgust any person not lost entirely to goodness.

It was straight to Thelma's uncovered delight that Daphne was drawn, as if to a magnet. Delia watched how she laid her hands on Thelma's parted thighs and bowed her head to put her mouth to the soft lips gleaming within a fiery-coloured thicket of hair. For one completely shocking moment Delia found herself envying Daphne her task, and wished it was her own wet tongue touching Thelma's pussy. Then decency reasserted its belated sway over Delia's better nature and she closed her eyes in horror to shut out the dreadful sight.

'Ah, ah, ah!' Thelma moaned. 'Lick me fast, Daphne dear, for I shall fetch off in an instant!'

As if this were a signal permitting the unleashing of their depravity, the young ladies about the bed closed in, gloating at Delia, lying there bound and helpless, face-downwards. Hands were thrust between her open thighs, and underneath her belly, and beneath her bare titties. Lascivious fingers probed her pussy and the little knot-hole hid between the reddened cheeks of her well-smacked bottom.

Other corrupt fingers sought and found and plucked the tender buds of her titties, and pinched the soft flesh on the inside of her thighs, performing unspeakable acts on all parts of her body. These were lustful acts which no gentlewoman ought to be capable of even imagining, far less performing.

At the bedside, close within Delia's range of vision, stood Thelma Fanshawe, her legs spread wide, and her hands clasping Daphne's head to her belly. Thelma's eyes were tight closed and her legs trembled under her – it was very evident to Delia that the form prefect was fetching off repeatedly under the stimulus of Daphne's vibrating tongue.

'More,' Thelma whimpered. 'Do me till I swoon and fall down.'

Even as Delia stared, transfixed by the lewd sight, Thelma's knees buckled and she sank slowly down to the dormitory floor. In her gradual descent she turned until her back rested against the bed on which poor Delia was bound helpless. If Delia could have moved her head but half a foot to the left, she would have been able to press her mouth to Thelma's nearest titty and suck at the prominent bud – but what horrid thought was this to come into Delia's mind? She banished it instantly, staring aghast at Thelma's spasms.

Thelma's legs were sprawled out most inelegantly on the floor and were wide apart to reveal her wet pussy.

'Don't stop, Daphne,' she said in a soft gasping voice. 'Put your fingers up me and keep me fetching off!'

Whilst Daphne squatted between Thelma's outstretched legs to obey, Thelma turned her head and stared at close quarters into Delia's shocked face – and Delia was immeasurably moved, though by what emotion she was not then able to say clearly, being so closely confronted by the form prefect's flushed face, on which was displayed a grin of lascivious delight.

## The Girls' Boarding School

Even while Delia gaped open-mouthed and gazed into those blue eyes in which lurked unfathomable depravity, Thelma reached out to put a hand behind Delia's head and pull her face toward her own – her mouth pressing hard on Delia's in a long wet kiss.

Delia would have pulled away, but she was bound down far too closely to have more than a few inches of movement possible to her. She closed her eyes and endured the unwanted kiss – even when Thelma thrust her tongue into her mouth! From the way it throbbed against her own tongue, Delia guessed that Thelma was again being fetched off.

'Ah!' Thelma gasped into Delia's mouth as the throes of her sensual climax shook her. 'Again, Daphne – do me again!'

The dreadful abandonment of their prefect inspired the young ladies of Form V to renewed endeavours of lubricity. They fell upon their bound victim with degenerate relish, and before they had finished with her, each of them individually, one after the other, compelled Delia to fetch off. She would have shrieked, but her own drawers were forced into her mouth to silence her cries while she endured the female spasm again and again.

It seemed to Delia in her agony of mind that each repetition of the climax was more intense and furious than the previous. At long last her tormentors withdrew, giggling and whispering, to their own beds to continue the practice of their vile habit on each other. Delia lay in utter exhaustion, her ravaged pussy and smooth thighs slippery with the dew of sensuality, and her tender young titties sore from handling, her innocent knot-hole penetrated and violated by depraved fingers.

They had left her bound to the bedposts, face-downwards and helpless, and in this plight she swooned away.

Sometime later – after an interval she had no means of estimating – she came to her senses to find gentle hands untying her bonds. With little sobs of relief and twinges of pain, she turned over from the cramped position in which she had been bound for so long.

'Maria,' she murmured, 'is it you come to my aid?'

'No it's me – Daphne,' a voice whispered close beside her ear in the dark, 'Thelma made me get into bed with her, or I would have been here to untie you hours ago. Whenever she punishes a girl, it throws her into a perfect frenzy and nothing will calm her but repeated fetching off till she swoons away from nervous exhaustion.'

'Poor Daphne,' said Delia, 'your ordeal has been as horrid as mine.'

'I truly think so,' Daphne replied, 'for there was precious little pleasure in it for me. I was made to crouch down at the foot of Thelma's bed between her legs and lick her pussy time after time. After I had fetched her off ten or a dozen times in a row without a pause she fainted clean away, and I thought my duty was finished.'

'Oh monstrous immorality and vice!' Delia said faintly.

'But I was wrong,' Daphne continued, a tremor in her voice, 'for even while I was creeping away from under the bedclothes, Thelma revived and asked me what I thought I was doing. Ah, she is so very strong of constitution. I'm sure I would be dead to fetch off that many times without a rest – but Thelma seized on my titties and opened her legs and told me to start again.'

Fatigued beyond all description by what they had endured in their different ways, the two young ladies sank into the deep slumber of the weary, their arms around each other for comfort.

It was almost morning when Delia next awoke. She saw that the dormitory was filled with the pale light of dawn

## The Girls' Boarding School

and somewhere outside was birdsong. Beside her lay the warm soft body of Daphne, who had released her from her cruel bonds and given her comfort, after her vile ordeal, by holding her in her arms all night long. A feeling of great tenderness towards her companion swept through Delia, and softly she touched her lips in a kiss of gratitude to Daphne's forehead.

As she became fully aware of herself and the circumstances of where she lay, Delia realised that she was naked, having been too utterly fatigued when she was unbound to seek out where her nightgown had been thrown by her persecutors. The plain fact was that she lay naked in bed with another person – and to make matters worse, if that were possible, the other person was also naked.

What was more, it slowly dawned upon her that Daphne's sleep-warm hand lay on her pussy, clasping it firmly. Delia lay still in amazement, a hot flush suffusing her face and neck, yet soon she was forced to accept that the clasp of her bed-mate's hand was something more than an innocent and accidental touch. To be completely frank about it, something unspeakable was going on. It was undeniable that Daphne's fingers were gently moving in a caress along the lips of Delia's bare pussy. There could be no mistake – Delia's person was being tampered with.

'Daphne,' she gasped, 'what on earth are you doing?'

'You're awake at last,' Daphne murmured. 'I've been fingering you for the last ten minutes to see how aroused I could make you before you woke up. Your pussy is beautifully wet.'

'Daphne, what has come over you?' Delia gasped. 'You were a witness to what they did to me last night – you cannot think I would submit willingly to further violation!'

'Don't talk rot,' said Daphne, 'I'm sure you loved

being felt by all the girls and fetched off by each one – I know I would.'

'Then you can never have been the victim of an ordeal similar to what they performed on my person,' said Delia.

'What on earth makes you think that?' Daphne asked. 'Many a time in my first term I had my bum smacked by the entire class and was fetched off by all of them. After the third or fourth time you fetch off the sensation is tremendous – I could hardly prevent myself screaming in bliss.'

'Daphne, I see that our opinions are poles apart and not to be reconciled,' said Delia. 'Let us agree to differ and go our own ways. What to you seems frantic pleasure to be sought after is to me a violation of my integrity.'

'A girl can't violate another girl,' Daphne retorted, 'only a gentleman can do that to her.'

'Why what do you mean?' asked Delia, attempting to press her legs together to deny her pussy to her companion's hand. 'What can a gentleman do to a girl more than another girl can?'

'What a silly question!' Daphne exclaimed. 'You cannot be so very simple as not to know what I mean.'

The way barred for the present to Delia's soft little pussy, Daphne's restless hand stroked her bare belly and then slid up to her titties and played with them. Delia crossed her arms to cover herself from this new assault, but Daphne was persistent and soon had both titties in her clasp.

'I do *not* know what you mean,' said Delia miserably, feeling her bedmate's hands interfering with her bare titties.

'What a gentleman can do to a girl more than another girl can do is that he can do her with his *thing*,' Daphne explained, though her lack of adequate words to designate clearly the male and female parts, and the action of one within the other, served to impair the comprehensibility of her explanation.

Seeing that Delia was utterly unenlightened upon the method by which the human race procreates itself, Daphne used her finger as a model to illustrate the fleshy projection which gentlemen possess between their thighs, in a place corresponding to that where females are endowed with a *pussy*, as the young ladies of St Agatha's named that private organ.

Furthermore, Daphne went on to demonstrate as best she could by means of the same finger how a gentleman's projection may be inserted into the natural female receptacle.

For this practical demonstration of the copulatory act, Delia was required to lie on her back with her legs well apart, in an attitude she found immodest in the extreme. That aside, Daphne made clear to her the motion of the male part within the female part by sliding the selfsame finger in and out vigorously, thus stimulating Delia's secret bud, with the inevitable result.

Delia gasped and panted and arched her back as sensations of utter delight sped through her naked body and found release in ecstasy.

'No!' she said faintly when she was somewhat recovered from the delicious spasms. 'This cannot be true. No gentleman would for an instant consider compelling a lady to submit to emotions of that type, even if it is true that they have this stiff part between their legs, which I doubt. Have you ever seen one with your own eyes, Daphne?'

'Well, no,' the other girl confessed, 'not with my own eyes, but I know they have them. Once when I was young I was with my cousin Hubert in the garden, and he helped me to climb up into a tree. It was very high and hard to climb, and Hubert held me close and pushed me upwards to grasp the branches.'

'He was below you?' Delia gasped in horror. 'You allowed him to see your legs? Fie for shame, Daphne!'

'I was wearing long drawers to my ankles,' said Daphne with a giggle, 'anyway, as we were climbing up Hubert pressed himself close against my bum and passed an arm round me to save me from falling if my foot slipped. I felt his hand upon my titties – I had quite big ones when I was hardly more than a child – but I took the touch to be by accident and made no reproach. When at last we sat in a fork of the tree high above the ground, Hubert was red in the face and had a strange bulge in his trousers I had never seen before. I asked him what it was, and he blushed even redder and refused to answer.'

'This is no proof,' said Delia, 'perhaps he had a penknife or a catapult in his pocket. Boys often have these horrid things.'

'Ah, but there's something else,' said Daphne. 'When I was at home for Christmas last year, my Uncle Oswald came to stay with us, he having recently become a widower. One afternoon we were playing at forfeits in the sitting room, and when my turn came to pay a forfeit, I had to sit on his lap and sing a verse or two of *The Vicar of Bray*. Whilst I was doing this, I could feel something stirring under my bottom in Uncle's lap. What do you say to that?'

'A movement of his leg, nothing more,' Delia replied, quite determined to remain sceptical.

'No, it wasn't,' said Daphne, 'for I put my hand down between us and felt – and there was this long and hard thing inside his trousers. When I touched it he put his arm round my waist and kissed my cheek and said I was a very pretty young lady and he would give me five shillings. I

## The Girls' Boarding School

think he would have kept me on his lap longer, but the song was ended and I got up. But it wasn't a penknife – I'm sure of that.'

Delia said nothing, being dumbfounded by what she had heard – could it possibly be true that gentlemen had a fleshy thing to fit inside ladies? It seemed very improbable.

'Your pussy is very wet,' said Daphne, and her finger tickled Delia's tiny bud, 'there's lots of time to fetch off again, you know, before the rising bell sounds.'

Poor Delia was so shocked and dispirited by her ordeal of the night and what she had been told about gentlemen that she made no further resistance. She lay still and quiet on her back for Daphne to have her lascivious way with her, and to her shocked astonishment, when the sensation of release swept right through her body at the crisis, she found it delicious as never before, though immediately afterward she was racked by guilt.

# CHAPTER 5
# A Disconcerting Discovery

On Saturdays the young ladies of St Agatha's enjoyed a half-day holiday from their studies. Their lessons were ended that day at twelve o'clock, and after lunch had been taken, they were at liberty until the dinner bell sounded at six-thirty.

Many of the girls chose to put on their outdoor clothes and walk to the town of Tupton St Mary, which was some three miles away by road. They had permission to go into the town, although very necessarily accompanied by a member of the teaching staff as chaperone, to protect them from any impertinent or unseemly comment by town boys, or any other molestation.

Those of the young ladies not disposed to walk there and back devoted themselves to their own interests – to sketching, or to embroidery, or reading from the excellent selection of books on offer in the school library, or whatever other diversion suited their leisure hours.

Delia was hardly yet on speaking terms with her friend Maria, whose desertion of her in her hour of need in the dormitory was still a subject that rankled. Maria went with a group of girls from several forms, conducted by Miss Harriet Jardyne, to town, where they would look into haberdashers' shop windows, and take tea and cream buns at Mrs Longhampton's Select Tea Room, which was to be found in the High Street.

Certainly Delia would not join in the outing, partly because she did not wish Maria to think all was forgotten and forgiven between them, but mainly because red-haired Thelma Fanshawe was a participant in the walk. Delia loathed and despised Thelma – or so she believed – for what Thelma had done to her and caused to be done. It was not so much the spanking, hurtful though it was, as the kiss forced upon Delia when she was bound hand and foot. During that vile and indecent kiss Thelma had been in the very throes of fetching off, and the knowledge of it raised in Delia's heart such powerful emotions that she was unable to get to grips with them.

Though she blushed scarlet only to think of it, Delia feared that if Thelma summoned her to her bed one night, the loathing she felt for the form prefect would be insufficient to prevent her from taking a depraved pleasure from toying with her ginger-haired pussy. Tormented in her mind by this hideous prospect of imminent moral ruination, Delia decided to remain behind in school when the others left for their walk.

After some considerable thought, Delia decided to spend her precious hours of freedom in the composition of a letter to her legal guardian, Sir Stanton Fortescue, addressed to him in care of his residence in London. The gist of this missive would be a statement, in as delicate a manner as Delia could command, of her puzzlement at the shameful abuse she had been subjected to, at the hands of the teaching staff and her fellow pupils of St Agatha's. She meant to let her guardian know her conscience was troubled by the constant violation of her person.

Her question to Sir Stanton was whether, in his experience of the world – in comparison with which her own

## The Girls' Boarding School

knowledge was as nothing – was what had been done to her simply the usual thing to be expected by young ladies at boarding schools? If so, she regarded it as a disgrace to be endured, though never approved of. On the other hand, could it be that the constant ordeal to which she was subjected by the other girls was something quite out of the ordinary and utterly deplorable?

If Sir Stanton advised that the former was true, then perhaps she ought to submit to her schoolmates' lustful onslaughts with a good grace, and if he so recommended, then she would attempt to do so, irrespective of her own private feelings. Yet on the other hand, if he informed her that what was being done to her was wrong, then she would resist with all her strength and try to preserve herself unspotted by the taint of sensual desire.

If Sir Stanton would be so good as to advise her by return of post, she would be most grateful, for in present circumstances she hardly knew which way to turn. Such was the gist of the letter Delia sat down that afternoon to compose.

Upright though Delia's intentions were, fate decreed that the letter was not written. Whilst she was settling herself at the library table with pen and paper, troubled in her mind how best to describe the molestation of her bodily parts by hand and by tongue, Rhoda Fitzwalter, who also had declined to go along on the walk, came to find her, with a forthright declaration that she had something of particular importance to convey.

If the truth were known, Delia was not unwilling to be torn away from her letter-writing, for she dreaded the heavy task of setting down in words that would not give offence an account of the very improper things that had been done to her. No doubt there were terms used by the medical profession for the private parts of the human body and the ways in which these parts could be stimulated by the touch of fingers. It might be that even doctors shied away in horror from such activity, – but for Delia the stumbling-block lay in the fact that she was entirely unacquainted with any such useful vocabulary.

It was out of the question to set down in black and white on paper the vulgar and indecent names used by the young ladies of St Agatha's. Delia was quite sure that *pussy* and *titties* could never be words employed in polite conversation. As for the term used by the girls for the sensual spasm itself – *fetching off* – she was certain beyond a doubt that Sir Stanton Fortescue would have an apoplectic seizure if he read it in a missive sent him by his seventeen-year old ward.

With a sigh of relief, then, Delia let Rhoda take her by the hand and lead her out of the library – and indeed right out of the school buildings altogether. They strolled across the lawn where croquet was played, between the elm trees that formed a boundary to it, and into the kitchen garden beyond.

During the course of this perambulation, Rhoda expressed her deep and sincere apologies for having been forced to take part in the smacking of Delia's bottom. If the truth were known, she had formed a fondness for Delia, she declared, and wished to be her friend. It was Thelma who had nominated her to take part in Delia's chastisement, and she had cried off as soon as she dare by claiming to be fatigued.

The two girls sat side by side on a low and sun-warmed stone wall that marked off the boundary of the kitchen garden. Delia was touched by Rhoda's words of apology and readily forgave her for her unwilling part in the dormitory punishment. They vowed to be friends, put an arm round each other's waist, and hugged affectionately while they conversed.

After a time it occurred to Delia to ask her new friend about the matter that was puzzling her: namely, the strange account that Daphne Grenville had given her in bed that morning of what gentlemen did to ladies – and the mythical fleshy part of their anatomy with which Daphne claimed they actually did it. Perhaps Rhoda could clear the question up, one way or the other.

'Well of course men have a long thick *thing* sticking out from between their legs,' said Rhoda in reply. 'Surely you know that much, Delia?'

Upon being assured of Delia's complete innocence, she took it upon herself to enlighten her – and not by the use of a finger, as Daphne had done, but with a demonstration from life itself. To this end she led Delia by the hand across the kitchen garden to where stood a little wooden hut. This was used by the school gardener, Mr Benjamin Horewood, for the safe storage of spades, hoes, rakes, and whatever other impedimenta he employed.

It was into this hut that Rhoda directed their steps. Inside, on a thick pile of empty sacks on the ground, they encountered the gardener's boy – Bert Horewood. He was a mild-mannered lad of some sixteen years, with hair like straw and a foolish expression permanently on his face.

Delia was astounded to see her friend – neat, slender, pretty Rhoda with the long dark ringlets and dimpled chin – sit down next to Bert on the sacking. Moreover, she proceeded to smile at him, in an unsuitably familiar manner.

'Rhoda, what has come over you?' exclaimed Delia, 'Shame on you – get up at once!'

'Don't be a silly goose,' said Rhoda with a giggle. 'Bert is the closest to hand male with what you want to see. Aren't you curious?'

'What do you mean?' Delia asked, standing with her head on one side as she gazed down at the grinning gardener's boy. 'You cannot seriously intend to ask him to exhibit his person!'

Rhoda giggled again and informed Delia boldly that boys liked nothing better than showing young ladies what they had between their legs.

'You go too far,' said Delia, her face blushing to a pretty pink, 'you will embarrass poor Bert if you speak like that.'

'Not a bit of it,' said Rhoda, 'he's quite used to it – many of the girls come out here to look at his *thing*. I've seen it dozens of times.'

'His *thing*!' Delia repeated faintly.

'Whereas you and I have a lovely soft split between our legs, which we are much too modest to show to a male,' said Rhoda in a fit of giggles, 'boys have a long hard shaft of flesh.'

'You are telling me a fib,' said Delia, far from convinced by her friend's assertion. 'The very idea is absurd!'

'That's what I thought when I was told,' said Rhoda with a grin of pure mischief, 'but I've seen it for myself many times. At least, I've seen Bert's, and he says every boy is the same – when you've seen one you've seen them all, he maintains.'

Whilst Delia watched in silent amazement, Rhoda reached down between Bert's thighs, which were somewhat parted, and ran her hand up the inside until she paused over a bulge showing in one leg of his countrified trousers of brown corduroy.

'There it is,' she said to Delia, pinching the bulge between her fingers, 'that's Bert's *thing*, limp and soft at the moment, but we can soon change that.'

'I cannot believe this,' Delia objected, 'it is too unlikely to be true. Perhaps Bert is misshapen, or even deformed.'

## The Girls' Boarding School

The gardener's boy grinned up at her from where he sprawled on the sacking.

'It ain't me what's deformed, Miss,' said he impertinently, 'there's nothing amiss with my dick.'

'Your what?' Delia gasped, while Rhoda laughed.

'If you ask me,' Bert continued, 'I reckon as how it's girls what's deformed, not having nothing between their legs, only a bit of a slit with hair round it.'

'Oh Rhoda,' cried Delia, 'surely you haven't let Bert look at your uncovered parts!'

'I had to, to get him to show me his,' said Rhoda, absolutely unperturbed, and still rubbing her palm on the bulge in Bert's trouser leg, in a manner that must be described as indecent.

The recipient of her attentions lolled back, leaning upon the planking of the hut. He spread his legs wider, and his foolish smile grew ever more idiotic.

'I'll show you,' said Rhoda to Delia, and she undid the boy's buttons from top to bottom, and pulled his shirt right up his belly. He wore no other garment, not even the simplest form of underwear, so that his body was exposed by Rhoda's actions.

Delia stared in fascination, though her cheeks blushed a red hue at her own immodest and unladylike forwardness in an affair that was, to say the least, unseemly. By uncovering the lower portion of Bert's body, Rhoda had made it possible for Delia to discern a light patch of straw-coloured hair at the base of his belly, but nothing more. From this she concluded that her friend was playing a trick on her, and that the gardener's boy had a pussy between his legs like any girl.

The illusion was shattered when Rhoda's dainty hand plunged into Bert's trousers and down the leg to find and extract an object the like of which Delia had never in her life seen – and at which she gasped when it emerged into full view.

Between Rhoda's fingers was held a long fleshy protuberance, pale of skin beneath, with faint blue veins, as plump and dark red as a plum above, where the head emerged from the protecting skin. Even as Delia stared wide-eyed, Bert's shaft became even thicker and longer in Rhoda's hand, to her stroking.

'Do you see, Delia,' said she, 'if you handle a boy's *dick* it becomes hard. Isn't that so, Bert – you go stiff?'

'Stiff as a poker, Miss Rhoda,' said he with a happy grin on his face. 'I reckon you like that.'

In the interests of teaching Delia all that she ought to know about boys' *dicks*, Rhoda was ready to ask of Bert a question or two of fact, requiring a short answer. She had no intention of entering into conversation with a low-bred gardener's boy or of bandying words on the topic of whether she took pleasure in looking at his sensual part. She bade him hold his tongue and concentrate upon making his part grow as big as possible.

Delia was wide-eyed at what she saw – Bert's *dick* was by now twice as long as it had been, and twice as thick, and stood out of his open trousers as hard as iron.

'When it's in this condition, it's called a *cockstand*,' Rhoda informed her staring friend. 'Remember that, Delia. I'm sure we shall see many a gentleman's in this condition when we leave St Aggie's to take our place in society.'

'Why does it grow so hard and big?' asked Delia, her lovely brow furrowed with lines of puzzlement. 'The purpose of this is not readily apparent to me.'

'My, you really know nothing!' said Rhoda, giggling slyly at her friend's state of innocence. 'Bert's *dick* goes hard so that he can fetch himself off.'

*The Girls' Boarding School*

'Oh!' exclaimed Delia, her pretty face blushing bright pink again at this rude allusion to the sensual spasm. Despite the embarrassment any mention of so indelicate a subject aroused in her, she had a great curiosity to learn more of this forbidden activity. It caused her infinite effort to make any mention of it, but she forced herself to stammer out a few words. 'Are boys fetched off in the same manner as girls are, with a finger inserted into their person to tickle the secret bud?'

Rhoda giggled again at that, and Bert's foolish smile became a broad and lecherous grin.

'Boys have no split like ours down between their legs,' said Rhoda. 'Feel for yourself if you will. Beneath Bert's *dick* hang his *pompoms*. Look, I will show you.'

With these words she delved with her unoccupied hand inside the gardener's boy's open trousers, and lifted out into sight a hairy skin bag for Delia's inspection.

'What on earth is that for?' Delia asked.

'It contains Bert's sap,' said Rhoda, 'in a little while you will see perfectly well what I mean. Boys like their dicks to be played with and that fetches them off. Isn't that the way of it, Bert?'

'Why yes, Miss Rhoda,' said the grinning lad, 'that's the way of it, right enough.'

'Then you are to demonstrate the proper way to Miss Delia at once,' Rhoda ordered him. 'She has never seen a boy fetch off.'

Having given Bert his instructions, Rhoda removed her hand from his upward-standing shaft. Bert's grin spread wider still across his face, and he clasped his *cockstand* in his own hand. Delia's eyes opened wider to see him pump it up and down, for never, not even in her most secret dreams, those most shaming visions of the night that could never be spoken of – not even in the most unseemly of them, ever, had she envisaged anything like this.

Bert turned a little on the pile of sacking to afford Delia a complete view of what he was doing to himself. He stared fully up into her face and, while his hand slid up and down, he spoke to her in the most insolent way possible. 'Is that right, Miss Delia? Ain't you never seen a boy fetch off before? It don't seem natural, you being grown up nearly.'

Delia could not meet his eyes, her attention was too fixed on his moving hand, and what it held, and what it did. To her eye it seemed that Bert's *cockstand* had grown thicker and longer in the brief time he had been manipulating it. The blue veins were more prominent along the column of flesh his fingers grasped to work up and down in well-practised and unbroken rhythm. To her it seemed that the head had darkened in hue and swollen up till it resembled a large and ripe fruit.

Strange emotions burned within Delia's breast, reddening her face. She felt guilt at what she was watching without protest, dread of what the unknown consequences might be, and desire to know all. At this moment she wanted above anything else in the world to stay to the end of this unfamiliar event and thus become a party to the knowledge of how males fetched off. Yet a feeling of intense mortification troubled her, and the strength of her own improper desires confused her.

Her ordeals to date at St Agatha's had educated her fully in the knowledge of how young ladies were fetched off – and of how she herself was, willy-nilly. She had become a reluctant expert in what happened to young ladies when the sexual spasm seized them – their cries and sighs and convulsive jerks, the slippery wetness of their parts, and the languor that followed.

## The Girls' Boarding School

She had many times, far too many times for so decent-minded and modest a young lady, been forced since her arrival at this vicious and evil school to experience the full sensual spasm in her own person. To be touched deliberately on her secret parts troubled Delia deeply, even after so many times, for she dared not believe it to be other than indecent. What followed – to be manipulated lewdly, was horridly unnatural!

Yet the blissful spasms in which the manipulation ended, when at last the orgasm was wrung from her, she had to confess that these sensations were divine beyond all imagining. The delight might even in time, she feared, reconcile her to being ravished nightly by one or other of the young ladies of Form V.

Yet that was by the way. The question in hand was – how did a boy fetch off? Did he fall into the same paroxysm of pleasure as a girl did when the sensations gripped her belly? It seemed virtually impossible to Delia that any creature lacking a soft and tender pussy to be fingered could ever attain the rapture reserved for girls.

Why, only to observe how hard and strong Bert's *dick* had now become – how very male and insensitive – this was all the proof required to show that, whatever happened to males in their time of climax, it must be very far inferior to the celestial bliss felt by girls – even girls held down and fingered against their will, like Delia herself.

Nevertheless, Delia could not take her eyes off the part that Bert was now manipulating furiously. He pumped at it harder and faster, his breathing harsh and irregular, his face turning to a dark red, his eyes staring. Delia's own pretty blue eyes were round and big with wonder to observe Bert's *cockstand* straining upwards in his clasping palm.

Upwards, ever upwards, as if the leaping part would

reach up past Bert's exposed belly-button to his chest. Then he gasped loudly and his body jerked to the gushes of white creamy fluid that came shooting out of the tiny eye in the purple head.

'Oh!' Delia echoed Bert's gasp, her knuckles crammed in her mouth to bite at in her agitation of mind. Meanwhile, her other hand was down between her thighs, pressing to her pussy through the folds of her skirt, for honesty compels the admission that sensations of strangely unexpected pleasure throbbed throughout her secret parts at the sight of those milky white spurts.

Bert's hand continued to flicker up and down, coaxing out the last drops from his jerking *dick*. He grinned shamelessly up at Delia, savouring her wide-eyed amazement at this revelation of the male sensual spasm.

Dare it be said? Perhaps in the depths of Bert's common and lustful imagination, he was pretending to himself that his sap was spurting freely into Delia's virgin slit, though fortunately for her peace of mind no such vile imagining could enter into her decent thoughts to contaminate her purity.

Then Bert was done, and lolled back against the planking of the shed wall with wide-spread legs and bared belly, down which dribbled the long trickles of his spent lust. His head was laid back against the wall behind him, and his eyes were half-closed in languid content.

'Now you've seen what it's like when a boy fetches off,' said Rhoda, leaning across Bert's semi-recumbent form to address her dumbfounded friend, a knowing smile on her pert face. 'Isn't it jolly to watch? When he's rested for a few minutes he shall do it for us again. Better still – you shall bring him off with your own hand, just for a lark.'

'I?' stammered Delia, outraged by the idea. 'What can you be thinking of, Rhoda, to imagine I would ever touch the person of a male? No, the suggestion is as shameful as the act itself!'

'Fiddlesticks!' Rhoda retorted. 'You cannot deceive me with your goody-goody talk. Your pussy is itching, from watching him fetch off – you've got your hand on it!'

Delia snatched her hand away from her body and blushed more furiously yet to be caught in so improper a gesture. What might Rhoda think, to observe her like that, in an act compromising beyond all rational explanation? Lubricious of her character as she was, Rhoda might reach a wrong and insulting conclusion, namely that Delia herself applied her fingers to her own pussy to bring on the sensual climax.

The very thought of being mistaken for a self-abuser, even by a girl who freely admitted to being one herself, caused crimson fiery flushes to rise to Delia's cheeks.

'You may blush all you want,' cried Rhoda, her look sly, 'but you can't hide the truth from me, Delia. I've fetched you off on your own bed – don't forget that! I know how easy you fetch off when your pussy is touched. You won't deceive me now!'

With that, she jumped up from where she sat on the sacking by the side of Bert, who seemed to have lapsed into a foolish sort of trance, and balancing on her knees she seized Delia about the thighs and tipped her over. With a cry of surprise Delia fell down on to the pile of sacking, her legs higher than her head, and at once Rhoda thrust a hand up her billowing skirts.

With breathtaking speed and insolence Rhoda's fingers found their way between Delia's thighs, and into the opening of her drawers. With ruthless skill she pried open the lips of Delia's pussy and pushed her fingers inside.

'Ha!' Rhoda exclaimed gleefully. 'I knew it – you're just as wet as I am between the legs. Watching Bert fetch off has made you all hot and bothered, so don't try to deny it. I'll soon put things to right for you, Delia.'

Delia was too shocked to reply, or even to resist, as Rhoda's fingers played over the sensitive little bud inside her split. The observation of Bert's lustful actions had indeed roused her far more than she was prepared to admit, even in her own secret thoughts. Soon the most delicious palpitations made themselves apparent between her spread thighs and in her quaking belly.

She would have died rather than admit it, but she shortly was in a veritable frenzy of hot desire, and found it necessary to clench her teeth together to prevent herself from begging Rhoda to finish her off! It shocked her to the marrow to realise she wanted not the cessation of this depraved rubbing of her pussy but the blissful spasm of release a continuation of the rubbing would bring. She lay on the rough sacking and let Rhoda have her way, knowing how it would soon end, and for once pleased by the thought.

Rhoda too had been highly aroused by Bert's demonstration of his male power of ejaculation, and her fingers dashed about in Delia's slippery pussy with a vigour that hovered on the narrow edge between excruciating pleasure and intolerable pain: that ambiguous area of sensations difficult to particularise exactly – but which are the most intense that the human nervous system can bear. For Delia in this desperate condition, a few seconds were sufficient to do the trick, as the common saying is: her girlish loins jerked hard upwards, and with a cry she fetched off strongly.

When she lay at last tranquil, clasped in Rhoda's arms, that mischievous young lady whispered another secret into her ear – a suggestion so shocking that Delia could not prevent a gasp of horror to hear it.

## The Girls' Boarding School

The true purpose of a boy's *cockstand* was very obvious, Rhoda claimed with a low chuckle – it was so he could push it up into a girl's split. Then he would slide it in and out quickly and by this means bring himself and the girl to the spasm.

'But Bert's *thing* grew to an enormous size,' Delia objected, 'it became far too large to go into a pussy without splitting it. What you suggest is a physical impossibility, Rhoda.'

'Not so,' replied that irrepressible young lady, 'perhaps you may not know it, but a pussy will stretch open wide enough for even the biggest *dick* to go in.'

Delia denied this could be so, and when Rhoda found she could not persuade her with words, she turned to a demonstration of her contention that male and female parts were shaped for each other. To this end, she transferred her attentions back to Bert and handled his limp and dangling part till it stood strong and stiff once more. He allowed her to do to him whatever she would and sat slumped and submissive, though his eyes were wide open and had a gleam in them.

'Now Bert,' said Rhoda, 'I've woken up your *thing* for a good reason – I want my friend to see how you go about putting it up a lady's pussy. Do it slowly, in order that she may observe the entire process.'

'Right, Miss Rhoda,' said Bert with his foolish grin back on his face, 'if you'll just lie down on your back, Miss, and pull your clothes up, I'll lean on my elbows over you, so Miss Delia can get a good look.'

Delia pulled her own skirt down, realising too late that the gardener's boy had been given a sight of her pussy when she lay in Rhoda's arms with her clothes up to her belly. The burning shame of that passed quickly enough in the interest of watching now what Bert did to her friend.

Rhoda had turned onto her back, her skirt up to her waist and her slender legs wide apart in the very lewdest of postures. In the front opening of her drawers, which were pulled gaping wide by the outward thrust of her thighs, there were displayed the darling little mossy curls of her pussy, surrounding the tender pink lips. None of that delayed Bert – aesthetic considerations played no part for him in sensual activity.

He positioned himself above Rhoda, his legs inside hers and together, his renewed cockstand poised above her split and very nearly touching it. His weight rested on his arms, the elbows bent outwards, so that only his chest touched Rhoda, brushing over the full titties inside her school frock, while his bared belly was raised clear five or six inches above hers.

'No, I can't believe it!' exclaimed Delia.

Nevertheless, it was true – before her eyes Bert lowered his belly slowly down, while Rhoda grasped his *cockstand* and guided it into the tender lips of her pussy. Inch by inch it slid in – drawing from Delia an exclamation of incredulous astonishment, as she stared wide-eyed at this slow penetration.

Then Bert's belly was on Rhoda's, and no more could be seen.

'I'm right up your *twat*, Miss Rhoda,' he said, enthusiasm in his voice at last, 'does it feel nice, Miss?'

'I think the fit is a little tight,' said she, unperturbed, 'but I must admit the sensation is pleasant enough.'

The unfamiliar word Bert used to designate Rhoda's delicate little pussy struck Delia as coarse in the extreme. It must be, it was, a vile, vile word! Yet what more could be expected of a low-class and ignorant boy? He possessed no finer feelings, had no appreciation of the better part of life, he was without an inkling of the decencies of polite

## The Girls' Boarding School

society, without a trace of the treasures of the mind, and he spoke the Queen's English very badly, yet notwithstanding all that, what a very uncouth word he used – *twat* – to describe the tender female organ!

In particular, it was a totally unsuitable designation to use in reference to Rhoda's pussy, which as Delia knew from playing with it, was pure delight to behold, the prettiest arrangement of soft curls and pink lips, that parted at a touch.

Not that Delia took any pleasure in either seeing or touching other young ladies' private parts! She pulled herself up sharp over that ill-judged thought. Nevertheless, in fairness it had to be admitted that the unmentionable female parts down between their thighs could be regarded – purely from the aesthetic and artistic point of view – as not without a certain loveliness of shape and colour and appearance.

No doubt *twat* was an adequate description of the rough hairy parts of common women, the females of the class of labourer to which Bert himself belonged. After some thought, Delia decided the division made good sense – common women had *twats*, whereas young ladies had *pussies*. A world of difference lay between the two, and young Bert Horewood ought to be properly appreciative of the immense and undeserved privilege he was allowed to enjoy in thrusting his common *cockstand* into a genteel pussy.

At that moment it occurred to Delia with all the force of a smack from a hand on her bottom that Rhoda was no stranger to this curious penetration of soft pussy by hard male *thing*.

Plain commonsense indicated it was impossible to believe this was the first time Rhoda had permitted herself to be pierced by a male – for Bert's great hard *thing* had slipped in too easily for that. Though Delia understood nothing of the way of it, she knew her own pussy would not accommodate so thick a fleshy male part without discomfort.

Rhoda was more slender of body and limb than Delia, it stood to reason that she could not have accommodated Bert's intrusion so easily unless she had been well prepared for it beforehand: not to beat about the bush any longer, her maidenly pussy must have been stretched – and more than once! Yet on the occasions when Delia had played with Rhoda, no particular dilation of the parts had been noticeable. A certain facility to fetch off quickly perhaps, but that was all. Nor was that out of the way in respect of the young ladies of Form V – the majority of them fetched off very easily when fingered.

Nevertheless, Delia reminded herself, in Rhoda's case it must be borne in mind that her own attention had been on Rhoda's bud and rubbing a fingertip over it, not on thrusting a finger up her pussy to see how far it would go, in the manner Bert probed her now with his stiff part.

She saw that Bert had started to jerk his bottom up and down in a rough yet regular rhythm, and from this Delia deduced that he was rubbing his *cockstand* in and out of Rhoda's pussy. From this she partly understood what had been obscure to her before. The slide of Bert's hard flesh over Rhoda's bud would bring her to the spasm, and no doubt pleasant sensations were imparted to Bert by the friction, to make him fetch off.

Rhoda seemed to be enjoying very greatly what was being done to her – her eyes were closed and her mouth open in continuous sighs of joy. They were much the same sighs she uttered in the dorm, when Delia or any other young lady tickled her pussy with a gentle fingertip. A pang of jealousy stabbed through Delia's heart to see her friend in the sensations of bliss with someone else. Someone who was not even a Form V girl! Rhoda was doing it with a boy. Worse than that, with a common gardener's boy. Oh, it was too much!

Before Delia could turn away in revulsion from this horridly obscene behaviour exposed before her, Rhoda exclaimed, 'Pull out, quickly!'

Bert grunted and jerked his bottom backwards. Delia observed the entire length of his *cockstand* emerge, wet and shiny, from Rhoda's gaping pussy. Instantly the white sap spurted from him in quick throbs, and splattered thickly on the front of Rhoda's drawers.

Whilst Bert was shaking in the throes of his fetch off, Rhoda reached down between her own thighs and thrust two fingers into her open pink pussy. With half a dozen light rubs upon the bud that was exposed by the spread of her legs, she brought herself to the sensual spasm, shrieking with delight.

Delia stared mesmerised at Rhoda's throbbing pussy, and then at Bert poised above her, his leaping *cockstand* pouring out its milky white fluid. This was the rudest and most disgraceful act she had ever witnessed – the perverted nature of it filled her with a strong loathing. At the same time, her pussy throbbed in sympathy with Rhoda's and she wondered what it could feel like, to have a hard male *dick* pushed up into her own pussy.

Suddenly the vicious spell that held her immobile was broken. She turned on her heel and fled from the potting-shed, hearing her own whimpers of distress as she ran.

The violence of her running undid her before she had taken a score of steps – from between her girlish legs a throb of bliss passed through her body. Her knees lost their power, her legs began to crumple. She gasped and clutched at the nearest fruit tree for support, lest she fall to the ground. A wild frenzy of sensation overcame her, she pressed her belly to the tree, her legs on either side of it, and surrendered to the sensations of delight. The spasms of her fetching off shook the slender tree, and brought down a shower of white blossom about her.

# CHAPTER 6
# A Truly Deplorable Development

It will undoubtedly be considered by persons of good sense and sound morality that the introduction of Delia Sempill-Shand to the mysteries of the male ejaculation at so tender an age as seventeen years must, of necessity, set her upon a course that could lead only to disaster. So the outcome proved to be, the dreadfulness of her fate not long in manifesting itself.

Though Delia fled in shame and anguish from the horrid vision presented to her shocked eyes and dismayed sensibilities in the small shed – the unbelievable sight of her friend Rhoda letting the gardener's boy ravish her sweet young pussy with his hard-on *dick*, as he called it – the hideous truth was that Delia in allowing herself to watch had become morbidly fascinated by the vile act. From that day on she could not keep herself away from Bert, the proud possessor of the unfamiliar bodily implement.

Needless to say, Delia would never permit Bert to take gross liberties with her as he had with Rhoda – and nor did she wish to grasp his *dick* into her own hand, for that would be terribly indecent, in her opinion.

What she returned at convenient times to seek of him was only a repetition of the act of self-gratification that first caught her imagination in so fervid and unhealthy a grip. In short, to watch him bring out his limp part and manipulate it between his own fingers to a hard *cockstand* – then finally to rub it up and down until his sap flew freely.

Bert was very willing to satisfy her desire to watch him in the act, sitting with wide spread legs on the sacks, a foolish grin on his face while he wielded his stiff-standing part. When the emission was finished, he was willing enough to satisfy her curiosity, although it is to be feared that the words he taught her were unsuitable to be used anywhere but in the very lowest and coarsest classes of society.

That notwithstanding, Delia learned much from him, as to what went on between men and women, and the mechanism by which they satisfied each other's desire. The erect male organ ceased to be a thing of amazement to her and the spurting emission of sap became a regular and ever-interesting occurrence, for Bert was in the habit of slaking his adolescent lust several times a day by hand, in the potting-shed.

Retribution dogs the heels of those who indulge themselves in shameful practices and it was not many days before Delia was made to pay dearly for her offence. In class one afternoon, as the hour of dismissal approached, Miss Jardyne instructed her to report to her study. A whisper ran around the class at once, as Delia's classmates speculated on what she had done to earn a smacking. The buzz was silenced when the beautiful black-haired form mistress glared her displeasure. Delia's mind was by then in a perfect whirl of fearful speculation – what could she have done to merit Miss Harriet's anger?

She had taken pains not to upset Thelma Fanshawe – she never now refused to allow other girls into her bed at night. Indeed, in the past fortnight Delia had actually permitted herself to be violated by each and every young lady in Form V. More even than that – she had swallowed

## The Girls' Boarding School

her scruples, gritted her teeth, and forced herself to play with the pussies of her bedmates to fetch them off. She was absolutely certain there was nothing to reproach her with on that score.

After the class was dismissed, Delia waited in the corridor for the proper five minutes before making her way towards Miss Harriet's study. In this time Maria came to offer her sympathy and to enquire the reason for Delia's disgrace. So too did two other members of Form V – first Rhoda, who kissed Delia on the cheek and with a friendly smile offered to kiss her bum better after the spanking was over, an unrefined offer Delia refused. Then, much to Delia's surprise, Thelma Fanshawe approached her.

'Look here,' said Thelma, 'this is nothing to do with me, and I want you to know that, Delia. I haven't reported you, believe me, because I know of nothing you've done to deserve it. Try to take it without blubbing, and you'll be all right.'

A minute or two later Delia tapped timidly at the study door, heard the clear tones of Miss Harriet bidding her to enter, and went inside. The form mistress was not seated at her desk, nor in one of her cosy armchairs. She stood beside the fireplace, one arm along the mantel, her long and slender fingers drumming an impatient tattoo upon it.

Delia flinched to see the stern expression on the beautiful but cold face that was turned towards her. Icy fire seemed to burn in Miss Harriet's eyes as she glared down at a large sheet of drawing-paper she held in her hand.

'Explain this if you can!' she cried, and flung the paper at the trembling girl. 'Is this your vile work? Answer me!'

It was one of the sketches Delia had made from life over the past week. She had taken as her life-model the gardener's boy, and the sketch Miss Harriet hurled at her in disgust showed him him in the vegetable-garden, sitting at his ease on an up-ended wheelbarrow.

Delia was talented with her pencil, and the sketch was a good likeness. She had caught perfectly Bert's features and foolish smile, as he sat with a hand thrust under his gardener's apron.

'Well?' Miss Harriet demanded ruthlessly. 'Speak girl – have you lost your tongue? Do you deny this obscene sketch is your own work? Speak – I will have an answer.'

'The sketch is mine,' Delia admitted in a quavering voice, her pretty face flushing bright scarlet with shame.

'And what is this wretched boy doing?' Miss Harriet asked in an ice-cold voice. 'Why is his hand under his apron – what is he doing to himself?'

'I don't know,' said the unhappy girl, her desperation making her tell a lie in the hope of avoiding punishment. 'He sat like that for me to draw, and I thought he was scratching himself.'

'Indeed?' Miss Harriet exclaimed in disbelief. 'And was his hand moving at the time?'

'I really did not notice, Miss Harriet,' said Delia, getting deeper and deeper into the quagmire of falsehood.

'You observed him closely enough to make what is otherwise an excellent drawing, but you did not notice if his hand moved or not!' said Miss Harriet, her voice heavy with sarcasm. 'But do you know with which part of his person he was interfering?'

Delia was inexperienced in lying, and very inexpert at it. A look of utter confusion on her pretty face testified plainly to her lack of decision in how to reply. She knew very well at the time the sketch was made that Bert's trousers were unbuttoned and his *cockstand* thrusting up stiff under his apron. She knew also that he was stroking it up and down, because she had asked him to do so. Her secret knowledge

## The Girls' Boarding School

and her falsehood in denying it now brought the flush of shame to Delia's cheek.

'Do not play the little innocent with me!' Miss Harriet said harshly. 'I have been in charge of girls like you long enough to become acquainted with their tricks and schemes. Confess now – you deliberately provoked this common boy to handle his male part. The expression on his face you have caught in your sketch shows him almost at the moment of sensual spasm and emission.'

Miss Harriet was correct in her assumption: Bert had indeed fetched off while the drawing of him was being made, not once, but twice. Delia thought she would faint away with shame. She stared at Miss Harriet, her lips moving but no words emerging.

'I thought as much,' said Miss Harriet, a cruel smile on her face. 'You are ashamed now that you have been caught out. And well you might be! Explain to me, if you can, how you came to be acquainted with the habit of self-gratification in boys?'

Delia burst into tears and hid her face in her hands.

'I doubt if even now you understand the shocking gravity of your offence,' said Miss Harriet, 'but at least you know enough to realise you must be punished severely for it. I have had one occasion to chastise you for interfering with another girl, but it seems the lesson was wasted. You have sunk to low tastes and low companions. You must be broken of these vulgar habits, and learn how a gentlewoman conducts herself.'

'I implore you, Miss Harriet – show mercy and I promise never again to give you cause for offence,' Delia stammered between sobs of fear.

'The offence is far too grave,' retorted the form mistress in a tone of cold cruelty. 'I ought in plain duty to report the matter to the headmistress, and leave your punishment in her hands. She will deal with you far more severely than I, you may believe me. But you are a new girl at St Agatha's and I incline towards compassion in these cases. Therefore I shall punish you myself and spare you the abject humiliation of chastisement by the headmistress. Bend over and raise your clothes behind.'

Terror stilled Delia's sobs. She bent over as commanded, and with trembling hands lifted her frock.

'Untie the string of your drawers and let them drop to your ankles,' was the next order. Delia did as she was told, baring the soft round cheeks of her bottom for chastisement.

'Six of the best,' cried the form mistress. 'Three on either cheek!'

At once her open palm smacked down on Delia's tender cheeks in a veritable tattoo of slaps that made her cry out for mercy.

When it was over, Miss Harriet ordered Delia to turn and face her, and to get down on her knees. The chastened girl thought this was preparation for kissing the hand that had punished her so viciously, and so it proved – Miss Harriet extended her arm and Delia pressed her lips to the dainty white hand offered to her. So shapely and slender of fingers it was – yet the spank of it had stung her bum hotly.

Her submission completed, Delia would have risen to her feet, but Miss Harriet had not yet done with her, and held her hand in a cruel grip, forcing the astonished girl to remain on her knees.

'How dare you be so impertinent!' Miss Harriet exclaimed in a voice of anger. 'Have you no shame? Does not even the threat of renewed punishment restrain your degraded thoughts?'

At these words Delia was overwhelmed by shock and

fright, for she had not the least idea of what unintended act of hers might so have enraged the form mistress.

'I beg your pardon most humbly, but I don't understand what you mean, Miss Harriet,' she gasped out miserably.

'Do not compound the insult by lying!' exclaimed the other, 'when you kissed my hand your eyes ought to have been downcast in shame to find yourself in this posture of subjection. But no – you were staring up at my chest, and the expression on your face betrayed your innermost thoughts. You were allowing your imagination to indulge in improper speculation as to the shape and size of my bosoms, if uncovered.'

'No!' Delia murmured, aghast at the very thought. 'No!'

'Yes, yes,' Miss Harriet mocked her, 'I could read everything that was passing through your mind in your eyes – it was all so clearly revealed. You were wondering how much larger my bosoms might be than yours, the tint and prominence of their tips, the colour of the skin, whether milk-white or not, what the texture would be to your hands if you cupped them. All this I saw in a flash when I caught your glance.'

'Miss Harriet – I swear to you I had no such unseemly thoughts about your bosoms. It would be dreadful beyond words!'

'What?' the form mistress exclaimed, her cheeks blushing to a fiery scarlet. 'You dare to say to my face that my bosoms are dreadful? For this you shall be thrashed to within an inch of your life!'

'No!' Delia gasped. 'The thought, not your bosoms, I meant, Miss Harriet! Your bosoms are perfectly lovely in shape and in size, objects of beauty and grace. To see them uncovered would be the greatest of privileges.'

'Ha! Then you admit you indulged freely in a desire

to view my bosoms uncovered. And that was not the full extent of your indecent imaginings,' cried Miss Harriet, her nostrils flaring. 'You dropped your gaze after you had stared your fill at them, but instead of staring decently at the floor, as befitted your humble position after being punished for the earlier offence, I then caught you exhibiting the insufferable impudence of gazing at the portion of my person below the waist.'

Delia gave a sob of terror at this new accusation. It seemed that whatever she did or said, her innocent motives were fated to be misunderstood by Miss Harriet.

'I have never been so embarrassed in all my days,' the form mistress said. 'It was almost as if your gaze penetrated my clothing to gloat over the sight of my private person. A blush of shame came to my cheeks at the thought of your indecency!'

Delia opened and closed her mouth without being able to utter a word, so numb was her mind. Miss Harriet seized the advantage to dumbfound her further.

'Of what interest to you can my private person be?' demanded she, in a high voice charged with emotion. 'Why did you gaze at me with that lubricious expression on your face? But why ask – my years of dealing with girls like you have enlightened me as to the depravity that can lurk in the youngest heart. Confess it – you were thinking you would like to do to me what you did to Edna Calthorpe-Brunton, when you were seen in bed together.'

'Oh no, Miss Harriet – there was no such thought in my mind, I assure you,' Delia managed to say, dumbfounded by the strange accusation, and by no means certain that she was wholly telling the truth now.

She could not in all fairness deny to herself that on the day she had by chance observed Miss Harriet in the act of stroking her own pussy, its beauty of form and of colouring had greatly seized upon her imagination. Indeed, so strong a hold over her fancy had it taken that she had dreamed of the scene, and while asleep she set her hand to Miss Harriet's black-haired pussy. When she awoke she was ashamed for dreaming so indecently, but that was another matter.

'Very well,' said Miss Harriet, with the strangest of smiles on her lovely face, 'since you do not admit to the offence of failing to control your lewd thoughts, but continue to tell me unconvincing lies, you shall get as much as you deserve.'

So saying, she bent down to take hold of her own skirts and a shocked Delia saw her raise them up to her waist, so revealing her stockings and her flounced *knickers*. Delia's face blushed as scarlet as her smacked bum to see Miss Harriet pull down her knickers to the top of her thighs, and expose to the kneeling girl, without any evidence of modesty, her black-haired pussy.

'Since you have fallen into undesirable habits, it is my duty to make sure you understand properly what is involved in the act of self-gratification,' said the form mistress, her voice animated, her face a pretty rose-pink, as her fingers opened up the soft lips of her own plump pussy.

'Observe closely where I am touching with my finger, Delia – this small pink bud of flesh. This is the most sensitive spot of the entire female anatomy – as I am sure you are aware.'

'I beg you, Miss Harriet, do not continue further!' Delia exclaimed, her face redder than ever.

'Do not be insolent,' said Miss Harriet, pulling open wider yet the lips of her pussy. 'You spent a night in bed with Edna Calthorpe-Brunton, whom I know for certain is depraved beyond her years – there is no point in pretending you did not handle her and she you, to the point of climactic spasm. And I have no doubt you have done the same with other girls in your dormitory – perhaps with all of them for all I know.'

At this shrewd guess, Delia blushed crimson, for it was only the simple truth that she had allowed herself to be manipulated to spasm by every girl in Form V – and she had done as much for them in return. Though under duress, it must be stated clearly, or so Delia insisted. Miss Harriet observed the blush and drew from it her own conclusions.

'Before our lesson is finished,' said she, somewhat blithely considering the circumstances, 'you will be thoroughly familiar with the many possibilities of sensuality. You may take down my knickers, Delia.'

Delia stared up into her face in astonishment, and saw that it was pink with emotion. Not daring to disobey, she raised her hands up and pulled the dainty garment downwards, hardly daring to look at the long round thighs she was uncovering. Yet gaze she must; her unspoken desires would not allow her to do otherwise – whether it brought down further punishment on her or not.

Delia sighed to observe Miss Harriet's lissome thighs move a little way apart, as if to afford a better view of her pussy. A stifled sob, whether of anxiety or of pleasure cannot be known, escaped Delia when her fingers touched lightly the satin-smooth flesh of Miss Harriet's bare thighs above her stockings.

'Now,' said Miss Harriet in a matter-of-fact voice, 'was this how you imagined my person would look, when you were committing the unspeakable insolence of trying to see through my skirts?'

'I wasn't, honestly,' Delia murmured, lost in wonder at the soft touch of Miss Harriet's flesh and wishing with all of her heart she dare plant a kiss on that creamy-white expanse.

'Little liar,' said the form mistress, 'you shall pay dearly for each untruth you tell. But first, I wish to be informed as to what impression you have now that you have been permitted to view what attracted your lewd curiosity.'

'Oh, Miss Harriet, you are so very beautiful,' Delia sighed.

'Of course I am beautiful,' said the older woman in a tone of disdain, 'I need no schoolgirl to tell me that. What comes into your mind while you stare with huge eyes at my bared person?'

'Such emotions fill my heart . . .' stammered Delia, 'I hardly know what I feel . . . I have no words to describe it . . .'

'There can be no room for doubt in your mind of my infinite superiority,' said Miss Harriet. 'I am shaped like an ancient Greek deity, white of skin and full of form, lovely beyond mere mortals as to all my parts, worthy of the deepest devotion and worship.'

'Oh, yes, yes,' Delia whispered, entranced by the beautiful pussy at which she stared so long.

'Then display your homage with an appropriate kiss,' replied Miss Harriet, with a thin smile of triumph.

Thus bidden, Delia could conceive no thought of disobeying so imperious a command, but swayed forward to press her lips against the warm flesh of a bare thigh.

'Good,' said Miss Harriet. 'Higher.'

As if in a dream, Delia moved her mouth upwards a little and kissed again in admiring salutation.

'Higher,' said Miss Harriet.

This time when Delia kissed, she felt the tickle of silky and jet-black curls on her nose.

'Higher!' said Miss Harriet again, parting her thighs wider.

Delia's lips had reached at last the warm and secret bower of Miss Harriet's femininity. Soft pussy lips met her mouth, and seemed almost to open beneath her kiss. Tutored for night after night by her classmates in the ways of titillating the female parts, Delia slipped her tongue between those enticing lips and gently touched the little rose-bud within.

'Ah,' sighed Miss Harriet, 'you know more than you pretend, Delia. It is just as I thought – you have a sensual nature and pretend to an innocence that has long departed from you. If you practice this shallow hypocrisy with others, that is only to be expected, the world being as it is. But not with me – I insist upon complete and utter frankness. You have tried to deceive me again and again, for which you shall be made to suffer in good time. For now you may continue to kiss me until I command you to stop.'

Delia plied her tongue briskly, in the way that she had been taught by her depraved and lustful classmates. Soon the growing irregularity of Miss Harriet's hasty breathing confirmed Delia in her supposition that her form mistress was fast approaching the climactic spasm. Delia lifted her head and stared up at the pink-flushed face of the older woman, awaiting an indication as to whether she should continue until the inevitable took place, or if she was to break off this dishonourable stimulation.

At once Miss Harriet swung her arm round and smacked Delia's face sharply.

'How dare you disobey me!' she cried. 'I ordered you to kiss me until I said stop.'

Her other hand swung round and smacked Delia's face upon the other side, tearing a sob from her throat. The demonstration of dissatisfaction spurred Delia back to her perverted task – she pressed her mouth to the pouting lips of Miss Harriet's pussy and plunged in her tongue as far as

## The Girls' Boarding School

it would go, vibrating it over the button that stood ready for her caress.

'Faster!' Miss Harriet exclaimed, her shining eyes staring down at Delia's head. 'If you won't obey me properly, there are ways enough to deal with girls like you!'

A sigh escaped Delia – a sigh in which resignation to her lot was mingled with despair at her treatment by the teaching staff and genteel pupils of St Agatha's. By reason of the fact that her mouth was in the closest proximity to Miss Harriet's pussy, the sigh communicated itself to the form mistress as a long and warm breath of air on that most delicate and sensitive part of her person.

At that sweet sensation Miss Harriet's soft belly and thighs stiffened and became rigid at the onset of spasms of delight – she moaned and swayed lightly on her long legs as she fetched off in elegant throbs.

When at last her pleasure was complete she leaned down to put a hand under Delia's chin, and turn up the girl's flushed face, to stare commandingly into her eyes.

'Hear me now, Delia,' said she, her voice hard, 'if ever you speak of this to another living soul, it will be the worse for you. You will not be believed, for who will take your word over mine? But you will come to the attention of the head mistress and be punished bitterly. Is that clear to you?'

'You may trust me to say nothing,' Delia stammered in terror.

Miss Harriet lowered her skirts and pulled up her *knickers* to conceal the beauties of her lower parts. Without commenting further on Delia's assurance of silence, a gesture of her hand brought the girl up from her knees to her feet, her eyes still downcast. Delia thought she would be dismissed, her punishment completed, but her form mistress had not yet done.

With an imperious flick of her long fingers she indicated

to Delia that she was to pick up the offending sketch lying on the carpet and hand it to her, whereupon she ripped the sketch into four parts and threw them into Delia's face.

'If I find out that you have been anywhere near this wretched gardener's boy in future, you will regret it for the remainder of your life,' she said, her eyes flashing with dark fire. 'You are to put out of your mind all lewd thoughts of male creatures handling their own persons – do you hear me?'

'Yes, Miss Harriet.'

'Take my advice – form a friendship with a suitable person of your own age and social standing among the young ladies of Form V, and conduct yourself discreetly. Do you understand what I am telling you?'

Delia nodded, her face crimson at the suggestion.

'Good,' said Miss Harriet, 'above all, do not let yourself be caught out. If you are seen in bed with another girl you will be punished, because that is the rule at St Agatha's. Therefore take heed *not to be discovered* breaking the rules, whatever you may do for your private amusement.'

So saying, she grasped Delia by the arm and pushed her across the room to where her desk stood by the wall, then made her sit on the edge of it, and then lie down on it. No sooner was Delia on her back than the form mistress thrust a hand up her skirts and into her open school drawers. Delia tried to keep her legs together, but found it impossible to do so, for Miss Harriet pushed them apart to stand between her knees, and then thrust a knowing fingertip into Delia's virginal slit and rubbed at the tender button within.

It seemed utterly pointless to complain, and therefore Delia lay with her eyes tightly closed, waiting for the ordeal to end as it must, by the induction of the sensual spasm. This was not long delayed. Truth to tell, she was already in a condition of excitation, it being necessary to confess that kissing Miss Harriet's pussy had aroused Delia's base passions in a shameful and abnormal manner, however bitterly she denied it to herself.

Only twenty seconds of stimulation by Miss Harriet's skilled hand were sufficient for the task in hand – Delia moaned loudly as her exposed legs jerked, and she fetched off.

'There, that's settled you.' Miss Harriet declared. 'Be off with you now.'

Her order was not obeyed, for Delia's delicious throes lasted longer than usual, and she lay helpless and shaking across the desk, sighing and gasping, her belly quaking in ecstasy.

'That's the way of it, is it!' Miss Harriet exclaimed in her surprise at this excessive sensuality. 'Your pose of innocence stands revealed for a sham, a pretence, an outright imposture. Well then, dear innocent little Miss Sempill-Shand – we'll soon find out what it takes to drain your lust dry.'

With that she employed both her long thin thumbs to separate the wet lips of Delia's pussy, sank gracefully to her knees and with her tongue recommenced the lascivious manipulation of the startled girl's throbbing little bud.

# CHAPTER 7
# Depravity Beyond Belief is Revealed

As the days passed and became weeks, Delia became duly resigned to her fate and settled into the general life of St Agatha's. She was reconciled with her friend Maria, and formed a type of mild friendship with ginger-haired Thelma, the form prefect.

Save for the three days in the month when her natural courses were upon her, Delia's nocturnal hours were entirely given over to enforced sensual activity, for each night a different young lady slipped into her bed. By this means, and in rotation, she found herself submitting to the lusts of Form V entire.

After the ordeal in Miss Harriet's study, when Delia had been forced to kiss her form mistress's uncovered pussy and then had been ravaged by her fingers until she could hardly stand on her feet without swooning, nothing more transpired between them. In class Miss Harriet treated her precisely as before, not better, not worse. Nor did she send for her to her study again.

Although Delia thought about it often enough, she was unable to explain to herself why Miss Harriet had behaved towards her in that manner. It had been punishment of a sort, that she knew well enough, but a form of punishment not entirely unwelcome or distasteful. In her secret thoughts Delia wished at times that Miss Harriet would again summon her to her private study, raise her skirts to reveal her dainty knickers and order Delia to get down on her knees and kiss her. Yet such thoughts were indecent in the highest degree, and Delia paid for them dearly in pangs of conscience and guilt.

The weeks passed and nothing of the sort happened. It seemed that Miss Harriet had completely forgotten what she had forced Delia to perform upon her – or perhaps it was a matter of total insignificance to her. Delia could hardly credit what Maria had told her of her own encounters with Miss Harriet and was too ashamed to enquire of her classmates if they too had been used by Miss Harriet in unusual ways. Or, perish the thought, if they each in turn made regular visits to Miss Harriet's study to assuage her improper desires.

Meanwhile, Delia by night was felt and fingered and handled and kissed and licked and forced to fetch off time and again by her classmates – pale blonde Edna Calthorpe-Brunton of the big titties, dark-haired little Maria, insatiable Daphne Grenville, and shy Amy Gore-Boothby, who fetched off so very silently that only she knew when she did, and often lay so still that she was brought to the spasm five or six times in a row before her bed companion guessed.

These and all the other girls had, by their lewd and perverse actions towards her, imprinted themselves on the virgin tablets of Delia's memory. There was big-bummed Dorothy Benson-Smyth, who had a heart-shaped brown mole on her broad white belly, close up to her pussy, and Martha Dalrymple, who had almost no hair between her thighs and gave the appearance, whenever she parted them, of being no more than twelve years old. Then too there was Selina Ripley, who liked to

## The Girls' Boarding School

have both of her lower orifices fingered at the same time.

There was little Myrtle Fookes who could be fetched off quite easily by handling her titties. When Myrtle found out that this was an ability Delia shared with her, she insisted they engaged in hours of mutual titty-stroking, causing Delia and herself to attain the female spasm at the same instant – not merely once, but in a long succession of repeated paroxysms, lasting an hour or more, until both young ladies fainted clean away from excess of emotion, and lay unconscious together in bed.

Naturally, Thelma Fanshawe insisted on her right as the form prefect to have Delia, sometimes two or three nights in a week, for Thelma had taken a strong fancy to the innocent young girl. Delia knew that when Thelma was with other girls she made them lick her ginger-haired pussy to repeated spasm, but strangely, when she came to Delia's bed she played the masculine role, and made Delia her sweetheart.

She would compel Delia to lie on her back with her legs apart and her nightgown up over her titties, then strip herself stark naked and lie on Delia's bare belly, pressing hot kisses on her reluctant mouth, whilst rubbing her ginger-haired mound against the lips of Delia's pussy.

Yet whichever young gentlewoman invaded her bed each night to debauch her, when daylight came and Delia rose to prepare for the day, these depraved hours of her utter submission to Thelma or Maria or Dorothy, or whoever it had been who had ravaged her body, were dismissed as if they were mere dream-fantasies soon forgotten.

She could not help but be aware that the other girls of Form V took every opportunity that served during the day to indulge their unnatural desires – she had herself been seduced by Maria Wendover on the bench under the tree

115

they called the love seat. She had been new to the ways of St Agatha's then, and ignorant of what went on. Since then she had been been tutored much against her will in the tortuous pathways and byways of vice.

There was no means by which she could safeguard and protect her maidenly virtue at night in the dormitory from the ravages of her companions, but during the day she kept aloof. Not that it was easy to do so, for she was a very pretty young lady and received constant invitations to stroll with someone or other out into the gardens *for a feel*.

These disgraceful invitations were usually accompanied by the touch of a soft hand on her bottom or bosom, but Delia replied firmly in the negative to all alike, and blushed as she removed the offending hand from her person.

Notwithstanding, there came a day when Delia found herself to be alone in the classroom with Thelma. The day's work was over and Form V had been dismissed. Miss Harriet had ordered Delia to clean the blackboard before leaving. The last lesson of the day had been in simple arithmetic, and Miss Harriet had written in white chalk on the board a problem for the girls to solve:

> At the draper's shop satin dress fabric is priced at 5 shillings and 8 pence the yard. The shopkeeper has for a good customer agreed to allow a rebate of 2 pence in the shilling. What is the cost of eight and three-fifths yards of satin, in pounds, shillings and pence, reckoned to the nearest farthing?

Whilst Delia was busily wiping the words and figures from the blackboard with a yellow duster, an arm was slipped around her waist, causing her to start in alarm. It was Thelma hugging her affectionately, a smile on her face.

'I came back to see you clean the board properly,' she said. 'Miss Harriet gets very shirty if she finds it badly done when she starts the day's lessons. And as form prefect, I'm the one who is blamed.'

'Is it clean enough?' Delia asked, anxious to please.

'You've done it well,' said Thelma, and led Delia away from the board and towards Miss Harriet's tall desk and long-legged chair.

Delia uttered a little gasp of surprise when Thelma displayed an insolent boldness by seating herself on the form mistress's chair. Her arm was still about Delia's waist, holding her close to herself, and Delia gasped again, though louder this time, to feel Thelma's free hand undoing the buttons down the bodice of her grey school frock. In a moment the bodice was wide open and Thelma was reaching inside, down the front of Delia's chemise.

'Thelma – this is insanity!' exclaimed Delia faintly.

The other young lady passed her hand over Delia's deliciously round titties a score of times, then asked her to hold open her frock, that she might kiss them. Delia was too much in awe of Thelma to refuse, though her conscience troubled her sorely at the thought of complying with this degenerate suggestion.

Being anxious only to please, and sure that nothing of moment could ensue here in the empty classroom, she did as requested.

Thelma thrust her flushed and burning face deep into Delia's gaping bodice, and her tongue was busy at the rose-pink tips of Delia's titties, sending tremors of guilty delight through her.

'That's enough now, Thelma,' said Delia most imploringly, 'I thought you only wanted to kiss me.'

'Silly girl,' replied Thelma's muffled voice from inside the frock, 'I'm sucking your titties till you fetch off.'

Whereupon she set her eager mouth to the nearest bud and drew it strongly into her mouth, while the tip of her tongue flicked over it without cease. Nor was that the complete extent of her sensual tampering – her hand slipped slyly under Delia's skirts and felt in a searching manner about her person. It moved ever upward, between Delia's soft thighs and into the front slit of her drawers, setting her blood on fire and rousing voluptuous emotions in her.

'No – we shall be discovered here!' Delia exclaimed in great dismay as thrills of forbidden pleasure coursed through her. 'I beg you to stop, Thelma – come into my bed after lights out, if you wish, but we must not do this here!'

Judge of Delia's indescribable horror when the door was flung open and there stood Miss Harriet with a dark look of sternest disapproval on her lovely face. She strode swiftly across the classroom, unheard by Thelma, who was too deeply engrossed in sucking Delia's titties, and then with a fierce jerk she pulled Delia away from her ginger-haired seducer, the pulled-down top of Delia's chemise exposing bare titties.

'Upon my word,' exclaimed Miss Harriet, 'I find you debauching another classmate, Delia. Have you no shame?'

Thelma jumped up from Miss Harriet's chair and stood with her hands clasped together and her face impassive, though pale.

'As form prefect I expect better from you, Thelma,' said Miss Harriet in a cold voice. 'I am aware that activities of a kind we need not discuss are practised by night in the dormitories of this school. But I never expected to come across so brazen a display of lewdness as this – two of the young ladies entrusted to my care engaged in sensual indulgence in my own classroom! What have you to say for yourself?'

## The Girls' Boarding School

'I humbly beg your pardon, Miss Harriet,' replied Thelma at once, by no means tongue-tied to be found out, as was Delia. 'I don't know what came over me – Delia brushed against me as she passed and in some manner I cannot explain or excuse I lost all control of myself.'

'Delia provoked you, did she?' said Miss Harriet. 'I am not surprised to hear that. She is in the habit of interfering with other young ladies and has been punished for it before today.'

Thelma wisely said nothing, her eyes downcast modestly.

'You had your hand up her clothes,' observed Miss Harriet, 'I couldn't help but see it. Did you touch her private parts?'

'I cannot tell a lie,' said Thelma, who was quite capable of telling any number of lies, 'I did.'

'Through her drawers, or actually on the bare flesh?' asked Miss Harriet with icy calmness. Delia listened to the questions and answers in fear and trembling, guessing that she and Thelma would be chastised severely.

'The bare flesh,' confessed Thelma, who seemed to be intent on making things worse for herself and for her friend.

'At least you have the good sense to be candid with me about your wrongdoing, Thelma. Did you put your finger inside her?'

'No, Miss, there wasn't time – you came in almost as soon as I put my hand up her skirts.'

'But you would have done, if I hadn't entered just then, I'm certain of that,' said Miss Harriet. 'What was your intention – to manipulate her until you brought on the spasm, Thelma?'

'Yes, Miss Harriet,' said Thelma, her eyes still downcast but no trace of shame in her voice.

119

'Now, Delia,' said the form mistress, turning her attention to the shocked girl, 'you have heard Thelma confess frankly to misdeeds, achieved and intended. What have you to say?'

'Only that I am most dreadfully ashamed,' Delia stammered.

'Ashamed, are you? I should jolly well think so!' exclaimed Miss Harriet, her jet black eyebrows rising up her smooth white forehead. 'But being ashamed is not enough – I hoped that I had instilled some sense of decency into you, but evidently I was wrong, for I find you in broad daylight, and in the classroom, provoking Thelma to lascivious acts. We shall try again and see what a good smacking can do to mend your ways.'

What followed was a mockery of all that is proper and right. From the drawer in her tall desk Miss Harriet produced several lengths of coloured ribbon, of the type used as decoration for ladies' hats and other garments, the type which is as strong as cord when doubled.

She ordered Delia to lie face down over the desk and told Thelma to assist her in binding the wretched girl's wrists together and then attaching them to the legs of the desk. Delia sobbed but offered no resistance, not even when her ankles were tied, so that she was well stretched out.

'Your bare posterior shall pay for your lubricity,' said Miss Harriet.

She commanded Thelma to turn up Delia's clothes over her back and pull her white cotton drawers down her legs. She would not listen to Thelma's plea for forgiveness on Delia's behalf, nor her insistence that what they had been doing was not so really wrong, but only a friendly touch between close companions. This excuse did not in any way abate Miss Harriet's wrath, or soften her obdurate mind.

'It is my duty to correct you, and I have never yet shirked

my duty,' she said, seemingly addressing her remarks to Delia's bare bottom. She raised her arm and brought her palm down hard on Delia's uncovered bum six times, each smack leaving a print in dark red to mark the place of its impact, thus bringing to the soft peach-like cheeks an angry glow.

Tears of shame and mortification welled up in Delia's eyes, but her loudest outcry was wrung from her when Miss Harriet had completed her *six of the best* and thrust her hand between her victim's legs.

'How far had matters progressed between you and Thelma?' she demanded. 'Had either of you succumbed? Ah, I detect here some slipperiness that ought not to be present – it is unmistakable. It betrays a condition of arousal. It is quite clear to me now that you had gone far before I interrupted you.'

While she spoke, her fingers were probing into Delia's virgin pussy, touching her secret button and rubbing it a little.

'Ah no, no, Miss Harriet – do not handle me in so indecent a way, I implore you,' cried Delia, her bum wriggling about while she sought to escape the fingers ravishing her maidenly modesty so very expertly.

'I intend to find out if you fetched off, as I believe it is vulgarly called by the young ladies of this school. Lie still – if you wriggle about I shall slap you again.'

In truth, her probing fingertip stimulated Delia's secret button with more zeal than her avowed investigation warranted. Even in her ordeal of embarrassment and shame Delia could not help recalling vividly the instance when she had knelt upon the carpet before the sternly beautiful form mistress in her study, and observed her pouting black-haired pussy, and then kissed it until the spasm overtook Miss Harriet.

To remember that, and how Miss Harriet had driven her almost mad with delight afterwards; this greatly aroused Delia against her will, and her belly began to squirm on the desk she lay on. The outcome could not be long in doubt – as Miss Harriet pried most expertly into Delia's slippery-wet split, the paroxysm of sensual pleasure seized the pinioned girl, and she fetched off with a long moan.

'What!' Miss Harriet exclaimed. 'You dare to do that in my presence? I shall beat your backside until you repent of your impudence and promise to mend your ways.'

'No, Miss Harriet,' cried Thelma, 'for you will only arouse her again, and make her fetch off a second time!'

'Keep your insolent remarks to yourself, girl,' Miss Harriet said. 'Her bottom shall suffer till she has learned her lesson and can fetch off no more, not even when I put my hand between her thighs.'

In this way she continued, dealing out a smack or two across Delia's bottom, then sliding a finger into her slit and playing with her until she succumbed to the sensual spasm yet again. At which Miss Harriet declared herself deeply offended by what she described as Delia's impertinence, and smacked her again. Then she brought her to the spasm again with clever touches of her fingers, and no sooner had the enforced rapture faded away than she once more smacked poor Delia's bum.

So it continued, Thelma watching pale faced, and wide eyed at the cruelty visited upon her helpless friend, until Delia lay half-fainting after five smackings and six increasingly intense fetch offs, all within the space of fifteen minutes.

'I venture to think she has had a lesson she will not forget in a hurry,' Miss Harriet said coldly, standing back from her handiwork. 'You may untie her, Thelma, and attend to her. After that you are to report to me in my study – do not imagine that *you* are to get off scot free!'

As soon as the form mistress had left the room, Thelma untied the ribbons that bound Delia and raised her gently to her feet. She passed an arm about the trembling girl's waist and helped her out of the classroom and upstairs to the Form V dormitory. Hardly aware of what was taking place, Delia allowed herself to be laid face down on Thelma's bed and her drawers removed.

'Your bum looks very red and angry,' said Thelma. 'It must be excessively painful, I am sure – Miss Harriet has a very hard hand when it comes to spanking. Sleep awhile, Delia – no one dare disturb you on my bed.'

'Thank you, dearest Thelma,' Delia murmured brokenly.

'I shall return when Miss Harriet is finished with me,' said Thelma with deliberate bravado. 'It won't take me long to fetch her off three or four times, the way she likes it.'

Although her bottom was stinging hotly, Delia was so entirely exhausted by the dreadful ordeal she had been put through that she closed her eyes and fell into a deep sleep. Some time later she became uncomfortable in her face down position and turned on to her back, but the sudden stabs of pain in her bottom when it rested on the bed caused her to turn on her side. That also was highly uncomfortable, she discovered, for her skirts seemed to press on her bruised flesh, and with a sigh she turned again to lie on her belly, and slept once more.

She was awakened by a hand smoothing lightly over her bottom, a soothing touch, she realised, for it was applying face cream to the angry cheeks. Delia turned her head on the pillow to see who it was, and saw that Thelma had returned and was attending to her hurt. She had turned up Delia's clothes to her waist and since her drawers had been removed before she fell asleep, bare fleshy cheeks were presented for Thelma's tender care.

'Does that help?' Thelma enquired.

'The agony is somewhat abated,' Delia confirmed.

Thus encouraged, Thelma's hand began to stray from the cheeks she had anointed with soothing face cream to parts that had not been subjected to a smacking hand, but only to the inquisitive touch of Miss Harriet's fingers. Delia lay still, knowing there was no escape from Thelma's attentions. She felt fingers dipped in smooth face cream pass over the lips of her pussy, applying the scented unguent to them, and she sighed in resignation.

'Thelma,' said she, hoping to divert her red-haired friend's attention away from sensual pleasure into other channels, 'did Miss Harriet smack you as thoroughly as she did me?'

'She didn't smack me at all,' said Thelma in a breathy voice, 'it was something quite else she had in mind for me.'

'What might that be?'

'Promise never to repeat it to another soul,' Thelma insisted vigorously, 'promise now!'

'I promise,' said Delia, her interest quickening at this show of confidence, although she noted at the same time with regret that Thelma was continuing to finger her pussy, and had gone so far as to part the soft lips and caress lightly inside.

'I thought I was in for a jolly good spanking,' said Thelma, 'to be followed by a mutual fetch off or two. But when I got to her study she said something very strange.'

'What? What?' Delia asked faintly, feeling quick thrills of delight passing through her body from the gentle stimulation of her secret bud by Thelma.

'She said that she had lost control of herself, and this

## The Girls' Boarding School

must be atoned for. She said she had in her temper punished you too hard and too much. I was glad to hear this because I thought it meant she would smack me very lightly, but as it turned out she didn't touch me at all. Instead, she ordered me to *cane* her, to atone for what she had done to you.'

'What?' cried Delia, her belly squirming on the bed to the tremors of bliss that shook her body. 'You *caned* her? I can't believe it!'

'It's the truth,' said Thelma, her fingertips moving slowly now over the most sensitive part of Delia's person. 'She opened a cupboard and produced a thin swishy cane of the sort never used on us. A cruel looking thing, believe me – it sent shivers up and down my spine just to look at it!'

'You are making this up,' Delia said dreamily, her thighs and belly quivering in pleasure.

'I swear to you every word is gospel truth!' Thelma replied. 'Then she lifted her skirts and took down the prettiest mauve knickers you've ever seen, and bent over the arm of the sofa! I thought I was asleep and dreaming when she ordered me to give her *six of the best*.'

'Oh!' gasped Delia. 'Oh!' and she fetched off in convulsive throes to the insistent tickle of Thelma's finger.

When she recovered her senses sufficiently to understand what Thelma was saying, she lay still and listened avidly.

'Such a beautiful bum she has,' said Thelma enthusiastically, 'the cheeks are perfectly round and milk-white. I hardly dared use the cane on it, but she made me. I gave her six quick cuts and saw the angry red lines where I had struck.'

'Did she cry out?'

'Not she, though I gave it to her hard and strong. I saw her body jerk to each cut, and she gave a little sigh. I thought the affair was finished when she stood upright again, and for three dreadful moments I thought perhaps she was going to swish me. But not a bit of it. She went to the sofa and lay down on it full-length and raised her clothes up to her waist. She ordered me to give her another six – across her belly and thighs!'

'You saw her pussy?' Delia asked quickly.

'With her knickers off I saw everything,' said Thelma, lying down on the bed beside Delia. 'Put your hand up my skirt and feel how wet my pussy is.'

To keep her friend talking about Miss Harriet, Delia hastened to do as was asked, and found that the lips of Thelma's pussy were slippery with excitement, and that inside she was soaking wet.

'What does Miss Harriet's pussy look like?' enquired Delia, who knew very well from personal experience by sight and touch of tongue the appearance and texture of it.

'It's gorgeous,' said Thelma, and her voice trembled with the force of her admiration. 'She has a lovely thick bush of glossy black hair, and below it a pair of pouting pink lips – I can't describe how lovely it is. And her belly is rounded and milk-white as the cheeks of her bum, with a dear little button deep-set in it. If I'd dared, I would have gone down on my knees and kissed all I saw.'

Delia closed her eyes and smiled secretly to herself at the fond recollection of the day she herself had enjoyed the superb and blissful privilege of licking Miss Harriet's black-curled pussy. At the memory, her titillating fingers moved a little faster in Thelma's slippery wet pussy, ravishing her bud with delight and drawing sharp gasps of pleasure and long intakes of breath from the enraptured form prefect, whose legs moved wider yet apart on the bed.

'But surely you never laid the cane across her lovely

belly,' gasped Delia, who had become almost as aroused as Thelma, only by hearing the description of Miss Harriet's naked charms.

The eager question fell on deaf ears – Thelma cried out aloud and writhed on her back as she fetched off, her legs kicking up in the air in a most unladylike manner. Her bliss lasted for some seconds, and before even it was finished Delia flung her friend's skirts up over her belly and jerked open her drawers, baring her from her belly-button to her strong thighs.

Then, to the long middle finger with which she had stimulated Thelma to the female spasm, she added the two adjacent fingers, pushing the trio of joined digits well into Thelma's wet split.

'I want to know,' Delia said. 'Tell me if you did!'

Thelma's loins bucked upwards convulsively to the assault of the fingers within her and their insistent caress of her secret bud – which naturally was in a condition of highest sensitivity from her recent fetch off.

'Yes,' she gasped, 'I raised the cane and brought it down in a swishing cut right across Miss Harriet's beautiful bare belly – just below her button. She shrieked and clenched her fists and I saw the long red line I had made on the creaminess of her soft skin. Oh Delia, you'll make me fetch off again if you go on fingering me like that . . .'

'Tell me,' said Delia fiercely. 'What did you do then?'

'I was reluctant to mar her loveliness, but she stared up at me with her beautiful dark eyes and commanded me to proceed. So I cut again – this time somewhat lower, across the front of her thighs, just below her glorious black bush.'

'Did she cry out?'

'She shrieked aloud again and her eyes closed for a moment – but then she told me to prepare to deliver the third and final stroke on her word. I didn't know what she meant.'

'I can guess!' said Delia fiercely, her fingers ravaging her friend's pussy.

'What she did was spread her legs wide open,' Thelma murmured faintly, 'so that the entire mound of her pussy was revealed to me – she pushed her belly upwards . . . oh, Delia, I am fetching off, I swear it . . .'

'Not yet,' said Delia firmly, but she continued her ravishing of Thelma's wet pussy. 'Control yourself. Stiffen your legs and clench the cheeks of your bum tight and by will power refuse to let your emotions run away with you, until you have told me the remainder of your tale.'

'Ah, ah . . .' Thelma sighed, perilously near to the instant of sensual release. 'I raised my arm and held the cane poised over Miss Harriet, but I could not bring myself to strike again – it was too lovely a sight, her pussy, to wish to hurt it. But when she saw that I paused, she commanded me to obey her. *Do it now* she cried out fiercely, and I begged her forgiveness in advance and cut down sharply across the upthrust mound of her pussy.'

'She shrieked at that?' demanded Delia, who was quite beside herself with furious sensual excitement.

'Yes. She emitted a high-pitched scream, the sort of sound a thin silk garment would make being torn in two. Her body jerked up and down nine or ten times on the sofa, her eyes stared wide open at me and I could see how her fingernails were digging in the palms of her hands. I could hardly believe what I saw, but the sting of the cane on her pussy had made her fetch off . . .'

Thelma's account of doings in the study terminated in a quick gasp of ecstasy as her orgasm was overwhelmed by the thrills of bliss that shook her. Delia rammed her close-pressed fingers as deep into her friend's ginger-haired split as they could be made to enter. She herself trembled from head to toe, ravished by the force of her emotions – corrupt emotions, it need not be said – which would require much attention from Thelma's tongue to alleviate. That she was contemplating such actions of moral turpitude, and even welcoming them, brought a vivid scarlet to Delia's pretty face.

Yet though her present acquiescence in unnatural vice surely betokened a collapse of Delia's virtuous principles and a lapse into depravity of an order almost too frightful to contemplate and incompatible with the retention a degree of self-respect, nonetheless it was Delia's determination to cajole Thelma into fetching her off until she collapsed of satiety and exhaustion.

# CHAPTER 8
# A Teacher Betrays her Sacred Trust

The effect on Delia's innocent mind of hearing Thelma's account of being compelled to cane Miss Harriet on her pussy was indeed intense and long-lasting. Whoever came into her bed at night to make her fetch off a time or two before sleeping, Delia dreamed nightly of the form mistress, her sleeping thoughts envisaging that lovely black-curled pussy and milk-white belly laid bare for her to adore.

Something of her aroused feelings for Miss Harriet showed in her manner by day in the classroom, perhaps in the way in which she responded to questions addressed to her, or the secret look of admiration she directed towards Miss Harriet when she thought herself unobserved.

Whatever it was that sufficed to betray her feelings makes no matter here. There came an afternoon when, at the end of class for the day, before Miss Harriet dismissed Form V she announced that Delia was to come to her study in five minutes.

'Oh Lord,' said Maria, 'what have you done this time, Delia? You're in for a smacking, by the sound of it.'

Delia protested that she had done nothing amiss, and appealed to the form prefect to disclose anything she might know of the supposed offence. Thelma shook her head and declared she was in total ignorance of any such misdeed, and even put her arm about Delia for a comradely hug, and wished her well, in whatever lay ahead in the study.

Greatly perturbed, Delia made her way towards the private den of the form mistress, reluctance in her every step, yet mindful that if she exceeded the five minutes she would incur the wrath that awaits the unpunctual. She stood silent outside the door, took a deep breath and straightened her back, then tapped at it and awaited the dulcet tones of Miss Harriet commanding her to enter.

The day was warm, being in the early part of June, and there stood tiny beads of perspiration on Delia's upper lip and under her delicate arms there was a faint prickle. Whether this could be entirely attributed to the heat of the room, or was in some part due to Delia's agitation of mind, is a fine point that may not be settled at this remove after the event. Miss Harriet sat in her arm chair, and she betrayed no signs of discomfort – she appeared remarkably cool and self-possessed. She had worn that day a soft white blouse with leg-of-mutton sleeves and a high frilled neck, together with a long close-fitting skirt of some dark material, and this simple but attractive ensemble enhanced the natural excellence of her form.

'Ah, Delia, it is you,' she said, her face without expression as she glanced at the trembling girl. '*You come most carefully upon your hour*, to make use of the immortal words of William Shakespeare. No doubt you recognise the quotation?'

'I believe it to be from *Hamlet*, Miss Harriet.'

'Capital! Stand here where I can see you properly without my neck straining round. I have a most serious matter to discuss with you.'

Delia kept silent, thinking that best, and went to stand in front of Miss Harriet.

## The Girls' Boarding School

'It is my privilege to have been a teacher of well-bred young ladies for some years now,' the form mistress commenced, 'and I am therefore guided by a wealth of practical experience. It has not escaped my attention, Delia, that your attitude in respect of myself has undergone a change of late.'

Delia was quite astonished by what she heard and raised her eyes to gaze at Miss Harriet's face.

'Yes, look me frankly in the eye,' said the older woman, 'and tell me if it is not so.'

'I humbly ask your pardon, Miss Harriet, but I fear I do not perfectly understand your meaning,' said Delia in a quavering voice.

'I think you do – have you not been directing burning glances at me in class? Has your pretty face not blushed pink whenever I have put a question to you? Have your knees not turned weak beneath you when you have observed me reaching up to write upon the blackboard? These are rhetorical questions, requiring no answer, for the answer is plain enough to see. In short, Delia, is it not true that you have developed what is vulgarly called a *crush* on me?'

'Oh, Miss Harriet!' Delia stammered, her face crimson.

'In proper parlance, an infatuation with my person,' said the form mistress. 'You entertain the warmest of feelings towards me but are unable to articulate them – am I correct?'

Poor Delia had been rendered speechless and could only blink.

'Your blush and confusion of manner are answer enough,' said Miss Harriet with a slow smile. 'I know what is in your heart, for this has happened to me before in my career as a teacher of females. Many, many pretty young ladies like you have felt the force of those same feelings towards me

133

– for it is no more than simple truth that I possess some measure of beauty, which I am proud to acknowledge and for which I am not bashful in any way. Do *you* think I am beautiful, Delia, truthfully now?'

Her deepest emotions in a perfect turmoil, Delia could do no more than nod her head timidly and gaze intensely into the dark and luminous eyes of the woman she adored.

'You've a bad case of it,' Miss Harriet declared, tossing her head back in what could be described, in a lesser female, as a flirtatious manner. Fixing Delia with her steady gaze, even as a stoat mesmerises a cornered rabbit, she continued her game of teasing the girl.

'When you gaze upon me your pulse begins to beat faster,' she said, 'your breathing becomes ragged, the blood mounts to your cheek – if it were possible you would hug me and shower kisses on my face. Is it not so?'

Delia was dumbfounded by this casual exposure of her feelings which she had thought to be a profound secret until now.

'Come closer,' said Miss Harriet.

Delia moved towards the chair on which the form mistress was seated. At once Miss Harriet reached out to pass an arm about Delia's waist and hold her fast, whilst with her other hand she raised the startled girl's long skirts and tucked them up above her waist, revealing the thin white cotton drawers which alone concealed the expanse of her youthful thighs and belly.

Before Delia could collect herself to utter a respectful, if totally insincere, protest at so very immodest an action, Miss Harriet's hand roamed freely between her thighs, plunging into the opening of her drawers, and playing lightly over her sweet and soft-haired split.

'Without the word of a lie, Delia,' Miss Harriet said

boldly, now that matters had advanced this far, 'you have the prettiest pussy in the school . . .'

Delia gasped aloud to hear the classroom word *pussy* from the lips of the greatly-respected Miss Harriet Jardyne. It was not possible to imagine that when Miss Harriet was herself a young lady at school she had participated in the impure and sensual fingering games of others her own age. Surely it was beyond all decency to imagine that she had allowed her lovely person to be handled and kissed until she fell into spasm?

The coldly calm beauty of Miss Harriet's face denied all hint of knowledge or experience of unwholesome emotions, for she had the features of a saint. Yet the lushness of her lovely body, even when fully clothed, suggested otherwise, and served as an indication of the immorality of her inner nature.

Appearances notwithstanding to the contrary, the excessively vile lewdness of Miss Harriet towards Delia, as towards the rest of the young gentlewomen in her charge, was proof positive that she had been given over to shameful and unnatural practices all her life, from the earliest age. It would be a fair conclusion to draw that when she was a schoolgirl herself, some ten years or more ago, Miss Harriet was the one who corrupted her classmates and taught them how to interfere with their own bodies.

'And you have the smoothest, whitest pair of thighs, with the possible exception of little Amy Gore-Boothby,' continued Miss Harriet, fondling Delia as she spoke. 'You may believe my words – there is not a girl at St Agatha's whose charms I have never laid bare and inspected for my own pleasure. All of them – from the juniors up to the Fifth Form. These slender fingers of mine have titillated every pussy in the school – I have fetched off every young Miss here – and very thoroughly.'

All the while she was running her fingers over Delia's naked flesh, in the most shameless manner, causing the mortified girl to blush scarlet.

'Oh!' she cried out, to feel Miss Harriet pressing a gentle middle finger on the junction of her thighs, where the softest of blonde hair adorned the lips there. To be assaulted in this way by the girls of Form V in bed had become a nightly routine, but to be fingered in so very intimate a fashion by the object of her dearest sentiments was quite another question. Delia was *in love* with Miss Harriet, as she thought, and it struck her as utterly indecent to associate that noblest of emotions with the base affair of feeling pussies.

Nevertheless, Miss Harriet's fingers fluttered and lingered, seeking out the maiden split in the soft nest of Delia's silky curls, the boldness of the action suggesting to the oddly confused girl that either the strongly heart-felt emotions she entertained towards her teacher were not reciprocated, or – and this seemed almost impossible to grasp – could there perhaps be some kind of unfathomable connection between true love and the induction of the sensual spasm?

Even while this unthinkable prospect was causing agitation in Delia's mind, Miss Harriet's fingers found what they sought so insistently, and began to caress Delia's secret little bud with insolent grace. The pleasurable nature of the thrills caused by her touch was enough to compel Delia to decide that there could not possibly be any connection between mere physical sensation and the sublime sentiment of love.

'Oh, Miss Harriet,' she murmured, 'I beg you, for the love of all that is wholesome and precious, do not do this to me. It is too shameful!'

'Is it so?' said Miss Harriet in a mocking tone. 'Then tell

me why your pussy is warm and wet to my touch, if you feel only shame at this moment.'

'You mustn't,' Delia pleaded, not knowing how to reply to the question that puzzled her young wits.

She spoke in vain, for the older woman's fingertip slid over that sensitive spot at the top of her slit, where sensation is the greatest. She twitched and gasped, but Miss Harriet held her firm round the waist whilst she spurred on her agitation of body to fever pitch.

'Shameful, do you say?' Miss Harriet exclaimed. 'You did not think it shameful to take Thelma Fanshawe into bed with you, or Edna Calthorpe-Brunton, for both of which misdemeanours I have chastised you. Did you feel only shame when Thelma had her hand between your legs in the classroom? Were you ashamed when you allowed her to feel you? Of course you were not! Then why is it shameful now – am I less worthy than your classmates to feel your lovely young body?'

'No, Miss Harriet, that is not what I meant!' gasped Delia in her confusion. I was taken by surprise when Thelma put her hand up my clothes, I swear it!'

'But you were not taken by surprise when she fetched you off, as the girls here refer to the female spasm, were you, Delia? You do not have to pretend to me to be innocent of the reasons why pussies are felt.'

Whilst Miss Harriet spoke thus, she tickled Delia's button in the most expert manner with her immodest finger, and in equal proportion to the increasing stimulus, her victim's breath came in shorter gasps that were interspersed with incoherent words that she had little or no knowledge of uttering.

'Oh, Miss Harriet ... the girls of Form V perform actions of unspeakable depravity upon each other, and upon me, despite my unwillingness to participate ... oh

Heavens, the sensation . . . do not make me do it . . . you are the one I truly love and cherish, and this seems so very wrong . . .'

'Ah, you love me, do you, Delia?'

'Oh, I am near to fetching off . . . stop, please . . . I adore you more than life itself, Miss Harriet . . . do not force me do this or all respect between us will be lost . . . too late, too late!'

Delia's hips jerked and her smooth uncovered thighs quivered. For some seconds she seemed quite to lose control of her limbs, and but for Miss Harriet's supporting arm about her waist it is certain she would have collapsed in a heap on the floor.

'Oh, what an eager girl it is, to fetch off so quickly,' Miss Harriet exclaimed. 'The feel of your tender pussy has undone me and I must have you again, little Delia.'

So saying, she pulled the half-fainting girl down on her lap and thrust her tongue into Delia's mouth. She opened the front of Delia's school frock and put a hand into the top of her chemise to handle her soft titties and tickle their rose-pink buds.

'Let us put aside this nonsense about respect, and think only of love and the bliss we may take from each other,' said she to the dazed girl, who sat with spread thighs, unable to do other than submit.

'You are mine to enjoy, Delia,' said Miss Harriet with a slow smile of anticipation, 'and by the time we part this evening we shall have brought each other off a dozen times. Your love will find its fullest expression in blissful sensation and only then become the sweet languor of desire satisfied.'

Delia's head whirled at these strange words, but the hand in between her parted thighs was inducing such delicious throbs of sensual pleasure that she was in no

## The Girls' Boarding School

condition to evaluate what was said or determine the truth. Miss Harriet's mouth pressed close against hers, her tongue insinuated itself slyly between Delia's lips and penetrated deep into her mouth. Delia's nerves were overloaded with sensation, more than they could tolerate, and with convulsive heaves of her belly she fetched off again.

When her youthful companion had in some measure recovered her self-possession, Miss Harriet rose and went to the door, where she turned the key twice in the lock. That done, she smiled at Delia and stood facing her while she undressed herself. Delia stared open-eyed and lost in adoration, as off came the blouse and the long skirt, to reveal a knee-length chemise over purple beribboned knickers of the latest style, and dark stockings.

She slipped off the shoulder ribbons to let the chemise slip down her body, baring her superb bosoms. Delia's tongue thrust out a little, unknown to her, and licked at the corners of her mouth as she gazed in joy at Miss Harriet's round creamy-white titties, the fullness and weight of them, and their prominent pink buds. Miss Harriet stared boldly into the girl's admiring eyes and passed her hands over her own bountiful globes, then lifted them onto her palms, and squeezed them gently.

Not content to rest with only so much adoration from the poor besotted girl, Miss Harriet laughed musically and stripped off her fine knickers. Delia gasped open-mouthed at being allowed to see her alabaster belly and the bush of black curls between her lissome thighs. In another moment Miss Harriet stood close to the sofa, her legs astride, thus presenting her loins to the astonished girl to be kissed.

Instantly Delia sat up straight and leaned forward to press her mouth to the pink and warm lips of Miss Harriet's beautiful pussy. The soft lips seemed to pout under her long caress, just as if they were returning the kiss gracefully.

Whereupon Delia pressed her tongue between them and licked wetly at the little rose-bud within.

'Ah, yes,' sighed Miss Harriet, her hand stroking gently over Delia's hair, 'how very nicely you do that, my dear, how every daintily. It will not take much to bring me to a fetch off.'

Indeed, it was evident that her earlier attentions to Delia had roused strong passions within the form mistress, and little more than a touch was needed to release those pent-up emotions in convulsive bliss. Delia plied her tongue busily, in heavenly rapture to be permitted to kiss so very intimate a part of the person she most adored. Very quickly, Miss Harriet began to sob softly, her long legs trembled as her knees lost their rigidity at the onset of the sensual spasm, and she dissolved into short blissful throbs.

When at last her pleasure was complete she leaned down to put a hand under Delia's chin and turn up the girl's flushed face, to stare deeply into her eyes, and then to press her full soft mouth to Delia's maidenly mouth. Her kiss was so very clinging and passionate that Delia felt herself becoming moist again in her pussy. Again and again Miss Harriet kissed her, thrusting her tongue into the girl's trembling mouth. After many kisses, so very sweet on Delia's lips, Miss Harriet ask her to lie back on the sofa, her feet on the floor.

Delia did as asked, though her cheeks were blushing, whereupon Miss Harriet stooped over her to remove her drawers completely, thus exposing her person from her knees right up to her belly-button. Delia became breathless with anticipation and agitated sensuality to think that her tender young body was so completely at the disposal of Miss Harriet. It was wrong, wrong, wickedly wrong, to submit to shameful stimulation – yet how delicious!

## The Girls' Boarding School

Despite her sadly mingled emotions, wherein shame strove with a lewd desire for sensation, Delia lay still in the position in which she had arranged herself on her back, her legs dangling loosely down to the carpet.

'Well now,' said Miss Harriet, 'I've already told you that you have a pair of lovely white thighs and well-turned calves. And to that I may add that you possess round and dimpled knees of the very sort that gentlemen admire. You are fortunate in this.'

'Thank you, Miss Harriet,' said Delia dutifully, 'but ought a modest young female to entertain thoughts of what gentlemen may admire?'

'You are right to rebuke me,' exclaimed Miss Harriet, 'let us pay no heed to what may please gentlemen. But you will not be surprised to learn that what I see of you pleases *me* very much, Delia.'

With that she knelt down, to Delia's delight, and kissed her uncovered knees, her fingers and lips wandering all the while up her bare thighs towards regions higher still. Impure fancies were raised in Delia's mind, even though she knew them for what they were – the marks of depravity. And yet how marvellous, she thought, were the passionate kisses rained on her bare thighs by Miss Harriet.

Delia's senses were swimming, her mind a tremulous whirl of sensual delight at the feel of Miss Harriet's tongue licking up the inside of her thigh, towards her maidenly pussy.

'Now Delia, dearest,' said Miss Harriet, 'I want you to put your legs on my shoulders – up they go now.'

A misplaced sense of joy invaded Delia's heart at these words of vile significance. Although she was about to submit without a protest to unspeakable acts of infamous and degrading intent, she silenced her conscience with the disreputable thought that it was her duty as pupil to obey the form mistress.

Without even a show of virginal reluctance, Delia raised her perfectly-shaped legs, separated them and rested one on each of Miss Harriet's shoulders, so bringing her bared pussy close up to the face of the form mistress, whose eyes were fixed upon it in an ardent gaze.

'How very pretty!' said Miss Harriet with warm emotion. 'Now I have a really good look at your darling little slit – and how very enticing it is. I feel it is begging me to make love to it until it is overwhelmed with wonderful sensation and sated.'

Delia shuddered lightly and sighed, entrapped within a most complex web of emotion spun by the feel of hands – the hands of someone she respected highly – touching her completely exposed slit. To Delia's way of thinking, the divine Miss Harriet could do no wrong, but surely what she was doing to Delia's person now was perverse and wanton! So far had Delia fallen away from her once high standards of morality that she was incapable now of resolving the contradictions in her mind.

Yet to look down the length of her own body and observe Miss Harriet staring with a cold smile on her face at the parts that lay between Delia's thighs – to watch how with her long white fingers she caressed the soft blonde curls there in a manner so improper that could be described only as debased . . . ah me, what a moral dilemma for a young lady. What was to be done?

A fingertip traced along the closed pink lips and brought a suppressed gasp from Delia – then she blushed crimson from her pretty face down to her belly-button to feel Miss Harriet's two thumbs gently parting the lips between her parted legs.

'O Miss Harriet,' she said sighingly, 'tell me that it is

all right for you to do this to me, and for me to let you!'

She knew very well that the form mistress's purpose was to ravish her to the spasm yet again. Secretly, down in the depths of her heart she rejoiced at the prospect and waited impatiently for the gentle touch on her secret button that would transport her to bliss. Yet the better part of her nature rejected it as unladylike, and demeaning in the extreme.

'There is no right or wrong about it, Delia,' Miss Harriet said in a murmur, 'we needs must worship beauty when we see it, and you are in the first flush of girlish beauty. You have read in the classroom the sublime words of John Keats, the greatest of our poets:

*Beauty is Truth, Truth Beauty,*
*That is all ye know on earth, And all ye need to know.*'

'But was Mr Keats thinking about intimate friendship between females when he penned those lines?' asked Delia faintly as in her groin fingers played softly and insistently.

'Naturally,' Miss Harriet assured her. 'He was deeply in love at the time with Miss Fanny Brawne of Hampstead in London, and as a poet he partly understood the emotions that rise in female hearts. Therefore it is impossible that you should even think of not letting me adore you, for it would be selfish and horrid of you to deny me an opportunity to convey some moment of truly celestial joy to you and to myself. Make your conscience easy, my dear, the worship of Beauty will lead to blissful Truth, and nothing shall be done which is not pure delight.'

Whilst Delia was attempting to reconcile these words with an uncomfortable sense that *bliss* and *goodness* might not be quite the same thing, a long gasp was drawn from her – on the inside of her soft thighs she felt Miss Harriet's hot breathing. A moment later the same hot breath transferred itself to Delia's uncovered and defenceless pussy.

Then a wet tongue touched the lips, and licked them with soft gentleness. That done, the probing tongue pressed between, and forced its way deeper and deeper yet. When Delia's female split was wide open, the tongue darted in and around, and lapped at the fleshy little button, unleashing such sensations that soon Delia's breath came in ragged gasps.

The feelings grew ever more intense, almost to the point of being unbearable, and Delia's whole body was shaking from Miss Harriet's ministrations, while the tide of lust rose higher in the girl's bosom, unbidden and unwanted, unsought and shameful. Yet so very great was Delia's excitement that she accepted her violation with a desperate eagerness that surprised herself.

'No more,' she stammered out, but her body betrayed her moral principles even while she made her feeble protest. Her girlish loins bucked upwards, and a raging heat swept her through from head to toe – so fierce that she thought she was about to faint away. All resistance dissolved in a lustful spasm of delight as the convulsions of ecstasy shook her.

'I love you,' she moaned, 'I love you, Miss Harriet.'

'I'm pleased to hear it,' replied the older woman when she at last removed her tongue from Delia's ravaged body. 'I find you a most attractive young lady – I mean to enjoy you to the full in the time that you are here at St Agatha's.'

She arranged Delia and herself on the sofa, lying close and facing each other, her mouth close to Delia's face so that she might bestow a kiss when it suited her to do so.

## The Girls' Boarding School

Somewhat less innocently, her hand lay between Delia's bare thighs, in reach of her private parts, for when she next chose to fondle them.

'Now that we are close friends,' said she, 'and so that I may best advise and guide you away from the pitfalls and problems of casual sensuality, you must reveal the whole truth to me and confide utterly. When did you first begin to stroke yourself to the sensual thrill?'

'Never!' Delia gasped in dismay, that she should be thought capable of so very immodest an act. 'No hand had ever touched my person before I arrived at St Agatha's, where I was violated most rudely on my first night in the dormitory.'

'Come now,' said Miss Harriet, tickling the fair curls about Delia's pussy with a fingertip, 'let us be frank.'

It occurred to Delia that Miss Harriet's inquisition was much the same as that she had been subjected to by Maria Wendover on the morning after her violation by Thelma. Maria had taken her to the love seat in the gardens, under the chestnut tree, there to abuse her body first and then to outrage her pride by asking if she was in the habit of *playing* with herself.

Delia's repeated denials that she had ever done such a thing only partly convinced Miss Harriet.

'Even after your nightly experiences in the Form V dorm,' she said, 'it is evident to me that you attach a sense of guilt and shame to the spasm, whether induced by another or by yourself. This we must cure, or you will carry this handicap with you all through life. Therefore, to impress upon you the simple truth that there is nothing blameworthy in stimulating yourself to a fetch off, you are to do it to yourself now, in my presence.'

Protest as she might that it was unthinkable and out of the question, Delia was unable to resist the strength of character of her form mistress, who seized her wrist and pressed her hand forcefully to her pussy, saying *Do it*!

'No, no – I cannot!' Delia moaned, her eyes tightly closed to shield herself from the burning gaze of Miss Harriet's dark and beautiful eyes. Yet nevertheless, she was all too aware of her own bush of soft curls under her hand, and the warmly moist lips of her own pussy that lay there.

'Do it,' Miss Harriet repeated, her nimble fingers unhooking the bodice of Delia's school frock to get at her charming young titties.

'I can't,' murmured Delia, her face a bright red with despair and mortification – and yet her hand had already opened her own pussy and her middle finger slipped within, to touch the ready button that awaited her caress. Delia could scarcely stifle the shocked gasp that rose to her lips on realising what it was she was contemplating doing to herself.

*This must not be!* thought Delia, her heart beating faster at the delicious sensations that flicked through her belly. It was utterly improper, she was certain, to abuse her own person for the sake of a fleeting physical sensation. Heaven above knew it was vile enough when she was forced against her will to endure the spasm by the manipulation of her parts by one of the other girls in the dorm . . . or even by Miss Harriet, whom she felt now that she loved and adored, and who could do whatever she wished to Delia and would be adored all the more for it . . .

Improper or not, the honest truth of the matter then was that Delia's belly and thighs were twitching to exquisite pangs of sensation brought on by the movement of her finger inside her own wet pussy. Miss Harriet had succeeded skilfully in baring her titties and was handling them firmly and with expertness of touch resulting from many years of playing with other females. All this added immeasurably to Delia's fast growing delight – debauched and indecent though it must be considered.

Into her head came the memory of the tale Thelma Fanshawe had told her – of how she had been required to punish Miss Harriet by swishing her with her own cane.

It had been done here, on this very same sofa on which Delia now lay with the form mistress. According to Thelma, Miss Harriet had taken down her knickers to bare her lovely white bum for the cut of the cane. When Thelma had used the swishy implement of pain on the cheeks and dealt with them cruelly, Miss Harriet lay full-length on her back with her clothes raised up to her waist.

As Delia knew from recent experience with the form mistress, this immodest posture on the sofa would have revealed to Thelma belly and thighs of superlative shape and texture – and a truly gorgeous bush of glossy black hair.

According to Thelma, she had been ordered to bring the cane down hard across Miss Harriet's beautiful bare belly, making a long red line on her creamy skin. Delia was gasping and writhing at this vivid picture in her mind whilst she plied her fingers furiously in her slit.

Clearly in her mind's eye she saw Miss Harriet on her back on this sofa, her legs spread apart and her belly pushing upwards to present the soft mound of her pussy to a stroke of the cane. The instrument of chastisement in Thelma's hand slashed down at her victim fiercely, landing full across Miss Harriet's tender and adorable split with its glossy curls, tearing a scream from her as she fetched off under the agony of the cruel slash.

'O mercy!' gasped Delia, and loud and long sighs racked her, her belly clenched hard and she fetched off furiously. This was the first ever time in her life that she had induced in herself the sensual spasm by manipulating her parts, and though she had been commanded to do so by her form mistress, the blame must be laid squarely upon Delia's own shoulders, in that she complied with so very improper an order.

In the meantime, Miss Harriet's long thin fingers tugged and rolled the little pink buds of Delia's titties, to prolong the spasms of bliss.

'Oh Miss Harriet,' she moaned, 'I want to kiss your pussy!'

She really wished to say that she wanted to swish a cane down across Miss Harriet's lovely black-haired pussy and watch her fetch off under the blow – knowing that if ever she were allowed to do so, she herself would fetch off at the selfsame instant! This perverted desire she was totally unable to put into words, for it seemed so very shocking. Therefore she substituted *kiss* for *cane*.

'And so you shall, Delia, you shall kiss it, and I shall kiss yours, I promise you, until you swoon for joy. But first rest a few moments to recover, and tell me what was going through your mind while you were fetching yourself off. Whatever it was, it aroused you in the most delightful way.'

'I dare not say,' Delia blurted out, her face crimson.

'Ah, then it is something deliciously improper and I insist on knowing at once. Tell me, or I will pinch your pussy with my fingernails until you scream in pain!'

It took a little time, but eventually Miss Harriet got it out of her. She was somewhat displeased that Thelma had given away her secret, even to Delia. Nonetheless, she was amused to hear that a little whim of hers excited Delia so intensely. As proof of that, Delia's pussy had grown wet and slippery again during the confession of her secret desire.

## The Girls' Boarding School

'We shall see,' said Miss Harriet, sliding two joined fingers into Delia to titillate her firm little button, 'when we know each other better, perhaps I may allow you to torment my pussy with the cane. For now we have more orthodox delights to share. It is my intention to find out how many times you can fetch off before you collapse and swoon in the exhaustion of complete and languid satisfaction. Spread your legs a little wider apart and we shall begin.'

# CHAPTER 9
## The Edge of Disaster

The brutally obscene way in which Delia was chastised by Miss Harriet for sketching the gardener's boy with his hand between his thighs taught the errant girl a lesson. She kept well away from the potting shed, afraid of punishment that would befall her if she were ever again caught there with young Bert. Worst of all – far worse even than a well-smacked bottom – would be the loss of Miss Harriet's love and affection.

Several times Rhoda Fitzwalter suggested that Delia should go with her to the potting shed, to see, as Rhoda expressed it, if Bert was abusing himself, and fetching off in his hand.

It is to Delia's credit that she declined Rhoda's invitations without hesitation, and yet the thought was firmly established in her mind that the occasions when she had watched while Bert stroked his stiff *dick* had been vastly interesting. She made an attempt to dismiss the idea, but it was lodged tight, and after enough time had elapsed for the memory of Miss Harriet's anger to fade from her mind, she went one afternoon clandestinely in search of Bert.

She found him in the hut, seated on the sacking, having eaten his lunch-time thick sandwich of cheese and onion.

The door was closed and the sun on the roof had made the interior of the hut stifling hot.

'It's you, Miss,' said Bert with a grin, making no attempt to stand up politely to greet a young lady condescending to visit his squalid domain, 'drop the catch across the door, and nobody can barge in.'

'Your suggestion is highly insulting,' Delia replied, having been taught how to deal with menials and keep them in their proper place. 'You appear to be of the opinion that my presence here indicates something may occur which I would be ashamed to have observed by others.'

'Don't know nothing about that, Miss Delia,' said Bert, his idiotic grin across his face, 'I thought you'd maybe come by to see me play with my dick. You used to come by every day, but I ain't seen you for a couple of weeks – not since you made that drawing of me. Somebody told me you got caught and leathered.'

His informant must have been Rhoda, Delia deduced, from which it was evident that Bert had not gone short of a partner in his daily vice. Not merely a female to observe his vigorous self-gratification with interest, but one willing to expose her own private parts to his sight.

Moreover, as a blushing Delia could clearly remember from the time Rhoda brought her into the shed, with her it did not stop at looking, not even with touching, but Rhoda had lain down on her back and allowed Bert to thrust his stiff part into her!

'You are very insolent,' said Delia, as she dropped the iron catch on the door into the metal hook set into the doorpost.

'That may be,' said the lad, 'but I ain't had your eddication and can only speak as I mean.'

With that, he unbuttoned his stained corduroy trousers

down the front, for he had laid aside his long apron before sitting down to his frugal midday meal. Grinning up into Delia's face, he felt inside with dirty fingers and fished out his limp and dangling male part.

'That's what you've come here to see,' he said, letting it hang down outside his rough trousers.

'Really, Bert!' exclaimed Delia, scarlet-faced with shame and embarrassment at his forwardness. 'Why earth do you imagine I want to look at your exposed person? Put it away at once – do you hear me?'

'Can't do that, Miss, not now I've got him out. Once he's out he has to be treated right and fetched off or I'll get no peace all afternoon.'

For all her protestations of dismay and shame, Delia's eyes were staring at the exposed male part, hanging so limp and soft and giving the appearance of being quite harmless and innocent. It was a source of wonderment to her that so small and tender a morsel could swell up into a long hard shaft of flesh, capable of piercing Rhoda's pussy. Yet she had witnessed this with her own eyes and knew it to be true.

'Why is it small and soft, Bert?' she enquired.

'Because nothing's been done yet to put it on the hard, Miss. If you was to touch it for a second with your hand, you'd see it get stiff right away.'

'Touch you? I?' cried Delia. 'How dare you suggest such an infamous thing!'

'Miss Rhoda don't get so hoity-toity,' said Bert, not in the least perturbed by Delia's petulance, 'she likes to get hold of my dick and give it a good feel to make it stand up.'

'I am aware that others do not always share my abhorrence of sensual matters,' said Delia, trying to sound very grand, even while she sank to her knees on the sacking, facing Bert and to his side. He grinned foolishly and spread his legs wider.

'I want you to understand very clearly,' she said, 'that I am not even faintly interested in sordid thrills obtained by the manipulation of physical organs. But there is something lacking in our school text book on physiology and biology, and for that the reason, I think, is because it was written for school by a clergyman – the Reverend Thomas Drooper, D.D.'

Bert stared at her blankly.

'The Reverend Drooper,' Delia went on regardless, 'has a most irritating habit of dealing with these matters in terms so very abstract that no clear picture can be formed of what he is writing about. It is only by personal experiment that the ambiguity of the Reverend Drooper's text may be elucidated. Do you understand?'

Bert stared open-mouthed at her, having understood hardly a word, and not believing the little he grasped.

'You're pulling my leg, Miss – parsons don't write books like what you said. Nobody writes *books* about it, they just does it, even parsons, I reckon.'

It was not his leg that Delia was pulling – she had taken his limp part in her dainty hand and was tugging at it to induce it to become stiff and hard. Bert was strong and uncomplicated by nature, and his *dick* responded quickly to the touch of a female hand. Delia felt it swelling up in her palm, and growing longer in a very satisfactory manner.

Her cheeks were blushing a fiery red hue at the untruths she had told Bert as to her motives for wishing to view his sexual parts, and also at her own immodesty in handling those parts. A truly modest gentlewoman would never in any circumstances clasp a male part in her bare hand, not even if she was threatened with instant execution if she refused to do so! Even now, with her girlish innocence ruined past repair, a passing thought did much to dispel the vague shame she felt at her own depravity – the thought that it was very pleasant to hold a stiff *dick* and feel the warm flesh of it against her palm.

'There now!' crowed Bert, totally unabashed by Delia's fiery cheeks and shaking hand, and enjoying the sensations imparted to his person. 'You've given me a cockstand like an iron bar. I'm ready for a fetch off now.'

'Oh,' Delia gasped. 'What a thing to say!'

She stared down at his upright male part, long and hard, pale of skin along the barrel, with a swollen purple head thrusting out of the loose skin. She changed her grip from a full-handed grasp to a light hold between her fingertips and flicked up and down swiftly.

'That's the way,' said Bert, contentment in his voice whilst he lay down lazily on the sacking, flat on his back.

'So you say,' commented Delia, 'though to be candid with you I fail completely to understand what enjoyment you can derive from this simple and repeated mechanical motion. Explain it to me, if you please.'

'Nothing to explain, Miss,' Bert said faintly, his eyes half closed as the sensations gripped him, 'it just feels nice when you stroke me – I can't say more than that.'

'And if the manipulation is continued, then in due course it brings on the spasm,' said she, 'accompanied by an outflow of creamy white fluid. This I have observed times enough in the past when you have abused yourself under my watching eye.'

So absorbed was she in her self-imposed task that she did not at first notice Bert's hand feeling up underneath her skirts, until it was between her thighs.

'Let's have a feel of your *twat*, Miss Delia,' he said softly.

Instantly Delia clamped her thighs together, to stop his hand gaining any further ground. Indeed, she was appalled beyond all words by the very idea of being touched between the legs – and on her pussy – by a male, and a lowly school employee at that! As for the coarse term he had employed to refer to her delicate pussy, his impudence was intolerable!

'Remove your hand at once!' she exclaimed, her soft cheeks a blazing red with shame.

'Fair's fair,' said Bert, his grin more idiotic than ever as he strove to force his hand higher up between her thighs, 'you have a feel of me, so it's only right I have a feel of you.'

'There is a world of difference,' cried Delia, pressing her legs very tightly together inside her skirts, 'and as for that word – it is highly offensive to a person of gentle breeding as myself and I forbid you ever to use it in my hearing.'

With the fingers of her right hand she continued to stimulate the boy's hard shaft with nervous little up and down movements, while with her other hand she delved under her skirts to grasp at Bert's wrist and endeavour to pull his hand away.

'What word do you mean, Miss Delia?' he asked, with a look of puzzlement on his face.

'You know perfectly well which word,' said she, tugging hard at his wrist now she had hold of it. It is perhaps needless to state that he was physically by far the stronger of the two and was able to resist her with ease, his hand remaining up between her thighs, so that only the thin cotton of her drawers guarded her soft flesh from actual contact with his prying fingers.

'I'm sure I dunno what you mean,' he said, his tone showing he spoke in ignorance of his offence against polite manners.

'The word that commences with the letter T,' Delia answered, blushing furiously again.

The look of incomprehension in Bert's eyes made her realise with a start that he was wholly uneducated, even to the point of never having learned the ABC. Not only the letter T but all other letters were to him a mystery.

Meantime, his *cockstand* throbbed in her grip and it seemed to her that it had grown to an enormous size and girth. The little eye in the purple head stood open, and from her own observation in the past she knew it to be a warning of a forthcoming sudden ejaculation of his creamy fluid.

Meanwhile, in some inexplicable manner during their exchange of remarks, Bert had wheedled his hand high up between Delia's legs and into the front opening of her drawers. She could feel his blunt fingertips groping across the light fur that adorned and covered the maiden lips of her pussy.

'Take your hand away from my *twat* this instant!' she cried, the urgency of the situation breaking down the high and very necessary barrier of gentility that prevents young ladies using – or even knowing – such crude words to denote the private parts of their bodies.

Now Bert had reached the goal his hand had sought, he made no attempt to tickle the warm lips, as did the girls of Form V who invaded her bed nightly in the dorm, as a prelude to a slow act of seduction by the insertion of a finger to touch, and then to titillate, her secret bud. Such niceties were not part of the repertoire of a gardener's boy. On the contrary, his clenched hand was grasping her pussy entire, holding it hard and fast in his rough palm, squeezing it as if it were a fuzzy-skinned and golden peach from which he was pressing the delectable juice.

For an instant Delia experienced pain at this rough treatment of her delicate portion, but then an extraordinary feeling of being mastered and used set up sensations so overwhelming that she was rendered quite helpless. Her thighs parted of their own will inside her skirts, not only betraying her high principles, but also leaving the way open and clear for Bert to manipulate her in whatever manner he chose.

'Ah, your *twat's* wet and mushy as an old dishrag,' said Bert with a knowing grin. Whatever he may have had in mind to do to poor Delia now she had completely submitted herself to him, the event precluded any further physical advance on his part – for her continuous rubbing of his hard-on shaft had conveyed him to the moment of sensual spasm.

His iron-hard dick throbbed and jerked in Delia's grasp and strained upwards towards his chest. He gasped loudly and heaved his belly upwards as his milky-white fluid spurted out in quick gushes.

'Yes! More!' gasped Delia, and her legs slid wider apart, to the limit imposed by the confines of her skirts, and Bert's wrenching grip on her pussy became stronger and tighter still in his blissful throes.

Delia maintained her rapid up and down movement on his part in order to drain him of his entire liquid stock, and the heavy grasp of his hand on her pussy as she did so wrung from her an emotion so overpowering that she closed her eyes and uttered a shriek of ecstasy. Her lovely young body was shaken and racked by rapid tremors, her belly clenched and seemed to turn itself inside out – and she was aware of Bert grinning up in her face, to see her coming off.

When they were both done, he pulled her down full length upon the sacking beside him. Delia was far too

## *The Girls' Boarding School*

overcome and weakened by the sensations she had experienced to resist. Her head lay on his shoulder, her long yellow tresses spilling over his old and tattered shirt onto the sacking on which they lay together. Bert remained on his back, a broad wet patch on his shirt where his sap had soaked in, his wet *dick* starting to shrink back to its normal proportions.

Delia lay on her side, her hand still clasping Bert's organ of pleasure as it dwindled, her skirt raised over her knees and his coarse hand up it. He still gripped her moist pussy, though now with a more relaxed hold, not the ferocious grasp that had precipitated in her the ecstatic spasm. She lay breathless and in some bewilderment at the outcome of her experiment with his male part: she had thought to assuage her unadmitted longings by handling it – but in the process she had been humiliated by the gardener's boy seeing her fetch off!

'You did it like a good 'un, Miss,' said Bert in his impudent manner, 'scrawking like a cat being done by our old ginger tom, you were.'

'Hold your impertinent tongue!' Delia exclaimed, shocked by his common words.

She tried her best to sound angry and indignant, but alas, in the gentle lethargy that held her in a soft delicious grasp she could manage no more than a murmur that conveyed nothing at all of her moral outrage. This wretch of a boy had touched her most personal part with his bare hand! Unthinkable as it was, even worse had followed – he had in some strange way she did not for an instant understand brought her to the female spasm!

Perhaps it was by the contact of his work-hardened fingers on her tender pussy or perhaps by some method of manipulation she had not encountered at the hands of the young ladies of Form V, but somehow he had achieved it.

It was quite true, of course, that the depraved pupils with whom she shared the Form V dorm fetched her off thrice nightly – but immoral and depraved though it was, a difference must be recognised between that and what Bert had done to her. A main consideration was that in the dorm all were females, as Delia was herself, born with pussies between their legs, whereas Bert was of the opposite sex, a male possessing an organ capable of standing up hard and stiff.

Furthermore, the young ladies who insisted night after night on violating Delia's virgin body as she lay helpless in her bed were gentlewomen by birth, and of her own social standing. Two of them were closely related to the aristocracy, and Delia had wondered more than once whether she could detect any difference between being made to fetch off by an upper class hand and the hand of a young lady of the middle classes. It ought to be so, according to the principles by which society arranged itself, with royalty at the top and the common herd down at the bottom.

Be that as it may, and she had never yet discerned any great distinction between having her pussy felt by Daphne Grenville, who was of a great landed family, the head of which was a duke, and having it felt by Selina Ripley, whose father owned no land but was a wealthy manufacturer. Both young ladies, irrespective of their ancestry, could bring Delia to the spasm with skilful fingers in very short order.

Nor had Delia yet recorded any difference between the pussies of Daphne and Selina, when she was required to feel them and to give their youthful possessors the cheap thrills they sought so very frequently – and that in itself seemed to her a matter of some oddity. In the darkness of the dormitory it was impossible to tell an aristocratic pussy from a middle class pussy, and it was equally impossible to distinguish between upper class moans of delight and any other, at the moment of spasm.

Be that as it may, the point at issue here was simple – Bert Horewood was nothing but a common gardener's boy, far beneath Delia in the scheme of things. She considered it to be no great lapse on her part to handle his *cockstand* and manipulate him to an emission in order to further her own education into sensual matters, but it was *infra dig* to permit him to handle her body, and demeaning to succumb to the spasm at his behest.

Altogether, the situation was most unsatisfactory, and Delia was miserably aware that she should spring to her feet and quit the potting shed at once, breaking off further encounters of any kind whatsoever with this common young fellow, who lay with his hand up under her clothes and clasped over her pussy. Yet she did not, for in her most secret heart she felt the touch of his hand between her legs to be pleasant, and she remained with him and savoured her contentment.

'Bert, there is a matter on which it may be possible you can inform me,' she said, 'though you seem to know little enough of the ways of your betters.'

'What then, Miss?' he asked, not in the least put out by the condescending manner of her address, being used to nothing else in his lowly station in life.

'The first time I came to this shed I was in the company of Rhoda Fitzwalter, a companion in Form V. Indeed, it was she who suggested we came here, I being utterly innocent of such things – and it was she who bore the responsibility of bringing about the circumstances in which I first clapped eyes on a *cockstand*, as I understand you call it, namely yours.'

'That's right, Miss Delia,' Bert murmured slyly.

His fingers were moving slowly over her pussy, exploring

the wetness of her recent spasm. 'Miss Rhoda held you down on your back, Miss, and fetched you off a treat, even though you would keep screeching and wriggling all the time.'

'Quite so,' said Delia, 'but that is not the point at issue. Miss Fitzwalter, after bringing you to an emission in my sight, lay down and permitted you to introduce your stiff male organ into her person, whereupon you experienced a second emission.'

'Ah, she do like being done, Miss Rhoda,' said the gardener's boy, with a foolish grin on his face. 'I expect as how you want to try it yourself, Miss Delia?'

'Certainly not!' she exclaimed, aghast at mere thought of a boy's low-class organ being thrust into her delicate body. 'I wish you to explain to me, if you are able, why this was done – why she allowed you to use her in this abominable way, and why you wished to do so.'

Thus encouraged, Bert set forth for Delia an account of how nature had shaped the sexual organs of male and female for the purpose of intercourse. Lacking any education or refinement, he did this in the very coarsest of terms, these being all that he was familiar with. What he told her was almost the same as she had heard from Rhoda, but rather more graphic. Nevertheless, it was with growing amazement that Delia listened to Bert's story of *cockstands* and *twats*, and of the means by which the precious male fluid was introduced deep into the female belly.

It was done to put girls in the family way, said the grinning and disrespectful gardener's boy, so they got big bellies from a baby growing inside them. Then there'd be more girls born who'd grow up big enough to be *done*, and enough boys born to grow up and *do* them. Besides which, it gave people a lot of pleasure – in fact, *doing* a girl beat ratting any day of the week.

## The Girls' Boarding School

Much of this was lost on Delia, for three excellent reasons – firstly, she did not truly understand the rude terms that Bert employed. She guessed that a girl was said to be *done* after she had lain on her back and a male organ had produced an emission within her pussy, but other words of Bert's were beyond guesswork and would remain a mystery, until there was an opportunity to ask Rhoda or Thelma if they could explain them to her.

Secondly, during his exposition of the secret facts of life, Bert continued to play with Delia most indecently, his hand up her skirts and in through the opening of her drawers. The slow tickle of his fingers on the soft lips and then her hidden bud, which was very wet and slippery, set up such sensations of deep delight that she heard only one word in six of what he said.

Thirdly and lastly, although she grasped the general theme of what he was saying, albeit in a cloudy sort of way, she refused absolutely to believe that nature was so arranged that a pussy must be assaulted by a stiff male organ for a female to become in the family way – the idea was undignified and ridiculous.

Meanwhile Bert had rolled on his side to face her and raised her skirt up to her waist and pushed her legs apart in the most immodest position. He untied the string of her drawers and made them gape wide, thus exposing the dainty curls and the softest pink lips.

Delia gasped aloud as she felt the boy's mouth pressed to her tender pussy and his hot tongue explore. This had been done to her a thousand times by her schoolmates in bed in the dormitory since she had come to St Agatha's – never a night passed unless she was kissed and licked to the spasm innumerable times. Yet to let Bert perform this rude act was another matter!

'Bert – you must not do that,' she said weakly.

The gardener's boy raised his head and grinned up at her.

'You like it, though, Miss Delia,' said he, 'I can tell from the way you're a-twitching.'

'Nevertheless,' said she, attempting to make her voice clear and firm, 'you must discontinue this unwarranted familiarity.'

It is probable that her words lacked meaning to Bert, who was accustomed to simpler and much more direct speech. His idiotic grin spread wider and his fingers slipped cunningly back into Delia's pussy.

'I do believe you're going to fetch off, Miss,' said he, 'then arterwards I'll do you, to give you a feel of what it's like.'

'No, no!' Delia shrieked, but in vain, for Bert had forced her to the very brink of sensual release, and in another moment her loins arched upwards from the sacking on which she lay and her soul left her body to hang suspended in the transcendence of a fetch off.

When she regained her wits at last after her wracking spasms, she observed with horror and dismay that Bert knelt upright between her parted legs, his hand rubbing furiously up and down his stiff shaft. She could remember very well how he had *done* her friend Rhoda, lying above her and bringing his *cockstand* to her pussy and forcing it right up her, until his belly was flat on her's, and no more could be seen.

'Stop, stop!' screamed Delia, terrified at the imminent and fearful penetration.

Bert's free hand was between her legs, opening her pussy to allow himself easy ingress.

'Why, you're still a virgin, Miss Delia,' he said, grinning at her. 'Who'd 'a thought it at your age?'

Delia twisted sideways, drawing her knees up to her

belly to clear Bert and then roll away from his threatening and purple-headed *cockstand*. The lad was slow in his responses and she was almost away before he roused himself to grasp at her. She tried to wrench herself free, but she was on her hands and knees and Bert had her by the waist.

'Whoa, girl, easy, easy,' he said in a soothing voice, as if quieting a restive horse or mare.

Delia gasped out loudly to realise that her lovely white bum and soft rounded thighs were wholly exposed to this monster of a boy.

'Let me go at once!' she cried, her face flushed to brightest scarlet as she glared back over her shoulder at him.

Bert was quite beyond the reach of all reason or authority. His face bore the foolish grin that characterised his debased level of intelligence and he was panting in the anticipation of fetching off in Delia's virgin pussy, for so it technically was despite the many and continuous nights of manipulation to which it had been subjected by the girls of Form V.

Poor Delia writhed and exclaimed at the vile outrage being perpetrated upon her helpless person, but all her protestations were to no real purpose – Bert had his stiff shaft in his hand and was rubbing the bulbous head of it up and down the darling cleft between the lily-white cheeks of her bottom. She shrieked at the hot touch against her tender flesh, dreading to feel at any second a violent penetration of her pussy.

Most fortunately for her, the gardener's boy knew of but one manner of ingress, and instead of taking immediate advantage of the young lady helpless within his tenacious grasp, he paused a moment or two in his vile intentions, while he rolled her over on her back and spread her legs wide. Delia shrieked piteously to feel Bert's weight upon her belly – and his hand sliding up and down his *cockstand* as he guided it relentlessly to the wet lips of her pussy.

'Hold still, Miss Delia,' he panted, 'while I get it up your *twat*.'

As if in heaven-sent answer to Delia's cries of dismay at her impending violation, the door of the potting shed was rattled and a sharp voice spoke outside: 'Open this door at once!' it commanded. 'At once, I say!'

The angriness of the tone succeeded in percolating through a haze of lustful sensation that enveloped Bert's mind, and his head jerked up to stare at the door in some amazement. His hand continued of its own accord the manipulation of his twitching shaft as he pressed the bulbous tip against the lips of Delia's pussy. Like the brute beasts of creation, his intelligence was far removed from, and connected but slightly, with the physical impulses of his body.

Before the distraction at the shed door he had been about to force his grossly swollen *cockstand* by main force into Delia's pussy and ram it deep into her belly, thus depriving her of the priceless gift of virginity.

Needless to say, the delicate membrane that is set across the female orifice by a wise providence had long since disappeared from her person, all trace destroyed by the nightly invasion of the lewd fingers of her friends in the dormitory. Nonetheless she was yet a virgin, for the obvious reason that no thrusting male organ had entered into her charming little split.

Yet she was in the very gravest peril, for in another second or two all would have been over for her – Bert's hard-on *dick* was on the verge of piercing her. Her honour would be smirched and her person ruined beyond recall.

Happily for her, the distraction of Bert's attention by the rattling latch saved her from a Fate Worse Than Death by purest chance. As Bert's fingers continued their mindless stimulation of his organ, the inevitable result made itself manifest before he could push it in – with a grunt he fetched off!

On first entering the hut Delia had dropped the metal hasp on the door into the eyelet that served to fasten it. In normal circumstances it sufficed, but the person outside was not to be deterred by this simple mechanical device – a vigorous pushing tore the metal eyelet from the wooden doorjamb with a great splintering sound. At the instant of Bert's lustful emission, when his hot fluid gushed onto the inside of Delia's thigh, the catch gave way completely, the door was slammed back and – oh horrible to relate! – in rushed Miss Harriet.

'Save me!' Delia cried out, 'I am being defiled.'

Miss Harriet took in the dreadful scene which confronted her, the girl half-fainting, her grossly abused body shuddering in horror, the gardener's boy lying upon her and grinning like an idiot as the movement of his hand drained him of his creamy sap on to Delia's thigh. She stepped forward and seized Bert by his ragged hair and dragged him forcibly from Delia.

'How utterly degrading,' exclaimed Miss Harriet, 'to permit yourself to be polluted by the lowest of the low! How vile and shameful. You have let me down very badly indeed, and I shall insist that the severest punishment is inflicted on you, Delia. Pull up your drawers at once, girl, and hide your shame from my eyes!'

Saying which, she averted her gaze from the sight of Delia's widely-spread legs and moist pussy, and the white trickle down her thigh.

# CHAPTER 10

# Morality Is Defied By The School Head

In Miss Harriet's study Delia stood with blushing cheeks and downcast eyes, her hands behind her back, whilst the angry form mistress upbraided her severely. Despite Delia's protestations that she was the victim of uncontrolled male lust, and innocent in the matter, Miss Harriet insisted that as she had of her own free will entered the potting shed, and had remained there when Bert exposed his person, she must bear the responsibility for all that had occurred.

The incident was too serious to be dealt with as a matter of everyday classroom discipline, said Miss Harriet, her beautiful features pale with rage and her perfect bosom heaving to strong emotions. There was no help for it but to report Delia's breach of propriety to the head mistress herself.

Poor Delia was dumbstruck by the contemplation of being hauled before the formidable Mrs Kenilworth, yet nothing she could say had the least effect in softening Miss Harriet's heart. *No, you have gone too far this time to be punished and pardoned by me*, was all the stern form mistress would say to her, clenching her hands in rage at the thought of any young lady in her charge offering her person to the attentions of a common lout.

Thus it came about that Delia was dragged through the school to the headmistress's commodious study. Half-fainting in shame and fear she stood before Mrs Kenilworth, unable to look her in the face while Miss Harriet described the dreadful circumstances and all she had observed in the potting shed.

Mrs Emily Kenilworth was a most distinguished lady of forty-five or thereabouts, stout of figure, broad of face and greying of hair but strong of character. What had become of Mr Kenilworth, if ever there had existed such an unlikely soul, was neither known nor speculated on, so greatly was she esteemed and respected by all who knew her.

She stared at the erring pupil in dismay and distaste while the details of her grievous offence were told, nothing being held back by Miss Harriet, who had changed on the instant from loving and affectionate to vindictive. At her cold description of Bert's emission of sap on Delia's bare skin, Mrs Kenilworth drew in her breath in a gasp of horror.

When Miss Harriet was done, there was silence for a moment or two while the headmistress considered. When she addressed Delia, it was in a stern tone of voice that boded ill.

'What you have done is quite unforgivable,' said she. 'I fear that instant expulsion from St Agatha's is the only course that I can follow, with a letter to your legal guardian setting out the reason for it.'

'No, I implore you – do not reveal what has happened to Sir Stanton,' Delia stammered. 'I could not bear the shame.'

'You should have thought of the consequences before you went to the potting shed and allowed the gardener's boy to interfere with you,' said Mrs Kenilworth, shaking her head sadly. 'Do you deny it was with your consent that he took down your drawers?'

## The Girls' Boarding School

By way of reply Delia broke into a torrent of tears.

'Stop that!' exclaimed the headmistress. 'I have a duty towards you and the other pupils at this establishment of learning. My duty indicates that I must hand you over to your guardian for proper and due correction, but I am disposed to be merciful to one who is an orphan. You may take your choice, Delia – expulsion now, or accept the severest punishment I can devise.'

'Beat me, Mrs Kenilworth!' cried Delia, through hot tears of despair. 'Cane me, flog me! Anything but expel me!'

'Very well then, the choice is made,' said Mrs Kenilworth.

The study was large and three of its walls were lined with leather-bound books from floor to ceiling. A short and highly-polished ladder of best mahogany leaned against one wall, for use in any part of the study to give access to the top shelves of volumes. Mrs Kenilworth nodded gravely to Miss Harriet, the two of them in complete understanding, and gestured to the ladder.

At once Miss Harriet took Delia by the arm and led her to it.

'Remove all of your clothing except for your chemise, Delia,' she ordered brusquely. 'You have chosen to receive the headmistress's punishment, and this is no small matter.'

Delia blushed furiously, yet dared not disobey. With trembling hands she undid buttons and hooks and removed her garments one by one, handing them to Miss Harriet, who watched her closely the whole time, until at last she was bare-legged and barefoot, her only covering to preserve her maidenly modesty a thin loose linen chemise.

The form mistress deposited the forfeited clothes on a nearby chair and continued with the preparations by ordering Delia to stand on the lowest rung of the library ladder and lean against it. A terrified curiosity filled the girl's mind as to what was meant to be done to her, but she obeyed without demur.

Behind her and out of her sight Mrs Kenilworth handed to Miss Harriet several lengths of soft-woven cord, which she took from a desk drawer, and with these the form mistress secured Delia firmly to the ladder, with her arms high above her head and her feet well apart.

Mrs Kenilworth had always preferred to use the short ladder rather than the whipping-horse, declaring that when it was not required for chastising errant girls, the engine of doom served another almost equally useful purpose, that of access to books.

'Excellent,' said she to Miss Harriet. 'You have prepared this wicked girl for her punishment most proficiently. Now that she is fully immobilised, you may expose her posterior – here is a packet of safety-pins.'

Delia gasped in shame and terror to feel her chemise raised, and then pinned above her waist.

'Ah, a nice white bottom!' said Mrs Kenilworth. 'Between us we shall soon redden it for her, Harriet. You may begin.'

Were the whole truth told, canes, whips and birches were not made use of at St Agatha's because Mrs Kenilworth held it cruel to spoil young female beauty by breaking the skin of a lily-white bottom and drawing blood. This sprang from no particular sentimentality in her nature, nor a kind-heartedness towards the young but, if the hideous truth be told the true reason was that she had an unnatural and perverted lust for young females.

Therefore the instrument with which miscreant young ladies were brought to an understanding of the error of their ways was the hand. An open palm, as Delia knew to her cost, was well able to make a loud smack when it landed on a bottom, stinging most painfully and bringing a hot red flush to tender cheeks.

Yet it did no damage, and the contact of her hand with warm and tender girlish flesh afforded the headmistress the keenest of depraved pleasure.

Miss Harriet made a last inspection of the cord bindings that pinioned Delia's wrists to the ladder above her head, and her ankles to the rung first off the ground. She crouched beneath her to examine the bonds from below and test with her hand that they would hold firm, however much the victim writhed. Meantime the frightened girl stared at her form mistress through the rungs of the ladder and pleaded for mercy in a whisper.

Without deigning to reply, Miss Harriet ran an immodest hand up under Delia's loose chemise to feel her bare titties, giving their plumpness a squeeze, and pinching their buds with cruel fingers, bringing fresh tears to Delia's innocent eyes.

'Oh, Miss Jardyne,' said she faintly, 'I must ask you not to touch me on that portion of my person.'

Her tormenter laughed at her and deliberately increased her agony of mind by putting both hands up the chemise, feeling her titties very freely. Then satisfied that she had asserted her authority, she fetched a cushion from the sofa and pushed it between the girl's belly and the ladder. This was not, as might be thought, an act of mercy to save her from bruising against the wood, but a cold-hearted action intended to force Delia's bottom outwards, as a better target.

Without her drawers on, and her chemise pinned up her back to present her nether cheeks prominently, all was in readiness and the victim awaited her dread fate. The cold cruelty implicit in Miss Harriet's nature found means of keeping her in suspense a while longer. She laughed harshly, and passed a searching hand over the terrified girl's bare bottom.

'Beautifully plump and round,' said she with relish. 'Do you not think so, Mrs Kenilworth?'

'Ideal!' cried the headmistress cheerfully. 'Soft sweet and delicate flesh for a good hard spanking. We'll soon make her shriek and sob.'

'Have mercy,' the hapless girl pleaded, her face stained with tears, 'forgive me, I beg you, and I will never offend again.'

'It is too late to ask for pardon now,' said Miss Harriet. 'Your crime was unspeakably indecent and shameful beyond belief – the very thought of perverting a common boy to have sexual connection with you cannot in any circumstances be forgiven. By this degraded act you have bitterly offended Mrs Kenilworth and let down the entire school. There can be no pardon until these young cheeks have blushed fiery scarlet under the bitter sting of chastisement, and a lasting understanding of how vilely you have behaved has been imprinted on your mind, as well as upon your posterior.'

Whilst she was adding to her victim's sufferings by her hard words, Miss Harriet's scornful hand roved over Delia's uncovered bottom, and slipped down below the cheeks, to probe shamelessly between the girl's thighs and touch her secret furry place.

'Oh, the ignominy of it!' exclaimed Miss Harriet, addressing her words over her shoulder to Mrs Kenilworth. 'This shameless girl bared these very parts to the view of a gardener's boy and tempted him to pierce her with his aroused organ. In another second or two it would have been too late – it was by the mercy of providence that I broke into their hiding place in the nick of time!'

Even in her mortal anguish of mind, Delia recognised

that in so speaking, Miss Harriet was expressing her own jealousy – her vicious and degenerate lust for Delia's body had been changed into hatred to see a male handling those parts she herself had so many times kissed and fingered.

'St Agatha's is disgraced,' said Mrs Kenilworth mournfully, shaking her head in sorrow, 'and but for your vigilance, dear Harriet, the tallow might have been spilt inside her and caused her belly to swell in some months' time. The shame of that would have killed me!'

During this exchange of remarks, Miss Harriet's fingers were roaming freely over Delia's bare pussy, fingering the lips and probing between them, touching the girl's secret bud fleetingly but enough to induce an unwelcome state of excitement.

'A smack or two here would serve to teach you better manners in future,' said Miss Harriet, her fingers prying further into Delia's split.

'Quite so,' agreed Mrs Kenilworth, 'she would not be so very eager for sensations of pleasure between her legs if she tasted a few hard spanks on the selfsame spot. Did I ever mention to you, Harriet, how I broke a young servant girl of her habit of self-abuse by whipping her parts?'

'Really?' replied Miss Harriet, keenly interested. 'I wish I had been there to observe the cure you undertook. As she was a servant, it was only right and proper to whip her. I venture to think you must have it found a most satisfying act.'

'Very satisfactory indeed,' said Mrs Kenilworth, and a note could be discerned in her voice which was akin to *gloating*.

'Was her flesh very sore afterwards?' enquired Miss Harriet, who had personal experience of the sensations, and relished the perversity of the infliction of pain on so tender a part of the human frame. 'Did it require long to cease to be swollen?'

'A day or two,' said the headmistress. 'For a day or two the girl limped about her work bow-legged, though the whip I used on her was a light one, the sort children use for whipping tops – no more than a stick with a length of string attached to it – and it drew no blood. Afterwards I insisted upon examining her morning and evening, to observe the way in which the puffiness of the lips was reduced. Regular bathing in cold water helped a good deal to take down the swelling, and to make sure the task was done, I performed this act for her myself.'

It may well be imagined that this conversation between Miss Harriet and Mrs Kenilworth added a thousand-fold to the terrors raging in the bosom of the pinioned Delia. She moaned softly to herself, but nothing lay within her power to improve the plight in which she found herself.

'At each examination I took the opportunity to issue a stern warning to the girl,' said Mrs Kenilworth, 'reminding her that she would be whipped twice as hard if it ever again came to my notice that she had abused her own person.'

'A shocking habit that some young women allow themselves to fall into!' cried Miss Harriet.

There was no detectable trace of hypocrisy in her voice, at least not to Delia's ear, though as the helpless girl had seen for herself, Miss Harriet was not averse, when alone, to baring her own beautiful black-haired pussy and fingering it until she fetched off.

'Naturally, her parts would have been too sore to be handled to a fetch off for some little time after you had whipped them, I suppose,' Miss Harriet said thoughtfully.

Even while she spoke, she insinuated two fingers between the soft lips of Delia's pussy and subjected her secret button to a most unwelcome tickling.

## The Girls' Boarding School

'But after normality returned,' she continued, 'your serving girl most probably made up for lost time?'

'She was handled briskly, sore or not,' Mrs Kenilworth said, 'twice a day, after bathing her parts in cold water, I gave her a smart fetch off. On the first day she groaned and complained and writhed about whilst she was being handled, and begged me to desist – but it never took long before her moans changed to gasps of pleasure, and her writhings became the lively jerking of a fetch off.'

'Imagine that!' said Miss Harriet softly, her perverted mind hot at the vision she had conjured up in it.

'I kept her on, but at half wages, for a few months after she was fully recovered,' said Mrs Kenilworth, 'largely because she had a certain coarse prettiness, and I found it interesting to make use of her body against her will. But the stupid creature was hot for the embraces of men and craved the insertion of the dreadful *things* they possess. She was ashamed to be fetched off by another female – which made it all the more piquant for me! Nevertheless, she was such a simpering and silly-minded wench that the pleasure palled on me in time. I discharged her, with thirty shillings and a reference.'

'How generous is your nature,' said Miss Harriet. 'Will you make trial of the capabilities of Miss Delia here, while she is bound and at your disposal?'

'I shall make use of her girlish plaything when she has been properly punished,' the headmistress replied. 'Assure her, if you please, that I shall make her shriek more than once while she is bound to the ladder – though the second time will be by reason of different sensations from those of a sound spanking.'

'Not that! Spare me, I implore you,' gasped Delia. 'You may beat me all you will, but do not outrage my modesty.

Oh, Mrs Kenilworth – I throw myself on your mercy! I beg you to spare me from further violation.'

'Tush, girl – hold your tongue,' her headmistress responded. 'As for the rest, it is my intention to give your pussy a good tousling, after Miss Harriet has had her fill of it. That is – if she has any desire for it. You'll be carried up to your bed senseless from fetching off, when we've done with you.'

'I want nothing whatever to do with her in a sensual manner,' declared Miss Harriet coldly, but her expert fingers gave the lie to her words by teasing poor Delia's pussy so cleverly that the helpless girl hung above the precipice of fetching off. She was wracked by violent sensations, but not allowed to achieve the spasmodic moment that would bring relief to her ruthlessly overstretched nerves.

'Do you say so?' exclaimed Mrs Kenilworth in surprise. 'I was sure you would be interested in any girl as pretty as this one. I take it you have had her before and found her disappointing.'

'I thought her a charming young lady once, and went out of my way to be loving and kind to her,' responded Miss Harriet, her middle finger as far up Delia's pussy as she was able to thrust it, at which the poor child whimpered, her eyes starting from her head as her organism attempted to achieve a fetch off, but was not allowed to do so.

'I offered her my friendship,' said Miss Harriet, 'but alas, it is the intimacy of servants and the lower class that appeals to her. She has vulgar tastes, I am grieved to tell you. After I have chastised her backside to a fiery red I shall leave her in your hands to cure her of these common leanings.'

When that was said, she withdrew from Delia's wet pussy the fingers which had for some time been abusing her so shamefully, and stood away from the bound

## The Girls' Boarding School

girl. Delia cried out as the headmistress's palm landed smartly on her bare white bum and stung her pitifully. Six times the agony was repeated, causing her to shriek, then there was a pause. Delia sobbed and hung at a near swoon in her bonds, trembling now her ordeal was over.

In this assumption she was entirely mistaken. Scarce had the headmistress completed her smacking than Miss Harriet stepped forward and made a mockery of her disclaimer of interest by the outrage she then perpetrated on Delia's maidenly modesty. One hand probed between the cheeks of the helpless girl's scalding-hot bottom, whilst her other hand came round about the ladder to plunge between Delia's thighs from in front.

Delia shrieked to feel the touch of two prying middle fingers inside her wet pussy, ravaging her excited bud. The sensations were greater than her nervous system could withstand – she gave a choked moan and fetched off in violent spasms.

At once Miss Harriet stepped away from her and delivered six more cruelly hard slaps to Delia's tortured backside, mingling the excruciating pain of the smacking with the ecstatic throbs of her spasm. A darkness descended on Delia as she swooned away from the fearful maelstrom of physical sensations that engulfed her. She hung limp and senseless in her bonds on the ladder.

When she came to herself again, her ankles had been set free and Mrs Kenilworth was unfastening her wrists. Delia gasped in fear and glanced over her shoulder. Miss Harriet was sitting in an armchair across the room, now her part in the brutal ordeal was accomplished.

'Don't make a fuss, girl,' said Mrs Kenilworth, as she untied the final bond. 'Step down from the ladder – be careful now.'

Delia got down from the lowest rung, but her strength had not fully returned after her swoon and her legs were still feeble. She swayed as she stood barefoot on the carpeted floor, and was like to fall down. The headmistress passed an arm about her girlish waist to support her, and in her weakness Delia leaned against her ample form, grateful for her aid.

Poor innocent Delia – too trusting of the motives of others! Mrs Kenilworth's helpful arm tightened about her waist and soon was clasping Delia in a most passionate embrace against her own body. The arm round the girl was tight as an iron band, whilst her other hand slipped down between Delia's legs.

Delia was taken aback by this assault on her person, although she had been prewarned before the smacking of her vile purpose by the headmistress herself, who had refered to a *tousling* of her parts. She struggled to liberate herself, to no avail.

'Oh, Mrs Kenilworth, what are you doing?' she gasped.

'Don't play the innocent with me,' said the headmistress in reply. 'You've been taught by your form prefect and classmates how we pleasure each other at St Agatha's – though I'm sure you knew it well enough already before you came here.'

'No, I assure you,' Delia stammered, wriggling her body in an attempt to get away from the hand that was feeling so lewdly in between her thighs, 'I knew nothing of such things, nothing at all. Yet since my arrival I have been compelled to submit to infamous and shameful acts, night after night!'

Mrs Kenilworth paid no attention. She guided Delia across the room to the sofa and pressed her down on it. She sat herself up close beside her, keeping control of the girl by a sturdy arm about her waist, her

## The Girls' Boarding School

other hand up Delia's chemise between her legs, holding them apart.

She brought her broad and plain face close up to Delia's face and kissed her, pushing her tongue into the girl's mouth. At the same time, her finger found its way between the lower lips, invading Delia's slippery-wet pussy, in measure with her tongue invading the startled girl's mouth. Soon this skilfully-wielded finger had the desired effect – Delia began to sigh rapidly and her titties heaved in agitation.

To ravage poor Delia in this manner drove Mrs Kenilworth near frantic with lust. She seized the girl's hand and conveyed it up her clothes. Even though Delia's mind was reeling under the insult offered to her person, she could not help but note that Mrs Kenilworth, unlike Miss Harriet, wore old-fashioned drawers with an opening front and back. Against her will, her hand was thrust into the slit of the headmistress's drawers until her soft little palm was pressed against a big hairy pussy.

Delia recoiled in dismay from what was being required of her, but Mrs Kenilworth was determined to have her way, and held the girl's hand hard against her. With a despairing sob, Delia slid a long finger into the moist split of her headmistress. Horror had seized her, yet she was keenly aware that the sensation of a finger in the headmistress's split was very much the same as one up Thelma Fanshawe's, except that this was much bigger than Thelma's.

A long gentle sigh of delight from across the room served to distract Delia's attention, and she turned her head to observe its source. She saw that Miss Harriet, lying back sensuously in her armchair opposite the sofa, had drawn up her skirts to her middle and parted her stockinged knees. Her knickers were down her thighs, revealing her bush of glossy black curls and gaping pink lips. As Delia watched, Miss Harriet parted those lovely lips with long genteel fingers and felt between them, to stroke the bud of pleasure she had thus exposed.

Her position, half-lying in the chair with her legs parted so immodestly, afforded Delia a most perfect vista into the moist and rose-pink interior of Miss Harriet's adorable pussy. Yet in this she was not alone – the selfsame blissful view was on show to Mrs Kenilworth, who nodded in approval. Furthermore, she was driven by the sight to quicken the movement of her fingers in Delia's pussy, driving her almost to distraction with unwanted sensual thrills.

'Well done, Harriet!' the headmistress called out in a most insensitive and improper manner. 'Fetch yourself off, my dear, while I attend to this wretched girl!'

Long sighs shook Miss Harriet's elegant form as she advanced towards the peak of her lustful pleasure. Delia stared in horror and fascination, her own sighs matching those of Miss Harriet, for her own culminating moment was drawing close, under the busily manipulating hand of Mrs Kenilworth.

'Oh yes! I'm fetching off – I feel it!' gasped Miss Harriet as the female spasm seized her.

At the same moment Delia surrendered to the sensations that held her in their grasp, and her body squirmed and twisted in the firm hold of Mrs Kenilworth's encircling arm.

Meanwhile, not to be left behind, Mrs Kenilworth had herself almost attained the same apex of sensual satisfaction, and her plump body began to tremble against Delia.

'Fetch me off hard!' she commanded Delia. 'Push your fingers up into my pussy – all of them!'

Notwithstanding the force of the spasm that was making her writhe in ecstasy Delia refused to abase herself in this way by becoming the handmaid of another's vicious desires.

'No, I will not!' she attempted to say, but Mrs Kenilworth's tongue forced its way into her mouth and thus gagged her power to speak, so that only a gurgle was the result. Delia wanted to remove her hand from the wet and hairy pussy it had been thrust against, but the headmistress clamped her thighs together in a close grasp, and Delia's hand was held prisoner.

Nevertheless, she would not – she could not – comply with the shameful wishes of her captor and arouse her lust further. Her hand lay still and motionless, held against its will, refusing to move the finger that had penetrated inside, denying the headmistress the titillation she craved in her wet-lipped split.

If only Mrs Kenilworth would desist now from her unwanted and disgraceful attentions to Delia! If only she would let her go, let her run from the room and hide her blushing face. Yet she did not – the madness of depraved desire was upon her to ravage and to be ravaged!

Only a few seconds had elapsed since Delia had fetched off, but Mrs Kenilworth carried on her vile fingering, continuing to work skilfully at Delia's concealed bud, till she had the poor girl's loins and belly quivering yet again with sensation.

'Yes, Miss Hoity-Toity, you know what's about to happen,' exclaimed Mrs Kenilworth, her heavy hips twisting this way and that as she rubbed her pussy in a frenzy against Delia's hand.

Delia said nothing, for she was incapable of forming rational words, so intense were the sensual thrills that shook her body. Her eyes closed tightly, her mouth gaped wide, and she uttered a long and loud shriek as the sensual spasm took her again and plunged her into a shameful bliss.

Her ordeal was by no means over – indeed, it had only begun. Mrs Kenilworth, her face red-flushed and her prominent titties heaving, snatched away Delia's hand from between her legs, and put her own hand up under her own skirts in place of it. Delia sat still, unable to free herself from the arm about her waist, conscious that her headmistress was now fiercely rubbing her own pussy.

'Harriet,' she croaked, 'let me see you doing yourself again while I fetch off.'

At once Miss Harriet flung her skirts higher, and slipped her frilled knickers completely off, thus baring herself from knees to belly-button. Her delicate hand lay between her own slender milk-white thighs, the fingertips plucking at the lips of her lovely pussy before parting them and gliding within.

'Ah, Harriet, I'll have my tongue six inches up your pussy before you leave me tonight,' moaned Mrs Kenilworth, her face flushed. To Delia she whispered words that froze her blood.

'As for you, you selfish little beast, you are going to learn a lesson you will never forget. You refuse to do it for me, do you? You would leave me high and dry while you fetch off. Well then, Miss Goody-Goody, you'll find out what happens to young ladies with no regard for anyone's satisfaction but their own.'

Mrs Kenilworth's words ended in a long moan as her busy hand between her thighs brought her at last right up to the topmost pitch of gratification she so urgently sought. She cried out in a shrill voice as she fetched off

## The Girls' Boarding School

forcefully, clutching Delia to her, her tongue thrust deep into the girl's mouth.

When at long last her shameful ecstasy was completed and she regained possession of her faculties, the headmistress sprang to her feet, dragging Delia up with her, to put into effect the brutal threats she had made. Miss Harriet lay in her chair, her eyes closed in contentment, her black-haired pussy bare and on show to all, her hand resting on her smooth thigh.

Yet on hearing a call to duty from Mrs Kenilworth, the form mistress also rose to her feet and lowered her clothes modestly to cover her long beautiful legs and her private parts.

Delia sobbed with apprehension, held fast in the firm grip of the headmistress. No time was wasted now in binding her to the library-ladder – her persecutor's blood was too hot for delay. She flung Delia face down upon her writing desk, and instructed Miss Harriet to take her wrists and keep her limbs extended.

Struggle though she might, Delia's girlish powers were not a match for the combined strength of the two women. She lay upon the desk, her arms drawn up above her head by the pull of Miss Harriet on her wrists, her legs extending backwards in the air. Her chemise was up in her armpits, so that her delicious young belly and titties lay bare upon the polished wood of the desk.

Miss Harriet was staring beyond Delia, the cruellest smile on her lovely face, a dark fire in her eyes. From her expression Delia guessed that Mrs Kenilworth was about to smack her again. The thought of that dreadful pain was more than the girl could bear – and with a sob of despair she cried out that she would obey the headmistress and comply with her every wish, if only she was spared the punishment.

'Ha, you've changed your tune,' said Mrs Kenilworth's voice from somewhere to the rear of Delia. 'What do you say, Harriet, am I to let this wicked girl off her due reward in return for a promise of loving attention to me?'

'Smack her!' exclaimed Miss Harriet. 'Smack her bum till she screams. After that she will be willing to pleasure you as many times as you like.'

'The thought is tempting,' Mrs Kenilworth admitted, running a hand over the sore cheeks of Delia's bottom, 'but no, I am too impatient. I shall smack her again later, if she does not carry out her duties skilfully.'

With that, Miss Harriet let go of Delia's wrists, and she got off the desk. Mrs Kenilworth returned to the sofa, removing her drawers entirely, and hitching her skirts up to her waist.

'Come, Delia,' said she, and parted her strong thighs to show the broad bush of dark brown curls about her pussy. 'Kneel down here between my legs and apply your tongue. It is my desire to fetch off three times without a pause between. After that we shall see.'

Delia stared in horror, her every virginal instinct causing her to recoil from the hateful vision presented to her. Yet she could not tear her glance away from the disgracefully exposed split that confronted her, try as she might. It seemed so large and so powerful of appearance, so *domineering*, in comparison to her own girlish slit. The lips pouting at her were fleshy and thick and stood boldly forth, and they were a little shiny with the moisture of the fetch off the headmistress had induced so angrily in herself.

*Oh no, oh no*, Delia sighed to herself in dismay, but for all her reluctance, she moved forwards, drawn in spite of herself, against all her moral principles, against her better judgement, to that dominating female organ. Her face was scarlet and her limbs shook in shame and embarrassment – yet she was incapable of controlling her own actions and recoiling from the monstrous command imposed upon her. She pressed her dainty mouth close to Mrs Kenilworth's hairy pussy and slipped her tongue between the warm lips.

# CHAPTER 11
# A Clergyman is Tempted Beyond Endurance

Total exhaustion set in after Delia was so disgracefully abused by Mrs Kenilworth, with the assistance of the cruelly depraved Miss Harriet. When Delia was released from the unspeakable ordeal to which they subjected her, she went to bed, although it was only seven in the evening. Her bottom was fiery hot from the smacking she had received, and her spirits were low. At the behest of Thelma Fanshawe, who understood that rest was a dire necessity after violation at the hands of the headmistress and form mistress together, the young ladies of Form V left Delia alone to sleep and recuperate.

It was towards morning when Delia awoke from the heavy sleep which had claimed her. The first faint light of day was at the windows and all around she could hear the soft breathing of her sleeping classmates. A hand lay on her shoulder, to shake her a little and rouse her from slumber. Delia gazed up and saw that it was Edna Calthorpe-Brunton, of the pale yellow hair and the large titties.

'Dear Delia,' Edna murmured, 'I have been so very worried and anxious for you. Was the punishment very fearful?'

'Oh Edna,' said Delia, touched by the sympathy thus

shown to her, 'it was awful beyond all imagining. You cannot begin to comprehend the things that were done to me!'

'Merciful Heaven,' sighed Edna, 'tell me what happened.'

Delia was pleased to have a chance to unburden her heart and mind of her afflictions and began to recount to her friend with sighs and sobs some details of the outrage of her modesty. She made way for Edna in the bed beside her, wishing to keep her voice low and not risk wakening anyone else in the dormitory. The two of them lay close, Delia's voice a mere whisper close to Edna's ear – and in the middle of her tale, when she least expected it, Delia felt Edna's shameless hand slip under her chaste nightgown, and between her legs.

Before Delia could give utterance to the protest that rose to her lips, Edna had hold of her pussy. Nor was that the end of her unwarranted depredations, for she inserted a finger into the sensitive spot at the top of Delia's virginal, though much handled, little split.

Delia trembled mightily and moaned in despair, but by her own acceptance of nightly defilement by her classmates, her fate was to become the plaything of the vile lusts of others. Like a shot, her treacherous friend rolled half on top of her, her big soft titties squashing Delia's smaller and more shapely pair. A passionate kiss by Edna closed Delia's mouth, the while her busy fingertip tickled the unfortunate girl's hidden nub.

Although poor Delia had been abused to the verge of swooning only the evening before – or perhaps even because the excessive stimulation had made her female parts more highly sensitive yet – both the young ladies were very soon aware of the slippiness of arousal within Delia's pussy. Silent tears of shame coursed down Delia's cheeks at this most unwelcome development. She had been dreadfully misused by the headmistress, and no less so by Miss Harriet. Surely a malevolent fate could inflict no more horror upon her. Yet Edna – whom she had trusted as a friend – was now plying the same course.

Try as she might to keep her thighs together, Delia felt them sliding apart of their own will, almost as if inviting Edna to do whatever she chose to the maidenly body of her victim – evil and loathsome thought! Struggle as she might – though silently so as not to awake the whole dorm and bring them to watch about her bed – there were thrills of most shameful pleasure coursing through Delia's belly. Deep in Delia's heart lurked a humiliating certainty that in another moment she would be fetched off by the hand between her legs.

It was too much for a gently-bred and tenderly-nurtured girl to bear. In the course of a single day she had been wrought up to the spasm a dozen times and more by Miss Harriet and by Mrs Kenilworth – and now she must suffer this renewal of the dread ravishment by one she had believed to be a true friend!

Mortifying though the situation was, it was a fact that Edna had so aroused her that Delia no longer knew what she did. Her groping little hands shook as if in a fever as they found their way up under Edna's nightgown and felt her unreliable friend's big soft titties. The touch excited Delia's raging emotions to a more intense degree, and also pleased Edna enormously.

'Oh Delia, give them a good tousling while I bring you off,' Edna murmured. 'Then you shall do me.'

So it was not to be once only. Edna was of a mind to repeat this shameful practice several times before leaving her alone. At the realisation of what lay in store for her at the hands of the other girl, Delia felt her back rise from the bed to thrust her belly and her pussy up against Edna's ministering hand.

The overwhelming sensations of the female spasm throbbed right through her, and although she squirmed in the throes of a reprehensible ecstasy, she cried out to her friend, 'Edna – you are a traitress! You have undone me – I shall never speak to you again.'

Later in the day, at mid-morning, a messenger in the form of a housemaid interrupted Miss Harriet's arithmetic lesson to say that Delia was to report to the headmistress's study at once. All the girls stared at Delia, and so did Miss Harriet, though her beautiful features bore no expression to give Delia a clue as to what was intended by this unexpected summons.

Trembling with she knew not what emotions, Delia proceeded to Mrs Kenilworth's study and tapped at the door, and entered when bid, to where the headmistress awaited her.

Delia's eyes fell to the headmistress's prominent bosom under a brown frock and in her mind's eye she again saw those vast titties she had only last evening handled and sucked, in the throes of lust encouraged by a spanking. She glanced down over the round belly she had felt and kissed, and to where, hidden under the headmistress's plain frock, there lay the big hairy pussy that Delia had been compelled to lick – and which she had come to like so much that she had begged to be let do it again and then again, until even Mrs Kenilworth herself had half-swooned in an excess of sensual pleasure.

Delia was hoping, in the dark privacy of her mind, that she had been sent for to repeat last evening's events, for vile as those events were, they had seized upon her imagination and she wanted very much to experience them once more – though without the spanking this time. She was on

## The Girls' Boarding School

the very edge of going down on her knees before the headmistress and pressing her face to that capacious lap, when she glanced up into Mrs Kenilworth's face. At once all thought of pleasure fled. Mrs Kenilworth bore a stern expression, and her cold blue eyes shone with severity – Delia sobbed in terror and begged to be spared.

'Enough of your complaining,' said the headmistress briskly. 'Even though you were punished severely only yesterday, you are so lost to all decency of conduct that you misbehave in a most abominable way instantly afterwards. You are now far beyond any correction that Miss Harriet can perform. It seems very clear now that I have been too lenient and forbearing with you, but that is now about to be changed.'

'But in what have I offended?' Delia asked miserably. 'I was told to report to you – no reason was divulged.'

'Former correction has achieved nothing in improving your behaviour,' Mrs Kenilworth replied. 'You have had your clothes up round your waist and your backside smacked to a blazing red, but still you persist in your wickedness. This time you are to be taught how pupils are dealt with when they persist in their offences against the School Rules.'

Until this very moment Delia's emotions had blinded her to the presence in a corner of the room of a third person. She had seen him before and knew who he was, but otherwise knew little about him. He was the Reverend Octavian Blenkinsop. This young gentleman of some six and twenty years was curate of the church of St Mungo's, in which parish lay St Agatha's Boarding School for Young Gentlewomen.

The young clerical gentleman was a nephew to the bishop, who had sent him as curate to Canon Grossmith at St Mungo's, seeing this as a stepping-stone to a higher ecclesiastical preferment, with a superior stipend, in due course.

As to the incumbent of St Mungo's himself, it was rumoured in the parish that Canon Grossmith, although married twenty years and the father of eight children, had lately developed the most lively interest in choirboys – their musical, their moral and their physical development.

Not just one, but all members of the St Mungo's choir, it was whispered about, were the objects of the Canon's regard, and in particular those of a tender age, whose sweet treble voices had not yet broken. These youngsters received the Canon's fullest attention and each spent hours alone with him in the vestry of St Mungo's, being personally tutored.

In the circumstances, the Canon had delegated to his curate the duty of attending St Agatha's School, for the holy purpose of conducting morning prayers, and to take classes in religious knowledge – an important part of the curriculum.

The Reverend Blenkinsop was no especial favourite of the young and lively gentlewomen of St Agatha's. He had fair hair and a weak chin, and eyes of watery blue. He was tall, but thin and rather round-shouldered. In all, not an imposing figure.

He wore a black frockcoat with his white clerical collar, his pale hands were joined together in a washing motion, while his gaze was fixed on Delia in dismay and doubt. Nevertheless, she begged him, as a man of compassion, to intercede with the headmistress on her behalf, that she might be spared further suffering. But the curate shook his head, saying it was out of the question to intervene in a matter of school discipline. He advised her to be brave and take her punishment in the spirit it was intended – for her own good.

'Then tell me what my offence is, if you know it, Sir,' Delia implored him, but he merely shook his head doubtfully.

'The Reverend Blenkinsop has not been informed of the details of your sly back-sliding,' said Mrs Kenilworth with a frown, her arms folded beneath her ample bosom. 'I hesitate even now to assail his ears with what can only cause him to despise you for your actions.'

'Oh, but I feel I should be made aware of what the young lady has done,' said the curate, most earnestly. 'You have my deep assurance that however hideous the offence, I shall never allow myself to entertain feelings of animosity towards her.'

'Very well, then,' Mrs Kenilworth agreed, 'since you yourself request it. This girl, Miss Delia Sempill-Shand, last night in her dormitory, inveigled one of her classmates into bed with her. This is strictly forbidden by the Rules of St Agatha's, as you may be certain.'

'Really?' asked the curate. 'Why is that? Perhaps they were saying a prayer together, and that would be an act of merit, to be rewarded with approbation, not to be punished.'

'I doubt if prayer was the intent,' Mrs Kenilworth replied. 'Experience has shown that proximity of young ladies clad only in thin nightgowns normally leads to an excitation of emotions better left dormant. The warmth generated by two persons close together tends to arouse improper thoughts. In extreme cases it leads on to actual *touching* of bodily parts.'

Delia listened in astonishment to this farrago of arrant hypocrisy from her headmistress. To hear her speaking thus to the reverend gentleman – she, the very person who had stripped Delia naked and violated her with lewd fingers. The person who had exposed herself wantonly to

Delia and compelled her to kiss her pussy and fetch her off. Oh, if the Reverend Blenkinsop only knew what went on at St Agatha's. If only Delia dare tell him! Yet without anyone having said so, she knew if she dared to breathe a word to an outsider she would be cruelly spanked, branded a liar, and expelled with ignominy.

'Great Scot!' exclaimed the curate, his eyes bulging from his pale face in shocked dismay. 'Whatever are you suggesting, Mrs Kenilworth? Do you think it possible that Miss Sempill-Shand touched the other girl with her hand on some private part of her person? No, no, the thought is quite outrageous – not for a moment would I believe it.'

'Whether she did or not, that is not the point,' said Mrs Kenilworth. 'She flouted the rule that forbids two girls to be in bed together. For that she must be chastised.'

'Have you asked her if she did invite a friend into her bed?' said the Reverend Blenkinsop. 'Perhaps there might be a mistake. Is your information reliable?'

'Completely. I was informed this morning by the housemaid who carries hot water up to the dormitories that she had seen Miss Edna Calthorpe-Brunton in the bed of this young lady before us. With her own eyes the housemaid saw that they were embracing as they slept. More than that is not necessary to convince me – as it must convince you – of the impropriety of the situation.'

'Quite so, quite so,' said the curate sadly. 'How fearful it is to encounter sin in one so young and fair of appearance.'

Without a word, but with gestures that showed clearly enough what she wanted done, the headmistress made it plain to Delia that she was to bend over the end of the desk and lift up her skirts to offer her backside for chastisement. Delia hoped that the presence of the reverend gentleman

## The Girls' Boarding School

would guarantee her some measure of protection against the worst excesses.

She arranged herself on the desk, her clothes pulled up over her back to reveal the white drawers that served as her last frail remnant of modesty. Immediately, Mrs Kenilworth slid her hands underneath Delia's waist to undo the string that held the garment about her.

'No, no,' exclaimed Delia pitifully.

Alas for maidenly modesty! Her drawers were stripped down to her knees. Thus face down and helpless, her posterior bared in the most shameful manner for what was to come, Delia knew that Mrs Kenilworth's eyes were fixed on the twin rounded cheeks of her exposed bum. Worse yet, a dark suspicion entered in her mind that perhaps the Reverend Blenkinsop was also gazing upon her lily-white cheeks, however recklessly improper that was for a man of the church.

'Confess your wrongdoing now,' said Mrs Kenilworth. 'Why did you inveigle Edna Calthorpe-Brunton into your bed last night?'

'Her presence in my bed was not my doing,' Delia stammered in fear and dread. 'More than that I cannot say. To tell tales on each other is wrong.'

'I suppose that the lustful games you played together are not wrong?' Mrs Kenilworth demanded. 'Away with this silly notion of schoolgirl honour. I mean to have the truth before ever you leave this room, and a full confession of what the pair of you did to each other.'

'It was not my choice!' cried Delia. 'I was forced against my will.'

In asserting this she was not being entirely truthful. It was the fact that Edna had initiated the disgraceful proceedings by thrusting her hand up between Delia's legs, but thereafter both young ladies had participated in the perverse handling of each other's parts indiscriminately, Delia becoming as eager as Edna to undergo the female spasm, time after time.

'Forced to it – a likely tale!' Mrs Kenilworth retorted with cutting sarcasm. 'Forced were you? Did you hear her impudent lie, Reverend Blenkinsop? She must think me a fool, to try out that old chestnut on me.'

'Dear me, dear me,' Delia heard the curate murmur.

He was not allowed to escape easily from his duties, for Mrs Kenilworth addressed herself to him at some length: 'Whilst you have been spiritual adviser to St Agatha's,' she demanded of him, 'have you ever heard of a pupil forced against her will by another young lady to commit an act of indecency?'

As she spoke she placed her heavy hand on Delia's bottom and pressed against the soft flesh, as token of what worse would be inflicted in due course.

'Never,' said the curate, a new note of urgency in his voice, almost a hint of a most unhealthy excitement, to see the girl's body being touched. 'Never once.'

'But I swear it is the truth,' Delia cried, her final hope gone now that the curate seemed set against her. Her words made him feel obliged to give some sort of explanation for his view.

'Unlike a certain type of young man, who finds a sinful and degenerate pleasure in handling females, and by brute force and strength forcing them to his shameful will,' said he, 'the truth is that well-bred young ladies are by their temperament too delicate, and possessed of a natural chasteness, for them even to contemplate such horrid acts. I much fear you are telling a falsehood to deceive us.'

'Mark me well, Delia,' said Mrs Kenilworth with cruel cheer, 'I have been headmistress twelve years, and in that time every lie has been told to me, every wicked untruth

## The Girls' Boarding School

young ladies make up when they are afraid their little vices have been found out. Do not try to deceive me with useless tales of woe. Speak out, what did you do to Edna Calthorpe-Brunton? I must know.'

It was in Delia's mind to retort that Mrs Kenilworth knew very well what she and Edna had done to each other, for it was the same that the headmistress had forced her to do here in this study not long ago. To think of rebellion on this scale was one thing, but to put it into action was another. The words did not form themselves, and were perhaps impossible ever to say.

'May I be forgiven for betraying a friend,' Delia confessed in a quavering voice, 'but when Edna Calthorpe-Brunton got into my bed early this morning, I tried to make her go away, but she is strong and she was determined to violate me.'

'Was she, indeed?' said Mrs Kenilworth, disbelief apparent in her tone as she drew her hand slowly along the back of Delia's left thigh, till her fingers lay in the cleft between the plump cheeks of her lily-white bum. 'And how were you *violated* – was it by Edna's fingers or by her tongue?'

'Both,' said Delia in a low voice. 'She would not go away and leave me alone, no matter how often I begged her. She was like a person possessed, and had her way with me several times, till I lay broken and exhausted.'

'Great Scot, did ever you hear such lewdness from the lips of a young lady, Curate?' Mrs Kenilworth demanded. 'Not just once but several times, she indulged her wanton desires!'

'The mind reels and draws back in horror!' said the reverend gentleman in a shaking voice, evidently in the grip of strong emotion. 'I am astounded that the female constitution is able to tolerate so prolonged a spell of sensation. You must advise me, Mrs Kenilworth

– is what this girl claims to have undergone humanly possible?'

'Very possible,' replied the headmistress. 'In this respect the male and female constitutions are very different in their capacities. Whereas any gentleman could well be too fatigued to continue further after experiencing the sensual spasm twice or so, a well-fed female is able to withstand half a dozen or more repetitions of it within a short space of time.'

'Good God!' exclaimed the young gentleman of the cloth, his agitation of mind betraying him into near-blasphemy. 'I had no idea. The thought is monstrous. Monstrous!'

'You see now the importance of checking this conduct between the young ladies of St Agatha's as soon as the least suspicion of it arises,' said Mrs Kenilworth. 'Otherwise debauchery would run riot in no time at all. Repeated indulgence in these acts by the young dulls their minds, stunts their bodies, and turns sallow their complexions.'

'Heaven forfend!' gasped the Reverend Blenkinsop.

'You may see the results any day by a simple observation of the daughters of the poor in any town or city in the land,' Mrs Kenilworth continued. 'They walk with stooped shoulders, and do not look you in the eye. Their cheeks are wan, their eyes lack-lustre their bosoms undeveloped.'

'Bosoms!' exclaimed the curate with a catch in his voice not very distant from a sob. 'By Heaven – I dare not allow myself to think of these female protuberances.'

'You must be bold enough to see life and humanity as it truly is,' the headmistress admonished him. 'The female portion of the human race is at least half of it, and every female above the age of thirteen or thereabouts is possessed of bosoms, small or large. It is idle and useless to shut your eyes to the truth. Glance about you at your congregation when next you conduct Sunday services in St Mungo's – you will be able to recognise among the poorer type of female parishioner the signs of incessant and forbidden indulgence.'

'Lord protect us!' sighed the curate so weakly that he might have been about to faint. 'What a fearful responsibility rests in your hands, dear Mrs Kenilworth – to guide your pupils along the straight and narrow path to mental and physical health.'

There reigned in Delia's mind great confusion on hearing the words of her headmistress. How was it possible that the girls of St Agatha's were tall and well-formed, keen of intellect and vigorous of body when Mrs Kenilworth said that indulgence in sensual pleasure had a devastating effect on mind and body? Here was to be found an unresolved contradiction, and Delia was unable to make sense of it at all.

'Good teaching, good plain food, good discipline – these are the the only methods I use or need,' said Mrs Kenilworth with pride in her professional abilities.

When she stopped speaking and remained silent for some little time, Delia clenched the cheeks of her bottom tight together in anticipation of the blow. But the hand of the headmistress lay lightly upon one cheek, deliberately stoking up Delia's terror, and affording her tormentor a degree of cruel pleasure.

There was another matter troubling Delia. If it was true in any degree at all that unrestrained sensual indulgence did harm to young ladies' health, then how was it possible to explain why Mrs Kenilworth herself had ravished so many of her pupils? For so she had given Delia to understand when she had recovered from the third or fourth tonguing. Nor was it the headmistress alone, for if Miss Harriet was to be believed, and no one could doubt the word of a lady so lovely in her person, then she had herself debauched every girl at St Agatha's taking them in turn one a day – including Delia.

If Miss Harriet did so, then it was not beyond the bounds of conjecture that every other teacher at the school did likewise; Miss Rodgers, Miss Gawsby, Miss Willimby, Miss Lumton – every one of them! Into Delia's innocent mind crept the first faint suspicion that hypocrisy played a large and necessary part in the workings of St Agatha's, and perhaps in the world outside.

'Now,' cried Mrs Kenilworth, interrupting Delia's train of thought, 'you have confessed to utterly disgraceful conduct in provoking Edna Calthorpe-Brunton to manipulate you five or six times to spasm last night. How often did you do it to her?'

'You wrong me with this accusation,' said Delia tearfully, but with no foundation in truth. 'I refused to take any part in the immodest acts that Edna wished to indulge in. But she threatened to manipulate my body to collapse, unless I consented to put my hand to her person and give her the sensations she craved.'

'Now we have it,' Mrs Kenilworth exclaimed briskly. 'What do you make of that for a full admission, Reverend Blenkinsop? She persuaded the other young lady to abuse her several times, then returned the abuse with her own hand an equal number of times.'

'Oh my word,' the Curate sighed, 'I can scarcely credit it.'

Mrs Kenilworth waited no longer. Her strong hand flashed down through the air and landed with a smack across Delia's bare bum and made her cry out in sudden shock. She gritted her teeth as another smack landed on her sensitive flesh, spanning the crease between her cheeks, stinging both.

## The Girls' Boarding School

'Open your legs,' Mrs Kenilworth commanded. 'Display the part of your body that leads you into temptation at bedtime.'

The thought of obeying a command so immodest, especially when a gentleman was present, caused Delia to feel bitter shame. She kept her legs close together, and was rewarded instantly by a stinging spank that made her jump and cry out. The agony seemed quite unbearable, and to prevent a repetition, Delia parted her legs a little.

She knew that by doing so she had exposed to the headmistress's eyes, and to those of the Reverend Octavian Blenkinsop, a glimpse of the pouting pink lips of her pussy, set in her thin fledging of fair hair.

Delia gasped aloud to feel Mrs Kenilworth's hand slide sideways up the inside of her right thigh, until it reached her exposed split. There it stayed, resting against the soft lips.

'Observe, Reverend,' she heard Mrs Kenilworth say, a distinct note of triumphant gloating in her voice, 'a gentleman in your respected position must not be in ignorance of the ways of male with female. Or in the individual case we are dealing with, the ways of female with female.'

'Quite, quite,' he gasped. 'We clergy must understand all if we are to speak with authority on sinfulness.'

'Observe closely,' said Mrs Kenilworth, 'there in between her legs is the fleshy organ that is the cause of so much mischief. Mark it well, Sir, and instruct me if you can how I may check the base urges of my pupils – except by a smart spanking?'

'Lord,' Delia heard him murmur softly, but with considerable interest, 'then that is what the female parts look like. Until this moment I did not know, Mrs Kenilworth. I am most grateful to you for enlightening me, though I would wish the occasion to be less ominous than this.'

'A sentiment with which I can only agree,' said the headmistress with a tinge of malice in her voice. 'To complete your knowledge of the female person while opportunity serves, set your hand to it and acquaint yourself with how it feels to the touch.'

'But surely . . .' the curate said gaspingly, as if to protest this was going a great deal further than was right or decent, as indeed it was.

In truth, the suggestion was monstrously wicked and past all belief in a female of mature years and of good family, who was in charge of an educational establishment for young gentlewomen. A long term in prison at hard labour – seven years at least – must surely have been the sentence on so depraved a person, had she been brought to book by the law and put on trial! Yet the meek acquiescence of the curate in this nefarious scheme was just as criminal, and if brought to justice, he surely deserved no less than to be unfrocked and despatched to Dartmoor Prison and set to breaking stones.

A moment or two passed, then the reverend gentleman's slackly trembling hand felt gingerly between Delia's parted thighs, and his fingers touched her bare pussy.

'Oh!' she heard him cry out in a shaky voice. 'But it is so very . . .'

He sounded so odd that Delia risked compounding the wrath of the headmistress by craning her head round to see what caused the condition. She saw the curate lurch a step or two back from her bare posterior, clutching with both hands at his own body, in the region of the lower belly. He was bent over, with his eyes shut and his mouth hanging loosely open. In his stumbling and unguided retreat the back of his legs struck a chair and he collapsed into it, gasping out *Oh oh oh oh* . . .

A very strange thought crept into Delia's mind then,

## The Girls' Boarding School

making her face blush. The manner in which the Reverend Blenkinsop's loins jerked, and the cries he uttered, recalled to her those of the gardener's boy, when he fetched off. She well remembered how his *cockstand* throbbed and jumped in her fingers and how he gave rapid gasps while his creamy fluid spurted.

To see the curate in this condition almost made her think he had undergone a similar experience, although no one had touched him, and he had certainly not handled his own person. Whatever it was that racked him, it was soon over and done with, and the reverend gentleman lay back in the chair with a look of foolish content on his pink-flushed face.

Delia was at a loss to explain it, for she was quite certain that clergymen were high above such degrading mortal weaknesses as succumbing to bodily thrills. She was convinced that it was only low class males, such as gardener's boys, and other base members of the labouring classes, who underwent the experience, or wanted to.

Among gentlewomen, matters were otherwise, and for excellent reasons, as Delia had learned at St Agatha's. Events had shown her that her fellow-pupils were madly devoted to the sensations the spasm afforded them, whether of aristocratic stock or only rich merchants' daughters. A difference set by nature between the experience of young gentlewomen and low-class young men was that females did not eject messy gushes of milk-white liquid in the throes of a fetch off. Furthermore, and this was of great importance indeed, female raptures were of a superior and finer type altogether, and almost could be described as aesthetic – it might not be going too far to claim an element of spirituality for them. It was certain that the young ladies of St Agatha's did not surrender their bodies to such common little thrills as males and the lower orders underwent.

Nonetheless, the curious throes into which the Reverend Mr Blenkinsop had fallen at the moment when he had touched Delia's uncovered person was odd in the extreme and quite inexplicable. Happily for Delia, Mrs Kenilworth's own attention had been so engrossed in the curate that she had not noticed Delia's short and surreptitious observation of the event.

'Dear me,' she addressed the languid young clergyman, using a tone Delia found slightly facetious and therefore inappropriate to the poor man's inexplicably enfeebled and bemused condition, 'what an unfortunate accident, to be sure! How very surprising a thing to occur to a young gentleman in Holy Orders. You must withdraw, Sir, and attend to your clothing. I fear the washer-woman who has the duty of laundering your linen next week will think you have fallen into moral turpitude and solitary vice.'

'Oh, Mrs Kenilworth,' the curate murmured in deepest dismay, 'what is to become of my reputation?'

'As to that, I cannot say,' replied the headmistress, in an unsympathetic manner, evidently intent on pressing home to the full the advantage she had gained over the crestfallen cleric, 'but of this I am sure – it is not proper for you to remain in the same room as a young lady, after what has happened to you.'

The words meant nothing to Delia, who lay very still across the end of the headmistress's polished desk, her innocent bum uncovered and awaiting the remainder of the *six of the best* she feared were her fate. She heard a mumbling by the curate as he made his apologies, though no word could be distinguished. When he had left the room and the door was closed behind him, Mrs Kenilworth addressed herself again to Delia.

## The Girls' Boarding School

'The sight of your bare backside had a curious effect on the reverend gentleman,' said she, 'but for that I cannot blame you – indeed, it is a pretty posterior, in all honesty. Perhaps we should not be too surprised that a young man as inexperienced and unworldly as the Reverend Blenkinsop allowed himself to be carried away by his emotions and succumb to your girlish charms to the point of *giving up the ghost*, as one may put it.'

Whereupon Delia felt a hand stroking over the bare cheeks of her bottom, and shortly afterwards enquiring fingers fondled at the lips of her pussy.

'To see a member of the male gender humiliated in so comical a way has put me in the best of tempers,' said Mrs Kenilworth. 'I have decided to forgive you, Delia – this time you shall not be punished severely for being in bed with Edna. But only this time, mark you.'

The headmistress's fingers probed expertly and Delia gasped to feel the little button within her split being caressed.

'You shall fetch off now,' said Mrs Kenilworth. 'I much enjoy watching young girls wriggling in the sensual spasm. Stand with your legs wider apart, Delia.'

# CHAPTER 12
# A Depraved Friendship Renewed

At the end of July St Agatha's broke up for the summer holidays and the young ladies were allowed to depart for their homes and families. All the previous afternoon there was a vast bustle as boxes were packed and brought down by the servants to the hall, ready for an early start on the next day. That night there was little sleep for anyone in the school, nor did the various form mistresses make the slightest attempt to enforce silence after lights out, for the pupils found much to chatter about.

In addition to the gossip fuelled by high spirits and happy prospect of six weeks of holiday from school-work, there were many warm goodbyes to be said between friends. This could only be accomplished by a regular and sustained movement from bed to bed by the young ladies in question, to exchange not merely the words of friendship but tokens of their abiding regard for each other in the indecency of shared spasms. There was not a pupil to be found in the entire school who was not brought off half a dozen times during the course of that night, by different hands and tongues.

It is needless to state here that every form mistress clearly knew what took place amongst her young charges during the last night of every term. The very air was charged with excitement – each dormitory was alive with whispers, sighs and gasps in the dark, as mouth was pressed to mouth in burning lustful kisses, while up inside nightgowns trembling hands stimulated wet young pussies. Indeed, it was the general opinion of the young ladies of Form V – and probably of Forms I, II, III and IV – that their form mistresses were similarly engaged with each other.

Delia came in for more than her share of fond farewells that night, for although her reserved manner seemed intended to fend off lewd approaches, her physical attractions brought her many admirers among the young ladies of Form V.

The first to violate her modesty on that night was red-haired Thelma, who as form prefect took priority. Afterward, with her mission achieved, she moved on to another bed, so leaving Delia with her nightdress up about her neck and her maidenly pussy still throbbing weakly in the aftermath of sensual pleasure.

After Thelma, big-bosomed Edna was soon to follow, slipping into Delia's bed in the dark and falling upon her bared titties with her avid mouth. Then came dark-haired Maria, her own split wet and slippery from coming off with another before entering Delia's by-then rumpled bed. Not to spin out longer this record of youthful depravity, by one o'clock in the morning every girl in Form V had visited Delia's bed in turn and had compelled her to take part in an exchange of shameful caresses and spasms.

When at last Delia was left alone, her lovely bare body wet with the sweet perspiration of continued arousal to the apex of human sensation, her thighs slippery with the dew of excitement which ought never to have been permitted – when at last no more girls slipped into bed with her and reached for her titties or ravaged slit with eager hands,

## The Girls' Boarding School

then and only then did she close her eyes and slide into the deepest of exhausted sleep.

Next day, as can well be imagined, there were moans and sighs of complaint when the rising bell was sounded. The young ladies were slow to struggle from their beds after the fatigues of the night, faces were paler than usual and dark shadows were to be seen under pretty eyes. By stages they stirred themselves into action, washed and dressed themselves not in school frocks but in their finest clothes, and descended for breakfast, where their spirits were raised and girlish chatter broke out freely, unchecked by the supervising mistress.

By nine o'clock the last arrangements were made and off went the young ladies of St Agatha's to enjoy their summer holidays. A long procession of hired conveyances took them to the railway station at Tuppington, where they were to embark on the branchline slow stopping train for Midsomer Rackham. There they would change to the London Flier when it rolled snorting and panting into the station, the mighty pistons of the engine thrusting so forcefully that the girls stared in breathless admiration and felt quite moist between the legs.

To chaperone them on the long journey Miss Uckworth had been charged with the grave responsibility of accompanying the party all the way to London, for it was rumoured that curious things could befall young ladies who travelled on their own in railway trains. It was by no means unknown for gentlemen seated in the same compartment to attempt familiarities of an obscene nature. Maria Wendover had regaled all of Form V, on the night before they were to travel by train, with a story she had been told by a chambermaid at home, who had been exposed to gross indignities, by a person on a train. He was not a gentleman, only a man, for the chambermaid travelled in a third class compartment, as befitted her position in life.

That notwithstanding, the man in question had unfastened his trousers, said she, and taken out a part of his person that was at least nine inches in length and as thick as a cucumber. Nor was that the total extent of his disgraceful behaviour, for he had suggested to the chambermaid, whose name was Annie, that it would pass the journey pleasantly if she were to take it in her hand and stroke it. She, being a respectable girl, blushed red and would have nothing to do with it, whereupon the man grinned offensively and manipulated his own person with his hand.

In the few short weeks between the first day of term and the last, Delia had learned enough not to be astonished to hear of a man pulling out a long stiff *dick* – she had with her very own eyes seen Bert the gardener's boy do so. Nor was she under any delusions of ignorance any longer as to the reason a male wanted to have his *cockstand* stroked – it was to make his creamy white fluid come squirting out.

Indeed, now Delia had thought it over several times, she had come to entertain a strong suspicion that the weak-willed and ineffecutal curate of St Mungo's had experienced an emission in his trousers when he had touched her with his fingers. She blushed in the dark dormitory to call to mind that he – a man! – had been afforded an open view of her bare pussy. To be told by Maria there were male persons, not gentlemen of course, who brought out their *cockstands* to show to women on railway trains – it was very strange and unsettling.

Every one of the girls to whom Maria told her story was quite sure that nothing so very exciting would ever happen to them if Miss Uckworth was present. The sturdily-developed Miss Uckworth was in charge of games at St

## The Girls' Boarding School

Agatha's, the croquet and lawn tennis, the shuttlecock and battledore. To the unprejudiced eye she was a woman of very considerable physical presence, in the briskest of good health, muscular in a way better suited to a male than a female.

Those young ladies who had come to know Miss Uckworth in an intimate way – and there were many of them, although Delia was not one – said she fetched off very quickly when handled. Her titties were flabby, they said, her pussy hairy and prominent, with the lips permanently open, and a nub that stuck out like a small pink tongue. Miss Uckworth was as fond of young girls as the rest of the staff at St Agatha's, and had two of them a day as her general routine.

Heaven help any misguided man, young or old, who exposed his person and asked her to hold it! She was capable of seizing it in her gloved hand and wrenching it away from the malefactor's body.

It was a pity, the young ladies agreed, that they would not be subjected to molestation on the express train to London, for the journey was excessively dull, and the sight of a young man stroking his person to a fetch off would provide entertainment. At Paddington Station they were all to be met by relatives or servants despatched by their families, to accompany them upon the remainder of their various journeys home. They hoped, being lively young ladies with an over-developed and demeaning desire for cheap sensual thrills, that occasion might serve during the summer holiday to be alone with young gentlemen interested in experimentation.

After the departure to catch the train a blessed silence fell and St Agatha's became still and solitary. Delia sat on her own in the library for an hour with a volume of Mrs Hemans' poems, but her mind wandered from the lines and ranged widely elsewhere. For Delia alone had not been of the party to be conveyed to the railway station and on to London and the bosom of a loving and kindly family – for she had none. Poor Delia was an orphan, and her destiny, until she attained the age of twenty-five years, lay in the hands of her legal guardian, Sir Stanton Fortescue.

Only very rarely had she been privileged to meet him face to face, he being a gentleman with a great many interests to claim his time and attention, interests which were social, cultural, artistic, financial and personal. Yet he never neglected for an instant his duty towards his pretty young ward. Ten days before the end of term, letters from him had been delivered to Delia and to Mrs Kenilworth, to the effect that he would be detained for some time yet in Paris.

In consequence, it had been arranged that Delia should remain at St Agatha's after the end of term, until Sir Stanton became free in due course from his important commitments there, and he would then arrive in person at the school to give his thanks to the headmistress and take Delia back to London with him to his town house for the remainder of the holidays.

The afternoon passed very slowly for Delia. She put down her book and went for a walk in the sunshine of the gardens and sat for a time on the bench under the tall chestnut tree where she had, on her second day at St Agatha's, permitted herself to be shamefully handled by slender dark-haired Maria Wendover – who was now her close friend, in spite of a never-ceasing desire to get her hand up into Delia's drawers.

Their acquaintance had been initiated here on this very bench where Maria had insisted on tickling Delia's sweet little pussy until she fetched her off in huge throbs.

## The Girls' Boarding School

Afterwards she wanted Delia to do as much for her. The most dreadful thing was that it was not the first time for Delia – that had been the night before, when she had been ravished to near collapse in the dorm by Thelma, who had, as the girls called it, *broken her in*.

How fearful it was to reflect that before she arrived here at St Agatha's Delia had been wholly innocent of such things – she had no inkling that cheap thrills could be obtained by the rub of a fingertip on the secret bud inside her pussy. Now, a mere twelve weeks later, for that was all the duration of the spring term, not only was this guilty knowledge etched upon her mind – but she had been subjected to the perils and shame of the spasm by every girl in Form V.

More than that, she had undergone violation of her person at the hands of her form mistress, the coldly lovely Miss Harriet Jardyne – and also at those of the headmistress herself, the very formidable Mrs Emily Kenilworth. Nor was it a only a question of occasional abuse – it had been done to her day after day and night after night, time and time again. It must total hundreds of times, Delia thought in dismay. Twelve weeks had seven days each, which multiplied together came to . . . she recited in her head the multiplication table until she acquired the answer eighty-four.

Frequency *per diem*? Ah, that was not easy to tell. Upon some nights it was only one girl who slipped into her bed and forced her to experience the spasm perhaps twice before they dozed off – but some nights were very different and more energetic. Last night, for instance, though being the last night of the term it was rather special, eleven girls had been in her bed, and each had insisted they do it to each other two or three times.

That came to a grand total of between twenty-five and thirty-five times in one night!

Moreover, on those instances when Delia had been at the mercy of Miss Harriet or, worse yet, of Mrs Kenilworth, she had been compelled to undergo the extreme of sensual passion many times, with hardly a break between. The treatment she had received at their hands was humiliating and degrading in the extreme . . . but on reflection, how very exciting to call up into her mind's eye the plump and hairy pussy that lay in between Mrs Kenilworth's strong thighs . . .

Miss Harriet was so excessively lovely of face and body that even to remember her creamy white belly and thighs laid bare, and the glossy black curls of her pussy, brought a feeling of moistness to Delia between her legs. Ah me, she thought sadly, if when the opportunity was ripe she had been able to retain the warm and close friendship of Miss Harriet! That would have been heavenly indeed. Alas, the goodwill of the form mistress had turned to contempt when she discovered Delia with Bert in the potting shed, and his stiff *dick* spurting all over her.

In search of distraction of any kind, Delia rose from where she sat on the wooden bench and made her way towards the fatal shed where she had come near to having a *cockstand* pushed right up her. What she wanted there, she could not say, but if Bert had been there, it was beyond doubt she would have had his male part in her hand and brought him to a fierce fetch off.

What dire calamity might have befallen her thereafter, it is impossible to say – in her downcast and lonely frame of mind an act of complete submission to Bert's low lust might not even be entirely beyond the realms of speculation. Her precious young maidenhood might well have been imperilled – but by great good

## The Girls' Boarding School

fortune the shed was empty, save for the sacking on the ground.

Dinner that evening was a lonely meal, even though Delia was not alone. Miss Uckworth had departed for London to supervise the young ladies on their long journey, and Mrs Kenilworth was absent on some business of her own, but the remainder of the school staff were still in residence and would be for some days while they discussed the term past and made plans for the term to come when the pupils returned at the beginning of September.

Sadly for Delia, the form mistresses were too deeply engrossed in their scholarly discussions to pay attention to the single pupil still remaining at table, save to make sure that she ate the food placed before her. After dinner Delia returned to the library and occupied herself until bedtime with a novel by Sir Walter Scott, *Quentin Durward*, which she found enthralling and she quite forgot her miserable condition.

It seemed very odd to sleep alone in the dormitory and Delia lay in bed somewhat discomposed by the unusual quietness around her in place of the normal chatter and giggles. At lights out one of the maidservants looked in to turn down the gaslight and close the door, a task performed in term time by Miss Harriet.

Alone in her bed – a most unusual condition for a young lady at St Agatha's – Delia relaxed the discipline of her thoughts and let her mind stray. She quickly found herself picturing the extraordinary event of which Thelma had told her in confidence – the caning of Miss Harriet's bare belly. With every fibre of her being Delia longed to have been present on that scandalous occasion. Before long, it was not merely Delia's thoughts that strayed, her hands were doing much the same, stroking herself between the legs.

Her breathing grew quicker and shallower till, in a

flurry of lustful impatience, she dragged her long school nightgown up to her waist and pressed a finger between the soft lips of her pussy. Whilst she played deftly with it, she recalled how only the previous night Thelma's finger had fluttered there between her parted thighs, and then Edna's, and Maria's, and Daphne's, and Selina's, and Martha's . . . but before she had completed the roster of names of the companions with whom she had shared the shameful thrills only twenty-four hours before, she became aware of a shadowy presence at the side of her bed.

With a gasp of fright she opened her eyes and stared up – and there at the bedside stood Miss Harriet in a dark dressing gown with her beautiful black hair unpinned and hanging loosely down on her shoulders. Even in the unlit dimness of the dormitory it was possible to make out that her face was as stern as that of an avenging angel. With a flick of her wrist she wrenched away the bedclothes and flung them to the foot of the bed, exposing Delia in all her shame.

'Ha! So that's what you get up to alone in bed,' she cried. 'I thought as much,' and she pointed a long slender finger at Delia's immodestly bared body.

Miss Harriet knew all there was ever to be known about young ladies of seventeen and she had chosen her moment to perfection. Delia was revealed lying on her back, her nightgown pulled right up to her belly-button and her hand down between her wide-parted thighs. Her middle finger was thrust between the delicate pink lips of her pussy.

'Miss Harriet!' the wretched girl gasped in her fright.

Her pretty face blushed crimson to be so caught, and with a shaking hand she made to pull down her night-attire to hide her shame. Miss Harriet seized her wrist and prevented her.

'How many times you assured me that you never had

## The Girls' Boarding School

nor would indulge in acts of self-gratification,' said Miss Harriet with a thin smile. 'How insistently you claimed that all was done to you against your will by your classmates. And yet I find you playing with yourself like any other girl in Form V. It seems to me that for all your avowal of innocence you are incapable of keeping your fingers away from your private parts.'

Delia sobbed in her anguish of mind, and rolled quickly over to hide her face in the pillow, her nightgown still up around her waist. Miss Harriet stared at the plump white backside the girl had unwittingly exposed to her, gleaming palely in the dim dormitory, and there was a glint of selfish delight in her cold blue eyes and a faint smile on her perfect lips. She did not allow that to soften the deliberate harshness of her tone.

'How dare you turn your back on me!' she exclaimed.

With her open palm, she raised an arm and brought it down in a mighty spank on Delia's bare bum, causing her to shriek aloud in surprise and fright.

'No more, I beg you, Miss Harriet,' Delia wailed, writhing and twisting about on the bed as if to dodge the next smack. To no purpose – the open hand descended in a firm slap on Delia's other creamy-white cheek.

'Stop that whining at once,' Miss Harriet commanded, but she spanked no more. Delia's backside was hot and stinging from the chastisement it had received, and she sobbed softly against her pillow. A gasp escaped her and she winced to feel Miss Harriet lay her hand on the fiery cheeks of her bum and fondle them.

'Hush, Delia,' she ordered, her voice less harsh now, and she pushed the girl's thighs widely apart. 'You have sustained no hurt, only the indignity of a couple of smacks.'

In another instant she was feeling between Delia's open

legs, her long cool fingers prying open the furry pussy that was the centre of her interest.

'The habit has taken a firm hold on you,' said she, her voice shaking with secret emotion. 'This is what comes of association with servants and underlings instead of paying due attention to the requirements of social class. I fear that the taint of the gardener's loutish son is upon you. When you cannot be with him to bare your person to his degrading attentions, you are unable to resist the temptation to seek out the sensual spasm by other means. Here in your private parts I detect a slippery wetness and a looseness that betrays the forbidden excitement which you were causing in yourself.'

'Oh, Miss Harriet,' Delia said faintly, 'please forgive me – but there are times when I am unable to resist touching myself. Many a time I wake up feeling wet and sticky, but I swear it is nothing to do with Bert, or any other male.'

'Be silent and turn over,' Miss Harriet replied, her fingers stroking her victim's pussy. 'Turn over and open your legs.'

Delia rolled over on to her back, and Miss Harriet pushed her legs very wide apart, disclaiming all modesty and decency. Her finger sank into the girl's unprotected pussy, rubbing over her secret button.

'Here is the source of your agitation,' she said, fingering it deftly, 'though I need hardly tell that to you, for you know very well that when it is manipulated it sets off the sensual spasm – the *female orgasm* as physicians term it, I understand. How often do you yield to self-gratification, Delia?'

'Very rarely, Miss Harriet,' the girl whispered faintly, 'for the girls of Form V are in my bed nightly to force the spasm on me. Tonight is most unusual, I assure you. I'm so ashamed.'

## The Girls' Boarding School

Miss Harriet paid no attention to the words. She slipped her hands under Delia's backside to grasp the soft cheeks, and her head ducked down between the spread thighs. Her wet tongue slid into Delia's pussy and lapped quickly at her tender button.

'Oh Miss Harriet – what are you doing to me?' Delia asked in a weak voice. 'You must stop – I respect you too much for me to think of you in the same way as I have come to think of Thelma and Edna and Maria and the others, who insist on doing this to me every night. Please stop, or you'll make me fetch off, and I shall die of shame if *you* see me!'

'Nonsense, it's not the first time I've done it to you,' said Miss Harriet, raising her head to stare up into Delia's tearful face.

'I love you so much,' Delia confessed, 'and I wanted you to love me – but everything went wrong when you found Bert trying to ravish me and blamed me for it. Now you hate me and despise me, and I wish I were dead!'

'Is this true?' Miss Harriet asked, suspending the action of her tongue while she considered the import of the words. 'It is easy to make such declarations – how can I believe that you are speaking honestly?'

'I would do anything for you,' Delia stated, a little bolder now that she was being listened to. 'I would die for you!'

'That would be a perfectly useless thing to do,' Miss Harriet said. 'What good to me are you dead? Alive you may be capable of persuading me that your so-called love is genuine.'

'It is, it is!' Delia babbled.

'Then I shall give you an opportunity to prove it.'

Whereupon Miss Harriet rose from the bed and removed her long dressing gown and then the fine white linen nightgown under it. Delia stared in rapt admiration at the dimly-discerned naked body by her bedside, the large and shapely titties, the palest gleam of the belly, and the bush as black as night between the alabaster of her thighs.

'You may take off your nightgown, Delia,' said Miss Harriet as she lay down again on the bed and parted her lovely legs.

Delia was naked in a trice, hardly able to believe that this was really happening, and half-certain that it was a wonderful dream. The beautiful Miss Harriet in the dorm and in her bed. Stark naked! Words were wholly inadequate to describe the joy – though it was a perverted and unholy joy – of that moment as Delia sat on the bed beside her idol and stared blissfully down at her superb body.

'Now,' said Miss Harriet, speaking more gently than she had done before, 'you may prove to me that you love me, Delia. I am quite sure you understand how.'

Infamy upon infamy! What is to be said of a person entrusted with the care of young gentlewomen who corrupts them and causes a complete destruction of their moral fibre? The language has not words of reprobation strong enough to designate enormities of depravity on this scale.

As to what ought to be done with the beautiful but perverted Miss Harriet Jardyne for reducing her young pupil to a constant and beastly craving for bodily sensation and cheap thrills – no high court judge in the land, not even the Lord Chief Justice, could mete out a sufficient sentence to punish her. The very severest punishment ought to be hers: to be stripped naked and exhibited in Piccadilly Circus while being whipped on her bare and beautiful backside – and then sent to live for the rest of her life in one of the colonies, as being unfit for the company of decent people.

'Oh, Miss Harriet,' Delia exclaimed, her emotions in turmoil, 'do you want me to fetch you off?'

'Let me feel your tongue on my pussy,' said Miss Harriet in a murmur. 'You are to bring me off three times without a pause – three times, do you follow? Then I shall do as much for you, and afterwards we shall rest a while and speak more of love. If your tongue is devoted enough to pleasure me to excess, I might decide to accept you as my dear friend.'

'Oh yes, yes,' Delia sighed, 'not just three times, dear Miss Harriet, but twenty times without pause if you wish. Command me, and I will kiss your darling beautiful pussy all night long to fetch you off times without number.'

Delia was convinced by now that she had passed gently away in her sleep and gone straight to heaven – a notion as blasphemous as it was criminal. Yet in her sensation-fuddled mind no other explanation seemed adequate for an eternity of ecstasy beside a naked and aroused Miss Harriet. Delia sighed in amazement and delight as she slid down the bed on her belly to set her tongue to Miss Harriet's open and ready slit.

# CHAPTER 13
# The Fate Worse Than Death

For seventeen-year-old Delia Sempill-Shand the three weeks that followed her nocturnal reconciliation with Miss Harriet were no less than sheer heaven. All the other young ladies who attended St Agatha's had departed on their summer holiday and the school was for all purposes vacated. The headmistress, Mrs Kenilworth, was out most days, and sometimes remained away overnight when she had gone up to London on school business. Miss Harriet, who had no family in Great Britain, remained at the school and took charge of the servants, who were set to work to clean and make good any damage wrought by high-spirited pupils during term.

It was in Delia's mind that the mattresses in the Form V dorm could with advantage be taken out into the sunshine and well beaten, after the exceptionally hard use to which they had been put by young ladies writhing in the throes of nightly spasms of delight. Naturally, she could not put this immodest view into words, and even to think it brought a faint blush to her cheek.

With the exception of Miss Harriet, the other form mistresses had departed on their holidays. Miss Uckworth had despatched a telegraph message to the school from Paddington Station itself, notifying her safe arrival with the young ladies in her charge at the metropolis, boasting that they were unmolested during the journey by men, shameless, drunk, or merely beastly.

Miss Harriet had become so well disposed towards Delia that she showed her the telegraph, smiling broadly, and said that she found it ridiculous of Miss Uckworth to be so very confident of her immunity against male lustfulness.

'But Miss Uckworth is so strong,' said Delia, 'what gentleman would enter a trial of strength with her? Moreover, though it is impolite of me to say so, Miss Uckworth is very plain in her appearance. Surely that is protection enough?'

'Not a bit of it,' declared Miss Harriet, her smile broader yet at the girl's innocence. 'You have much to learn about the male sex. If only pretty women were the subject of men's abject lust, then the population of the world would be scarce half of what it is, and three-quarters of all females would be virgins to their dying day.'

'What do you mean, Miss Harriet?' Delia asked, wide-eyed.

'It is a social convention, and a fiction, that men's desires are aroused by female beauty, by which is generally understood a pleasing aspect of face and figure – a fine complexion, large and lustrous eyes, a straight nose and a dimpled chin, an hour-glass figure, with swelling bosom and rounded hips.'

'Just like yourself, dear Miss Harriet,' sighed the love-sick girl, seizing Miss Harriet's hand and kissing it.

'This is a falsehood which is put about by poets and writers of romantic novels,' Miss Harriet declared. 'The truth of the matter is otherwise, Delia. The urges of men are stirred not at all by a woman's face but by her pussy. She may be miserably ill-favoured, her titties drooping, or none at all – and yet a clever woman can

## The Girls' Boarding School

get men into her bed as easily as the prettiest young girl.'

'How can this be so, Miss Harriet?' Delia asked, puzzled by the form mistress's words. 'Our faces are displayed proudly for all to see and admire, but our pussies are never, never seen by gentlemen.' Delia blushed furiously when she said this, recalling how the curate of St Mungo's had seen hers.

'It is not necessary,' said Miss Harriet with her cold and enigmatic smile. 'The force of imagination is so strong in men that merely to see a woman is to set them wondering instantly about the shape and size of her pussy, the colour of the curls on it, the tightness or looseness of its grip on their private part. Believe me, men think of very little else but pussy, from morning to evening. At night they dream of it, I am sure.'

'Oh Heavens!' Delia exclaimed. 'Then Miss Uckworth stands in some danger whilst she is in London, among so many people.'

'She may not see it as danger,' said Miss Harriet. 'I have an idea that, for all her devotion to the bodies of young ladies and her protestation of despising the male sex, Miss Uckworth is secretly fascinated by the thought of what a man might do to her if he had her on her back in a quiet place.'

'No,' Delia cried in horror, 'poor Miss Uckworth would be ruined forever!'

Miss Harriet laughed at her and remarked only that it would be interesting to question Miss Hortense Uckworth when she came back to St Agatha's for the beginning of next term, to find out if she had allowed herself to be *done*. The word struck Delia as coarse and unfeeling, and she blushed to hear it.

Every night, soon after Delia had retired to her bed in

the empty dormitory, Miss Harriet would appear at the bedside, clad in her dressing gown, her long black hair unbound and brushed, hanging down below her shoulders like a silk curtain. Under the dressing gown she was naked, and with a little smile of delight she would slip out of it and into bed with Delia. They handled and kissed and licked each other for hours and hours, in long and blissful love-bouts that left them both gasping for breath, and wrung out by the force of the sensations they shared.

Not only at night did they indulge themselves so unashamedly in these forbidden pleasures – they took full advantage of the emptiness of the school to manipulate each other to excess in the daytime also. It had been decided by Mrs Kenilworth that if Delia was to remain at St Agatha's until it was convenient for her legal guardian to fetch her away, then she should continue with her lessons and not be allowed to idle away her time. Each day she presented herself to Miss Harriet in the Form V classroom at the usual time and was taught in the ordinary way.

It need not be thought, in the circumstances, that Delia was taught in a proper way, or even a decent way. Miss Harriet proved to be insatiable when opportunity served – as it did now. The morning class began in the ordinary way, Delia at her desk with her school book open before her, and Miss Harriet at her high desk by the blackboard – but before long the form mistress made Delia leave her seat and stand beside her.

Whilst the eagerly attentive girl stood there beside the high desk, Miss Harreit would invariably reach under her frock and stroke her soft young pussy. It took only a short time before Delia was gasping and near to a fetch off, holding on to Miss Harriet's desk for support as her legs shook under her.

At other times Miss Harriet would instruct her to write

up on the blackboard an arithmetic sum or equation, and while she did so, stand behind her and fondle her titties through her clothes until she was breathless with desire. Often Miss Harriet would hitch up her own skirts as she sat on her high chair, part her legs, and ask Delia to kneel down and kiss her. There were many other ways she invented to indulge the pair of them, so that lessons were never dull and boring, and by the end of the day Delia had been fetched off half a dozen times at least, and had a night of bliss still to look forward to.

The intense frequency of their pleasures gave Delia a healthy appetite and she ate heartily at every mealtime. Miss Harriet smiled and warned her that if she became stout from overeating and developed a fat belly and heavy thighs, she would lose most of her charm. At that, Delia reminded her of her own words – to the effect that it was not good looks, but the thought of pussy that stirred up desire.

'That applies only to men,' said Miss Harriet, frowning. 'Did I not make that perfectly clear? Men are coarse creatures with ravenous lusts. When their organ becomes long and stiff – which happens very easily – they will thrust it into any female slit within reach, whether that of a beautiful young woman, a grand lady, a greasy servant wench or a drab picked up in the lowest public house. All they require is an orifice in which to spurt their raging desire.'

'Great Heaven!' Delia exclaimed in dismay.

'Nor are they particular as to which opening they make use of as the receptacle for their fluid. To quote the well-known old proverb: *any port in a storm*.'

'What do you mean?' cried Delia, horrified.

'Simply this – that a fully aroused male will, if given only the least chance, thrust his erect part into a female mouth, or even up a female bum, and there discharge his lust.'

'Oh horror beyond belief,' Delia said in a shaking voice. 'A male organ spurting its vile essence into my mouth! Never, not if I must remain single all my natural life. As for doing it up my bottom – the mere thought causes me to shudder and question if men are part of the same race of humanity as we females.'

'We women are totally different,' Miss Harriet continued, 'we are made of finer stuff than men, our nature is refined and our character turns us towards higher things.'

'Yes, yes,' Delia breathed fervently.

'To return then to the question of female beauty and what it may achieve, and what it may not. The plainest female has not the least difficulty in getting herself done by any man she may select, if that's what she wants. On the other hand, she would find it difficult to secure the loving and intimate attentions of other females, if she is so very plain. This you must have observed during the term you have spent at St Agatha's.'

'In what way, Miss Harriet?'

'The prettiest girls in the dormitory are the most popular – and have company in bed every night of the week. Those who are less pretty are sought out only after the most desirable are already partnered and therefore unavailable. The plainest girls of all must fetch each other off, or sleep alone.'

'Oh!' said Delia, recognising the truth of the words.

'You, dearest Delia, are exceptionally pretty, and I am sure that you never have a night alone. The same is true of several of the members of Form V. Edna Calthorpe-Brunton, for the sake of example, and Maria Wendover. Like you they are bound to be in great demand. On the other hand, Rhoda Fitzwalter and Selina Ripley are instances of the second category, those whose refuge against rejection is each other. Do you not agree?'

'I have never thought about it,' said Delia, quite overcome to learn that she was regarded as belonging to the most highly sought after minority. It explained why she had never spent a night alone – hitherto she had thought it a normal part of the awful depravity of the young ladies of Form V that they took turns to visit her bed and abuse her body. To be told by Miss Harriet of her popularity gave Delia a perverse pride in herself.

'At the far end of the spectrum of desirability,' continued her mentor, 'there is, for example, Dorothy Benton-Smyth, poor child, so very plain of feature and lumpy of figure. I fear she must spend most nights alone, and be wanted only when there is no one else at all available. Is it so?'

'I cannot say,' Delia replied.

If the truth were told, there was a warm spot in Delia's soft heart for Dorothy, who could be relied upon to know the answers to sums set for prep. In the darkness of the dorm after lights out, thought Delia, feeling mildly guilty, it was as exciting to be licked to a fetch off by plain Dorothy as by pretty dark-haired Maria.

At once she recoiled from the thought – could it be possible that there was in her nature some share of the coarseness that Miss Harriet had said was a male characteristic? To be greedy only for pussy, no matter what female form surrounded it? From now she would share her bed only with the very prettiest. Poor Dorothy must console herself with her own fingers in future.

During these days of continuous delight with Miss Harriet, Delia asked all she wished to know about males and their parts, what they did with them and why. Miss Harriet answered freely, and Delia was astonished to learn that what she had been told by Bert the gardener's boy, and by her classmates, was largely correct. Gentlemen were in this respect not different from the lower classes – their male organ rose up to a *cockstand* at the slightest provocation, whereupon they desired to thrust it into the nearest pussy and discharge their fluid. By these strange actions is the human race propagated, Miss Harriet explained.

'Then when I am married,' Delia stammered, 'my husband will require me to lie on my back with my legs apart for him to push his organ into me?'

'Quite so,' said Miss Harriet with a grimace of distaste at the very thought of a lovely young pussy being barbarously used and stretched by brutal male importunity. 'So undignified and impolite a prospect needs must be displeasing to a young lady of taste and refinement, but for a young person as intelligent as you, there may be compensations.'

'I cannot imagine any,' said Delia, quite shocked and longing to feel Miss Harriet's soft fingers playing with her pussy.

It was evening and they were seated comfortably together on a sofa in the form mistress's study. The selfsame sofa upon which Delia had, in the very first week of term, secretly witnessed her idol lay bare her beautiful black-haired slit and caress it until she fetched off.

'Listen and learn,' Miss Harriet said, her expression calm as her hand toyed with Delia's nearest titty down the front of her frock. 'A husband is easily satisfied. Once that duty is done, a wife is at liberty to pursue her own pleasures when he is out of the home and about his profession or business. She may then pay visits to her female friends, for an hour of talk and tea, and of pleasuring each other as it should be done – as we do.'

'But how can this be? You have said that men are little more than raging beasts in their lustfulness.'

'That is so, my dear, but fortunately for us this coarse lust is soon quenched. Once a man has his organ up a pussy, he will fetch off within a minute or two. If he is young and vigorous, he will wish to repeat the performance after a lapse of about ten minutes. In the early months of marriage he may wish for a third connection after another fifteen minutes, but more likely he will drop off to sleep.'

'Heavens!' Delia cried. 'Must it be twice – or even thrice? How very fearful is a woman's lot.'

'Patience a while,' Miss Harriet admonished her. 'As in every aspect of life, familiarity brings changes quite soon. Twice a night becomes only once a night. And after a year or two, every night is reduced to twice a week.'

'So the ordeal is of limited duration?' asked Delia.

'Male desire is very feeble,' Miss Harriet confirmed, fingers tweaking the sweet pink tip of Delia's titty to transmit little shudders of delight through her. 'It is soon done with.'

'But how?' Delia asked, feeling her darling pussy positively ache at the mere thought of having a stiff male *thing* rammed into it night after night. 'Surely it is very *common*, this thrusting of male organs into our bodies?'

'Only a foolish women allows her natural refinement to stand in the way of her judgement,' said Miss Harriet. 'A foolish wife denies her husband access to her person if he wants it for two nights in a row – she keeps her legs together and pretends she has a headache, or some such footling excuse. Men become angry and confused if they are fobbed off and denied the relief of their pressing emotions. The affection and generosity which ought to exist between husband and wife wears thin, much to her disadvantage, for the unsatisfied man finds another female who will oblige him – and it must not be forgotten that in nearly every case it is the man who controls the purse-strings.'

'I never thought of that,' said Delia with a shiver.

'An intelligent woman gives the appearance of encouraging her husband to make use of her natural orifice,' Miss Harriet went on, 'crude though the act must seem to her. She parts her legs every night whether her husband requests her to or not. And if he does not at once grow stiff, she handles his part into a fit condition to thrust into her.'

'How very immodest,' Delia gasped, 'to take a man's part in your hand!'

'As I have explained to you, men are capable of very little. There is not a man living, nor ever has been, who can fetch off a dozen or more times in a day, as you and I do. By rousing up his lust, the intelligent woman makes sure it is quickly dealt with, and causes her no problems. A man brought to satisfaction by these simple means becomes a slave to his wife and will give her whatever she asks for, and do anything she may require.'

'Truly, Miss Harriet?'

'To put it crudely, in order to make my point clear, a clever woman takes a firm hold of her husband's organ and can lead him where she pleases, as a bull is led by a brass ring through his nose.'

'It may be as you say, but I want nothing to do with men and their long stiff ugly organs, not even if they have rings put through them,' cried Delia. 'I want only you, Miss Harriet!'

With that she flung herself off the sofa and on to her knees, her hands burrowing up under Miss Harriet's long skirts to get at her beautiful black-haired pussy and ravish it again.

This remarkable idyll in which the two of them, form mistress and seventeen-year-old pupil, were engrossed came to a surprising end after it had lasted a day short of three weeks. After lunch one fine summer day they were out taking a stroll in the sunshine before going back to the classroom. Proceeding at a ladylike pace along the quiet country lane which joined the school to the nearby hamlet of Cocksworth Parva, they met the Reverend Mr Blenkinsop, busy about the good works of the parish. He doffed his clerical hat to them, and paused for some moments of polite conversation.

During the course of this he enquired why Delia was still in residence at St Agatha's during the holiday break. On learning the reason, and that her lessons were continued daily, he declared that he had been remiss in his duties and that he would attend at the school on the next day to continue her education in the scriptures. He thereupon raised his hat once more and bade them a good day, and proceeded on his way.

Delia pulled a face at the curate's retreating back, and Miss Harriet smiled and said that for the good of her immortal soul she must endure the reverend gentleman's tedious lesson.

'I would rather have *your* lesson,' Delia retorted, pink-faced with emotion, and threw her arms about Miss Harriet's lissome waist. The youthful ardour of her words and action suggested to the form mistress that a lesson was in order there and then.

In a moment she put an arm about Delia and drew her under the shade of a beech tree that stood in the hedgerow. With a smile on her coldly beautiful face, she set Delia's back against the trunk to support her, then put her hand up under her skirts for a feel of her pussy inside her drawers. When Delia's sighs of delight became quicker, Miss Harriet transferred her fingertip to the puckered little node between the satin-skinned cheeks of her bottom.

'Since you request to be taught by me, I shall today

acquaint you with something new,' said the form mistress, the strangest smile upon her face.

'What might that be, dearest Miss Harriet?' gasped Delia, as she wriggled her girlish bum to the tickling of her teacher's skilful finger.

'That vile and vicious though it is for a male to make use of a female's rearward orifice for his degraded pleasure, if it is properly stimulated by a close female friend, you will find you fetch off as surely as if my finger were in your pussy.'

Thus it proved to be, and for the remainder of the day Delia applied herself to learning this lesson, and how to make use of it on Miss Harriet herself. At eleven the next morning the Reverend Blenkinsop appeared at the school and was shown into the classroom where Miss Harriet taught her pupil some elements of the French language. Delia watched dismayed when her beautiful dark-haired form mistress yielded her place at the tall desk to the young curate.

'Our lesson is the *Lamentations* of the prophet Jeremiah,' he informed Delia. 'Open your copy of the Holy Scriptures.'

For ten or fifteen minutes the lesson proceeded, the curate asking exceptionally difficult questions and showing every sign of impatience when Delia was quite unable to give him a correct answer. At his weekly lessons during the term past, never once had he been abrupt or put out, however incompetent the girls of Form V had shown themselves to be in their grasp of Jeremiah's gloomy chapters. Today he was in a very different mood.

Eventually, he put down his Bible and shook his head sadly at Delia, declaring that she was an idle and inattentive scholar, and worthy of severe punishment. His pale face became very red when he uttered these words, and poor Delia feared the worst.

## The Girls' Boarding School

Nor were her fears groundless. The Reverend Blenkinsop commanded her to come to the front of the class – which consisted only of herself and three rows of empty desks. She did as he bade her, but with reluctance and foreboding.

'I am aware of how discipline is maintained at St Agatha's,' he said, his eyes seeming to start from his head with the force of some secret emotion that gripped him. 'You were punished by your headmistress in my presence. Very well then, you shall be punished in the usual way now, your inattention and total lack of effort having deserved it. Assume the correct posture – with which you are well acquainted, young lady.'

With a tiny sob of dismay, Delia turned about and bent over a desk in the front row. With trembling hands she reached down to take hold of the hem of her school frock and raise it up at the back, to uncover the clean white drawers that decently covered and concealed her lovely young bum and thighs.

'I beg you not to be cruel,' she said, tears in her eyes. 'It is true I do not know the writings of the prophet Jeremiah as well as I might, but if you will give me another chance, I vow to study his *Lamentations* until I know them by heart.'

'Too late,' the curate answered in a voice that was no more than a croak. 'Prepare yourself for chastisement!'

'Oh no, no!' Delia stammered.

Nevertheless, he insisted, and in the belief that a clergyman was not like other men, and could gaze upon the intimate female parts without being aroused to brutal lust, Delia obeyed him. A trembling of her fingers unnerved her as she untied the bow of her drawers and slid them downward to her knees, fully exposing the cheeks of her bottom for the smacking. Behind her she could hear the

Reverend Blenkinsop mutter to himself and give utterance to a low moaning sound, but she dare not look over her shoulder to ascertain why.

For her maidenly peace of mind it was fortunate that she lay with her belly on the desk and stared down at the floor, for if she had glanced round, she would have seen a sight to strike a bolt of fear into her young heart. The dread facts of the case were these: on the occasion when the Reverend Octavian Blenkinsop had caught his first sight of the female parts, his innocently blank mind had received so tremendous an impression that he had been quite unable to think of anything else ever since.

The parts in question had been Delia's, on the day the curate had been present by chance at her chastisement at the hands of the headmistress. Naturally, it was not deemed suitable by the educational and ecclesiastical authorities responsible for his upbringing and training for the Church to acquaint him with the appearance of female organs, nor except in a sketchy way, with the manner of their use for the pleasure of mankind. Therefore it came as a frightful shock to his sensibilities to experience an involuntary emission of sticky juice in his underwear at the sight of Delia's silky-curled young split.

Since that time his newly-awakened sensual desires had given him no respite. At the most inconvenient times of day his organ stood up fiercely in his clothes and threatened to embarrass him by calling attention to his condition. When in company, he was unable to do more to hide his predicament than draw in his belly tight and pretend that nothing untoward was happening.

If he chanced to be on his own when his unruly male portion elongated itself and swelled thick, he would thrust a hand down the front of his trousers and pinch it painfully, in an attempt to check its unwanted activity. Rarely did this

## The Girls' Boarding School

have the effect desired – more usually his engorged part continued to twitch in rhythmic time, and cause a vision of Delia's uncovered split to appear in his mind's eye. Nor did it achieve much to remove his trousers and dash cold water over the offending part, though he had done that frequently.

At night he dreamed of Delia's lovely young bottom uncovered, as he had spied it in Mrs Kenilworth's study, and the delicate pink lips of her person. This dream was accompanied by feelings of intense delight, and he woke each time to the pulsing of his stiff organ and the wetness of spilled sap in his nightshirt.

Haunted as he was by what he had seen, the conviction grew in the curate's mind that to rid himself of his obsession the only possible way was to bring about a connection of his rebellious part with that which had set off his longing. Namely, to push his organ into Delia's! Needless to say, this was out of the realm of possibility – no young lady at St Agatha's was left on her own in the presence of a male person, even a clergyman.

Yet fate had intervened to bring about the very opportunity he had so desperately wished. He was alone with Delia, and for reasons she thought proper and he knew quite well were not, her lovely young pussy was fully uncovered to his gaze.

Had she looked round from where she lay face down on the desk she would have seen that the very worst fears she had expressed to Miss Harriet were fast becoming a reality. The Reverend Octavian Blenkinsop had removed his long black frock-coat and opened his waistcoat. He unbuttoned his long black trousers, all down the front from waistband to seam. He pulled out his long clerical pink *thing*, so very stiff and hard with lust, and clasped it in his hand, working it up and down.

With a tread as soft and soundless as a tiger in the Indian jungle stalking its unsuspecting prey, the curate approached the unwitting girl, until he was close enough to lay his hands on the bare cheeks of her bum. Delia gasped aloud and thought this irregular, but accepted it as part of his preparations to deliver the spank of chastisement. His fingers shook, but were remorseless in drawing apart the milk-white cheeks of her sweet and smooth young bottom, so that he might peer at her.

Delia flushed as red as fire to realise the most intimate and delicate portion of her person was laid bare for the inspection of a member of the male gender.

'There – now all is revealed to me,' she heard him mutter as he gazed down upon her. 'Oh how lovely, how very, very lovely, how flowerlike in her innocent bloom!'

The outraged girl emitted a forlorn shriek to feel a hand of the reverend gentleman roaming freely between her parted thighs and over her silky-curled pussy. The horrid truth was presented to her startled mind in all its disconcerting reality – a *male* was touching her pussy! Her dear little pussy – that dainty shrine where only Miss Harriet's tongue had the right to play.

Nor was this to be the full extent of his molestation – which surely amounted near to sacrilege, given the circumstances and persons involved. The Reverend Octavian Blenkinsop panted aloud for breath as he sank to his knees and pressed his mouth in hot wet kisses to the cheeks of Delia's quaking bottom.

'No, no – this must not be, Sir,' she cried. 'You may spank me if you must, but do not subject me to this indecency!'

The clerical gentleman was lost to all reason, his male part jumping in his hand like a wild creature. He stood up and bent forward over the hapless Delia, who uttered shriek after shriek as she felt him part her maidenly bum-cheeks once more to press the end of his stiff length to the lips of her pussy.

'I know it is terribly wrong,' he gasped, 'but I can do no other! Forgive me, dear girl, for what I am about to do.'

Delia shrieked louder yet to feel the swollen end of his male part pushed into her. She felt the opening of her pussy being stretched to the limit, and feared it would never recover after usage so vile. A loud moan escaped the curate, who was unaware until that moment of the narrowness of the virgin passage that he was attempting to enter.

He tried harder to force himself into Delia's unpenetrated and undefiled slit, but fortunately for her, he was ignorant of the best angle of approach. He huffed and puffed and pushed and jabbed this way and that in futile effort, his emotions rising until they became too excessive to be borne by his vibrating nervous system – whereupon his creamy fluid came gushing out.

At this moment of near-consummation, Miss Harriet burst into the classroom. Some female instinct had given her warning that all was not well – perhaps in some way not understood by common sense the scores of shared spasms she and Delia had enjoyed had set up a bond of fellow-feeling between them, causing Delia's distress to register at a distance in the form mistress's mind.

Whatever the rights of it, she was there, aghast at what she observed to be going on. With a cry of outrage she flew across the room to seize the reverend gentleman by his braces and drag him away from Delia just as once she had dragged Bert from her. As the curate reeled back from Delia's bare bottom, his jolting shaft continued to spurt his creamy emission onto the floor.

'What have you done!' Miss Harriet cried, her face

white and terrible in its icy hatred and disdain for male lust.

'May Heaven forgive me,' he moaned, 'I have committed the sin of Onan, who spilled his seed on the ground. I am accursed!'

Miss Harriet had no time for his foolish self-recrimination. She pushed him aside and went to Delia, who lay half-swooning on her belly across the desk. Swiftly she employed a fine white hankie to wipe away the white trickles of clerical sap, before pulling up her drawers for her, and tying them firmly.

'Stand up, Delia dear,' she said, 'I must get you away from here before this brute attempts to ravish you a second time. My poor girl, I fear you have been *done*!'

Delia raised herself and stood swaying on her feet, clutching at Miss Harriet for support. She gazed uncomprehending into the form mistress's eyes, her wits whirling in shock, then with a despairing moan she sagged at the knees and fainted away.

'Wretched man!' cried Miss Harriet at the bemused curate, as she supported Delia in her arms. 'You have ravished my darling girl and ruined her. Don't stand there like an idiot with that hideous thing sticking out like a coat-peg – get help!'

# CHAPTER 14
# A Trust is Shamefully Betrayed

The sickroom to which pupils of St Agatha's were consigned, if their normal rude health should by minor illness or by accident become affected, was no more than a large and sunny room, set a little apart from the ordinary accommodation of the school. Two beds were the extent of its provision for the unwell, and it was presided over by a pleasingly plump woman of some thirty-five years, who went by the name of Mrs Remply.

This female custodian of the unwell laid no claim to any kind of medical training, nor was any required of her. In a case of more than minor indisposition she summoned old Dr MacGavel from Midsomer Rackham to determine what ailed the patient, and then to prescribe a course of treatment. Mrs Remply's duties were to ensure the young ladies placed in her charge were kept warm and properly fed, to ensure their bowel movements were regular, and to administer their medicines.

When Delia recovered her senses after her cruel ordeal at the hands of the Reverend Octavian Blenkinsop – and not his hands alone, for it was a stiffer portion of his person with which the vile-intentioned curate had attempted to abuse her maidenly modesty – she found herself lying full-length on a bed having her forehead bathed by someone seated beside her.

Her cheeks burned with fiery shame when she became aware of a moistness and stickiness between her legs which was causing her drawers to adhere clammily to her skin. She started upright and stared wildly about her – then recognised Mrs Remply and sank back with a sigh of great relief.

The quiet of the sick room calmed her nerves, and in thankfulness for escape from her inhuman and hideous ordeal she smiled weakly at Mrs Remply, who nodded sympathetically and put aside the cloth and bowl of water she had been using.

'Awake at last,' said Mrs Remply cheerfully. 'You had a nasty shock, Miss Delia, and fell into a swoon. But we'll soon have you right again – put yourself in my hands and leave all to me. You're not the first young lady brought here in your condition, and restored to perfect health within a few days at the most.'

With these comforting words, she rose from her bedside chair and bent over Delia to reach under the hem of her long skirts to remove her shoes, which she set neatly on the floor. Delia closed her eyes and let her whole body lie loose and limp when Mrs Remply began with skilful fingers to undo the fastenings of her school frock.

'What has happened to me, Mrs Remply?' she asked, her pretty face pale.

The last conscious memory she was able to summon up when she tried was fearful beyond normal belief; it was of the clerical gentleman putting his hand between her legs, as if he proposed to fondle her pussy – but surely a clergyman would not perform so very indecent an act! As to what may have taken place after that, she had not the least recollection.

'Lord, Miss Delia, you've had a bad fright and from

what I've been told, you had a near miss, to put it no worse. Now we must make sure no harm comes of it in nine months' time.'

'Why, what do you mean?' she asked, unwilling to believe the worst, though she feared it, without knowing what it was.

'I mean we must take steps right away to get rid of the risky fluid that was squirted in you, every last drop, before there's any chance it can take hold. Have no fear, I've taken care of many a young lady when she's been a trifle careless with a male friend. Sit up and let me slip off your dress.'

Thus partly reassured that all would turn out well, Delia sat up on the bed. Though Miss Harriet had explained to her those aspects of human propagation which in general are referred to as the Facts of Life, Delia still did not wholly comprehend the dire implications of Mrs Remply's words – or what sort of harm might befall her. In the state of languor that possessed her as the aftermath of the ghastly shock she had received, she was content to allow herself to be undressed down to her chemise.

Mrs Remply went out of the room for a few moments while Delia sat on the edge of the bed and wished that darling Miss Harriet would come and explain everything to her. She had been present when Delia fell into her swoon and had taken immediate charge of the situation. Yet it was not the wished-for form mistress who entered, but kindly Mrs Remply, bearing a bowl, and several towels draped over her arm.

She set down her bowl, which proved to be half-full of warm water, and spread out a towel on the rug, then put the bowl on it and set a plain wooden chair close. She helped Delia to rise from the bed and walk with feeble steps to the chair and sit on it. An instant later she knelt at

Delia's feet and took hold of the astonished girl's chemise, raising it to uncover her thighs and then her belly.

'What are you doing?' Delia gasped, pressing her legs close together to preserve a semblance of modesty.

'We must wash away all trace of the gentleman's essence,' the older woman replied. 'Part your legs wide, Miss Delia.'

Before the startled girl could take in the fullest meaning of these words, Mrs Remply had pushed her knees apart and placed the bowl of warm water between her feet. Delia stared down with wide-open eyes as Mrs Remply soaped her dainty white belly and the silky curls that adorned her pussy. These measures taken to protect her were at last bringing her to some understanding of her plight.

'Mrs Remply,' she said, her voice quavering, 'tell me truly – have I been violated by a male organ?'

'Bless you Miss, it wouldn't be the end of the world if you had been. I wasn't there, my dear, and I only know what others have told me. The Reverend Blenkinsop tried to get his hard-on part up you, but he hadn't got much of it in when Miss Jardyne found him at it and hauled him away in the nick of time, at the very moment he started to fetch off. Most of his cream ran down your leg and was wiped off by Miss Jardyne, but we have to take proper precautions.'

'Then I am a virgin no more!' Delia exclaimed in horror.

'That all depends on how you look at it,' said Mrs Remply in a soothing tone, while her fingers worked gently on the lips of Delia's pussy, to wash away any lingering trace of the curate's immoderate passion. 'To most people's way of thinking a virgin is a girl that's never had a hard-on shaft up her, or received a man's load in her belly.'

## The Girls' Boarding School

'Oh horror!' Delia cried, aghast at the very thought of her lovely slit awash with sticky male fluid.

'By my way of reckoning you're a virgin yet, Miss Delia,' Mrs Remply reassured her, then added thoughtfully, 'even though we both know well that there isn't a young lady to be found at St Agatha's who doesn't know more about being fetched off than any married woman twice her age.'

'Oh, thank you for your words of comfort,' said Delia softly, her eyes closing in silent gratitude to providence.

Truth to tell, the touch of Mrs Remply's fingers in her pussy was extremely pleasant, most especially when she washed gently over Delia's secret bud – that tiny organ of bliss which had so very often been fingered and manipulated and ravished by every young lady in Form V, not to mention Miss Harriet's attentions to it during the past three weeks. Not to put too fine a point on matters, Delia was aware of what was shortly going to happen to her, and she did nothing to prevent it.

'There, my pretty,' Mrs Remply murmured, her fingers tickling with skill on precisely the right spot to bring on the sensual spasm. With that, Delia moaned blissfully and her girlish loins jerked to the spasm. Mrs Remply continued to manipulate her as she watched her squirm and gasp, and there was a smile upon her friendly face at the sight of such youthful ecstasy.

'Oh – that feels very nice,' Delia moaned, her legs forcing themselves wide apart to reveal the delicate loveliness of her pussy to the busy attendant. 'But it's too bad of you to take advantage of me like this!'

Mrs Remply made no reply, but used her fingers deftly to draw out the pleasure to the utmost. When Delia had become calm once more, she gently wiped dry with a towel the tender young female slit she had washed and then abused so indecently.

'Back to bed with you now, Miss Delia,' she said, and offered her arm in support. 'You need to rest and get your strength and courage back, after what you've been through. Trust me, I shall look after you.'

She conducted the unresisting girl to the bed and supported her with a hand under her head while she lay down full length.

'My nightgown,' said Delia, recalling her condition of near nakedness. 'I cannot lie here in only my chemise – it would be improper.'

'Quite right,' Mrs Remply agreed. 'We shall send for it from your dormitory. But first we must make certain you have taken no other harm from that monstrously wicked clergyman. What the Church of England is coming to I do not know when a man of the cloth tries to ravish an innocent young lady in broad daylight! He should have his bare bum whipped till he repents – and then be thrown out of his place.'

She had not covered Delia with the bedclothes. The physical and mental relief of the sensual spasm she had experienced had restored much of Delia's natural reluctance to permit her body to be seen, much less handled. She blushed slightly to consider that only the thin material of her chemise concealed her nudity from Mrs Remply's eyes. Hypocritical this may perhaps seem, but it is not easy to comprehend the emotions that engage the mind of a young lady of quality, most especially one whose moral sensibility had been subject to the appalling perversions that were the nightly occurrences in the dormitories of St Agatha's.

'Turn over, Miss Delia,' said Mrs Remply, and she complied at once, pleased to be able to remove her titties and

## The Girls' Boarding School

belly from the field of vision of the other woman, covered as they were.

In another moment, not even her thin chemise served to shield her modesty, for a swift flick of Mrs Remply's wrist turned the garment up over Delia's back, to leave her posterior cheeks as bare as the palm of her hand. Delia blushed scarlet at the very thought, but her confusion passed unseen by the female who was gazing with interest at the lily-white bum she had exposed.

'Mrs Remply, pray what are you doing?' cried Delia, feeling a hand stroking her bare cheeks.

'The question is, Miss Delia, apart from trying to force his *cockstand* up your pussy, did the curate try to force his way in by the back door as well? Open your legs and let me see.'

'Great Heaven!' Delia groaned, appalled by the possibility that she may have been ravished rearward as well as forward.

She spread her legs wide on the soft bed and felt Mrs Remply part the cheeks of her bottom to examine her.

'Did he touch you here, Miss Delia?' she enquired, rubbing a fingertip over the little knot of muscle she had revealed.

'Yes, I do believe that he did, the cur!' Delia exclaimed.

'With his finger, or with something else?'

'A finger only,' said Delia, 'isn't that bad enough?'

Nevertheless, the friendly touch of Mrs Remply's finger could hardly fail to summon up the memory of how dearest Miss Harriet had touched her on the selfsame spot, when they stood together under the beech tree. Ah, how delicious the sensations she had experienced that afternoon, how blissful the spasm when it came – was it only yesterday?

Lost in her joyful memories, Delia said nothing more,

but lay breathing softly and quivering, while Mrs Remply continued her slow massage of the crease between Delia's cheeks and then down the insides of her thighs.

'I think it tolerably certain we can say there was no actual insertion up here,' said Mrs Remply in a hushed voice. 'Thank heaven for that, my dear. Be still a minute while I make very sure.'

All unnoticed by the girl, Mrs Remply's fingers had slipped a little way down below the puckered knot which was her declared subject of concern. Not to shilly-shally about with the truth, she was easing open Delia's maidenly slit and her fingers were playing within. Having been slyly manipulated once when her parts were washed not two minutes ago a decent and respectable young lady would been on her guard against further attempts – but sad to say, Delia was so far gone in her craving for sensation that she merely thought it would be very pleasant if she could drop gently off to sleep while these lovely thrills ran through her.

'Yes, that's it, make yourself at ease,' said Mrs Remply with a chuckle. She slipped a hand under the girl's belly, and down, in order to employ both hands in fingering Delia's furry pussy, from front and rear at the same time.

'Oh,' said Delia in a tiny voice, 'I know what you are doing to me, Mrs Remply. You really must not!'

'I'm making sure there's been no damage to your most precious parts,' answered the sickroom nurse with a further chuckle, as she opened the soft lips of Delia's split as widely as possible and probed deftly within to stimulate the secret nub.

'Oh yes – please make absolutely sure,' said Delia in a voice that quavered to the intensity of the sensual thrills rippling through her belly, 'leave nothing to chance, I beg you.'

## The Girls' Boarding School

'Trust me to know what's best,' said Mrs Remply, and in only another moment or two her manipulation of Delia's private parts brought on the expected female spasm. Delia jerked and writhed on the bed, her legs kicking out in ecstatic jerks.

'What a pretty sight you make when you fetch off,' Mrs Remply declared. 'Your bum jibs up and down beautifully, and your legs open and shut like a pair of sewing-scissors.'

When Delia's tremors had faded at last, Mrs Remply helped her turn over in the bed to lie on her back, then pulled down her chemise and covered her decently with the bedclothes.

'There now, Miss Delia,' said she with a warm smile, 'you'll be more at ease now your nerves are settled. I'll sit here with you a while.'

With that, she took the liberty of sitting on the side of the bed. In other circumstances Delia would have taken umbrage, and made clear the distinction between the two of them that made it out of the question for someone of Mrs Remply's station in life to be seated on the bed of a social superior. Yet she had been so kind to Delia in her distress, so thoughtful and careful in her intimate ministrations, and clearly meant so well, that the girl decided to overlook the lapse this one time.

'Mrs Kenilworth will be extremely relieved to hear that there is no lasting harm done,' said Mrs Remply. 'I was instructed to report to her as soon as I was certain of the position.'

'She wishes to know about me?' Delia asked.

'There's no one more jealous of the good name and reputation of the young ladies of St Agatha's than Mrs Kenilworth,' stated Mrs Remply, 'and yet there have been times . . . not that I would ever dream of revealing shameful incidents in the past.'

'What incidents?' Delia asked, her interest caught by these hints of depravity taking place in the School.

'Well, without wishing to alarm you, Miss Delia, in the five years I have been in charge of the sickroom, I have seen three young ladies packed off home with big bellies – a very sad and distressing event when it occurs.'

'Good Heavens,' Delia exclaimed, 'how fearful a thing!'

'Bless you, Miss, it certainly was a man's *thing* that did the damage each time, and though I've heard them called many names, *fearful* has never been one of them. Rampaging, if you like, or rummaging, and even ravaging. Breakers of maidenheads they most surely are, and they make young girls' bellies swell up like balloons. But it's only natural, Miss Delia, and when they leave school most females welcome the shove of a hard-on shaft inside them.'

'How very common and degrading!' said Delia, aghast at the thought. 'How on earth could it ever happen that a male person was able to debauch pupils at St Agatha's? It must have been a forcible ravishing, as was very nearly perpetrated upon my body by Mr Blenkinsop.'

'Not a bit of it,' declared Mrs Remply. 'It was all done by cajolery and consent – the young ladies concerned lay down and opened their legs without a murmur. In fact, I know for certain that two of them deliberately led the man on, by lifting their clothes.'

'Great Scot! What man was this, Mrs Remply?'

'It was different men at different times that was giving out free membership of the Plum Pudding Club. The first time that I recall, it was thought to be Thomas Hames, who was employed as the odd job man, though the young lady refused to name him. And once it was known to be a young officer in the Horse Guards, who came on leave

## The Girls' Boarding School

to visit his sister here. You'd hardly credit it, you being still innocent of the ways of this wicked world, but that gentleman managed during a single afternoon to ruin three of the young ladies, out by the big tree with the bench, though only one of the three fell into the family way.'

'But I'm sure that can't be right,' said Delia. 'Miss Harriet told me that gentleman aren't up to doing ladies more than once before their organ shrinks. Or twice at most.'

'Don't you believe it. Some of them can keep getting it stiff enough times to do half a dozen girls. The young gentleman in question was named by all three he'd ruined. Needless to say, by the time his dastardly deed came to light, he was long gone, the handsome devil, back to his regiment.'

'And the young ladies?'

'The one whose belly swelled up was sent home. The other two who hadn't clicked were given a stern warning by Mrs Kenilworth and not allowed out into the grounds for the rest of their time here. Though I doubt if that did much good, for if a determined young gentleman meets a willing young lady, the desperate deed will be done, indoors or out, believe me.'

'My word,' said Delia, 'what goings-on at St Agatha's! Till now I thought the only sensual spasms experienced by the pupils were those brought on in the dorm at night by other girls.'

'That's the usual way of it,' Mrs Remply agreed, 'but there are times when a fox gets in among the hens, so to speak. Last time it happened was another mystery, though I'm sure in my own mind it was that gardener's boy Bert who did it. He knows more than he should for a lad of his age, if you ask me.'

'But this is frightful,' said Delia faintly, calling to mind her own disgraceful episodes with Bert in the potting shed.

'For these reasons I was instructed to examine you closely,' said Mrs Remply. 'I'm sure you understand. Tell me truthfully, and with no shame, what sensations did you feel in your pussy when I touched it?'

'There were no unusual sensations, I assure you,' Delia said, wondering what would constitute *unusual* in these circumstances. 'I experienced a sensation impossible to convey in words, but which is wholly familiar to me.'

'That's encouraging,' said Mrs Remply with a nod, and within her plain blue frock her ample bosom heaved. 'The sensation was well known to you from being played about with by your friends in the dormitory, I take it?'

Delia nodded, reluctant to engage in further discussion about her nightly activities, though finding a strange exhilaration in hearing such matters spoken of openly by an adult person. It emboldened her to enquire of Mrs Remply something she wished to know, which none of her friends in Form V had explained to her satisfaction, but which she guessed the sickroom nurse would be acquainted with, she being of baser stock.

'Mrs Remply, there is a matter which puzzles me,' said she, a sense of propriety making her choose her words with some care. 'By merest chance I overheard two persons conversing together, not pupils of St Agatha's, and they made use of a word which is unknown to me. I think it must be a lower-class word, for it is not to be found in the large dictionary in the school library.'

'Lord, whatever can it be?' said Mrs Remply with a smile on her broad face. 'I'm sure I can't guess.'

Now that the moment had arrived, Delia was unwilling to speak the word out loud. Her face coloured prettily, and

## The Girls' Boarding School

she tried to circumvent the issue by making Mrs Remply say it instead.

'I do believe you know the word,' said Delia, 'the meaning of it, so far as I could make out from the strange conversation of which I overheard only a fragment, is the private parts between a female's legs.'

'Her pussy, do you mean?' asked the other, her brow furrowed in doubt. 'That's a word the young ladies here use every minute and I cannot think that mystifies you.'

'The word to which I refer begins with the letter T,' Delia said in embarrassment.'

'Let me see now . . .' Mrs Remply mused, 'what begins with a T? Why, I do believe you mean *twat*. Was that the word?'

Delia nodded and put the question which mystified her: 'What is the difference, I am most curious to know, dear Mrs Remply, between it and a young lady's pussy?'

'The difference? Bless you, there isn't any difference.'

'I feel there must be,' Delia insisted, 'for why should there be a word so very different in sound and implication if no true distinction existed?'

Mrs Remply considered for a moment or two, then announced she would demonstrate what difference there might be, if any, in a way Delia could grasp. Whereupon she drew aside the bedclothes covering the girl and hitched up her chemise, to bare her body up to the belly-button, exposing her thighs and her little patch of silky curls.

'Open your legs, Miss,' she said.

Delia was most reluctant to comply, but Mrs Remply had been so kind and helpful that she was persuaded the request formed a part of her explanation of an anatomical or biological mystery. She slid her legs a few inches apart and waited.

'Lie easy, my dear,' said Mrs Remply, and she pushed Delia's legs far apart and pulled her chemise up to her throat, baring her well-grown titties. Her fingers flicked over Delia's curly bush and tickled the soft lips for a moment or two without any attempt to penetrate them.

'This is a *pussy*,' she said, with a chuckle having about it an open ring of lewdness.

'I am aware of that,' said Delia, 'you may stop now.'

'Be patient,' said the other woman, 'for you have asked me an interesting question, and the answer cannot be given in just two words. A pretty young lady like you has been taught by her friends here at St Agatha's how the female spasm is brought on by playing with the button that lies hid within your pussy.'

'No, no! I forbid you to touch me there again. Enough is enough,' Delia exclaimed, as Mrs Remply's finger slid into her maidenly slit.

It must surely be possible, Delia thought wildly, somehow to assert her superior position over a servant, for that was what she knew Mrs Remply's status to be.

'You must allow me to know best, young lady,' the other woman answered firmly, her fingers busy in Delia's slippy pussy.

In spite of the deliciousness of the little thrills coursing through her belly, Delia strove to rise from the bed and break away from the fingers that were interfering with her. Alas, for her good intentions – Mrs Remply put a large hand flat on her chest in between her bare titties and thrust her down again on her back.

'Hold your tongue, Miss Delia,' she said in the friendliest sort of way, 'for we haven't finished yet.'

'I thought you were a friend,' Delia sighed faintly, 'but you are just like the rest of them here – you want to take advantage of me and shame me!'

## The Girls' Boarding School

Mrs Remply paid not the least attention. With a smile on her round face she felt Delia's bare titties with the hand that was pinning her flat to the bed, whilst with the other she dabbled in Delia's open split and manipulated her tender button. Aghast though she was at what was being done to her against her will, Delia was unable to close her legs and squeeze her thighs tight together, in order to deny Mrs Remply access to her person.

Willy-nilly, little spasms of shameful pleasure were quickly throbbing through Delia's belly, and her legs were trembling in spite of all she could do to hold them still. Deep in her heart she knew that she was about to fetch off – and she urgently wanted to feel the blissfulness engulf her. Mrs Remply closely watched her rising excitement, and a bare instant or two before Delia succumbed to the spasm, she removed her hands from the girl's trembling body and stood up.

Wide-eyed and open-mouthed, Delia watched in a throbbing heat of frustrated emotion while Mrs Remply very quickly removed her skirts and parted the front opening of her old-fashioned white drawers – the same type as those the pupils were forced to wear – and there displayed to the girl's sight was a large and hairy mound, divided by long plump lips.

'Now that's a *twat*,' said Mrs Remply to the fascinated girl.

'Let me see,' Delia sighed in fascination. 'Come closer.'

Mrs Remply grinned and took off her other clothes remaining standing at the bedside stark naked, to be looked at. She was what is commonly called a buxom woman, among the low, for benevolent providence had bestowed on her a pair of titties the size of pumpkins. Now she had passed her thirty-fifth year they had become somewhat slack, but they were luscious enough still to cause Delia's aroused pussy to pout – for by her handling of Miss Harriet's person she had acquired a keen appreciation of the pleasures of big titties.

Mrs Remply spread herself stark naked on the bed beside Delia with her legs well apart. The sight was more than Delia could bear in silence. She uttered a shrill cry of excitement and knelt with her bottom in the air, to stare at Mrs Remply's twat – for it was obvious to her now that that word alone was the proper one to describe it, and its thick bush of dark brown hair.

Delia sighed, then Mrs Remply chuckled. Below her broad round belly, where the columns of her thighs met, her fat and hairy split seemed almost to smile in friendly welcome, as if to say to Delia that here was a grown-up female organ to play tunes on – not the tight little slits of young ladies that she was used to in the dormitory. Delia was almost beside herself with joy as she parted the wet lips before her, and burrowed a couple of fingers within, to feel how slippery it was.

'Well, Miss Delia,' murmured the sick room attendant, 'now can you tell the difference between a *pussy* and a *twat*?'

'Yes, yes,' Delia murmured in her excitement, 'it's so large and plump and hairy. Oh, I wish I had a *twat* like yours!'

There, she had spoken the word at last! Inspired by her own boldness, with gleeful but shaming lust she wiggled her fingers inside its wet warmth, causing its naked owner to utter moans of delight.

'I'm sure you want to see it fetch off,' Mrs Remply suggested slyly, 'and see if it does it otherwise than a pussy does when the spasm takes it. The young ladies at St Agatha's have more than enough experience of fingering young girls to see how they twitch in their genteel little

## The Girls' Boarding School

spasms. But I'll lay odds you've never seen a big hairy crack like mine before.'

Were the truth to be told fully and candidly, as it rarely is in matters concerning sensual indulgence, Delia would have been able, had she wished, to contradict Mrs Remply's assertion, for she had viewed Mrs Kenilworth's female organ. What is more, she had been forced to touch it and stroke it, and she had kissed it – and seen how it clenched tight in the spasms of pleasure. Naturally, there could be no question of discussing the headmistress in so intimate a fashion with a school employee.

Moreover, the fact was that Delia had allowed herself to grow most shamefully aroused by the sight of Mrs Remply's plump and hairy thick-lipped split. With no more ado, she threw herself on top of the sickroom nurse, her lovely girlish belly pressed upon the older woman's broad and slack belly, her legs between the plump legs spread wide on the bed, and her maidenly pussy on the coarse *twat* that had been exposed to her gaze.

This posture of lying flat on top of another had been taught to Delia by Thelma Fanshawe, who delighted in rubbing her pussy against another pussy, her ginger curls mingling with the brown or black or yellow curls of whichever bedfellow she had chosen on any particular night to abuse and deprave. Others in Form V also liked to assume the upper position, and had compelled poor Delia to endure their weight on her body, including dear Maria, her friend, who happily was slender and light yet who fetched her off with only a score of rubs of pussy on pussy.

Hitherto Delia had not herself ventured to adopt the posture of lying on top of another – something in her rejected the idea as unnatural, though she knew not why. Yet now, confronted as she was by Mrs Remply's body, bared for her gaze, her plumply hairy female parts awaiting whatever attention might shortly be bestowed upon them, it seemed to Delia entirely proper to throw herself upon that broad round belly and slide her pussy against the large one beneath.

'How delightful a feeling!' she cried out, as she thrust her loins at Mrs Remply in fast tempo.

Mrs Remply grinned and slid her hands between their bodies to hook the tips of her middle fingers in the lips of her *twat* and pull it widely open, so that the wet lips of Delia's maidenly pussy rubbed smoothly on her secret button.

'Do me hard, Miss Delia,' she gasped, 'you'll make me fetch off like a bomb exploding!'

The strongest sensations that the human organism can tolerate possessed Delia at that moment. She whimpered in delight while she rubbed forcefully at Mrs Remply's wet split, and in moments the climax of voluptuousness seized upon them both. Mrs Remply moaned and sighed and her belly shuddered under Delia's, to the spasms of her fetch off.

'Lord, these young girls love it!' Delia heard her gasp.

# CHAPTER 15

## News of a Wrongdoer and his Fate

After her shameful experiences at the hands of a person who was employed to tend her and to care for her well-being and not take advantage of her shocked condition to vent her own lusts upon her lovely young body, namely Mrs Remply, Delia slept very well in the sickroom that night, even more so by reason of the fact that it was the first time she had slept alone in a bed throughout a night for many weeks.

On the morrow she awoke happy and cheerful, ready to rise and resume her regular lessons, but it transpired the headmistress had sent strict instructions to Mrs Remply that Miss Sempill-Shand was to keep to her bed for a day or two. The purpose stated was to ensure a dispersal of any lingering shock to her nervous system caused by the dreadful obscenities that the Reverend Octavian Blenkinsop had attempted on her person.

During the morning Miss Harriet came to visit, bringing her a bouquet of fresh flowers from the school gardens, and a special treat – a novel by Mr Thackeray from the school library to pass away the time, until she was allowed up again. Mrs Remply found a pretty vase for the flowers and placed a chair by Delia's bed for Miss Harriet, then withdrew and closed the door.

They were no sooner alone together than Miss Harriet reached out to take Delia's hand, whilst informing her of her regret at the unspeakably vile and unwholesome ordeal that had befallen her favourite pupil.

'You saved me,' said Delia, her beautiful blue eyes filling with tears of gratitude. 'But for you that beastly curate would have had his way with me, and I would be ruined for life. I owe you my reputation and my honour, Miss Harriet, and I love you.'

'Dearest Delia!' cried Miss Harriet, her free hand entering under the bedclothes to untie the ribbon bow that held Delia's nightgown closed over her bosom. In a trice she had bared the girl's soft young titties and was fondling them.

A sensation of delight made itself felt within Delia's body – a sensation very familiar to her, and most welcome, now that it was induced by the hand of her beloved form mistress.

'The criminal and degenerate clergyman who tried to violate you,' said Miss Harriet, 'did he in any way cause harm to your dear little pussy?'

'I am very pleased to report that you arrived in time, and so forestalled his dastardly intent,' Delia murmured.

Deep in her heart was a desire that Miss Harriet might wish to examine her person closely, to confirm the truth of what she had claimed. Her hope was quickly rewarded; Miss Harriet turned back the bedclothes, and raised Delia's nightgown, to expose her lovely young body from her toes to her belly-button.

'It is good to be sure,' said she, her fingers playing gently over the neat tuft of fairish curls gracing the mount between Delia's thighs. 'No doubt our good Mrs Remply satisfied herself that no harm had been done to your precious parts, but a second opinion never goes amiss.'

Tremors of pure bliss from the soft caress of Miss

Harriet's fingers on her pussy caused Delia's body to quiver. She sighed and her legs slid apart, permitting full access to her person, whereupon Miss Harriet's playful but skilful digits eased into her split and glided over her secret bud with delicacy.

'Yes,' Delia sighed, attempting to continue the conversation, 'Mrs Remply satisfied herself completely as to . . . oh!'

A little cry escaped her as the tremors of delight within her belly became ever more powerful.

'Did she, indeed?' said Miss Harriet. 'She shall answer to me for her satisfaction, the hussy!'

'She was very kind to me in my distress,' said Delia, trying to erase the impression she had not meant to create in the mind of her dearest form mistress.

'It is not her place to be kind,' said Miss Harriet.' She is a servant, and has no right to lay a hand upon a young lady – did she abuse you very greatly, dearest Delia?'

'Hardly at all,' sighed the girl, her bare thighs shaking in bliss as Miss Harriet's caress urged her ever nearer the brink of sensual ecstasy. 'She examined my parts and washed them . . .'

'I warrant she did more than that to them,' Miss Harriet said with a meaningful chuckle. 'Well, for that she shall have a piece of my mind.'

Delia gasped loud and long as the female spasm claimed her at last and wrought in her sensations of divine pleasure. When she recovered herself she found Miss Harriet smiling down at her.

'You have sustained no harm from the unfortunate event,' said the form mistress. 'Your bodily responses are all that could be wished for and the sight of your pretty face wreathed in smiles is enough to delight the heart of anyone.'

'Dare I ask,' Delia murmured, 'does it delight you, dear Miss Harriet?'

'More than that,' cried the other, 'it arouses me!'

'Ah,' Delia sighed, 'may I be permitted to see your beautiful pussy, dearest Miss Harriet?'

What changes had been wrought in Miss Delia Sempill-Shand by one term at St Agatha's! On the day of her arrival, not more than twelve weeks before, she had been wholly innocent of physical and sensual matters, whereas now she surrendered her person to the manipulation of another female without the slightest qualm.

Three short months before, in the time of her virgin modesty, she had been horrified and shamed by the depravity of assaults on her body by Thelma Fanshawe, and outraged when the spasm was first induced in her. Yet now she was pleading to be allowed to look at another female's person. How soon is virtue despoiled, and how easily is innocence turned to guilty knowledge.

By way of answer Miss Harriet drew up her skirts into her lap as she sat on the chair Mrs Remply had brought for her, showing her stockinged legs and dainty frilled knickers of blush-pink. Her fingers pulled down the front of the garment, her slender knees moved apart, and there revealed to Delia's ardent gaze was the raven-black and glossy bush of curls she adored.

'Out of bed, lazy-bones,' cried Miss Harriet. 'Come here and kiss me properly!'

Delia was inflamed by the immodest words and slipped from the bed to kneel on the floor between Miss Harriet's feet. Her face bore an expression of the sheerest bliss as her trembling hand stretched out to touch the tender object of her desire. To her gentle fingering the long lips parted, and shudders of delight ran though her, no less than through Miss Harriet.

## The Girls' Boarding School

With a sob of joy Delia bowed her head and brought her tongue to bear on the throbbing split she had titillated. Miss Harriet sighed deeply in lewd impatience and sensual agitation of mind.

'Kiss me,' she sighed, gazing fondly down at Delia's face.

Thus urged on, Delia licked voluptuously at the long pink bud within the slit she held wide open. She could hear Miss Harriet gasping at the force of the fierce sensations that were running through her body and making her shake like a leaf in a tempest. Quite soon those long and gracefully-shaped legs of hers began to quiver strongly, in announcement of the imminent arrival of her spasm.

Delicious feelings racked Delia also from top to toe, induced by the sight and touch of her plaything. She was quite certain that Miss Harriet's black-haired pussy was the most sensual and the most beautiful specimen she would ever see in her life. All the same, she was forced to admit in her secret heart that she had been excessively aroused the previous day by the sight of Mrs Remply's big hairy *twat* – common though it was, of course. The strange word for those exciting parts found between female thighs reverberated in Delia's mind and stirred her feelings.

By way of mitigation for the disgraceful yielding to vulgar thoughts, Delia comforted herself with the excuse that she had been in a state of nervous shock yesterday – and Mrs Remply had taken shameful advantage of her by tampering with her parts and then compelling her to lick her common *twat*.

Miss Harriet gave a loud shriek and arched her back, her feet leaving the floor as she drew her knees up. Her belly shook and she hooked her legs over the kneeling girl's shoulders whilst her entire body convulsed in the throbs of her climactic bliss.

'You've fetched me off, Delia!' she gasped. 'Oh, do it again – slow and gentle this time – and then I'll do you again.'

When she was again in possession of her faculties, she was as good as her word, stripping Delia naked and spreading her flat on her back on the bed to fetch her off a second, a third, then a fourth time.

It was when they had paused to draw breath that Delia seized the opportunity to make an enquiry of her beloved form mistress that had often been in her mind, though hitherto she had never dared to ask.

'Miss Harriet,' said she timorously, 'have you ever permitted a man's organ to enter your pussy?'

'Heavens,' exclaimed the form mistress, 'what a question to put to an unmarried woman! Do you not realise how insulting it is to her honour?'

'Forgive my rudeness, dear Miss Harriet,' said Delia, blushing a bright pink, 'but you have shown yourself so knowledgeable in answering my questions in the past on this delicate topic that I cannot but feel this depth of understanding must spring less from medical books on human anatomy than actual experience.'

'You are quite right,' Miss Harriet admitted, a roguish smile on her beautiful face, 'and since we are such close and loving friends, you and I, you shall be let into my confidence.'

Thereupon she related to the astonished girl certain private events of her life prior to embarking upon a teaching career at St Agatha's. From the age of two-and-twenty, she explained, she held the post of governess to the Hon Melissa Blaby-Riddle, the only daughter of Lord Clacton, her days being spent in comfort and style at his lordship's country seat in Huntingdonshire.

Lord Clacton was a cultured gentleman of substance and

## The Girls' Boarding School

wealth who had travelled extensively abroad. Although he was more than twice the age of his daughter's governess, a sincere friendship developed between him and Miss Harriet. Indeed, this warmth of feeling between them developed to a point to which no modest or decent female would have permitted.

One evening after dinner, when the Hon Melissa had been sent off to bed, Miss Harriet was seated beside his Lordship in the drawing room, the two of them on a sofa. Of a sudden, his lips were upon hers in an affectionate kiss – and a moment later his aristocratic hand was up her clothes and between her thighs.

The shocked reader will be able to form a clear judgement of the moral character of Miss Harriet Jardyne from the fact that she did not scream and smack his lordship's face in outrage. On the contrary, she permitted him to fondle her between the thighs to his heart's content, and not long thereafter she even let him lead her up to his bedchamber – where he laid her on his four-poster bed and removed all her clothing.

'In short,' said she to Delia, 'Lord Clacton rogered me three times that night.'

'*Rogered?*' Delia asked, breathless with excitement. 'Is that the word for a gentleman putting his *thing* into a pussy?'

'Quite so,' said Miss Harriet, and went on to explain how she had remained in Lord Clacton's household and his employ for two years, and on most nights had received his intimate attentions.

'How can this be possible?' Delia enquired. 'You informed me that the male emission in a pussy causes the unfortunate female concerned to fall in the family way, at which her belly swells up large, and in due course she becomes a mother.'

'In the usual way of things, it is so,' Miss Harriet agreed, 'but I make no doubt that Mrs Remply showed you yesterday this may be avoided by a careful washing with warm water to remove all trace of the male fluid.'

'But how did you endure His Lordship's embraces for so long a time?' Delia asked. 'To have a huge stiff thing pushed up you nightly is a fearful fate!'

Miss Harriet agreed with a knowing smile that it was indeed a dire Fate for a young lady to suffer, yet her employment was in all other ways so ideally to her liking that she was reconciled to permitting Lord Clacton the use of her person.

In the main, she said, smiling knowingly at Delia, it would be true to say His Lordship's passion lay in handling her titties and fingering her pussy, bringing her up to the spasm several times. Whereupon he would mount her belly and *roger* her with a brisk motion. His penetration was never of a tedious duration, his emission taking place within a few seconds of insertion.

She would, said she, have continued happily in this mode with his lordship, but alas, on an ill-fated afternoon he discovered her with his daughter Melissa in a state of undress together. A knowledge of passionate friendship between females offended his sense of propriety. Indeed, it would by no means be overstating the case to say that he was outraged to learn that the virginal Melissa was enjoying regular sensual bliss day after day – and with the woman in his employ, whom he thought was his property to use for his own pleasure.

Not to put too fine a point on it, he took it badly amiss that rampant sensuality was taking place in his stately home without his knowledge, consent, participation or approval. He sent Miss Harriet packing forthwith, giving her only an hour to pack her trunk and be gone. Nevertheless, being a woman of considerable self-possession and intelligence, she was able to extract from His Lordship a glowing reference, and what was even more useful – a considerable sum of money, in return for a promise not ever to reveal what had happened in Huntingdonshire. The simple fact was that Lord Clacton would have been mortified greatly if it had become known in Society that he had entered into relations with his daughter's governess – and that the selfsame governess had debauched his daughter.

'What a beastly person he must be,' Delia exclaimed, and she threw her arms about Miss Harriet and kissed her a dozen times, 'to turn you away, after abusing your beautiful pussy with his despicable male *thing*. Poor darling pussy – how brutalised and violated it must have been by all that *rogering*!'

It is needless to record that Delia and Miss Harriet embraced and comforted each other for the next hour, by means of a shameful manipulation, by hand and mouth, of the intimate parts of their bodies. When at last Miss Harriet adjusted her clothes and departed, Delia sank into the sweet slumber of the fatigued and remained so until Mrs Remply brought her lunch on a tray.

In the middle of the afternoon the headmistress arrived at the sickroom to bring Delia news of two very different people. One of them was the Reverend Octavian Blenkinsop, formerly curate of the parish, but no more so, now that Mrs Kenilworth had visited the bishop and put him in possession of the unseemly facts. The young clerical gentleman had been sent far away, Mrs Kenilworth reported – he was even at that moment on his way to Southampton to board a ship sailing shortly for West Africa.

Given a choice of leaving the Church of England or becoming a missionary, the offending clergyman had selected the jungle and the opportunity of bringing the comforts of Christian doctrine to tribes of naked savages.

'Though I greatly fear he will endeavour to wreak his vicious and despicable lusts on dusky maidens, inflamed by the sight of their young bodies, for I am given to understand that they wear no more than a single banana-leaf to shield their private parts from prying male eyes,' said Mrs Kenilworth, her lips pursed in disapproval, and her arms folded beneath her heavy bosom, as if to support the weightiness of her titties.

'Poor creatures, I pity them!' cried Delia.

A vision had arisen in her mind's eye of the lustful curate, his stiff and menacing part sticking out of his trousers, as he flung himself upon a naked and dusky-skinned female of tender years, to commit an act of ravishment.

'In the absence of someone present to restrain his degenerate lusts,' Delia continued, 'he will surely accomplish his purpose and push that long thing into an innocent pussy, and discharge his lust in a flood of defilement.'

The very thought of it made Delia go quite pale.

'If he does,' said the headmistress, 'he may discover that he has trespassed on territory claimed by the tribal chief and a penalty will be exacted from him.'

'Will they cut off his *cockstand*?' Delia asked, wide-eyed.

'No, no, he is more likely to be made to pay a cash penalty,' Mrs Kenilworth said with a frown at hearing so vulgar and very indecent a word on the lips of a young lady, 'although there is justice in what you suggest. But that aside, I must forbid you ever again to use that horrid word to signify the male part.'

'I beg your pardon humbly,' said Delia, 'I was carried away by the horror of the situation and forgot myself. But there is no sufficient sum of money in the

## The Girls' Boarding School

entire world to compensate a maiden violated by a male organ.'

'Let us not overstate the case,' Mrs Kenilworth replied. 'But perhaps the despicable fellow will be compelled to marry one or more unclothed young women with rings through their noses if by his disgraceful behaviour he gives them big bellies.'

Delia nodded her agreement and said nothing, her aversion to the erring Blenkinsop being too great for comment on his future fate. In her heart she hoped for some dread plight to overtake him, such as having his offending male part bitten right off by a man-eating lion in the African jungle.

She had naturally put on her nightgown after Miss Harriet had left her before lunch, but being sleepy at the time from over-indulgence in sensual pleasure with the form mistress, she had forgotten to tie up the pretty ribbons that closed the bodice.

Observing that Mrs Kenilworth's gaze was fixed on her bosom, Delia glanced down and noticed that the ribbons were undone and a considerable portion of her titties was laid bare to view. A vivid scarlet blush came to her cheeks, and a smile to the face of Mrs Kenilworth.

'I have this day received a letter from your legal guardian,' she informed Delia. 'He will be here tomorrow before noon.'

'It is gratifying to hear that Sir Stanton is coming to take me to London,' said Delia, 'yet I hardly know him, being these many years at boarding school, ever since the tragic demise of my parents when I was a mere child. It will be a great pleasure to make his acquaintance properly. This holiday affords me an opportunity to get to know him better.'

'Better than you may think,' said Mrs Kenilworth, 'for

in the friendliest of ways his letter makes it known to me that he has formed the opinion that too much education is the ruination of young ladies. He concludes that you have been at school quite long enough, and ought now to take up your rightful position in society.'

'What does this mean?' cried Delia.

'Why, it means that you will not return to St Agatha's at the beginning of the next term,' Mrs Kenilworth replied. 'You are instead to be a debutante, my dear.'

Sorry though she necessarily was to lose a fee-paying pupil, Mrs Kenilworth could not but agree with Sir Stanton, that Delia would benefit less from any further scholastic studies than she would from making an entrance into the world of fashion and the social round, under the protection of so worthy a gentleman as her legal guardian.

Whilst Delia regretted leaving behind her friends in Form V, not to mention Miss Harriet, the prospect of grown-up life and greater freedom appealed to her prodigiously.

'If you will accept a word of advice from one who has seen a little more of the world than you,' said Mrs Kenilworth with an air of caution, 'it would be unwise to trouble Sir Stanton with the details of your misadventure at the hands, if I may so put it, of the Reverend Blenkinsop.'

'Surely as my legal guardian he has every right to know of an attempt upon my virtue,' Delia replied, somewhat puzzled.

'No doubt he does,' the headmistress said, 'but it has been more than once brought to my attention that gentlemen often may misunderstand these matters. He might wonder why you had bared your posterior for the reverend gentleman's inspection, and for what reason you took down your drawers. In short, Delia, it is quite possible

## The Girls' Boarding School

Sir Stanton might jump to a wrong conclusion, as to your willingness or otherwise to take part in this shocking act of sensuality.

'But I was wholly innocent!' Delia exclaimed. 'Surely no one would believe otherwise?'

'Parents and guardians have very strong views in respect of the virtue and chastity of young ladies,' said Mrs Kenilworth, shaking her head gravely. 'They tend to assume the worst about the young. Now I know, dear, that you were taken advantage of, and that your only experience of the sensual act is provided by the fingers and tongues of other young ladies upon your person – for in charity we will say nothing of your earlier adventure in the potting shed with the gardener's boy.'

'He too tried to ravish me!' Delia insisted.

'That may be so,' said Mrs Kenilworth in a tone indicative of her extreme doubt, 'but in regard to the former curate of this parish, a young gentleman in Holy Orders, Sir Stanton might not be persuaded that you were entirely unwilling to oblige, if he got to know of the dreadful episode. If he in error should form the opinion that you are no longer virginal and untainted, who can say what form his displeasure might take?'

'Then what am I to do?' Delia cried out in distress.

'Take my word for it, Delia,' said the headmistress, '*least said, soonest mended* is the best precept in these matters. Keep your pretty mouth tightly shut, and we of St Agatha's teaching staff shall do likewise.'

'In view of what you have said, you may be sure that I shall say nothing to Sir Stanton of the curate's depraved attempt on my virginity,' Delia assured her.

'Good, it is for the best,' said the headmistress with a nod of approval. 'Now, Delia, I cannot help noticing you have taken the liberty of abusing yourself, whilst lying here alone in the sickroom. This wanton behaviour is unworthy.'

'Oh no, Mrs Kenilworth – believe me I have not.'

'Then why is the front of your nightgown undone, girl? Ah, I see you blush pink for shame. And rightly so, for solitary vice is bad for the health of mind and body. Moreover, it is quite unnecessary at St Agatha's, where so many are ready to join you in friendly play.'

So saying, she seated herself upon the bed to face Delia, and thrust a hand into the open front of her nightgown, to grope at her soft young titties. Not content with this act of indecency, Mrs Kenilworth pulled the nightgown open and leaned forward to apply her mouth to the pink buds of Delia's titties, sucking at them with gusto. Her other hand was thrust down the bed and up inside Delia's nightgown between her legs, to finger her pussy.

'Oh Mrs Kenilworth . . .' Delia murmured, held fast in the other woman's firm grip and unable to free herself, though tremors of lustful pleasure warned her that she would quickly achieve the female spasm if this indecent abuse of her parts were continued for another minute.

Mrs Kenilworth said nothing, but brought her red-flushed face close to Delia's face and kissed her, thrusting her tongue deep into the girl's mouth. Delia began to breath rapidly, feeling the onset of the sensual crisis. Her titties heaved in pleasant agitation and her pussy turned slippery-wet to the manipulation of the headmistress's finger within it. Five seconds more, and Delia moaned to the clenching of her belly, in sudden spasms of sheerest bliss.

'There,' said Mrs Kenilworth, 'how very nicely you always do fetch off, Delia, as I've remarked before. I'm sure you must be a favourite with the entire dormitory after lights out. Are you had every night, girl?'

'Yes,' said Delia, half-ashamed to confess the truth, yet

she was also half-proud of her own popularity. 'Some nights by two or three of the girls before falling asleep.'

'You are no stranger to tickling a pussy, as I have reason to know,' declared Mrs Kenilworth with a friendly smile. 'You may feel me, Delia.'

'Oh yes,' said Delia, showing herself delighted by a prospect which only a few weeks before would have filled her with horror and dismay, 'do let me look at your lovely big pussy, dear Mrs Kenilworth, I beg you.'

The headmistress was overjoyed by this display of enthusiasm and quickly removed her black bombazine dress, her underskirts and her chemise, her shoes and her drawers, before getting into bed beside Delia in only her stockings.

At once Delia slipped down inside the bed to handle and kiss Mrs Kenilworth's vast soft titties, and tug and nibble at their long buds, until she had made them stand firm. She slid further down inside the bed, to press her lips to Mrs Kenilworth's bare plump belly, and further down still, getting between her parted thighs, to look at the thick bush of dark-brown curls.

How large and protruding it was, the headmistress's pussy – how prominent below the dome of her belly, how the lips bulged out as if pouting. So powerful of aspect, so *dominating* – as if it would squash a young lady beneath its fleshy weightiness and ravish her to the most fantastic fetch off. Mrs Kenilworth was a lady and therefore had a *pussy*, but, thought Delia, it is so very much like dearest Mrs Remply's that I truly believe it is less a pussy than a *twat*; a bold strong hairy split seeming possessed of the power to actually *roger* a girl.

With that improper thought in her mind arousing degraded lust in her, Delia pressed her lips to the female organ in question and thrust her wet tongue into it.

'That's it exactly,' exclaimed Mrs Kenilworth. 'Fetch me off slow and gentle, Delia – I mean to stay all the afternoon.'

# CHAPTER 16
# A Remarkable Journey by Train

On the next morning, after breakfast, Delia's belongings were packed and her farewells spoken – with admiration and esteem to Mrs Kenilworth, and with deepest affection to Miss Harriet. This latter fond parting took place in the pleasant privacy of Miss Harriet's study, and, as might well be expected on so very emotional an occasion, Miss Harriet took quick advantage of the moment to slide a hand up under Delia's clothes and finger her. She skilfully brought the girl to a most satisfactory *Farewell Until We Meet Again* spasm, all the while kissing her hotly upon the mouth.

To demonstrate her affection for her form mistress, nay, her abiding *love* for her, Delia sank to her knees on the hearth-rug and pleaded with Miss Harriet to raise her skirts to her waist, so she could press her face between her beautiful white thighs. In only a few moments she caused Miss Harriet to moan and sway, by ardent use of her tongue on the form mistress's beautiful black-haired pussy. Then at last, her fingers twined in Delia's hair, Miss Harriet fetched off to a loud cry of bliss.

A little before lunchtime, Sir Stanton Fortescue arrived at St Agatha's to take charge of his ward. He was a gentleman in his middle years, handsome of face and figure, tall of stature, fair-haired and blessed with great personal charm, his manners impeccable, his conversation in the best of taste, his clothes in the very height of fashion. Mrs Kenilworth was almost swept off her feet by the appeal of his person, while even the coldly beautiful Miss Harriet took to him on sight.

By mid-afternoon Delia and Sir Stanton were in an otherwise empty First Class carriage on an express train from Midsomer Rackham to London. Her trunks were safely stowed in the guard's van, her hat-box on the luggage-rack over her head, her schooldays behind her. Sir Stanton placed his shiny silk top hat on the rack, unbuttoned his elegant grey frock-coat and sat beside Delia to converse in an affectionate manner.

To Delia his mode of life sounded most pleasing. She looked on him with the greatest favour, as her future guide, mentor and friend, in addition to his legal responsibility for her and her fortune. She took no exception when he passed an arm about her waist in the friendliest possible manner, for she regarded this as no more than an avuncular gesture.

After some little time had elapsed Sir Stanton suggested that as a sign of the warm affection between them, she should sit on his knee. This astonished Delia, who replied with a pretty pink blush that, if she might bring to his attention a point of some importance, she was no longer a child, nor had been these past two or more years.

That being so, she declared, although hesitant lest she seem impertinent or ungrateful to her estimable legal guardian, many would deem it improper for her to do what he had suggested.

'Not a bit of it,' cried Sir Stanton with a merry laugh that dispelled her qualms, 'for although you are seventeen, my dear, and in every way grown up and shall be treated with due courtesy, I do not believe you are beyond a show of true affection. In my fond eyes and heart you are still my dearest little Delia, as first I saw you, ten years ago, when you became my ward, on the tragic demise of your natural parents.'

Thus encouraged, Delia thought there was no wrong in sitting on Sir Stanton's knee. She placed herself in that position, and he chatted cheerfully to her of the very many sights of London he intended to show her, now school was behind her forever – of the dressmakers and milliners, the pleasures of strolling in St James's Park, theatres and musical concerts at the Royal Albert Hall, of gourmet meals in good restaurants, and the plethora of other amusements which were to fill her days.

Delia listened happily, for she entertained no suspicion that anything other than what Sir Stanton spoke of was going through his mind. After the elapse of a little time, by degrees did she become aware of a stiffening inside his trousers, where her hip touched lightly against him. It grew into an unmistakable bulge against his belly, getting bigger and harder.

The memory of surreptitious visits to the potting shed in the grounds of St Agatha's to see the gardener's boy's *dick* swell up and go stiff – this memory made Delia aware of the condition into which her guardian had progressed.

Her stolen hours in the gardener's hut handling Bert's stiff part to a sticky emission were not the sole memory that flitted through her mind at that moment. Only too vivid in her memory was the dread occasion when the Reverend Blenkinsop had attempted a wicked violation of her person by thrusting his male organ into her from behind.

In Delia's mind confusion reigned as to the intentions of Sir Stanton. She reminded herself of Maria Wendover's warning that gentlemen on trains often attempted familiarities with female travelling companions. There was a peculiar rhythm to the beat of the mighty pistons and the clickety-clack of powerful wheels on the steel rails that had an insidiously arousing effect upon the male organism. So Maria had claimed, when on the last night of term she had regaled the young ladies of Form V with a lurid account of what had befallen her Mama's housemaid on a train.

According to Maria's second-hand description, the person who had molested the housemaid had pulled out a *dick* at least nine inches long and as thick as a cucumber. Despite her maidenly fears, Delia found herself wondering whether the stiff shaft in Sir Stanton's trousers was of a similar size.

On the frightful day the depraved clergyman had attempted his act of ravishment on her maidenhood, Delia's back was turned to him, thus protecting her delicate nerves from even a glimpse of his male organ. In consequence it was quite impossible to guess at the size of it – but in her fevered imagination it reared up to the level of his chin, with the thickness of a blacksmith's muscular arm, and a swollen crimson head large as a beetroot.

The subject of male organs and their length and thickness in full erection was a highly improper subject for a young lady's speculation, and it is a measure of how far Delia had descended into the morass of sensuality that she succumbed to unwholesome thoughts of this nature.

She wondered to what extent age was a determining factor in the extensiveness of a gentleman's part. Dearest Maria had not particularised the age of the man on the train who had exposed himself obscenely to the housemaid, but it stood to reason that a certain number of years must surely be required for any organ to attain a length of nine inches.

What then of Sir Stanton's male part when it stood, as it did now, at full stretch? Sir Stanton was a gentleman of forty-two years, by Delia's reckoning. It seemed to her a reasonable assumption that his organ must have grown much bigger than Bert's, exposed for her inspection in the potting shed. She recalled Bert's as about four inches long, and evidently Sir Stanton's had attained a size superior to that. But had it reached nine inches?

Delia had certain knowledge from observation that the female organ increased in size with the years, she having many a time compared her own and Miss Harriet's more prominent and longer-lipped black-haired delight. She had also made comparison with the even bigger and plumper and hairier pussy of Mrs Kenilworth – who was twenty years older than Miss Harriet.

Delia was not certain if Mrs Remply's *twat* ought to be taken into comparison. Her acquaintance with it during her time spent in the sick room had revealed it to be as large and well-grown as Mrs Kenilworth's – though Mrs Remply was much younger than the headmistress.

Perhaps the the discrepancy was accounted for by the inferior social class of Mrs Remply. To Delia's way of thinking, women of the lower orders were abused by their menfolk, who nightly made them lie on their backs and forced distended *cockstands* up into their pussies, a practice as repulsive as it was unnatural. Abuse on this monstrous scale would surely result in a serious stretching of the female parts. Mrs Remply evidently had been married at some time, and been brutally misused by her husband in this manner – which would explain why her *twat* was quite as capacious as the headmistress's.

Whilst Delia's girlish mind occupied itself with unseemly speculation, Sir Stanton had slipped an arm round her waist to hold her lightly to him. His thick blond moustache tickled her ear as he brought his mouth close to whisper to her of lingerie that would be purchased for her – choicest items of finest lawn linen, embroidered by hand, trimmed with Brussels lace. At this Delia turned her head to gaze fully into his blue eyes, certain now that he meant to take advantage of her in some way.

Leaving aside her near-ravishment by the Reverend Blenkinsop, a fate she did not expect or fear from the hand of Sir Stanton, he being a perfect gentleman, she pondered other possibilities. Would Sir Stanton open his trousers and handle himself to an emission while she looked on? This was a question Delia could not answer, for she was unaware of whether it was only low boys in garden sheds, and other similar common sorts, who brought on their own emission by hand, or if gentlemen did also.

She uttered a tiny gasp to feel Sir Stanton's hand dip under her skirts and glide up between her legs. A bright red blush suffused her pretty cheeks, even while her thighs moved apart without her willing it. She tried to persuade herself to press her knees together, but being touched on her pussy constantly by the girls of St Agatha's had implanted in her an impulse she could not now reverse – an impulse to let her legs move apart.

Nevertheless, she gasped again when Sir Stanton's hand passed through the opening of her drawers. The sweetest agitation made itself felt throughout her whole body to feel his fingers among the soft little curls growing about her pussy.

'How very delicious,' he murmured in her ear. 'I do not doubt that you were very sought after by the other young ladies at St Agatha's. Were you fingered much, Delia?'

She blushed crimson to realise that Sir Stanton was aware of what young ladies did to each other in bed at St Agatha's Boarding School. He noted her colour and smiled

## The Girls' Boarding School

in a most sympathetic manner and assured her that he understood the way of things and she should entertain no feelings of misplaced modesty in regard to nightly episodes involving her and her friends in the dormitory.

Thus emboldened Delia explained how she had been subjected to the appalling indignity of having a friend come to her bed each night to raise her nightgown and bare her body to manipulation of hand and tongue. Sir Stanton listened with great interest to all this and enquired about special friends. Delia told him of Maria and her roving hands and of Edna Calthorpe-Brunton of the large titties.

She spoke of Daphne Greville and of Selina, who took ages to reach the spasm, so that one's fingers became quite numb with tiredness, of Rhoda and her insatiable tongue which would bring her victim off five or six times before she paused to rest. She mentioned Myrtle Fookes, who adored having her titties sucked – and naturally she had much to say of red-headed Thelma.

Sir Stanton's face grew pink and his eyes gleamed, to hear of these young ladies and of their nocturnal plundering of Delia's maidenly pussy. The bulge in his trousers grew bigger and still harder, until he tugged his buttons open and pulled it out into the light of day. Delia gazed in fascination to estimate by how much his stiff *cockstand* exceeded in length the gardener's boy's.

'There now, Delia, you've never seen one of those before!' exclaimed Sir Stanton proudly. In this he was much mistaken, of course, but Delia had no intention of correcting his impression of her ignorance of male organs.

'My,' she murmured, her eyes modestly downcast, 'please, if you will, dispel my ignorance, Sir Stanton – what is the proper name for this portion of your person?'

'Why, there are many,' he replied, 'but the one I prefer to make use of myself in regard to this splendid fellow of mine is *John Thomas*. Don't you think that an excellent name?'

'Quite enchanting,' said Delia, pleased to be able to abandon Bert's rural word for the male organ and learn another – which naturally would be more *au fait*, coming as it did from the lips of Sir Stanton.

Meantime, she gazed at his exposed person with a careful eye, until finally she was satisfied that in length it was about six inches, and of proportionate thickness. When she reached this conclusion, she began to wonder what he intended to do next. He seemed somewhat apprehensive of her response to the view of his up-rearing *John Thomas*, and leaned back on the seat to wait for her to become more accustomed to it.

Though he had no inkling of what was in her mind, to Delia it was utterly absurd to suppose that any female in the Kingdom – even dear Mrs Kenilworth – had a pussy that could be stretched wide enough to admit Sir Stanton's hairy monster – or any other man's – without atrocious suffering and agony. That established in her mind, and taking into account that Sir Stanton was born a gentleman and would never cause pain to a young lady, it was evident to Delia that he would employ some other means to reach his goal that did not entail her suffering.

Perhaps he would fetch himself off, she speculated, in the way Bert the gardener's boy did daily. At this point a strange and unnerving thought occurred to her – was he waiting for her to handle his swollen part till his sap flew out? She knew the manner to do it, of course, but was unwilling to let him know that. In accordance with Mrs Kenilworth's advice, she intended to feign total ignorance of male parts and their workings.

## The Girls' Boarding School

She smiled shyly at Sir Stanton, allowing an air of innocent puzzlement to appear on her face. He kissed her cheek lightly and settled the question by putting his hand over hers to wrap her dainty fingers round his throbbing length.

With a winning smile, he begged her to remain just so and do no more for the moment – namely, to clasp him but not to move her hand on his person, lest she hasten on without intending an accidental emission, before he was ready for it.

She did as he requested, clasping *John Thomas* firmly, whilst Sir Stanton thrust his hand boldly up her skirts again to feel her pussy, until he made it wet with the dew of her virginal desire. Indeed, so delightful were the sensations he stirred up in her that she reached a most immoral and vicious conclusion – that if a gentleman like Sir Stanton deemed it not improper to play with her pussy, then it must be perfectly in order for him to do so!

What followed from this utterly disgraceful and wrong thought was that Delia had become perfectly willing to give her legal guardian a whole-hearted freedom to indulge himself on her body at any time he wished in so pleasant a pastime! Pause, gentle reader at this point, and reflect on how in this we truly see commonsense and decency turned upside down, and stood on their heads, for Delia ought to have fled away from her debaucher as from the plague, not surrender herself to his degraded tastes.

Meanwhile, her eyes were lightly closed, the better to savour the blissful little tremors that rippled through her body, and her knees were well apart in her skirt.

'Oh how very nice that feels,' she murmured, blushing faintly at her own boldness. 'I never knew gentlemen did this to ladies before now. In my ignorance I was under the mistaken impression it was only something girls did to each other.'

Sir Stanton chuckled at her words and played with her deftly, his middle finger gliding round and over her hidden bud till in another minute she sighed loudly and her belly quaked in joyous spasms. He let her rest for a while to recover, with her pretty head lying on his shoulder, his hand remaining up between her thighs.

'Tell me more of your friend Thelma, the ginger-headed young lady,' he suggested, 'though I have not seen her, I feel she is of importance to you. Did she get often into your bed?'

Her confidence in Sir Stanton secure after the understanding way in which he had pleasured her to the spasm, Delia informed him it was Thelma who had got into her bed on her first night at St Agatha's to *break her in*, as the girls called it. Thelma it was who had first sucked the tender pink buds of her titties and introduced her to the fierce sensation of the sensual spasm by causing her to fetch off for the very first time ever.

'What a wonderful moment!' exclaimed Sir Stanton, 'I'd have given a hundred guineas to be present.'

Delia was somewhat surprised to hear so open a confession but pleased that he understood what she had experienced against her will. She went on to tell him how, after her first fetching off she had in confusion begged Thelma to leave her in peace – but it was not to be. In a rage of lewdness, Thelma stripped off their nightgowns and lay on Delia, reversed head to foot.

'By George,' said Sir Stanton, his organ leaping strongly in Delia's soft and lily-white hand, 'Thelma is a real goer and no mistake, if she enjoys a sixty-nine at her young age. You shall write to her and invite her to visit you, and stay with us for a few days, while she is on holiday from St Agatha's.'

'I was much taken aback at the time,' said Delia with a fiery blush, 'for I had not the least idea of what she proposed to do in adopting this strange position on my body. I found out very quickly, when she ran her tongue up and down my open pussy. The sensations she aroused were so totally overpowering that, when she pressed her own pussy to my mouth, I could do no other than thrust my tongue in it and lick until she uttered terribly loud moans of delight and came off.'

Without being aware of it, Delia was freely using the word to describe the female organ which is not spoken in polite society – and this may be attributed to the newly-acquired confidence she felt in Sir Stanton's presence, and the ease with which he had encouraged her to converse. Yet how frightful an omen for the future, that indecent words should be used so casually in talk between a female and a male!

'And while you were attending to Thelma's pussy, her tongue was busy with yours, eh?' Sir Stanton asked merrily.

Her cheeks a pretty pink at the memory, though whether it was shame or pleasure in recollection there was no way Sir Stanton could tell, Delia confessed that she had indeed been compelled to succumb to the sensual spasm at the same instant as Thelma.

'I like the sound of this very lively young lady,' said Sir Stanton. 'Ask her to stay with us before she returns to school – and she can share your bed and repeat her naughty games.'

Not the faintest suggestion escaped of what he was thinking, nor did poor innocent Delia suspect for a moment what depravity was in his mind. Yet the truth was that Sir

Stanton fully meant to be present at any such resumption of nocturnal games between his ward and flame-haired Thelma, and to be a participant.

The train steamed furiously on towards distant London, wheels singing their clacking song on the rails, the engine puffing in effort, the carriage swaying. Delia became aware how pleasantly affectionate was her dear guardian's clasp of her pussy in the warm palm of his hand.

'This lovely little split of yours,' he whispered in her ear, 'so maidenly and sweet – yet I know it must have been ravished to delight many hundreds of times by the tongues and fingers of your schoolfriends. I find that thought to be arousing in the extreme, as you may observe from the jerking of *John Thomas* in your hand. Tell me, dearest Delia, which of your chums did it to you the best?'

How was she to answer him without betraying the confidence of a person she adored? Yet her very hesitation gave Sir Stanton a hint that here lay a particular secret, and he set himself to ferret it out of her. This he accomplished by reminding her of their closeness, as legal guardian and ward, and of the ties of affection that must flourish between them, of his care for her well-being, and half a dozen other pressing reasons. Delia in all honesty could do no other than agree there should never be secrets withheld from him.

After swearing him to life-long secrecy, to which he readily agreed, she confessed that the person she adored beyond all the others to play with was none other than Miss Harriet.

'My word!' Sir Stanton exclaimed, his eyes bright. 'I found Miss Harriet Jardyne when I met her to be a very handsome woman and extremely self-possessed. She is a woman much to my liking – fine features and a full bosom, good hips, and, unless I miss my guess, good legs too. Tell me, Delia, for you have seen them and know, does Miss Jardyne have good legs?'

'They are lovely beyond compare,' Delia replied, 'being long and very shapely, full in the thigh and slender in the ankle.'

'And her pussy, my dear – what of that?'

Her voice trembling a little with emotion, Delia described to him the bush of glossy black hair between Miss Harriet's creamy white thighs, and of the elegant long pink lips that split it. She praised it as quite the most beautiful natural object she had ever in her life beheld. Her girlish enthusiasm impressed Sir Stanton, in view of the simple truth that in the course of her single term at St Agatha's Delia had become most intimately acquainted with at least a dozen of the female playthings that pleased him.

'By Jove,' he murmured, 'to think you have enjoyed the great pleasure of being allowed to touch Miss Jardyne's pussy.'

'Very often,' said Delia proudly, and went on to tell him she had done more than touch it – she had kissed it, she had thrust her tongue into its moistly pink interior, and she had brought it to throbbing spasms, many and many a time.

'And she did as much for you?' her guardian suggested.

'O yes, in these past weeks since the term ended Miss Harriet has been tireless in her attentions to me,' Delia sighed. 'Ten or a dozen times a day she has induced the sweet sensations in me by the application of her tongue.'

'Nine or ten times a day, eh?' said Sir Stanton, enthralled by what he heard. 'I find myself warming more and more to Miss Jardyne, the more you tell me of her. Nine or ten times! What absolute bliss.'

'A bliss not entirely unalloyed,' said Delia. 'Perhaps I am foolish, but the pleasure of the sensual spasm was shadowed for me to some extent by a suspicion that what we did to each other was somehow wrong – perhaps even forbidden and immoral.'

'That would make fetching off even more delicious,' said her guardian in a voice that shook with emotion as his fingers slid in her open yet virginal pussy. 'Retain these suspicions for as long as you can, for they add most tremendously to the joy of a good fetch off. Tell me, though, do the same qualms trouble you when I feel you, my dear?'

*John Thomas* was leaping in Delia's hand – leaping so strongly that she guessed he was about to discharge his lust, for it was exactly so that Bert the gardener's boy's *dick* had jerked and twitched in the moments before his cream came pouring out.

'Oh!' she cried, sighing and shuddering under the soft touch of Sir Stanton's fingers in her pussy. The sensual spasm seized her exactly at the instant his sticky white sap spurted through her fingers, and on to her dress.

When he had recovered himself, he apologised for smearing her skirt and wiped it away with his own handkerchief. Delia found herself enchanted to be so courteously treated, and went so far as to return the favour by taking the handkerchief to wipe him dry. Her only experience of the behaviour of male organs after emission was limited to Bert in the potting shed, and she fully expected Sir Stanton's to go limp and small at once.

To her surprise, it did not. On the contrary, her gentle wipe with the handkerchief seemed to give it new strength – before her eyes it bounded, and seemed to become yet thicker.

'That was quite delightful. And now you shall take off your drawers, dear little Delia,' said he, with so warmhearted and loving an expression on his handsome face, that never a thought of disobeying entered her mind.

## The Girls' Boarding School

'I shall assist you to remove them,' he added, with his eyes glowing. 'Lift your skirts, my dear.'

She slid from his lap and stood upright, using both hands to raise her skirts and petticoats right up to her waist, letting him see the plain white drawers which were required to be worn by the regulations at St Agatha's. Sir Stanton's face beamed in unseemly pleasure to observe her old-fashioned underwear.

'I am sure you have no great liking for drawers of this cut,' said he, 'since young ladies naturally prefer to cosset their lovely girlish charms in knickers with frills and lace on them. Yet I am sorry to see the old style pass. Many's the sly feel of a warm pussy or a bare bum I have enjoyed by reason of the ease and convenience with which a hand may be slipped into the useful openings in old-fashioned drawers.'

Whilst speaking thus, he leaned forward on the carriage-seat to untie the bow that fastened the drawstring about her slim young waist. That done, he let the garment slither down to her ankles, and leaned forward further to press a warm kiss on her bare and maidenly belly.

It cannot be denied, after all that has been revealed before, that Delia's belly had been kissed many a time, by night and by day, by each and every young lady, jointly and severally, to be found in Form V of St Agatha's. Nevertheless, there seemed to her to be something different about the way Sir Stanton kissed. The soft tickle of his moustache over the smooth flesh of her girlish belly caused the most heavenly sensations. Very soon she found herself hoping he would kiss her lower down, so that she might feel the thrilling touch of his moustache on the soft lips of her pussy, but for the time being he did not.

Instead, he sat upright again and held her steady whilst she stepped out of her fallen drawers. She picked them up from the dusty carpeting of the carriage floor, and would have put them away in her travelling bag up on the rack above his head, but Sir Stanton smiled and took them from her, folded them and put them into a side pocket of his frock-coat.

'They shall be a keepsake of this wonderful day,' he stated, 'I shall treasure them forever and hug them to me if I am away from your dear presence for any length of time.'

That said, he drew her close to him until she sat astride his knees, her legs forced to splay wide apart. She blushed faintly while sliding forward, her intuition telling her that was what he wished her to do. He raised her clothes in front to let *John Thomas*, who was bounding for joy, press close to her underneath her chemise. The feel was warm and pleasant against her skin, and Mr Thomas was throbbing strongly. Delia put her arms about Sir Stanton's neck to press her hot cheek to his, in a gesture of spontaneous affection.

Sir Stanton's hands were under her clothes – he gripped her bare bum and stroked it. She could feel his amazingly stiff and long part slide against the warm flesh of her belly and against its darling little button, and she was forced to conclude that the sensation was most pleasant – perhaps almost as nice as the feel of Thelma's ginger-haired pussy rubbing on her belly.

Delia was quite sure now that Bert had been mistaken when he said that men always wanted to push their big thick *dick* up a pussy. Moreover, it appeared that unnatural advantage had been taken of dearest Miss Harriet by Lord Clacton, in his unseemly desire to push his *thing* into her nightly to ensure himself the pleasure of an emission.

Delia based this view on the plain fact that Sir Stanton gave no indication of wishing to push enormous *John Thomas* into her, but was content to rub it against her bare belly in a friendly and comforting manner. She presumed the error arose because a common boy like Bert was ignorant of the proper way of things among persons of a better class, and thought they did the same base things to each other as he and his like.

As for dearest Miss Harriet, she had been seriously misled by Lord Clacton. Aristocrat or not, he had evidently picked up low habits, which he had then perpetrated on her.

Member of the House of Lords he might be, but in Delia's view the former employer of Miss Harriet was a vulgar sort of fellow to have repeatedly pushed his thing up her. It might be he had risen to the top of society from being a mere manufacturer, who had accumulated a fortune by making and selling articles of use in households. When that sort acquired a sufficiency of wealth, they purchased country houses and estates and by large donations to politicians secured a title.

Sir Stanton Fortescue was a gentleman to his fingertips, who knew the ways of the world, and at this very moment he was busy about the process of showing Delia how it was done between the sexes, she firmly believed. The proper way to go about it, she understood from his present actions, was for a gentleman to rub *John Thomas* against the lady's belly. It was not in the least offensive – indeed, it could be described as quite pleasant.

She heard him sighing blissfully while he tupped against her smooth skin, and she uttered a tiny cry of surprise to feel his fingers probing between the cheeks of her bottom. The touch was very arousing, all things considered – his fingertips gliding tenderly along the crease between the cheeks, as Miss Harriet's fingers had done, many a time, since that first caress standing under the tree on the way back to St Agatha's.

Delia murmured in happiness to feel Sir Stanton caressing her so delicately, from the soft wet lips of her pussy to her tight little knot-hole. Then with a cry of purest delight he released his creamy essence in a long shuddering fetch off, that sent it spurting on to her bare belly under her clothes.

When he had finished his emission and got his breath back, he offered Delia the use of his handkerchief to wipe herself, and then made her stand on the swaying carriage floor, her hands on his shoulders to balance herself, while he pressed his lips in warm kisses to her girlish belly. He murmured the while of how delicious he thought her, and how wonderful he meant their life together to be.

# CHAPTER 17
# The Wages of Sin

Sir Stanton Fortescue's town residence was to be found in Pont Street, a fashionable part of London, between Cadogan Place and Belgrave Square. Here, Delia learned when they arrived from the railway station in a cab, he employed seven servants in all – a housekeeper who oversaw the others, and regulated the domestic expenditure, a parlour-maid to answer the door and to serve at table, two housemaids for cleaning, a cook, a skivvy for rough work such as vegetable-peeling, floor-scrubbing, washing-up and pan-shining, and a boots – who in addition to polishing Sir Stanton's footwear also did the odd jobs about the place.

To this establishment he proposed, he informed Delia, to add an eighth servant – a personal maid for her, for in his opinion it was necessary for a young lady to have the attendance of a personal servant, rather than to rely on a parlour-maid.

Delia thanked him warmly, quite certain that she would enjoy life in Pont Street with her dearest guardian.

Until a suitable person could be found, Sara the parlour-maid, was instructed to assist Miss Delia. Her first task was to help her dress for dinner, for it was already well after six before the cab brought them to Sir Stanton's residence.

Delia found Sara to be a pleasant young woman, some

ten years older than herself, buxom of figure and appealing of face, in a lower-class way.

The room assigned to Delia was large and well-appointed, with a good view of Pont Street below. With the assistance of one of the housemaids, Sara brought hot water to fill a bath, helped Delia out of her clothes, and washed down her back when she was seated in the scented water. Nor were her attentions confined entirely to Delia's back – her soapy hands slipped round to her titties and handled them firmly, which attention caused a soft blush to grace Delia's cheek.

'Oh Miss Delia,' said Sara, in a manner that struck Delia as pert, 'how your nubbins stand up at the slightest touch!'

'You're a wicked girl to touch me there,' Delia replied, for she was minded to exercise her superiority over the servant, so as to establish her position in the household.

'Wicked am I, Miss?' said the maid with a chuckle. 'Whatever can you mean by that? I'm only washing you, I'm not trying to interfere with you – I leave that to others.'

This impudence made it apparent to Delia that the servants of the Pont Street household were out of hand. She was sure it was not the fault of Sir Stanton, for she thought him perfect in every way. Her conclusion was that the housekeeper, a woman in her middle forty's by the name of Mrs Frigginton, had slipped into laxity during Sir Stanton's absence abroad, and allowed the servants too much liberty.

Words of rebuke came to Delia's lips, but remained unspoken, her curiosity caught by Sara's odd reference to *others* who, it seemed, might interfere with her.

'What are you insinuating, Sara?' she demanded, tossing her head in high dudgeon. 'Who is capable of such a thing?'

'I cast no aspersions, Miss,' the parlour-maid said, with the broadest of smiles on her face. 'Stand up, if you please, while I wash you down below.'

'I insist that you answer my question,' said Delia, rising to her feet in the bath. 'To whom did you refer?'

'My word, what a taking,' said Sara, with a mock sigh, 'what can be bothering you, Miss? Not my little joke, surely.'

Whilst speaking thus, she washed over Delia's charming belly with her hand, and between her tender thighs. She worked upward from the knees until her palm was sliding over Delia's pussy.

'Mind what you are about, Sara,' Delia said sharply, all too aware that the parlour-maid was taking the liberty of handling her as if they were social equals. But this was not St Agatha's and a servant was very far beneath young ladies of Form V such as Rhoda Fitzwalter or Amy Gore-Boothby, or any of the others who had delighted in stroking Delia's pussy, with the exception of Mrs Remply, of course, who was a sort of upper servant.

'Yes, Miss,' said Sara with a chuckle, 'I'll be very careful – we must keep this little treasure sweet and pure. We never can tell when a gentleman might want a feel of it, can we?'

The wretched indecency of the servant's words, no less than her improper actions, ought to have brought the severest rebuke from Delia, but did not, which shows how deeply tainted she had permitted her maidenly character to become, in her acceptance of the impure standards of others. Instead she stared stupefied at Sara's impudent remark, her eyes wide and her mouth open.

Meanwhile, letting not an instant of this opportunity escape her, Sara parted the soft pink lips between Delia's long white thighs and was washing within, her soapy fingers paying special attention to the secret little button.

Delia's anger died away as she trembled and sighed to feel a familiar sensation course through her belly. She moved her feet wider apart in the warm water, thus parting her thighs to allow the parlour-maid easier access to her parts.

'I'm sure I don't know what you mean, Sara,' she murmured, as her legs started to shake.

'No, Miss,' the parlour-maid agreed with a knowing leer, 'but you'll very soon find out, if I'm any judge.'

'Is it Sir Stanton you are accusing of gross immorality, Sara – or some other person?' Delia asked, her voice trembling in a manner that demonstrated how high her emotions had arisen.

'Accuse, Miss Delia?' the wanton maid said with a lewd wink of her eye. 'Accusing a gentleman is not for the likes of me. I know my place.'

'Then what?'

'Sir Stanton is the best of masters, kind and generous,' said Sara, rubbing gently at Delia's throbbing bud, 'and like many a gentleman about town he has an eye for a pretty young girl. And not just an eye for them, if you take my meaning. Many a young lady has come to Pont Street for a visit, and gone away wiser than she was before.'

'In what way wiser?' Delia gasped, hardly able to speak for the intense sensations in her belly. 'How wiser? Tell me!'

'Why, about what makes the difference between men and women, of course,' Sara replied pertly. 'Only don't say I told you so, or I might lose my job.'

Delia abandoned herself to the pleasure she was deriving from the insistent tickling of the parlour-maid's fingers. In only a few seconds she fetched off strongly, sighing to the tremors in her girlish loins and belly.

'That felt nice, I'll be bound,' said Sara, with an impudent grin, as she rinsed away the creamy soapsuds from Delia's fair haired pussy when the spasms had faded. 'Was it your first time today, Miss?'

'That's none of your business,' Delia retorted.

The fearful and indecent truth of the matter was that she had become so accustomed to being abused several times daily by her friends at St Agatha's that she was no longer abashed to have a question of such infamous impropriety put to her. Furthermore, since she had been interfered with so fully by Mrs Remply in the sick room, the touch of a servant's hand on her intimate parts no longer appalled her.

'Bring a towel and dry me,' she said, running her own fingers over her well-washed pussy now that Sara had finished with it.

She was aware that she had signally failed to exercise proper authority over the servant. Indeed, it could even be said that the parlour-maid had gained an ascendancy over Delia – who alas had so easily submitted to the inducement of the sensual spasm.

Yet was it of any importance, Delia asked herself as the maid towelled her dry. After all, the sensations were very delicious and the fetching off wonderfully thrilling – she could think of no reason why Sara shouldn't do it to her every day when she took her bath, so long as the girl remembered her proper place, and spoke politely.

In this, Delia had, as the observant reader will have noted, allowed herself to be outwitted by Sara, who had aspirations to better herself by rising from mere parlour-maid to the far more privileged position of personal lady's maid. Her background and upbringing among the poor had given her a cynical understanding of sensuality, and being in service in Sir Stanton's household had acquainted her with the foibles of the gentry.

She had with ease taken the measure of Delia's character, at one time so admirable, so proper, so correct in thought and in deed, but now, alas, morally tainted by excessive and improper indulgence in sensual pleasure. Here was a young lady, Sara had concluded, who was accustomed to being fingered to the spasm by her schoolfriends. By insinuating herself into Delia's favour by giving her the regular thrills to which she was used, Sara hoped to make herself indispensible and be awarded the position of lady's maid.

Dinner that evening was not a heavy or lengthy meal, the cook not being sure that Sir Stanton would arrive back in time from the country. Nevertheless, a good cook is never put out, and at the curtailed notice available a scratch meal was provided. It fell short of the ordinary delights of Sir Stanton's table, yet was very acceptable to hungry travellers, consisting of a thick pea soup and a dish of mutton chops, followed by orange syllabub, and Stilton cheese.

After the rigours of St Agatha's, even this very simple meal seemed to Delia almost a feast, and she ate with a will. At Sir Stanton's bidding she drank a glass of excellent Burgundy wine with the chops, and the merest thimbleful of port to accompany the cheese. Afterwards she and he sat in the drawing-room while coffee was served, and he thought it best she did not join him in a glass of old Napoleon brandy.

When the parlour-maid who had waited on them at last withdrew and left them alone, she winked secretly at Delia in a manner that must be described as lewd and suggestive.

## The Girls' Boarding School

Delia returned a haughty stare, refusing to be made a participant in whatever base imaginings filled Sara's common mind. She was good enough for stroking Delia's parts and providing daily the sensations she required, but that was very different from letting her know what transpired between Delia and Sir Stanton.

When he was quite sure he and Delia would be undisturbed for the remainder of the evening, Sir Stanton took from the inside pocket of his evening tailcoat the neat white knee-length and very plain drawers Delia had removed at his request during the journey by express train to London.

'See, my dear,' said he, 'I keep them close to my heart, as a memento of our first journey together.'

Whereupon he raised the dainty drawers to his lips, pressing a reverent kiss upon them. A faint blush rose to Delia's cheek, but she was in truth flattered by Sir Stanton's gallantry.

'Whilst I was upstairs dressing,' he continued, 'the memory of our bliss together in the train so raised my emotions that I wrapped this precious garment about *John Thomas* – who, needless to say, was standing to attention as stiffly as a guardsman.'

'Oh!' Delia exclaimed, astonished by this unexpected glimpse into the depravities of a gentleman's inner desires.

'How he bounded and squirmed to feel close about him the very garment that had been in proximity to your darling pussy,' said Sir Stanton, a smile of pleasure on his face at the memory. 'In the end the thrill of it was more than *John Thomas* could bear – he brought me to my knees by the dressing-table, felled by his sudden fierce emission.'

He held them out towards Delia, to show her the

damp patch on the thin white linen where his emission had soaked in.

'Oh my goodness!' said Delia faintly, astonished by what she heard, though Sir Stanton took her surprise to be caused by the large stain he was displaying. This he found flattering.

In truth, her astonishment arose from her clear recollection of Miss Harriet informing her that gentlemen were able to fetch off only twice, or at most three times, before they lapsed into lethargy and were unable to summon up another *cockstand* until they had slept and recovered. Yet on the train Sir Stanton had three times discharged his lust, which should have reduced him to langour for some hours, but in his dressing-room it seemed he had attained the acme of sensual pleasure again – and with no other stimulus than the touch of her discarded drawers!

On the other hand, Delia recalled, Mrs Remply had told her it was not unknown for some males to achieve a *cockstand* again and again, and do the dastardly deed half a dozen times. It had to be borne in mind that Mrs Remply spoke from personal experience of some years of marriage and, no doubt, unwholesome adventures with any number of lower class males, before she was led to the altar to be made respectable. Delia found herself wondering if dearest Miss Harriet may have underestimated the staying-power of gentlemen.

Could the solution to this perplexing puzzle be perhaps that Lord Clacton, who assuredly did not behave like a gentleman in his violation of Miss Harriet's lovely body, had in some manner impaired his own strength by vile abuse, so that he was capable of only a single emission before his male organ dwindled into a flaccid and harmless appendage? If Sir Stanton and not Lord Clacton was to be taken as the very picture of a gentleman, his ability to perform the sensual act repeatedly must necessarily be no exception, and must be regarded as the rule.

Whilst these highly improper considerations occupied Delia's thoughts, Sir Stanton continued with his account of how he had fetched off into her drawers in his dressing-room.

'It was during this pleasant interlude that a particularly interesting thought came to my mind,' said he, with a confident smile upon his handsome features. 'It is a certain course of action which I believe will bring you great joy and contentment – and therefore to me, since your happiness is mine.'

With this as introduction, he began to question Delia about Miss Harriet Jardyne and their pleasures together. Certain that she could trust his discretion, Delia revealed some details of Miss Harriet's former employment by Lord Clacton, as governess to the Hon Melissa Blaby-Riddle, previous to taking up her post as a form mistress at St Agatha's. When Sir Stanton learned the reason for Miss Harriet's dismissal from Lord Clacton's service his eyes sparkled and he stroked his thick moustache pensively.

'I wonder, my dear,' said he, 'if the delectable Miss Harriet could be persuaded to quit St Agatha's and take up an important position in my household? You are too old to have a governess, but you are certainly at a proper age to have a lady companion, someone to perform the duties of chaperone, when you leave the house.'

'Oh, I would be the happiest person alive if she would accept the position,' Delia cried, 'but after her ghastly experience as victim to the beastliness of Lord Clacton, I doubt she would agree to enter a private household again. Unless, of course, she had a solemn promise that her person would not be molested.'

'Except by you, my dear, eh?' said Sir Stanton with a manly smile. 'My fond hope is that you would molest her continually. Well, I am certain we can reach an amicable arrangement with so intelligent a young person as Miss Jardyne.'

He marvelled at Delia's innocence, and congratulated himself on coming into possession of so pretty and so biddable a young lady. As to Miss Harriet Jardyne, he entertained not the least doubt that the beautiful form mistress would gladly lie down on her back for him and part her legs to be *rogered*, in return for a well-paid and comfortable post in London, as a trusted member of a fashionable household.

'I shall write to her tomorrow,' said he, 'to offer her terms she will find most rewarding – for I doubt if teachers are paid more than a pittance, even at so estimable an establishment as St Agatha's. You must write a personal letter to be enclosed in mine, saying how much you would like her to accept the offer of employment.'

'Oh, bliss!' said Delia.

She noticed that whilst they had been talking *John Thomas* had grown full-size and was showing as a long bulge under the cloth of Sir Stanton's close-fitting evening trousers. It was not the place of a well-bred young gentlewoman to comment on any such condition, and she averted her eyes modestly, waiting until the event should declare itself.

Sir Stanton himself was without any trace of modesty, being a gentleman entirely given up to the satisfaction of his lustful bodily urges. He reached for Delia's dainty hand, and rubbed it over the hard bulge. A gleam came to his eye at the touch of so fair a hand upon his unmentionables, and his own manly hand was up Delia's skirt and between her thighs in an instant. He felt for the opening of her drawers, for as yet the only underwear she possessed consisted of regulation school uniform, and until he took her shopping she could not dress her girlish loins and bum in frilly-legged silk knickers of the most modern type.

'During your term at St Agatha's,' said he, 'I suppose there were occasions when you played in bed with more than a single friend at a time? A threesome, perhaps, or a foursome?'

'Yes,' Delia admitted faintly, a pink blush rising quickly to her soft cheeks. 'Myrtle and Daphne and I sometimes shared the same bed together.'

'Excellent,' Sir Stanton cried, his unseen finger parting the lips of Delia's pussy, to caress the bud concealed within the soft pink folds, 'then it will come as no surprise to you if we have a three-in-hand here sometime.'

'But with whom?' she enquired.

'Allow me to explain something of my intentions to you,' said he. 'I do not mean to take your virginity.'

'I should hope not,' Delia exclaimed in high alarm, 'what an inhuman and disgraceful course that would be!'

Sir Stanton flicked at his blond moustache with a finger and smiled at her innocent reproach.

'We have known each other less than a day,' said he, 'yet you exercise the strongest fascination for me, Delia. I might even say that I have become infatuated, my dear, by your beauty and youth, your sweet mind and pleasing ways.'

'You are very kind,' she responded, flattered by his words.

'The fascination I feel is to be found in this circumstance,' he continued, 'your darling little pussy has never been pierced by a male organ. It remains girlish and virginal, and you, dear Delia, are therefore a sweet young maiden, notwithstanding that you have been fetched off a thousand times by young ladies.'

'That is true,' Delia said, putting firmly from her mind all thoughts of the depradations of the Reverend Blenkinsop, 'with all proper modesty I may say that I am undefiled.'

'Therein lies your charm,' Sir Stanton exclaimed. 'If I were to ravish away your virginity, my dearest, by thrusting *John* up you and permitting him to achieve an emission in your belly, it would be bliss beyond all imagination.'

'For you – but it would be a dreadful agony for me!' Delia cried in horrified tones.

'How little you know, my dear. But never mind that, my point is this: I have *rogered* hundreds of pretty young women, and I have learned, to be candid about it, that after a few weeks the novelty is quite gone.'

'Then what do you mean to do with me?' Delia asked.

'To enjoy you to the fullest, in every way I can imagine, yet always denying myself the final pleasure.'

Delia stared at him, not entirely sure what he meant.

'I shall preserve your virginity most carefully,' he went on, 'whilst allowing *John Thomas* to revel in every other part of your beautiful young body, except for your pussy.'

The thought arose in Delia's mind that what Sir Stanton meant to do to her was not so very different from what had been done to her again and again at St Agatha's. The only real difference was that it would be a gentleman's hand or tongue that induced the spasm in her, not a girl's. She herself, instead of feeling another pussy, would handle *John Thomas* to a regular fetch

## The Girls' Boarding School

off. It was strange to contemplate the change, but not displeasing.

In this it may be observed not only how low she had sunk in her flight from decency, but also how little she understood of the ways of lascivious men. For a little while, while she was becoming accustomed to the life of shameful indulgence in every bodily perversion that awaited her, Sir Stanton would content himself by feeling her lovely young titties and pussy, and then letting her handle his male organ, satisfying his vile lust by an emission into her hand. Later on, when she was committed in her deepest emotions to him, he intended to take full advantage of her bodily beauty, by *rogering* her every orifice, save only her unbroached pussy, which would be defiled only by finger and tongue.

'You shall be my beautiful virgin,' said Sir Stanton, smiling most cheerfully at her, 'and I shall adore you to distraction. For the purpose of *rogering*, I shall make arrangements to have another young woman available.'

'*Rogering!*' Delia cried. 'But that's what common people do! Gentlefolk have nicer ways of displaying their affection – as you showed me so very nicely on board the express train when I sat across your lap.'

'Be that as it may,' said Sir Stanton with a chuckle, 'I have a great need to put *John Thomas* up a female receptacle at very regular intervals. Since I intend you to be my eternal maidenly playmate, for the purpose of *rogering* I hope to persuade Miss Harriet Jardyne to become resident in my household.'

His middle finger caressed Delia's little button lovingly and made her feel weak with pleasure. The thought that Sir Stanton would thrust his stiff organ up Miss Harriet's beautiful pussy with the black-haired bush about it was shocking beyond belief. Nevertheless, the tremors of bliss running through Delia tended to soften her anguish of mind at the hideous suggestion.

'You and she shall play with each other as often as you wish, day or night,' Sir Stanton said meditatively, 'and I shall play with you, dearest Delia, whenever I wish – which will be very frequently. In addition, to crown my delight, I shall *roger* Miss Harriet nightly, the three of us in one bed.'

'She will never agree to it!' Delia cried in dismay.

'I think you'll find that she will,' said Sir Stanton, with a lewd smile. 'I know a little more of the ways of the world than you, my dear, trust me.'

Delia's moral fibre was completely sapped by the stimulation of her parts by Sir Stanton's skilful fingers, for on further reflection, it occurred to her that it would be a most arousing sight to observe *John Thomas* sliding into Miss Harriet's wet pussy. It was not as if Miss Harriet was a virgin, after all – for she had been defiled nightly for two years by Lord Clacton. To feel her pussy immediately after Sir Stanton had *done* her to the spasm, and filled her with his creamy fluid – that to Delia seemed a most exciting prospect. A *three-in-hand* he had called it, and Delia found herself longing for the day when it became a reality.

Sir Stanton stood up, and lifted Delia in his arms as if she were light as a feather, for he was a strongly-built gentleman. In firm strides he carried her across the handsomely-furnished and extensive drawing room, along the hall, and up the stairs. She lay contentedly in his arms, with her soft cheek against his, whilst his fair moustache tickled her in a pleasant sort of way.

It was not to her own room he took her, but to his – a square and masculine room, panelled in polished wood, with a high bed set against the far wall. On this he laid her tenderly, sinking to his knees beside the bed, where with impatient hand, he cast her skirts above her waist. In an instant he had her drawers untied and gaping wide open, and showered hot lustful kisses on her bare belly and thighs.

'Oh!' she exclaimed at the sudden touch of his tongue on her darling pussy, and 'Oh!' again as he opened her with careful fingers and licked rapidly over her tender bud. It felt so very delicious that her legs trembled rapidly and she knew the spasm would not be delayed more than ten or twenty seconds.

'This is new and strange to me,' she murmured, 'to be used in this way by a gentleman and not a female – yet some instinct or other seems to tell me that it will be as enjoyable, perhaps even more so, for you are a gentleman of large experience and ardent imagination, who will teach me to enjoy wilder thrills than any schoolgirl has ever shown me.'

Thus may it be seen how utterly depraved Delia had become as a result of the corrupting influences at work in St Agatha's Boarding School for Young Gentlewomen. On her first night in that den of depravity, at the beginning of the spring term, she had been shocked and humiliated when ginger-headed Thelma Fanshawe squeezed her maiden titties and felt her pussy.

Three months later she was so lost to every consideration of human decency that she could, without even a blush, contemplate a life of shame and degradation, as the plaything of a rich and perverse man about town.

Not for Miss Delia Sempill-Shand, alas, the sweet and sacred joys of marriage and motherhood in the prime of her youth. No and no and a thousand times no – her destiny lay down another and unwholesome path, the wayward and wanton road that tempts those who are morally weak to step aside from the straight and narrow and give themselves up to dalliance. To make no mystery of it, her feet were now set firmly upon the primrose path of constant indulgence in sensual pleasure.

She had been detached from all common sense and virtue by her precocious and excessive exposure to bodily abuse by the young ladies who were her friends at St Agatha's. In consequence, she was all sadly unaware that, by allowing her bodily parts to be stimulated continuously she was acquiring a vicious habit which she would lack the moral power ever to break.

Yet it was not entirely her own fault, it must be recognised, that she had tumbled into this trap – Mrs Kenilworth must bear great blame for permitting the young ladies in her charge to go to each others' beds by night and defile each other's modesty.

Miss Harriet Jardyne, too, was equally guilty – perhaps even more so. It was her clear duty as a form mistress to check the depraved habits of young ladies for whom she was responsible, and lead them to sweeter and saner ways. This she failed to do, and worse, she had herself a warped habit of choosing delicate young ladies from Form V, on whose bodies she customarily sated her own dissolute and immoderate lusts.

The shameful outcome of this deplorable and criminal neglect of morality is to be seen in a thousand bedrooms the length and breadth of the kingdom. Without let or pause, young women well-bred and tenderly nurtured are so innured to impure thoughts and habits that they think nothing of taking part in practices so wholly debauched that words are inadequate to describe them.

Although the ordinary person must shudder away from perusing an account of females of this sort, it remains an inescapable fact that many of the best-descended ladies in society are lost to decency and virtue, to the unbelievable point at which they take horrid pleasure in sensual perversities practised on them by licentious men. Of the labouring classes it is needless to speak, for the depravity of male and female alike are too well known to require comment. Leaving these debased wretches aside, it cannot be gainsaid that those in a superior station in life ought to know better, and to set an example to the unfortunate.

We may take our leave of Delia Sempill-Shand, upstairs in the master bedroom of the house in Pont Street, stripped naked, a scandalous state in which no modest young woman should ever let herself be observed, not even by a lawful husband. There Delia lay stretched out fully on her back, her person laid bare from head to foot – titties, belly, pussy – nothing veiled from the lewd eyes of her legal guardian. The situation is so shockingly indecent that the virtuous mind finds it almost impossible to visualise.

Sir Stanton's wicked tongue was at its work between Delia's widely parted thighs, sending tremors of pure bliss through her entire body, and bringing her quickly to the crisis of sensual emotion. Her arm hung over the side of the bed, and she reached out eagerly to take Sir Stanton's exposed and stiff organ into her dainty hand, and rub it up and down.

'My dear,' he murmured, raising his mouth for an instant from her wet and pouting pussy, 'you have bewitched me. I confess I am utterly infatuated with you – and you will make me fetch off in another instant if you stroke *John Thomas* like that.'

'Oh yes,' she sighed in return, as his tongue returned

to its former ravishing of her pussy, 'let me feel the warm gush in my hand!'

Even as she spoke, her snow-white bum bounced rapidly up from the bed as the spasm overtook her. With outcries of shamefully abandoned pleasure, she surrendered herself, body and soul, to Sir Stanton's depraved and libidinous will. Three months only had been required to transform a modest maiden into a creature cut off from all decency and devoted to a life of disgraceful sensation-seeking. Parents of young unmarried daughters – take heed of Delia Sempill-Shand's dreadful plight!

# A Message from the Publisher

Headline Delta is a unique list of erotic fiction, covering many different styles and periods and appealing to a broad readership. As such, we would be most interested to hear from you.

Did you enjoy this book? Did it turn you on – or off? Did you like the story, the characters, the setting? What did you think of the cover presentation? How did this novel compare with others you have read? In short, what's your opinion? If you care to offer it, please write to:

> The Editor
> Headline Delta
> 338 Euston Road
> London NW1 3BH

Or maybe you think you could write a better erotic novel yourself. We are always looking for new authors. If you'd like to try your hand at writing a book for possible inclusion in the Delta list, here are our basic guidelines: we are looking for novels of approximately 75,000 words whose purpose is to inspire the sexual imagination of the reader. The erotic content should not describe illegal sexual activity (pedophilia, for example). The novel should contain sympathetic and interesting characters, pace, atmosphere and an intriguing storyline.

If you would like to have a go, please submit to the Editor a sample of at least 10,000 words, clearly typed in double-lined spacing on one side of the paper only, together with a short outline of the plot. Should you wish your material returned to you, please include a stamped addressed envelope. If we like it sufficiently, we will offer you a contract for publication.

## *A selection of Erotica from Headline*

| | | |
|---|---|---|
| FAIR LADIES OF PEACHAM PLACE | Beryl Ambridge | £5.99 ☐ |
| EROTICON HEAT | Anonymous | £5.99 ☐ |
| SCANDALOUS LIAISONS | Anonymous | £5.99 ☐ |
| FOUR PLAY | Felice Ash | £5.99 ☐ |
| THE TRIAL | Samantha Austen | £5.99 ☐ |
| NAKED INTENT | Becky Bell | £5.99 ☐ |
| VIXENS OF NIGHT | Valentina Cilescu | £5.99 ☐ |
| NEW TERM AT LECHLADE COLLEGE | Lucy Cunningham-Brown | £5.99 ☐ |
| THE PLEASURE RING | Kit Gerrard | £5.99 ☐ |
| SPORTING GIRLS | Faye Rossignol | £5.99 ☐ |

Headline books are available at your local bookshop or newsagent. Alternatively, books can be ordered direct from the publisher. Just tick the titles you want and fill in the form below. Prices and availability subject to change without notice.

Buy four books from the selection above and get free postage and packaging and delivery within 48 hours. Just send a cheque or postal order made payable to Bookpoint Ltd to the value of the total cover price of the four books. Alternatively, if you wish to buy fewer than four books the following postage and packaging applies:

UK and BFPO £4.30 for one book; £6.30 for two books; £8.30 for three books.

Overseas and Eire: £4.80 for one book; £7.10 for 2 or 3 books (surface mail)

Please enclose a cheque or postal order made payable to *Bookpoint Limited*, and send to: Headline Publishing Ltd, 39 Milton Park, Abingdon, OXON OX14 4TD, UK.
Email Address: orders@bookpoint.co.uk

If you would prefer to pay by credit card, our call team would be delighted to take your order by telephone. Our direct line 01235 400 414 (lines open 9.00 am–6.00 pm Monday to Saturday 24 hour message answering service). Alternatively you can send a fax on 01235 400 454.

Name ..................................................................................

Address ..................................................................................

..................................................................................

..................................................................................

If you would prefer to pay by credit card, please complete:
Please debit my Visa/Access/Diner's Card/American Express (delete as applicable) card number:

| | | | | | | | | | | | | | | | |
|---|---|---|---|---|---|---|---|---|---|---|---|---|---|---|---|
| | | | | | | | | | | | | | | | |

Signature .................................................... Expiry Date...............